**THE EAST IS ABOUT
TO MEET THE WEST**

Based Upon True Events

Trey Aven

Copyright © 2018 by Trey Aven

ISBN# 979-8-80702-389-6
Second Edition

PROLOGUE

I reckon I must have been the first cowboy to come to Kyiv. That's when the notion of building a cowboy bar in the middle of the Soviet Union came to me. Maybe it was a crazy idea. I still don't know.

"I first came to Kyiv in the summer of '89, right after the fall of the Berlin Wall when Ukraine was still part of the Soviet Union.

"Seven years later, sitting in this dingy, cockroach-infested apartment overlooking the boulevard called Prospekt Pobedy, I can't help looking back on how it irreversibly changed the course of my life and turned everything upside down.

"Prospekt Pobedy ... It's Russian for "Avenue of Victory." What a fucking joke! I've lost everything and don't know what's going to happen from one day to the next. I'm not even sure if I'll be alive tomorrow. I've been left to survive the best I can, but I've got the Soviet Union in my blood. It's like a disease and I can't get rid of it.

"I left everything behind to fulfill my destiny in Eastern Europe. Quite simply, I've lost my mind."

—

Kyiv ... what an interesting place, an ancient and beautiful city with a rich and brutal history. One moment you're looking at the palace of Catherine the Great. The next, you're watching some drunken derelict falling down on the street and puking his guts out.

Older than Moscow or St. Petersburg, she was the capitol of what had once been the Kiev-Rus Empire, the crossroads between the East and the West, the Arabic and the European.

Kyiv was the mother of Russian cities, the center of merchants and traders from every corner of the civilized world. She flourished until overrun by the Mongol hordes of Kublai Khan and the Tartars who sent the Slavic people fleeing northward to Russia.

From that point on, the Ukrainians were a conquered people ruled by the Tartars, the Turks, the Poles, Austrians, and Russians, among others. They endured centuries of brutal occupation that covered their rich land in the blood of their people.

She didn't even have a name until the latter part of the nineteenth century. In 1916, the League of Nations finally recognized her as a sovereign nation. She became Ukraine . . . "The Land."

Two years later, the Communist revolution swept through Eastern Europe into Asia and Asia Minor. The "red" armies of the north crushed the "white" armies of the south, and for the next seventy years, Ukraine existed under the yoke of Communism and "Russification." Unfortunately, the process created a severe identity crisis in the Ukrainian people as the eastern part of the country, as well as Odessa, spoke Russian and identified as Russians, while those in the western regions spoke Ukrainian. As a result, the nation developed a split personality that would haunt the people for the decades to come.

In the 1930s, Stalin sought to break the spirit of the troublesome and rebellious province. He seized the grain and engineered a famine resulting in the mass starvation of millions. Those who managed to survive were sent to the *gulags* of Siberia and other remote regions of the vast Soviet Empire.

3

Millions more perished when the Nazis invaded in what Eastern Europeans called the "Great Patriotic War." By the end of World War II, eighty percent of Kyiv had been destroyed.

Stalin ordered that the city be rebuilt along with Leningrad, Stalingrad and Moscow. What couldn't be restored was transformed into a magnificent tribute to Socialism that reflected the power and spirit of Soviet Society.

Kyiv became a part of what was called the Golden Triangle, one of the top three cities of the Soviet Union. Then she was also closed to the outside world.

In April of 1986 came the disaster of Chernobyl. It signaled the cracks in a decaying society. Moscow tried to cover up the explosion and did not inform the citizens of Kyiv of the danger. It was only discovered when abnormal levels of radiation began flowing over the borders into Western Europe. By then, much of the damage had been done. For the Soviet Union, it was the beginning of the end.

In 1991, as the Soviet Union rapidly disintegrated, Ukraine declared independence. However, not all the circumstances that surrounded the break up and the establishment of the Newly Independent States were as noble as one would think.

On the contrary, the statement made on August 24th by Stanislav Hurenko, the head of the Communist party, should go down as one of the oddest declarations of independence in history.

On that day, Ivan Plyushch, chairman of Ukrainian Parliament, called for a short recess announcing that the first order of business upon reconvening would be a vote on the resolution for Ukrainian independence.

Everyone was in a state of shock as Parliament adjourned. The politicians hurriedly conferred to see what they would do in order to save their sorry asses. They were aware that Yeltsin had sent a plane to the Crimea to retrieve Gorbachev and feared a purge in classic Stalinist fashion. They remembered from Russian history how disloyalty was rewarded and were torn between their fear of who had taken power in Moscow and an even greater fear of how life would be without the Soviet Union.

When Parliament reconvened, the atmosphere in the chamber was tense and emotional. Someone said, "I don't see why we should be independent. We've done nothing wrong."

That's when Hurenko stood up. Everyone fell silent as he looked over the room and replied, "Today we will vote for Ukrainian independence . . . because if we do not, we are all in the shit." And with that, Ukraine took its first step towards independence. Shortly thereafter, the other republics followed suit and the Soviet Union collapsed, fading into the history ... I love that story.

Western eyes turned to Ukraine, believing it had the best chance of achieving stability. It had inherited a disproportionate amount of the former Soviet Union's industry and armaments, plus it was the "bread basket" of Eastern Europe and potentially an agricultural dynamo.

Unfortunately, most of the Soviet era factories were "dinosaurs" in a post-industrial age, and half of the agricultural production would lie rotting in the fields due to poor distribution and mismanagement.

The economy collapsed as inflation rose to over 6,000% in the early years. There was a lot of change, but it seemed that it was all for the worse.

The new oligarchs quickly took control over anything of value that could be converted to hard currency as Western vultures flooded into the country eager to pick over the remains of the former Soviet republic. Suddenly, the new boss was the same as the old boss. The more things changed the more they stayed the same as the communists quickly converted to born again capitalism when in reality, they always had been capitalists.

Over the years, Ukraine repeatedly looked to the West for acceptance. Sometimes peacefully, other times not. Unfortunately, she was like a battered wife desperately trying to escape the misogynistic nature of an abusive Moscow. If Russia couldn't have her, no one could. As a result, true independence would never quite come to fruition.

THE BIRTH OF THE COWBOY BAR

"The Old West is not a certain place in a certain time, it's a state of mind. It's whatever you want it to be."   Tom Mix

I

A Cowboy in Kyiv

In the Fall of 1992, Rhett Avery joined the Peace Corps, which at that point was an eclectic group made up of mercenaries and misfits. While some were looking for a new experience or adventure, others were trying to escape a past that had somehow gone terribly wrong. It was a toxic mixture of idealism and espionage. That's when fate stepped in and, with a sick sense of humor, royally screwed him.

Rhett was assigned to the PR department of a company in Kyiv as an advisor on advertising and public relations and as he walked out on the streets of Kyiv, they could tell from his outfit that he was a cowboy. From his cowboy hat, boots and his duster he would walk every day. He appeared on television shows, at press conferences and was written about in newspaper articles that bore headlines like *THE COWBOY IN THE STETSON.* Before long it seemed that everybody knew that there was a cowboy in town.

All the while, he held onto a dream -- that someday, he would build a cowboy saloon in Kyiv. However, he failed to realize that sometime dreams can become nightmares.

During his first year, Rhett met a friendly former intelligence officer by the name of Volodimir, who had been taught English as an interrogator

7

during the "Cold War." With the Cold War at an end, Volodimir had been re-assigned from intelligence work to the Ministry of Foreign Affairs.

Volodimir had developed an interest in the cowboy of the group. So, Rhett invited him to his apartment for some vodka and to experience what Rhett called his "Cowboyskie Chili." Volodimir liked the chili. Evidently, so did his wife. She ate three bowls.

After the two men put away a couple of bottles of vodka, served straight up out of shot glasses, the conversation took an unexpected turn.

"Volodimir, I've heard that nearly everyone in the Soviet Union thinks we are really CIA agents."

"This is true. It was what we were taught. From our point of view, it seemed entirely plausible. America sends advisors into a country; they live among the people and learn about their way of life. How better to gather information?"

Rhett thought for a moment. "I can see your point. Unfortunately, we never get any of the perks that the CIA dishes out. In hindsight, with all the CIA agents that sold secrets to your people, maybe they should have hired us."

"Perhaps you are right," Volodimir laughed.

However, what Volodimir had told Rhett made him curious. "Then why in the hell would they let us come if that's what they truly believed?"

"The issue was brought up when it was first learned the Peace Corps was coming to our country. It caused serious debate among the powers that be. However, in the end, the conventional wisdom was, since the Cold War was over, Ukraine had more to fear from Russia than she did from the

Americans. So, since Ukraine was now on friendly terms with the U.S., we all decided what the hell and let you come anyway."

Rhett leaned over the table, looked Volodimir straight in the eye, and whispered. "You know? They were right. I am CIA." Things got quiet as Volodimir's eyes began to get bigger. He had a dazed look of shock. Rhett had his attention.

Rhett brought himself even closer to Volodimir and said, "Cowboys in Action!"

Volodimir's eyes blinked for a moment. Then Rhett broke into boisterous laugh slapping him on the back. Eventually, Volodimir joined him while his wife sat there wondering what had just happened.

Rhett was glad he had a sense of humor. It was the beginning of a long friendship.

The conversation turned to cowboys as Rhett told him of his dream of a cowboy bar. Since Volodimir had tasted his first bowl of Cowboyskie Chili, he rather liked the idea.

"Let me hear some of your cowboy music on the *magnetaphone*."

Rhett walked over to his portable tape recorder and put in a Garth Brooks tape. Volodimir listened as Rhett poured another vodka. "So, what do you think of the music? Would it go over in Kyiv?"

Volodimir wasn't sure. But after the chili and the vodka, he seemed to enjoy the music. "Why don't you do a radio show?" he suggested.

"Chomu Bini? (Why not)" Rhett answered in Ukrainian.

The next day, Volodimir arranged for Rhett to do a weekly country music program on a local radio station. And that's when "The Kowboy of Kyiv" was born making Rhett the first Country Music DJ in the former Soviet

Union. However, with his limited command of Ukrainian, the show turned out to be half music, the other half comedy.

The first time he announced a song by Reba McEntire, Volodimir nearly fell out of his chair laughing.

"What the hell's so funny?" Rhett could not imagine mispronouncing her name.

"Well," Volodimir answered, "vodka usually goes very well with fish."

Rhett thought for a moment before he realized that *reba* was the Ukrainian word for fish.

Trying to speak Ukrainian was easier said than done and Rhett always required a liberal intake of vodka to get through a program.

"Dobri vechir pani ta panove, Kyiv ta Ookrayino. Vwee slooxhayete goloc Kovboya v Kyivi po Kyivski naibilshi popoolyarni radiostantsi, Radio Kyiv Art. Na protyazi nactoopnoy hodeeni ve boodete sluxhati naikrashi kantry muzikoo v Kolishnomoo Radyanckomy Soyuzu." (Good evening ladies and gentlemen, Kyiv and Ukraine. You're listening to the voice of the Kowboy of Kyiv on Kyiv's most popular radio station … Radio Kyiv Art. For the next hour you'll be listening to the best country music in the former Soviet Union.)

Then there was the problem with his accent. Listeners kept calling asking why was a *"Pollyak"* on the radio playing Country Music.

It wasn't exactly "Good Morning Vietnam," but the program gained a cult following. As an article published by Cowboy Hall of Fame read, he was "sharing his Western heritage abroad in the Wild East that had once been known as the Soviet Union."

II

"Crazy" Dave Seigal

Rhett met "Crazy" Dave Seigal at an American Chamber of Commerce meeting. In those days, the meetings were always followed by a period of socializing and meeting new people, both American and Ukrainian. There was always plenty of food and of course, a whole lot of vodka.

Dave seemed like a regular fellow, always willing to buy a Peace Corps Volunteer a drink whenever he saw them. He knew they could rarely afford to go out. So, whenever he had a party, he invited the volunteers.

According to an article in the *Wall Street Journal*:

There are two types of Western-style businesses that can survive the environment of the Post-Soviet Market, "the big AT&T-style behemoths that make the ground shake when they walk and the one-person companies that hope they are too small to be noticed.

Dave Seigal is one of the latter. When he first arrived in Kyiv, Mr. Seigal chased the sort of deals that are the stuff of fantasy for post-Soviet Prospektors. Everything fell through, and after eleven months of earning not a kopek, Mr. Seigal took his guitar out to the city's main square and began singing country and western tunes, pulling in 6,000 Ukrainian coupons. After that, he figured he had made enough mistakes to qualify as a consultant, and now arranges housing and gives advice to companies doing business . . . He is also a fountain of scuttlebutt.

Well, that pretty much summed Dave up.

On occasion, Rhett would run into Dave. He was a good talker, always hustling the ladies, especially on one evening, when Dave noticed an exotic looking woman on Rhett's arm.

Baxheet was a Muslim of Asian descent from the city of Sumy in Eastern Ukraine. She owned a restaurant and when Rhett told her of his dream, she became intrigued by the American's idea of a cowboy bar. As she poured him a vodka, she began talk about the possibilities of transforming her restaurant.

"Rhett, I would like to know, if I wanted to make my restaurant like the one you describe, would you come to Sumy and help me?"

"Sure. Why not?" She poured him another drink.

"And could you help me with the menu?"

"No problem." She poured another.

"Then you could come to my city and help me design the restaurant?"

"Of course." And another drink.

"And you could help me train my people when you come to Sumy?"

"Yes, I'd be glad to." And another.

"And when you come, we can have our wedding?" She kept pouring.

"Yes, of course . . ." Rhett choked on his drink. "Uh, wait a minute. Would you run that last one by me one more time?"

Baxheet was a sly one. While she had been pouring, getting Rhett into an agreeable state, she thought she just might be able to wrangle herself a husband out of the deal.

"I'm sorry, darlin'. Of course, I'd be glad to help you with a restaurant, but I'm really not looking for a wife at this particular moment."

"I understand, my darling. We'll talk about it some other time." But he could tell Baxheet wasn't going to give up that easily.

She was looking for an American husband and had set her eyes on Rhett. Not that she couldn't have had any man she wanted, but an American could offer her something that no European could — a green card.

After that night, Baxheet would come to Kyiv every so often. She would always try to convince Rhett of her undying love, while trying to get him drunk enough to agree to marry her. She swore that he was the only man for her. So far, he had been lucky enough to successfully dodge the subject. However, Baxheet was a very determined woman.

—

When Dave offered to buy them a drink, Rhett was only too happy to oblige, because Baxheet had expensive tastes and couldn't seem to get it through her head that he was a poor volunteer. She had seen too many episodes of *Santa Barbara* and believed that all Americans had to be rich.

As the three sat talking and drinking, Dave leaned over to Rhett. "I want this Oriental. Is that all right with you?"

"Hey, Dave, what you want isn't up to me. I don't own anyone."

Then Dave made a suggestion "What do you say we all go over to my place for a party?"

Rhett saw a way out of a sticky situation.

That night, over another bottle of vodka, he discovered they shared the same dream of opening a cowboy bar in Kyiv.

Dave brought out a series of crude drawings he had produced of a facade and interior of a Western saloon. During the course of the evening, Rhett drank himself to sleep as the party continued without him.

When he woke the next morning, Rhett found Baxheet in bed with Dave. A smile came over his face as he walked into the kitchen and poured himself a drink. In his lust for the exotic Baxheet, Dave had inadvertently given Rhett the out that he had been looking for.

Nevertheless, Baxheet would continue to come to Kyiv and try to persuade Rhett to marry her. When she couldn't find him, she called Dave.

III

The Passazh

As Rhett neared the end of his Peace Corps service, he began looking around for any work that would enable him to stay in the Kyiv. After living in Europe, the idea of going back to Oklahoma was no longer appealing to him.

He hadn't seen Dave in about a year, not since that night with Baxheet. He had moved several times and Rhett didn't have a phone number for him.

Not until he met Kolinna, a chatty little American of Ukrainian descent, fresh off the plane from Chicago. She had been sent by a multinational ad agency to open a branch office in Kyiv and was running the agency out of an apartment that she rented from Dave.

Dave had established a real estate company that rented apartments to foreigners, particularly those who were working in Ukraine on fat government contracts and could afford to pay inflated prices for an apartment in the center of the city. Ukrainian real estate was a risky business, but the returns were high for anyone who could offer apartments that were up to Western standards. A choice apartment in the center of Kyiv that had been remodeled could go for as high as $10,000 a month.

He recognized the opportunity early on and began renting apartments from Ukrainians, negotiating low prices. He found a group of unemployed construction workers and hired them to remodel the spaces one by one.

Rental rates had gone through the roof and Dave was making a bundle simply by providing convenient living accommodations. It was quick and easy money and most of the time everything was handled in cash. In other words, he had a pretty good thing going.

It seemed that he had his fingers in many pies. After all, he was the virtual "fountain of scuttlebutt" according to the *Wall Street Journal* and was beginning to catch those "big deals that fantasies are made of."

When Kolinna told Rhett of Dave's plans to build a cowboy bar in the center of Kyiv on a quaint little street called *The Passazh* he saw an opportunity to make that dream come true.

—

Rhett wasted no time calling Dave. They agreed to meet at a little bistro called the Carambol located in the center of the city.

The Carambol was something straight out of a cheap detective novel. A marble stairway descended down into the basement where the bar was located. It was somewhere Dashiell Hammett or Bogart would have fit in perfectly. The intrigue was so thick you could cut it with a knife. There were gangsters, Mafia, locals and foreigners from all over Europe, as well as a few Americans and Canadians. A stocky-built doorman stood guard outside in case some rival Mafia should arrive unexpectedly. The decor was flashy and cheap but, by Ukrainian standards, quite posh. A smoke-filled room to the side housed billiard tables where Ukrainian pool sharks hustled each other for hard currency. It was a bit pricey, serving only imported liquors. The locals considered Smirnoff a status symbol, because it was American and accordingly, ten times the price of Stolichnaya.

When Rhett walked in, he found Dave sitting at the bar wearing a cowboy hat. Rhett, as usual, was dressed head to toe in his trademark black Nocona Boots, Resistol Hat and leather duster. Dave greeted him like a long-lost friend.

The patrons and the bartenders seemed to be amused. To them, it must have looked like a scene straight out of an American western.

"Nice hat. Where'd you get it?" Rhett asked.

"Brought it back with me from California."

Sitting down, Rhett lit a cigarette and ordered vodka, downing it in one gulp.

Dave looked at him and grinned. "So, everybody's taking bets on whether 'Crazy' Dave Seigal will actually be able to open this bar or not. I say fuck 'em. I'm going to do it and I am going to show them all."

"I've heard the rumors," Rhett replied, "but if you can pull this thing off and do it right, those same assholes will be spending their money in your bar, acting like they're your best buddies, patting you on the back and telling you they knew you could do it all along."

Dave laughed. "You're right! Fuck 'em."

Then Dave began by talking about his *krusha*. It was Russian slang for "roof" and used to signify Mafia protection. "My *roof* is Chechen. They're the biggest and baddest Mafia in Kyiv."

16

The idea was intriguing, as well as a bit disconcerting. Rhett wondered if Dave really knew what he was getting himself into. He knew about the Chechens and their reputation for ferocity. He had heard the old stories from Russian literature that read: *Beware the Chechen, who crawls on his belly at night along the banks of the river with the dagger in his mouth.*

"Are you fucking serious or just plain nuts?"

"Don't worry about it. I've got it all under control. I struck up a friendship with the leader of a group of four brothers. He heads up the Chechen Mafia in Kyiv. We're planning on doing some business deals together. The cowboy bar is only one. They're very well connected with officials high up in the government. We're going to build cowboy bars throughout Ukraine."

"Why not spread them out in major cities of Europe?" Rhett suggested. "There are a lot tamer markets than Ukraine."

Dave thought for a moment. "That might not be a bad idea."

"It might hedge your bets and be a bit safer."

"I'll think about it."

"But I don't know about this Chechen thing. That idea's got me a little spooked."

"Look, every business in this country's got a roof. I've just got the baddest motherfuckers in town behind me. Everybody's afraid of them. Matter of fact, when the manager of the German pub down the street asked me who *my* roof was, I told him. His eyes got real big and he told me, 'Now I guess I will have to worry about you taking over my bar.'"

Dave began to laugh.

Rhett took it to mean that it was merely a good-natured joke made by the manager. Still, he wasn't completely sure about the involvement with the Chechens. He was wondering if Dave could really trust the Chechen Mafia. Were they really his friends? "Have you ever run a bar before?"

Dave grinned. "I've been to enough bars in my life, so I figure that makes me an expert. Anyway, what's to run? Once I build the place, people will flock to it. It'll basically run itself."

"But what's to stop your roof from moving in and taking the business away from you once you've built the place?"

"Look, Rhett. They don't know the first thing about running a cowboy bar. Salom needs me."

"Who's Salom?"

"He's the one who heads up the Chechen Mafia in Kyiv. Besides, he wants me to help them set up legitimate businesses. They're involved in the financing of the war in Chechnya and they need to set up some way to expand in other European cities. That's where I come in. I'll be their front man and help them set up those legitimate businesses throughout Eastern Europe."

"Other businesses?"

"Yeah. Salom told me that he bought a freighter in Odessa. It's loaded with contraband and is on its way to South Africa, where they have buyers waiting. As soon as that happens, these guys are going be rich and will be able to finance all of their operations, including the chain of cowboy bars. Like I said, Salom needs me and he knows it."

"Well, I just hope you know what the hell you're doing, because if you fuck with these guys, they're liable to bend you over and make you bark like a poodle."

Dave laughed. "Listen, do you know what the war in Chechnya's really about?"

"Yeah. Oil. Chechnya's sitting on top of a huge reserve of some of the purest oil in the world, so pure that it requires little or no refining. Am I right?"

"Very good." Dave appeared surprised when he heard him mention Chechen oil. "You've done some homework. Not too many know about that and that's why if the Chechens are successful in gaining their independence from Russia, the nation's going be incredibly wealthy and so will the brothers. If that happens, I'll be in a good position to help them with all of their business dealings."

—

However, everything had not started as rosy as Dave was painting it. He neglected to tell Rhett how he had become involved with the Chechen Mafia in the first place.

The fact was, Salom and his men showed up at his door one day to see how much money he could extort from him. But Dave fancied himself a player and figured he could get them off his back by telling them of the various deals he was putting together, including the bar on *The Passazh*. And he must have been a good talker because they had evidently decided to listen to his offer.

If Salom wanted in on the projects, Dave was ready to take him on as a partner. In any event, he didn't have much of a choice. From that point on, they acted as if they were his best buddies and closest confidants.

"So, what are you going to call the place?"

"The Cowboy Bar. What else?"

"Why don't you spell it with a 'K?' Call it The Kowboy Dance Hall & Saloon."

"Sounds good, real Soviet. I like that," Dave responded.

"And where's it going to be, exactly?"

"I've got an area that's four hundred square meters situated directly under *The Passazh*. It's one of the best locations in Kyiv."

"How'd you find it?"

"My partner Sergei."

"Wait a minute. Who's Sergei? I thought this Salom was your partner."

"Sergei's an old friend. I've known him ever since I first arrived in Ukraine. He's my partner in the bar. He owns this place and he owns the space for our bar. It used to be a small billiards bar underneath *The Passazh*. Sergei was going to turn the place into a bowling alley until I convinced him that a cowboy bar was the way to go. I told him it would bring in a lot of Westerners with plenty of cash to spend. So, we became partners. Sergei provides the location. I build the bar. That way I don't have to pay a lot of rent for a choice location. It was simply too good of a deal to turn down."

"But what about Salom?"

"He's my roof and my silent partner. He's in on the bigger things, like the chain of cowboy bars."

"Then what does Sergei think about Salom?"

"Don't worry about it. I said I'm the one who's in control."

Dave also neglected to tell Rhett that since Sergei was in business on *The Passazh*, his ties were linked to a Moscow-based Mafia that ran the center of the city.

Ordinarily, the Mafias didn't infringe on each other's territories. Over the years, there had been an uneasy truce between them with no serious incidents of violence. However, Dave's unholy alliance with the Chechens was threatening to change all of that.

At first, Sergei opposed the deal. But when Salom's men abducted one of his employees, he didn't have much of a choice. If he wanted to see his employee alive again, he had to play ball. Reluctantly he acquiesced to Salom's demand to be Dave's silent partner.

Dave continued telling Rhett about his ambitious plans. The bar would have live country music and dancing every night. He was going to fly in a group of musicians from the states and make deals for them to tour bars throughout Europe.

He had also found financial backing through a couple of Americans working in Kyiv. Each had ponied up about twenty-five grand for a small percentage in the bar.

One was Valerie, a Texan. She'd arrived with Rhett as a Peace Corps volunteer. Within a year, she had wrangled herself a lucrative job with the International Finance Corporation.

At first, she was wary of the deal, but Dave could be very persuasive and eventually convinced her that it was better than money in the bank.

Todd was the other, a young redheaded collegiate type from Connecticut. Good looking and clean-cut, he had been working in Kyiv for about three years initially coming over to work on USAID projects. When those dried up, he began putting together a few deals on his own.

Another investor was a young Ukrainian named Lucy, who worked with Valerie at the IFC. She had saved close to ten thousand dollars and was intending to buy an apartment with her savings. However, Dave made promises to her, too.

He told her if she would invest in the bar, he would buy her an apartment and have his work crews remodel it to Western standards. It would enable her to move into a place almost immediately, without have to go through the never ending and grueling process of finding materials and doing the work herself. As a result, she convinced her family to sell their home and turn over their life savings to Dave.

———

Rhett kept listening as Dave continued. "Look, I was on the verge of packing everything in, but this deal looked so good I couldn't afford to turn it down. I called my wife in California and told her about it. She told me to go for it."

"Your wife?"

"Yeah. Didn't you know I was married?" Dave laughed. "I've got a great wife."

At that point, the subject turned to Rhett and his interest in the cowboy bar.

"OK. What do you want out of this deal?"

"Well, I've lived in Kyiv for three years and I'd like to find some work so I can stay. I surely can't go back to Oklahoma. They all but revoked my reputation there. Besides, there's not much left for me in Oklahoma."

"I need bartenders. You could be assistant manager. I'll give you all you can drink for free."

"Dave, I'm looking for a job, not a drink." He was annoyed by the offer. "Look, almost everyone here knows me as 'The Cowboy.' I think I can help you make this bar a success." Pulling out a drawing pad Rhett slid it across the bar. "I thought you could use them for your place."

Dave looked surprised again, but he was impressed. "These sketches are great. Who did them?"

"I did … used to be a designer. I won a lot of awards back in the States, and can organize a great advertising campaign to promote your bar."

"Don't need any advertising." Dave replied. "Once I open the bar, people are going to pay me to advertise the place."

Rhett knew that he was going to have to do a little persuading. It was obvious Dave was thoroughly convinced that all he had to do was open the doors and Westerners would immediately come pouring in.

But before he could continue, a group of Westerners entered the bar. One of them was a Canadian-Ukrainian Diaspora named Bogdan.

Dave stood up to greet him.

"Hey, buddy, what's going on? Have you met my advertising guy?" Dave's comment made Rhett feel a little better.

"Yes, we've met. You've obviously got the right man for the job."

Rhett smiled. He had sent Bogdan a resume a year earlier applying for a job at his public relations agency. He never received a reply.

"Did you ever receive that fax I sent?"

"Yeah," Bogdan answered tone and that was it. It was evident by the pompous tone in his voice that he wasn't interested. Anyone wearing a cowboy hat wasn't qualified for the job.

Rhett let the matter drop.

It was getting late and Rhett knew he had to make it home. He was still a cash-poor volunteer who had to travel by mass transit. He didn't have the money to spend on a taxi and knew the Metro would be closing soon. It was the middle of the winter; the snow was deep and he didn't relish the idea of walking home in the dark. Not that he hadn't done it before, but he remembered it wasn't a very pleasant experience. He got up to excuse himself. "Well, I've got to catch the Metro if I'm going to make it home tonight."

"OK. Call me in the morning." Dave told him. 'We'll set up a time and place to meet. I want to show you the bar before I leave for California."

"You're going to California?" Rhett was a little surprised.

"Yeah, gotta make an appearance with the wife," he laughed.

Rhett walked out of the Carambol as the other Westerners discussed where they were planning to go next. They were talking about going to the *River Palace*, a large cruise ship moored on the banks of the Dnieper River that had been converted to a casino. They were all highly paid fat cats on lucrative government contracts. With their wives back home in Canada or the States, they were free to go drinking and whoring 'til their heart's content.

Rhett hurried to the Metro. He was just in time to catch the last train. It would take him to his apartment located in the *Polytechnichny* region of

Kyiv. There weren't many people on the platform, only the drunks and derelicts who inhabited the streets and underground late at night. He was tired and a bit drunk himself. But he felt good about the possibilities that lay ahead.

IV

The Chechen

The ringing seemed to go on forever as Rhett waited for someone to pick up the phone.

"What!" Dave barked; his voice was raspy from drinking all night.

"Not what, where? Where do you want to meet?"

"Oh, yeah. Right. Uh, let me think for a minute. OK. How about ten o'clock on *The Passazh*." Dave gave him some muddled directions on how to find a door by which the construction workers entered. "I'll have Lena, my secretary, meet you. Do you know her?"

"I don't think so."

"Well, don't worry. She'll find you. You're not too hard to spot in that goddamned cowboy hat."

Rhett got dressed and walked out of his apartment onto Prospekt Pobedy. He lit a cigarette and looked around. "Well, this sure ain't Oklahoma." He chuckled to himself. "Nope, but that's what I like about it. It sure as hell ain't Oklahoma!"

—

When Rhett arrived on *The Passazh*, he couldn't find the door. Wandering up and down the street, he asked people if they knew of a bar being built. No one knew anything.

He was freezing and shivered as he lit another cigarette as he huddled underneath an arched passageway in the middle of the street.

A petite young woman walked up and spoke to him in English. "Are you looking for Dave?"

"Yeah. Are you . . .?"

"I am Lena, Dave's secretary. We have met before. It was at one of Dave's parties. I have always remembered the cowboy."

She led him down the passageway to an alley behind *The Passazh*, to a heavy steel door. Opening it, she led him down a flight of stairs where he saw Dave waving his arms about in the middle of the room shouting out directions to the workers in his pigeon Russian.

Sawdust and dirt were everywhere from the construction. A huge, thick brick wall had been knocked out, leading to another room. It was cavernous and much bigger than Rhett had imagined.

Rhett walked up behind him. "I don't think they understand a damn word you're saying."

Dave turned to greet him with a smile and a handshake. "Yeah? Well, fuck 'em. So what do you think?"

Rhett had to admit, 'It's got potential."

Dave led him through the cavern describing his plans for the club. "There will be a facade of an old cowboy town here, and there is where the Mexican restaurant will be. That room over there is going to have the electric bull."

"You're going to have an electric bull?"

"Yeah, going to fly it in from the States." As always, Dave thought big.

"As I said, if you can pull it off, this will be a great place for the ex-pat community, and the Ukrainians."

"To hell the Ukrainians! It's the foreigners who have the money."

Rhett shook his head and shrugged.

"I'm planning on a New Year Eve's opening in six weeks."

"Six weeks? Can you make that?" Looking around, he couldn't see how Dave could possibly do it. The wooden floors hadn't been laid. The bar, the kitchen, the bathrooms, the plumbing, the electrical system, the tables and the stools, and so much more. It would take nothing short of a miracle. "What about the equipment for the restaurant?"

"I'm not really planning on having too much of a restaurant." Dave answered. "Valerie told me it would be too much trouble. I'm thinking more along the lines of a watering hole and music venue."

"Well, I think you ought to reconsider. I read an article in *Newsweek* about a Russian who opened a Tex-Mex restaurant near the Kremlin in Moscow. It was so popular, he recouped his initial investment in only six weeks. And with the lack of good restaurants in Kyiv, a restaurant would bring in twice as many people as the bar. The Western community's desperate for new restaurants."

"I'll think about it. Do you know how much they had to pay to build the Arizona Bar-B-Que?" Dave asked.

"No idea."

"Two hundred and fifty grand. How much do you think it's going to cost me to build this place?"

"I'm sure you're gonna tell me."

"About half that amount. The way I figure it, it'll take somewhere between eighty and ninety grand. A hundred and twenty-five thousand, tops. Do you know why?"

"Nope."

"Because I tell everybody I have no money." He laughed. "I'm real good at telling people I have no money. That's why I don't have to pay as much as the other foreigners usually do. I get the best deals on everything. Besides, I've already got over sixty grand from my investors. This place is going to cost me next to nothing. Now, come on. Let's go to the Carambol, have some coffee and talk over a few things. It's colder than a witch's tit down here."

———

As they sat down at a table in the back of the Carambol, Dave put his head in his hands. "Shit! I've got a fucking headache. I didn't get in until five this morning. I need a beer and tomato juice. What'll you have?"

Rhett lit a cigarette. "Coffee will be fine. I drink enough at night as it is. Besides, I've already had a half-dozen aspirin and beer makes me piss like a race horse."

"Okay. What do you want out of this deal? Like I always say, I don't have a lot of money."

"I figured you'd say that. I think I've got enough to last me until things get going. But I'm telling you, I can't hold out indefinitely. I need to make a living."

"So what do you want?"

"I'll tell you what. I'm willing to throw in with you. I'll back your play, and if this thing's a success, then I'll expect you to pay me for the time I put in and cut me in for a percentage."

"Sounds fair to me. You've got a deal." They sealed the deal with a handshake.

"Anyway, I figure it will be a hell of a lot more interesting than going back to Oklahoma or working for some boring bureaucratic assholes that everyone seems to be sending over here."

"You got that right."

"But there's one thing that you've got to realize."

"What's that?" Dave asked.

"There's no middle ground here. You either wind up being a hero if you're successful or a fool if you lose. It's a hard game and people are only going to like you if you're a winner."

"You sound as if you know."

"In a way, I guess I do. But, I've been surviving and killing myself all my life. It's probably how I wound up in this godforsaken place. Besides, I've got to figure out something to do after the Peace Corps. But, hey! It's a cowboy's life ain't it?"

At that moment, Rhett looked up to see Lena. She was accompanied by two of the workers from The Kowboy.

One was Andrei, a fine-looking young Ukrainian who could speak English. The other was Sasha, a former sergeant in the Soviet army, was accustomed to handling men. Together, they would be in charge of the construction crew in Dave's absence.

Dave began explaining what would be needed while he was in California. Andrei hung intently on Dave's every word as Lena translated to Sasha.

"I have this bar right up here in my head." He told them. "It will be up to you to help me make it a reality. Now, Rhett here, as you can see, is a cowboy. So he knows what's in my head and how to make this bar look authentic. If you have any questions while I'm gone, ask him." When everything was apparently clear, Dave decided it was time to return to the bar.

As he stepped into the street, Rhett saw a pair of new Mercedes abruptly pulled up in front of him. He watched as six men filed out of their cars to greet Dave. It was Salom and his Chechens.

The Chechens were all smartly dressed in thousand-dollar suits and more closely resembled successful businessmen rather than the Mafia. Salom, in particular, was dapper … friendly and smiling. His reddish hair made him look more Irish than Muslim.

"Rhett, I want you to meet Salom."

Lena translated the introduction as Salom held out his hand to Rhett. She explained that they had seen him walking the streets of Kyiv and told him that Salom already knew who he was.

"Chuck Norris," Salom said as he shook Rhett's hand. *"Odeenokie Volk."* It meant Lone Wolf. Since he was wearing a cowboy hat, had longish long hair, a black leather duster, and because Chuck Norris was associated with cowboys, it was enough for them.

Rhett smiled. It wasn't that he really looked like Chuck Norris, but he kinda liked the name.

Dave turned to him. "I've got to go straighten out some details with Salom. After that, he's going to take me to the airport. You'll be in charge while I'm gone, so begin working on things. I'll call you when I get back."

With that, Dave got into one of the Mercedes. The Chechens quickly whisked him away as Rhett watched the cars disappear quickly down through the back of *The Passazh*. It was just the way Dave did business, very fast and very loose.

V

"Cowboys in Action"

Every night, while working on plans for the bar. Rhett would drink until he was too drunk to see, then fall asleep or pass out. He wasn't sure which. His mind was working so hard he couldn't relax. He found himself waking up in the middle of the night, worrying about the smallest of details he might have overlooked. Even with the massive doses of alcohol, he couldn't make himself sleep, no matter how he tried.

Whenever he would call Dave in California, Dave would always laugh and ask, "What time is it there? Don't worry, go back to sleep. I've got everything covered." Yet, despite Dave's self-assuredness, Rhett knew the bar was going to need a lot of work and help.

—

Rhett was aware that his friend that Volodomir still had contacts with the intelligence community. Thinking that it might be helpful, he telephoned to tell him about the restaurant. He also invited Volodomir and his wife to join him at his apartment for another Cowboyskie dinner.

After dinner and a few bottles of vodka, Volodomir wanted to know more.

"So tell me, Rhett, this is your restaurant?"

"No, it's going to be Dave Seigal's place. I'm helping him with the project. Do you know him?"

"Is he the one who played his guitar at the Metro under Kreschatik?"

"That's the one."

"Yes, I remember him. He is one of Kyiv's most picturesque adventurers"

"Xto? (Who)"

Volodomir explained to his wife in Russian who Dave was.

She laughed.

Volodomir turned back to Rhett. "When will it be open?"

"It's still under construction, but Dave wants to open it in January."

"What are you going to do for security? You know about our problems with the Mafia, especially with the nightclubs. If you would like, I will call someone. I know a man who will post *Militsia* outside. It will guarantee your safety and protection from the Mafias."

"I agree. The *Militsia* is the way to go, but Dave has made … how to say, *different* arrangements."

"And what would those arrangements be?" Volodomir asked.

Their friendship was built on trust and Rhett knew that he could confide anything to Volodomir. But he also knew of Volodomir's disdain for the Mafia. He reluctantly told him.

"Dave has made an agreement with some Chechens. They are his partners and he thinks they will be his best protection."

Volodomir was clearly shocked. "Does he know what he's doing? You can't trust the Chechens. They are Mafia. Only a fool would work with them. Dave's been here long enough. He should know better. The Chechens don't take anyone as partners. They'll take his club from him before he knows what's happening. He'll end up with nothing after he builds that bar. Does he know that?"

"I agree with you Volodomir. If it were my decision, I'd do it just like you said, but it's not my bar. It's Dave's. He's the one who's putting up the money, and ultimately the decisions are his."

"Durak! Fool!*"* Volodomir muttered. Then he turned to Rhett and with a stern tone said, "Well, you tell him what I said. And I will say this to you: If you need any help, I'll make the phone call for you, because you're my friend."

"Thanks. I appreciate it. I'll try to talk to him and tell him about your offer." But he really didn't think that Dave would listen, because Dave thought he had all of his bases covered. It was left at that.

—

Over the following weeks, Rhett would visit the bar every day, monitoring the construction and the progress. He also waited for Dave's return. On occasion, he would have the opportunity to get information from Dave through Lena.

One afternoon, when they ran into each other at the bar he asked. "Lena, when will we have a phone?"

"I don't know. I believe it is a problem for Sergei." She rubbed her fingers together, indicating it was a matter of money for a bribe to speed things up.

"Well, then, when will we have some money?"

She didn't know that either. "It is a matter that will have to be solved between Dave and Sergei upon his return.

The issue about where money would come from was always a vague issue. Only Dave really knew. Usually, he would give just enough cash to Lena to pay whatever was the most pressing need of the moment or whoever was screaming the loudest.

Rhett remembered the conversation he had with Volodomir a few days earlier and decided to approach the subject with Lena. "Who's going to be responsible for security?"

"I don't know. I believe that is an issue for Dave and Salom to work out."

"Listen. I've got a friend in one of the ministries. His name is Lakamov. Do you know him?"

"I don't think so."

"Well, he told me he could make a call for us and arrange our security. I personally don't think that Westerners are going to feel all that comfortable walking into a bar with a bunch of Mafia types standing outside."

"What do you mean?"

"I mean, if we have ordinary policemen standing outside, customers are going to feel a lot safer coming to this place. You go to any respectable club or restaurant in Kyiv and there are *Militsia* standing outside. Right?"

She nodded her head in agreement.

"They have them outside other Western clubs and restaurants, don't they?"

"Yes, they do."

"It only makes common sense. The *Militsia* are authorized to carry weapons. If there's any trouble, they have the legal right to make an arrest. After all, they are the law. They can do that, can't they? However, if one of Salom's guys shoots somebody, the police will come down on us very hard. If something bad does happen, this bar could be in for a lot of trouble, not to mention all of the bad publicity that would come right along with it."

"It sounds like it makes sense," she replied. "What does Dave think? Did you talk to him about it?"

"Not yet. I wanted to run it by you first. When he comes back, I think we ought to talk to him. Don't you agree? That's another reason why we need a phone. If there is a fire in this place or some kind of emergency, we need to be able to call the proper authorities. We might not have time to go up on the street and find a phone that works."

"You are right."

"Listen, I know this is Dave's bar. I'm just trying to think of everything now so we don't have any problems later."

Together, they agreed to talk to Dave when he returned. Then Lena left to take care of other business. Rhett was glad that Dave had someone like her. She was like his right arm. She was intelligent and as concerned with the bar's success as anyone.

———

Slowly, the bar began to come together. Still, it was nowhere near fast enough.

A few weeks later, Dave returned and they met once again in the Carambol.

"I've found our singin' cowboy to play at the bar."

"Really?"

"Yeah. I sent out an e-mail announcement looking for a musician to teach Ukrainians country music. I found one in Texas. This kid's been studying country music at some junior college in Odessa and noticed the Internet job posted on a teacher's door. He called up me up and said, 'I'm your man.' I liked the kid's attitude over the phone, so . . . I hired him sight unseen. Haven't even heard him play yet."

Rhett choked on his cigarette. "You haven't heard him?"

"Nope. I'm planning on bringing him back with me the next time I return from California. I know of a popular musical group here in Kyiv. My new plan is to bring him in to train them to play country music. It'll be much cheaper than flying in an entire group from the States. Besides, most musicians in Ukraine have trained in music conservatories."

"I understand your logic, Dave. I just hope this kid can play."

Rhett began bringing him up to date on what had been occurring at The Kowboy. Things had been going slowly. About half the floor was installed in the main bar room, and part of the facade had been built. Nevertheless, if Dave wanted to get the place ready by January, there was still a lot to do.

Then Dave began to fill him in on his strategy. "Everyone is getting tired of getting ripped off at places like the Arizona Bar-B-Que. My strategy is simple ... sell more for less. That's what'll bring in the customers. The way I look at it is, we're not going into competition with them. We're merely going to offer another alternative in a market that's begging for more places to patronize."

Rhett agreed. "Sounds like it makes sense … seems that there's a shortage of everything. Besides, the word is beginning to get around about The Kowboy and Westerners are starting to look for any sort of alternative to those high-priced nightspots of Kyiv.

"Hey! There's plenty of room for everybody. Plus, we'll have music and a dance floor. Folks will be coming for that."

Dave was anxious to see how his bar was coming along. So, they left the Carambol and began walking toward The Kowboy Dance Hall & Saloon.

Once inside, Dave took one look and a broad grin appeared ear to ear. "Now I can picture this place a reality. I didn't know for sure earlier. I couldn't really see it. But looking at these Old West facades, it tells me that this place is, by God, going to happen."

—

The Studio Restaurant was slick and modern. Decorated in a neo-fifties' style, it was a posh oasis where the ex-pat community could dine on delicacies rarely served in the other restaurants of Kyiv. Plenty of neon to accented the place and photographs of Marilyn Monroe hung everywhere. Everything was clean and sleek.

When Rhett arrived, he saw Dave sitting at the bar sipping on a Mimosa. He was obviously well known by many of the Westerners and if he wasn't hopping from table to table trying to get some deal going, people were coming to him.

After ordering Rhett a drink, Dave turned to him. "OK, Rhett. What am I going to have to pay you?"

"I told you, Dave. If the place is successful, I'm going to want a piece of the action. Right now, you don't have to pay me anything. However, in few months I'll expect you to pay my rent, plus a retainer.

"Well, we should be open by then. Shouldn't be a problem."

"Just make sure you don't forget."

"Don't worry, I won't." Dave slapped Rhett on the back, causing him to spill his drink down the front of his shirt.

Grabbing a napkin, Rhett looked up to see a petite, attractive blonde approaching. She was wearing glasses, which served to accentuate her intelligence, as well as her beauty.

Dave put his arms around her kissing her on the cheek. "Lucy, have you met Rhett yet?"

"No, I don't believe I've had the pleasure." She was polite and spoke softly in fluent English.

Wiping his hands with the napkin, he then extended one to shake hands. Dave looked around the bar. "Let's find a table."

As soon as they sat down, Dave continued with the introductions. "Lucy's one of the investors I told you about. She doesn't know it yet, but she is going to be working for me." He laughed, reaching over and giving her a hug.

She responded with a polite smile.

"Rhett's going to be in charge of our advertising. We're lucky he's going to help us out, because there is no way I could afford him. Look at some of the things he's doing for us. Do you have any of that stuff?"

Rhett reached inside his valise, pulled out the sketches and handed them to Dave.

As Lucy looked at them, he tried to correct Dave's explanations of what they were. Suddenly, Dave grabbed the sketches and got up from the table to show them around the restaurant leaving Lucy and Rhett alone.

"So, what do you think of the bar?"

"Dave does so many things. Everybody seems to know him. If he does what he says he is going to do, I think it should be very popular."

Rhett nodded. "Well, if he stays with the plan, he stands to be very successful."

"I hope so." She answered softly. "I've given him $10,000. It is my family's life savings."

Investing $10,000, for an average Ukrainian, was like a working-class American risking ten times as much. Lucy had put everything on the line for Dave and his bar.

It seemed that Dave was traveling at warp speed, holding meetings during the day while "chasing those deals that were the stuff of fantasy." At night he was the social butterfly, keeping a high profile and making sure that everyone knew that The Kowboy Dance Hall & Saloon was coming to Kyiv. Every night, he drank into the early morning hours at the bars and casinos that made up the nightlife of Kyiv.

When Rhett called him at his apartment, Dave would answer incoherently in his whiskey voice. It was amazing, but somehow Dave miraculously managed to pull himself together and start all over again.

Meeting Dave at the bar or his apartment Rhett accompanied him along with his ever-present Lena as he moved fast trying to confer on matters that concerned the bar between this deal or that.

Dave didn't have a regular office, being content to handle all his business dealings on the run. In its present condition, The Kowboy was not a suitable place for holding any sort of business. It resembled a bombed-out wreckage and didn't have a phone. There was no way to communicate to suppliers or sponsors except from the phones on the street and they didn't always work. Anyone could plainly see that Dave badly needed some organization in the way he did business.

Things were easier for Dave. He had a driver, Boris, who would drive him all over Kyiv.

Rhett had to take either the Metro, a tram or trolleybus. The Ukrainians always seemed confused why an American cowboy would be traveling by such a means of transport rather than a car.

The Metro wasn't too bad though. The stations were like monuments, great marbled, granite and steel monoliths that had been built as tributes to the Socialist State at the end of the Second World War. In fact, it was cleaner than the New York subway system and a lot safer.

However, the trams and trolleybuses could be a nightmare. They suffered from a lack of maintenance and were constantly overpacked.

It was while Rhett was travelling on the transport system that he first saw him. He wasn't sure at first, when he stepped onto the trolley car. But there he stood, from cowboy hat to cowboy boots. He was even carrying saddlebags — but he clearly wasn't American.

Rhett looked at him. He looked at Rhett.

There was no telling what the other passengers thought.

After several stops, he quickly stepped out of the train and disappeared into the crowd. Rhett had seen his first Ukrainian cowboy.

—

And that's how it continued, Dave getting drunk at the bars, money flowing like wine. Rhett, he got drunk in his apartment thinking about the woman he left behind in Oklahoma.

Three weeks later, Dave hopped another plane for California. The bar was far from finished and the date for its opening had been moved back.

VI

The Texas Troubadour

Dave was gone for a month. When he returned, he telephoned Rhett and told him to come to the Carambol to meet the young Texan he had brought back from Odessa.

When Rhett walked into the bar, he saw two cowboy hats. Underneath one was a clean-cut nineteen-year-old kid. By this time, the waitresses were really getting a kick out of seeing the cowboys rendezvous at the club.

Dave turned around as Rhett walked up. "Rhett, I want you to meet Toby."

"Pleased to meet you, sir." He spoke in a polite tone and seemed to be a fine upstanding example of west Texas American youth. Wide-eyed and bushy-tailed, it was obviously the first time he had ever been outside of the U.S. As he looked around, he couldn't believe he was actually sitting smack dab in the middle of Eastern Europe.

"I'm going to make this kid a star." Dave patted the kid on the back.

41

"Sounds okay by me," Rhett replied as they shook hands. "You know, Dave? Maybe we can arrange for him to play the main stage on Kyiv Day."

Kyiv Day was a celebration held at the end of May and drew tens of thousands to Kyiv every year.

"Got it under control. It's already in the works," Dave answered. "I told him he would be performing before an audience of seventy thousand."

Toby replied in a pure Texas accent, "Gosh, that's more people than Garth Brooks has ever played for." His demeanor seemed almost too good to be true.

Spotting a few Westerners at the end of the bar, Dave got up and walked over leaving the two cowboys to get better acquainted.

"So, what do you think of Kyiv?"

"It's awesome! I can't believe I'm actually sitting here."

"Sure is a far cry from Texas, ain't it?"

"You can say that again," Toby laughed.

"What do you think of the food?"

"It's great! Dave's been taking me to the Studio and the Arizona Bar-B-Que."

"Oh! Well, those are two of the best American restaurants in town, so you really haven't had any authentic Ukrainian food yet. Do you cook?"

"A little," he answered.

"If you would like, I'll take you around the markets and teach you how to shop. If you can cook, you can eat pretty much like you do back home. The markets have basically everything they have got back in the States. The only thing is, they're not quite as attractive as they are in American supermarkets. Plus, they eat some things here that you wouldn't dream of eating in the States. If you'd like, you're welcome to come over to my apartment some night and I'll cook us up a batch of my cowboy chili."

"Sure."

"Have you traveled the Metro yet?"

"What's that?"

"It's the subway. Basically, it can get you anywhere you want to go if you don't have a car. Do you speak any Russian or Ukrainian?"

"Nope, but I have a cassette that says it can teach me Russian in about six weeks."

Rhett laughed. "Well, I think it may take a little bit longer than that. I've been here for about four years and I think I can pretty much have an intelligent conversation with a three-year-old. It's a tough language with a different alphabet and they've got sixteen ways to say 'to go' here."

A waitress placed a napkin in front of the kid and asked for his order in Russian. Toby refused, waiving her off.

"Dave told me you didn't drink."

"Nope, I don't drink or smoke."

"That's just fine," Rhett coughed as he lit a cigarette. "You'll probably live longer than either us."

Toby laughed. Then he looked over his shoulder in Dave's direction. "He sure drinks a lot, doesn't he?"

"We all do over here. It goes with the territory … part of the culture."

Tossing back a shot of vodka Rhett noticed Toby ogling one of the waitresses.

"So, what do you think of the women?"

"Gosh," Toby gushed, "I never seen so many good looking girls in my life."

"Gosh? The boy doesn't cuss, either? Rhett thought. Then he ordered another shot.

Toby was right about one thing, though. Ukrainian women had always been famous for their beauty.

"Did you ever hear that Beatles' song 'Back In The USSR?'"

"Yeah, it sounds kinda familiar. I think my folks had that record when I was a kid.".'"

"Probably a little before your time. Anyway, it contains a chorus that says 'The Ukraine girls really knock me out. They leave the West behind.' I never really knew what it meant, until I came here."

"They don't seem to like it when I try to pay them a compliment or a lot of attention. Is that considered something bad here?"

"Not really. Maybe they're not used to it. Most likely, they're embarrassed."

"Boy, howdy. They sure are beautiful. I really wish I could talk to them."

"Well, they say the best way to learn the language is to get yourself a Ukrainian girlfriend."

"Might as well. My fiancée broke of our engagement when I told her I was coming here."

The heavy smoke in the bar seemed to be getting to Toby. "Excuse me. I can't breathe in here. I need to get me some fresh air." And with that, he abruptly stood up and left the bar.

When Dave noticed him leave, he walked back over. "Well, what do you think?"

44

"He seems a bit wet behind the ears, but I suppose he'll be fine. When does he meet the band?"

"Tomorrow. I've got a place for them to rehearse and they'll work every day until The Kowboy opens. I figure it'll take 'em about two months until they're ready."

"Have you heard him play yet?"

"He played me a song on the guitar the other night."

"And?"

"He sounded all right. Plus, one of his friends will be flying over in about a couple of weeks. He's from Oklahoma and it seems they played together back in the States. I've also got a second group. It's three girls who play rockabilly. Sort of a female version of the Stray Cats. They call themselves the Rockland Ladies. So, they'll be our opening act."

Noticing that Toby had returned and was checking out the hustlers in the billiards room, Dave nodded in his direction. "Evidently, he was in flight school back in the States, but he washed out. They gave him a discharge for a developing ulcer. I think it really meant that he couldn't take the pressure."

Just as Toby was about to pick out a pool cue, Rhett pointed at him "Well, you'd better do something about Opie over there before one of those sharks start using him as a toothpick."

"Right. I'll take him over to the Arizona and get him some dinner. Call me in the morning."

"Can you send a car for me? I'm getting tired of walking through all of this goddamned snow. I'll do it if I have to, but if you can send a car, I'd just as soon avoid walking around freezing my ass off."

"OK. As soon as my driver drops Toby off at rehearsal, I'll have Boris come pick you up. Say around ten o'clock?"

"Sounds fine."

It was late again, and as Rhett left to go home Dave took his new country singer to show him off. He wanted everyone to see his new sensation and wasn't about to waste any time.

At the Metro station, Rhett slid a few *karbovenetz* under the teller's window.

"*Nye rabotat*! (Not working)" The woman replied without looking up.

"*Nye rabotet?*" Rhett replied.

She explained that a drunk had fallen in front of the train and the Metro would be closed for the rest of the evening.

"Rhett walked out of the Metro and onto the street. It was snowing. He cursed under his breath, lit a cigarette and started the long walk home.

—

The following morning, Boris picked up Rhett and drove him to Dave's apartment.

When he arrived, Dave was going over the accounting system with his partner Sergei and his accountant Kolya. Rhett sat down and listened as Lena translated.

"Tell Sergei I want Kolya to keep two sets of books, one for the tax inspectors that will show a minimum profit. The taxes are too high in this country and I don't want to pay them if I can avoid it. The second set of books will be for us and those will be a true reflection of what the bar is really taking in."

Sergei conferred with Kolya, who nodded, indicating he understood and assuring Dave that it could be done.

"Good! Now tell him that since he's already a bar owner, I'm relying on his experience to put the system in place."

Sergei nodded again.

"Okay! That does it. Have you met Rhett? He's going to help me manage the place and handle the advertising."

Sergei and Kolya shook hands with Rhett, exchanged pleasantries, then left.

As soon as they were gone, Dave turned to him. "So, tell me what's going on."

"Look, Dave, I can't go on working out my apartment. For one thing, I'm starting to go stir crazy. For another, I don't have any place to file anything and I'm spending hours trying to find stuff. Besides, having an office will show everyone you're serious about this bar."

"Okay. I guess you're right. I'll get Salom to find us an office."

"Good. Where's Toby?"

"He's rehearsing with the band. I've decided that they're going to be called 'The Kowboy Bar Band.' What do you think?"

Rhett wasn't surprised. Since half of Dave's time was spent drinking at the bars, almost everything he could think of had the word "bar" in it.

"Fine by me. How are they doing?"

"They're coming along pretty well, but Toby doesn't like Anton."

"Who's that?"

"He's the group's manager. Toby doesn't trust him. He thinks he's a sleazy hustler and doesn't understand why his band would need a manager. Plus, he thinks Anton's undermining his authority as leader of the band."

"So what are you going to do?"

"Nothing. Anton's got the connections with the music scene here. Toby will have to deal with it."

Three weeks later, like clockwork, Dave flew back to the States again to spend the holidays with his family in California. Toby was on his own.

VII

The Kowboy Bar Band

"No! No! No! No! Nyet! Goddamnit, don't you guys understand English?"

The band members stood looking at Toby. They didn't speak much English, but they understood "No!" and they sure as hell understood his tone.

"This ain't rock and roll, its fucking country! You understand?"

"But Mister Toby, they do not have any music to read. If you will give them the music to read, I am sure …"

"Look, Anton, I don't need to read any music. I learned everything I play by listening to tapes. These guys got ears, don't they?"

"Yes, of course, but …"

"What do you mean 'but what?' I was told that these guys are the best musicians in Kyiv."

"Yes. They are one of the most popular groups in the city."

"Then why can't they play what I'm tellin' them to?"

"I'm sure that if they had the music to read, they could learn to . . .."

"I told you already, I didn't bring no sheet music. And what's with all this heavy metal crap with the lead guitar? That ain't country."

"I understand. But this group has many fans and they are known for playing the rock music."

"I don't care what they've been playin'. This is supposed to be a country group. You tell them if they can't learn to play it like I tell them to, then I'm going to have to start lookin' for somebody who can."

"Yes, of course. I will speak to them."

"You'd better, because if you can't do anything with them, then you're going to be looking for a job too."

Anton turned to the musicians and interpreted what Toby had told him.

"*Durak!*" replied one of the musicians.

"What'd he say? What does that mean?" Toby asked.

"He said he agrees with you," Anton replied.

"So, how's our troubadour doing?" The question came from behind him. He turned around to see Rhett standing behind him. "What? How long you been here? I didn't hear you walk in."

"O.I.T."

"What?"

"Old Indian Trick. So, how's it going?" Rhett repeated the question

"Pretty good. For the most part I'm satisfied with the band, but I'm having a hard time cleaning the hard rock out of them. Every time the lead guitarist comes to a break, he lets loose with that heavy metal shit. I have to stop everything and tell them about the finer points of country music."

It was starting to look like Toby was beginning to lose a bit of that good ole boy country charm. "I'm having an even harder time finding a fiddle player. Most of these guys are trained in classic music. They're not fiddle players at all. They're violinists. They don't know it yet, but there's going to be some shake-ups in the band and I'm planning on doing that as soon as my friend gets here."

"Well, I like all kinds of music. You name it — classical, rock, country. Besides, I think rock had a lot to do with bringing country into the mainstream, making it more popular."

"Not me. I don't go in for any of that new shit." Toby replied.

"Don't worry. I'm sure they'll get the hang of it."

"They'd better. I'm a purist as far as it goes with country music. I like Bob Wills, not this new crap they're playing on the radio nowadays."

Rhett decided to change the subject. "So, how are you getting along by yourself with Dave off in California?"

"To tell the truth, I'm glad he's gone," he replied. "He was taking me out every night and keeping me up until all hours. To be honest, it was starting to wear me out. I'm not used to that stuff. It was okay for him, but like I said, I don't drink or smoke. Anyway, you he's an alcoholic."

Rhett didn't reply, but he was surprised that Toby was talking about Dave in such a manner. It didn't make any difference whether it was true or not. Dave was Toby's boss and he didn't know Rhett well enough to be complaining about him or his drinking.

"Well, it's like I told you. A lot of Americans drink more over here than they do back in the States. God knows I drink more than my share. So other than that, how are you doing?"

"I called home the other day," he replied. "My folks told me it was almost ninety degrees in Odessa. I can't wait 'til I'm back there next week."

"You're going back?"

"Yeah, Dave's flying me back to the States for New Years. I'm ready too, after spending six weeks freezing my nuts off."

"Well, when you come back, be sure to bring some chili seasoning. The Ukrainians really like it once they've had a bowl or two. Matter of fact, I'm having some people over tonight and I'll be cooking up some chili. If you want, you're welcome to come on over to my … "

"No, thanks. I made plans to meet some Marines at the Arizona Barbeque."

Since Toby had been disappointed for not making it through flight school, it made sense he found some solace hanging out with the Marines from the American Embassy. He was far from home, they were around his age, gung-ho, redneck, and someone he could relate to. Whenever he wasn't rehearsing during the day, he would hang out with the Marines at night.

"Well, if you change your mind, you're welcome." With that, Rhett turned and walked out the door.

—

A few nights later, Rhett found himself working alongside a group of former Peace Corp volunteers in a Tex-Mex food booth at a charity event sponsored by the wives of the embassy personnel.

He was dishing chili and serving tacos in full cowboy regalia when Valerie walked up to him. "How's the bar coming along?"

"Slowly. Dave's pushed the opening back to February fourteenth"

"Yeah, right!" She laughed. "I doubt it. I'm going outside for a cigarette. You want to join me? I want to hear what's happening with the bar."

"Sure. Why not."

As soon as they were outside, Valerie turned to him. "Listen, I'm glad you're helping Dave out."

"Well, I needed to find a job and I figure this thing's right up my alley."

"Have you met our little cowboy Toby yet?" she asked.

"Yeah, Dave introduced us a few days after he arrived."

"He sure is a little bit of Texas, ain't he?"

"I guess you could say that. So what's the deal about the restaurant? Why did you tell Dave not to put one in?"

"I thought it would be too hard, you know, with getting all the food and stuff."

"Listen, Val. I'm not talking about anything fancy. He can make ninety percent of what he needs from the food that's available here."

"Yeah, well, it's Dave's place. I'm just an investor. And you know Dave. It's hard to convince him of anything. He's going to do whatever he wants."

"How much did you put up?"

"About twenty-five thousand. I can afford it since I'm working for the IFC. They pay me about seventy-five a year and Dave told me he could double that in six months. That's a better return than I could get anywhere else. So, have you talked about what he's going to pay you yet?"

"We haven't really discussed it."

"Well, just don't sell yourself too cheap. Get at least eight hundred a month."

Rhett was stunned. Valerie was making over seventy grand a year and she was telling him to get at least $800 goddam dollars a month.

"Don't worry, when I open my Tex-Mex restaurant, I'll hire you." She flicked her cigarette off into the night and walked back inside.

Rhett just sat there for a moment thinking of what he had just heard.

"Thanks a whole helluva lot, Val." he muttered to himself.

———

The following week, Toby flew back to Texas to spend Christmas with his family. When he returned, he brought back his cowboy friend from the panhandle of Oklahoma.

In the meantime, he had become engaged to his high school sweetheart — for the second time. They had overcome their problems and once more had decided to tie the knot. He proudly showed everyone her photograph, swearing up and down that since he was now engaged, he would not look at any other women. Rhett wondered how long that would last with all those world-class beauties walking on the streets of Kyiv.

The new musician was Tim. He seemed likable enough and was just as excited about being in Eastern Europe as Toby had been.

As soon as Tim had a chance to catch up to speed, Dave scheduled the band to make their debut at the Arizona Barbeque since it was always packed and would be excellent venue for Dave to show off his Kowboy Bar Band.

Rhett had never been to the Arizona, so when he walked in, he could hardly believe his eyes. It looked as if it had been snatched right out of the American experience and transplanted smack dab in the middle of Kyiv.

It was packed with Westerners and for a moment, he thought he might be back in the States.

Dave moved through the crowd, working them and doing his best to promote the Kowboy Dance Hall & Saloon. Being the frustrated showman, he eventually got up on stage and played harmonica with the group. Fortunately, the music was so loud that it drowned out his playing. So, it was hard to tell whether or not he was any good.

Nevertheless. he played on, relishing every moment.

A local television crew had set up and was filming the band. And due to the lack of decent local television programming in Kyiv, it was almost certain to make it on several television stations before the week was out.

Toby was eating it up too. Clean cut, with his white starched cotton shirt, blue jeans, and his hair buzzed short in a Marine-style haircut, he jumped up on a table where everybody could see him strut his stuff and sing his songs.

Lena and her husband were there and enjoying themselves along with dozens of Dave's friends, both foreign and Ukrainian. Before long, everyone was up dancing away as the Kowboy Bar Band played their country music.

The only ones who weren't there were his partners Sergei and Salom. It wasn't really their scene. Besides, a Western nightspot was too high profile for the likes of Salom and his Chechens.

All in all, it was great publicity for Dave's bar, and the Arizona didn't seem to mind too much either. The band had packed the place and they were making money hand over fist. It appeared that even though the

Arizona had only been open for three months, they were already turning a hefty profit.

It was late when Rhett left the Arizona. As he walked down the dimly lit streets of Kyiv, he could hear country music in the distance. As it spilled out into the evening, it sounded like things were looking mighty good for The Kowboy Dance Hall & Saloon.

VIII

The Cowboys Are Coming

A few days later, Dave returned to California and over the following weeks, Rhett didn't see much of Toby and Tim. Unfortunately for Tim, he had taken some of the limelight away from Toby at the Arizona and it had caused friction between the two. Friend or no friend, it was Toby's band and increasingly Tim found himself sitting on the sidelines Eventually, he became disillusioned and homesick, until he finally decided it was time to return to Oklahoma.

Even though Dave had paid a lot of money to have Tim flown to Ukraine at Toby's request, it didn't seem to make any difference. Tim was long gone by the time Dave returned to Kyiv.

———

When Dave did return, Rhett showed up at his apartment accompanied by a young Ukrainian. Igor was a nineteen-year-old Rhett had trained in advertising. Gesturing toward Igor, he introduced him to Dave. "This is Igor. He's bright, intelligent, a hard worker, and we need good people.

He's a good kid and comes with my highest recommendation. Besides, I need an assistant. So, what do you say?"

Dave gave the kid the once over. "What do you want?"

"Whatever you think is fair." Igor replied.

Always looking for a bargain, Dave winked at Rhett and gave Igor his favorite line. "Well, I don't have a lot of money, but I can give you twenty dollars a week. Can you live with that?"

Igor didn't really have much of a choice. He needed a job.

"I suppose it will be sufficient. I live with my parents."

"Then, I guess you're hired, kid."

When he noticed Igor eyeing a stack of cowboy hats in the corner he began to grin. "Try one on."

Then he turned to Rhett, "I bought them in Mexico for about four bucks apiece.

Dave saw Igor was looking at his reflection in a mirror. "You like that hat?"

"Yes, I do/ It is a fine hat!"

"Well, take it. It's yours."

"Thank you, Mr. Seigal. Thank you very much!" Igor was the proud owner of his first cowboy hat.

Rhett looked around the apartment. "Where's Tim?"

Toby had been sitting in the corner. He answered without looking up. "He went back home."

"How come? Didn't he like it here?"

"He and I ran into a little problem. He didn't like the way I was running the band. I had to straighten him out real quick over that issue. So, he left."

Rhett decided to let it go and said nothing more.

Instead, he turned back to Dave. "While you were gone, I found us a photographer to do a publicity shoot for The Kowboy, but it's going to cost a couple of hundred bucks."

When Dave started complaining about the money, Rhett was ready and explained his idea for the photoshoot. "What I envision is you, Toby and me dressed as three cowboys walking down *The Passazh*. Believe me, the photoshoot will be well worth the cost."

Considering himself the ultimate idea man, Dave suddenly had one of his grand epiphanies. "Yeah, yeah. You know what? Since I have all these cowboy hats, what if I call up a bunch of my friends and have them standing around in the background. You know, then it would look like Kyiv was full of cowboys. What do you think?"

Rhett thought for a moment. It wasn't quite what he had envisioned. "I was hoping to keep things as simple as possible. All those people might make things more difficult to coordinate. But it's an idea. Let me think about it."

Then he told them not to shave for a week, because he wanted the cowboys to look as rough as possible for the shoot.

"That okay with you Toby?"

"It's not my style."

"Don't worry about it," Dave interrupted. "He's supposed to be the star. I figure if you and I look rough and Toby's clean cut, it'll look just fine."

Again, it wasn't what he had planned, but Dave was on a roll and Rhett thought it was better to let him go with it if he could get Dave to pony up the money for the photoshoot. Besides, he was used to dealing with clients who wanted to do things their own way. "I guess it'll work. I just need to rethink everything. for a minute. Anyway, I have a meeting scheduled with the photographer this morning and we can scheduled the photoshoot for some time next week."

———

Within the hour, they were sitting in the photographer's studio.

As Igor interpreted, Dich elaborated on his ideas while the photographer patiently explained anything was possible. *Oo Princapi* (In principle).

Anytime one heard that phrase in Eastern Europe, it usually meant maybe, but probably not. Then the photographer explained if Dave wanted him to do everything he was asking, the shoot would take longer than one day and would probably cost more money.

"Okay. Here's a hundred dollars. Tell him to go ahead and get started, Igor." And with that, everything was apparently agreed upon. At least it appeared so as far as Dave was concerned.

———

The following week, it was snowing and was cold as Igor and Rhett walked out of the underground and onto the street. They saw Toby standing in front of a gastronome talking with the girls of the backup group, The Rockland Ladies as they were showing him their publicity photos.

Rhett walked up to them. "Where's Dave?"

"Don't know," he replied. "He hasn't been to the apartment all night, but I talked to him on the phone and said he'd meet us at the shoot."

"Well, at least he hasn't forgotten. Where's the band?"

"I think they are on their way."

Worried they wouldn't make it to the photoshoot, Rhett asked Igor to give the photographer a call and to check if everything was ready at the studio. The photographer confirmed that it was and he was waiting. Fortunately, the studio was only a fifteen-minute walk through the snow.

Rhett had become accustomed to the harsh Ukrainian winters. Of course, for the Ukrainians this was simply their everyday reality of life. Nevertheless, it must have been a strange sight to see. A group of cowboys walking down the streets of Kyiv in the Ukrainian Winterland.

As they crossed the street, two ladies turned around and looked at them. They said something, but Rhett couldn't quite catch what they were saying. However, Igor was laughing.

"Igor, what did they say?'

"They said, 'That's all we need in this neighborhood. If things weren't already bad enough in our country, now we have cowboys.'"

As the group approached the photographer's studio, Dave pulled up in a taxi. It was obvious he had been out drinking all night as he waved a bottle of Southern Comfort in his hand. "Hey, guys. How's it going?" He laughed. "Bet you didn't think I was going to show. Did you?"

As Rhett was ringing the bell of the building's front door, Dave walked up behind him. "I've been out all night, I'm in a bad mood and I'm pissed off. So don't anybody fuck with me. You got that?"

"Fine with me. You look just the way I want you to."

They heard the door latch as the door swung open. Initially, the photographer was smiling as he greeted them, but that look quickly changed when he saw there were more people standing outside than he was expecting. Nevertheless, he motioned everyone in and led them up three flights of stairs to his studio.

While Dave elected to stay outside in the hall with the members of the band, the photographer invited Igor and Rhett into his office and asked why so many people had come to the photoshoot.

Rhett could hear Dave laughing and kidding around in the hallway speaking in that raspy whiskey voice of his. Again, he was using his unique style of 95% English and 5% Russian.

Through Igor, Rhett explained the situation to the photographer. "Tell him I apologize. It wasn't my decision and not worry about it. We'll just go along with him and concentrate on the shots that we planned. I'll handle Dave."

Suddenly, Dave burst into the room waving the bottle of Southern Comfort about. "Why don't we have the show on the road? I know exactly what I want." It was typical Dave.

"Give me that bottle!" Rhett grabbed it out of his hand and took a swig. "We're almost ready. We just have to do a little makeup to do and we're ready to go."

"Hell, we don't need any makeup!" Dave roared. "We're supposed to be ugly. Put the makeup on the girls and Toby. They're the ones that are supposed to look good. We're supposed to look like rough and rugged cowboys! Ain't that right?" He looked the photographer straight in the face. "You know, ugleee! Forget wasting time putting makeup on us."

"Goddamnit Dave!" Rhett shouted. "This is a theatrical shoot and even as ugly as you are at this moment, you still need some makeup to make you look even uglier. Now, let's get started on this shoot! Just go into the other room and relax. When we're ready for you, I'll call you. OK? OK!"

Dave grabbed the bottle back and left to join the others in the hallway.

The photographer was obviously concerned and confused as Rhett continued to apologized. "Igor, tell him to relax, everything will work out fine. I'll handle Dave. Let's just get started on my makeup."

Igor translated as Rhett explained to the make-up artist that Doc Holliday was an old consumptive gunfighter and that was how he wanted to look. She understood perfectly and didn't have to work long. Within minutes, he had the circles under his eyes than the circles that were already there. The effect was perfect. He was even more gaunt than he was in reality.

He stood up and thanked her.

He then proceeded to go find Dave, who was still hitting the bottle. When he saw Rhett, he belted out with a "Jeezus Christ! You look terrible! You look like you're about to die! Damn, you look like shit!"

"That's the idea, asshole! Now, if you would be so kind, just go into the other room, sit down, shut up and let the lady do her job." It took her less time on Dave as he was practically there even before she started.

While the makeup artist worked on Dave, the photographer took Rhett into his photo studio and began to rapidly click off the shutter of the camera. Although he seemed pleased with the shots of Rhett, but he appeared even happier with Dave. As Igor translated his directions, Dave mugged before the camera. Being the frustrated showman, it didn't take long for him to get into the part. The photographer looked absolutely delighted.

The idea of wearing makeup was rubbing Toby the wrong way, and being a nondrinker he, was becoming impatient. And by the time it was finished, it was obvious that if anybody needed a drink it was Toby. Yet, it was that very uptightness that gave him a celluloid cowboy hero look.

While Toby was being photographed, Dave continued to keep up his pace of drinking set the night before. Rhett thought the best strategy was to try to drink some of the whiskey before Dave downed the whole bottle. As it turned out, it wasn't the best idea he'd ever had.

Finally, the photographer was ready to shoot the three of them together. Dave and Rhett were like an old pair of salt and pepper shakers in the background, just to add some authenticity and a little spice … and to sell a hell of a lot of whiskey. Toby, he was the centerpiece, the star attraction, clean cut in his starched white shirt. He stood smack dab in the middle, with that million-dollar smile of his. And oh . . . did he know how to use that smile. No doubt, it was part of his arsenal when it came to charming the ladies, which was exactly how Dave wanted him portrayed.

After all, Toby was his fine upstanding, young example of west Texas American Youth, straight from the good ole U.S. of A., sent by Uncle Sam to "wow" them all in the bleak and barren totalitarian wasteland known as the former Soviet Union. You could almost hear someone say, *"God bless America and, by God, bless Toby Smith!"*

———

The photographer managed to get some good shots in the studio before the Southern Comfort settled in. Unfortunately for Rhett, by the time the photo shoot moved to *The Passazh*, the whiskey was history, and he was feeling no pain. What little control he had over Dave and the photoshoot;

he was losing fast. Still, it made interesting entertainment for the locals as they watched three cowboys stepping out of the Old West and American history and walking into the modern-day depression that had become Ukraine. It was truly a sight to behold.

As for Rhett, he was simply thankful to be out in the cold air.

Since the whiskey was gone, Dave switched to beer. His friends from the foreign community were beginning to gather on the street with more were arriving by the moment. They had been invited to an after-party in the bar immediately after the shoot. In other words, it meant that before the night was over, there would be an all-out drunken debacle.

It appeared the bar was picking up support and even his detractors were beginning to be won over. Although the bar was far from finished, everyone was beginning to sense that Dave might just pull it off. After all, he had risen from the ashes in the past, and now even money was riding on him and his The Kowboy Dance Hall & Saloon.

The photographer set up his camera at the head of the street. All in all, it was supposed to be a pretty cut-and-dried shoot. The only thing the cowboys had to do was walk straight forward into the lens of the camera.

As Igor helped Rhett confer with the photographer, he could hear Dave in the background bullshitting and drinking with his buddies. Suddenly, he heard sound of glass breaking followed by a commotion. Dave had sent a beer bottle flying over the back of his shoulder that had narrowly missed a little girl. Fortunately, Lena was on hand to move in and apologize to the child's furious parents

Rhett quickly called for Toby and Dave to join him in the middle of the street. "Okay, let's get this over as quick as we can. It's going to be real simple — just like falling off a horse. All we have to do is walk down the street, right at the camera. Is that clear?"

"Sure, no problem. Let's do it," Dave replied. Then he went looking for another beer.

Rhett waived everybody back and turned to the photographer who was patiently waiting. Then he felt somebody put their hand on his shoulder. It was Dave, laughing as he fell down into the snow, pulling Rhett down with him.

Toby stood by looking irate. It was cold and he wanted to get inside and pout of the cold. Brushing off the snow, Rhett stood up as Dave laughingly toasted the crowd. "Here's to success. The cowboys are coming and by God, we're going to pull this thing off!"

For the next half-hour, the cowboys walked up and down the street until the photographer signaled he had the shots he needed. Plus, the sun was going down and he was losing the light.

It was getting colder and Rhett knew if they stayed out in the street much longer, things were likely to get much uglier. So, with a rousing "C'mon everybody, let's have a party!" Dave led everyone through the alleyway, down the back steps and into the bar. The pandemonium was just getting started.

IX

Kyrill, the Kife and a Cheshire Cat

The bar was in shambles. The wooden floors weren't finished and electric wires had been jerry-rigged for the band. Only seventy percent of the old western façade had been constructed and was leaning against the wall. Everyone was bringing plenty of alcohol to drink in anticipation of one hell of a drunken party.

The Southern Comfort had just about done Rhett in, so he propped himself up on a stool and leaned against the wall trying to regain his composure. Calling Igor over, he took off his leather duster. "Try it on."

Igor looked a bit confused as he put on the duster.

"What do you think?" Rhett asked.

"I like it."

"Well, then, I guess it's yours now. Take good care of it. It's been with me for a long time."

"Really? Are you sure?"

"I suppose I'd better be," Rhett laughed, "because it wouldn't be very nice to take it back after I've already given it to you, now, would it?"

"Thank you. Thank you very much, Rhett."

Rhett stood up to take a few steps, but tripped over a pipe extending out of the wall and fell flat on his face, literally biting the dust.

The people in the bar saw it and he knew it. Sheepishly, he got up and dusted himself off. Rhett knew that there was no getting around it. He had royally stepped on his Dave.

He made his to the bathroom and spent the next half-hour throwing cold water on his face. When he then returned, he sat down on the stool trying to sober up and regain whatever was left of his dignity. He knew that he wouldn't be the only one in that shape before the night was over, but he had been the first one.

Dave was in the corner talking to a young man and motioned Rhett over. "Rhett, I want you to meet Kyrill. I've just commissioned him to do a large painting of the three of us, you, Toby and me. Then I'm going to hang it in the entryway of the bar."

"The Kowboys of Kyiv." And with that Rhett had given the painting its title.

Kyrill was cool, hip, bohemian and very European. He also spoke English much better than Rhett spoke Ukrainian. He had exhibited in other cities of Eastern and Western Europe, as well as exhibits in America. Rhett had already seen a painting he had sold Dave and felt fairly confident that, given enough time, Kyrill could do the painting. But he also knew Dave was impatient and always in a hurry. He was already prodding Kyrill to have the painting ready as quickly as possible. Kyrill simply looked at Dave with a catlike smile. Rhett instantly liked him.

"So how much am I gonna have to pay you?" Once again, Dave employed his favorite excuse. "I don't have much money.".

"It is a big work," Kyrill replied. "I think it will cost at least a thousand dollars."

"Tell you what I'll do. I'll pay you twelve hundred, but I'll pay you half in cash and the other half in trade. Is it a deal?"

Kyrill shrugged and nodded in agreement. "To begin, I need two hundred to buy the paints and canvas."

Dave reached in his pocket and counted out a hundred. "Here. This is all I can afford right now. Get started. I want the painting in two weeks." Suddenly, he spotted an attractive woman by the bar. "Now, you two work out the details. I'll see you guys later."

And with that, Rhett and Kyrill were left to discuss how the painting should look. Three cowboys, using one of the photos that had been taken that day with a landscape of Kyiv behind them, lit up by a blazing sky. Kyrill seemed to grasp everything.

Rhett felt much more comfortable around him than he did with the high-pressured businessmen he had become accustomed to. Kyrill was calm, relaxed and refreshing. He lacked that bullshit intensity that everyone seemed to have in the desperate hustle and bustle of making a buck, putting together those big deals that permeated the Kyiv business community. Rhett thought Kyrill was alright. After all, he was an artist.

They were joined by two of his friends, other artists, a man and a woman. Kyrill suggested that they move further back away from the party, back into the remote darkness that led up a stairway at a spot where the future entryway to The Kowboy would be.

As they were talking, Rhett noticed the woman, a leather-clad redhead, pulling out a pouch and begin to roll a joint. He was a bit surprised, but not too much. Even Dave had a fondness for getting high. When he would fly back and forth from Kyiv to California, he often stopped in Amsterdam, frequently going to the city's Red-Light District to procure pot or hashish. On occasion, he would even smuggle some back to Kyiv.

The four of them stood in the darkness of the stairwell as the woman lit up the joint and handed to Kyrill. He took a long methodical hit and then extended his arm to Rhett.

In the former Soviet Union, people who used marijuana were called "*narco-men*." Nevertheless, he thought he would give it a try.

67

Rhett hadn't smoked marijuana in years and had forgotten what marijuana was like, but he recognized its sweet pungent odor. He was opting for what was called the *kife* — the high one got without having to pass out in a drunken stupor. At first it felt kind of good, the relaxation, that floating peaceful effect. But then, after a few moments, he began to feel the disorientation, the paranoia. He'd forgotten about that.

As they stood smoking in the dark, Todd appeared from around the corner. Kyrill offered him the joint, but he waived it away. Shaking his head in apparent disapproval, he turned around and walked down the stairs and back into the bar. That's when Rhett's paranoia really kicked in. That naughty little feeling a child gets when his mother catches him doing something very bad. It was strange. Sure, Todd was an investor and a collegiate jock type, but he was a lot younger than Rhett. He tried to shake the feeling off. Feeling guilty, he quickly ended the conversation and descended back down into the bar.

Entering the room, he saw Igor standing in the corner, but avoided him. He didn't feel like talking to anyone, ever again, for the rest of his life.

To him, the party had taken on an almost surrealistic aura. In fact, he found himself wanting to hear "Whiter Shade of Pale" rather than listening to "All My Ex's Live in Texas."

He returned to the stool leaning against the wall, taking it all in as Kyrill and his friends circulated through the room. Occasionally, they would catch each other's eye. Kyrill would look over and simply smile at him like a Cheshire cat.

Toby and the band were on break and Dave was beginning to get an urge to do a little singing himself. He immediately signaled up the musicians to pick up their instruments and grabbed Toby's guitar and began to play. The band was capable of making anyone sound good.

As Toby walked past him, he looked at Dave, then back at Rhett. "I hate it when he does that."

Rhett smiled. He understood exactly what Toby meant. He loved his guitar and the last thing he wanted was a drunk playing it. However, Toby knew he didn't have much say in the matter. It was Dave's bar.

Dave had the habit of making up his own lyrics to generic country tunes. They usually contained a basic country blues riff that lent itself to just about anything anyone wanted to do with it. This time he was playing something he called "The Ukrainian Cowboy Bar Blues" and although his whiskey-rasped voice was less than melodic it lent itself to country music. Then again, the band was capable of making anyone sound good.

Rhett was content to sit there, spacing out and watching the evening unfold.

Valerie walked by holding a six pack of beer and offered him one. Even though he hated beer, he took one anyway. He was still feeling paranoid and thought he might be standing out without a drink in his hand. At least, he could nurse it along for as long as possible. Besides, no one could tell if the can was empty.

As she handed him the can, she noticed his bloodshot eyes. "Jeezus, Rhett! You look terrible. What's wrong? Have you been taking drugs or something?"

That was the last thing he wanted to hear. However, she was right. He began to feel those little pangs of guilt all over again. There was no doubt about it. He was stoned! Plus, he failed to realize his appearance was due to the fact that he was still wearing his Doc Holiday makeup from the photoshop.

"No, no, no, no, no!" He answered nervously. "It's just been a real long day and I'm just tired. That's all. Really!"

"Okay, okay. Chill." Valerie gave him a strange look, turned and walked away, but not before giving him one more backward glance. Her expression held a combination of confusion, concern, and a little suspicious. Rhett didn't really know which it was.

"Damnit!" he whispered to himself. "Why did she have to ask me that? I sounded guilty as hell. Do I really look that? Shit!"

A fashionably dressed lady in a fur coat stopped next to him and leaned over. "Excuse me. Excuse me. Did they fly you all the way over from the States for this party? You sure do look like the real thing. Are you a cowboy?"

"Yes Ma'am. I'm a Cowboy. Thank you very much."

As soon as Dave finished playing, he walked over to Rhett. "Are you OK?"

"I'm fine, Dave, just fine. Okay?" Rhett snapped.

"Sure. Fine by me. My, aren't we all full of piss and vinegar."

At that moment, Rhett hoped nobody would ever talk to him again, for as long as he lived, for the rest of his life — forever! At that point Kyrill caught his eye. He simply looked at Rhett and gave a little smile.

—

The party was in full swing, and Dave was just getting started. Rhett couldn't believe he was still on his feet.

That's when he noticed Dave looking at an axe a workman had left sitting on top of a ledge. "You know, Rhett? I want this place to look really rough. Know what I mean? I mean really rough!" And with that, Dave grabbed the axe, bringing it down with all his force on a barstool.

"Oh, real good." Rhett muttered. "Now Dave's going to start acting like an axe murderer. Great. Just fucking great!"

Dave began to rant and rave, telling a group of Scotsmen, "I want this place to look like it's been through hell!" He then proceeded to demolish another barstool. Needless to say, it was attracting a certain amount of attention.

Toby and the band quickly picked up their instruments and began to play. Some people were watching the band. Others chose to watch Dave as he chopped the barstool into little pieces.

He then grabbed a beer bottle, throwing it against a wall as it shattered into flying pieces of broken glass. Laughing maniacally, he threw another one, encouraging others to join him. Rhett couldn't tell if he was turning into the Mad Matter or a serial killer. He looked around half expecting to see a hookah-smoking caterpillar

The band played louder as two Scotsmen and an Englishman in business suits cheered him on. He walked over and placed a wine bottle in the Englishman's hand, screaming, "Go on! Do it! It's my bar. It's Okay!"

The Englishman hurled the bottle at the wall. It didn't break, but bounced off. The Scotsmen chided him. "Awwwww."

Then one of the Scotsmen hurled his. It was half-full of beer and shattered into suds and shards of glass. This was greeted with cheers from the crowd. Some people were still watching the band, but others were beginning to turn their heads nervously to see if any debris was getting too close. Everything seemed to be reaching a crescendo.

Dave picked up the axe again. He hurled it over the head of the Englishman, who had gone to the wall to retrieve his unbroken bottle barely missing him. A cheer went up from the participants in Dave's destruction derby.

Rhett leaned against the wall about halfway in the middle of the room and started to light a cigarette. At the same time, one Scotsman hurled yet another bottle at the wall. It didn't break either. Instead, it ricocheted freakishly off the wall, becoming a missile whose trajectory jettisoned it directly towards Rhett with a sudden force that amazed everyone.

The bottle slammed into his hand, destroying the lighter he was holding and knocking the cigarette out of his mouth. He felt an excruciating pain surge through his hand as his middle finger fractured. He closed his eyes, gritting his teeth as he felt the bone crack. Luckily, it hadn't hit him in the mouth and his teeth were still intact.

Suddenly, everything became quiet. The Scotsman's eyes widened as he apologized in a thigh Highland accent. "Arrre ye okay, Mon? I'm terrribly, terrribly sorrry. Did ah hurrrt ye?"

Rhett took a deep breath. He knew it was an accident, but it didn't take the pain away. At this point, he wished he had been drinking. He tightened his stomach muscles and looked up at the Scotsman. "Was that a legal throw?"

For a brief moment the tension subsided as onlookers nervously laughed. But that didn't help his finger. He knew that going to a hospital wasn't an option. Nobody was in any shape to take him. The hassles of explaining to a night attendant at the emergency room in Russian or Ukrainian was out of the question and Dave for damned sure didn't have insurance. There was no other choice. Rhett grabbed his finger, pulled it hard and set it as best he could.

The Scotsman was still apologizing. Rhett, not wanting to put a damper on the situation, sloughed it off. "By God, you son of a bitch! You get no bottles when this bar opens,"

Rhett glanced in Kyrill's direction. He was still smiling like a Cheshire cat.

And with that, the party started to break. People began saying it was getting late and they ought to get home. They had a lot of work to do the next day.

The last ones to leave were Dave, Rhett, the two drunken Scots, and the Englishman.

Rhett watched as the three smartly dressed gentlemen in their Lord and Taylor suits stood howling like dogs in the middle of Kreschatik Boulevard as they tried to stop a cab to take them on to the River Palace and another night of debauchery.

When Rhett arrived at the door to his apartment, he dropped the keys several times as he tried to fit the key into the lock. He was on the verge of sitting down to spend a very cold night in the corridor when the key finally went in.

It was dark as he stumbled around before finding a chair and sinking into it. He sat alone in the darkness. His finger was throbbing.

X

The LA Express

Dave was in rare form when Rhett met him the following morning. "How're you doing? How's the finger?" he laughed.

"It'll be fine. I think I set it all right."

His driver, Boris, sped through the streets of Kyiv, toward a meeting with Salom. According to Dave, Salom was arranging for office space with the local chapter of the Red Cross.

As the car weaved in and out of the traffic Dave began boasting about his exploits of the previous evening. "Well, after the party, I went drinking at the Arizona, where I ran into a Carl. He's a friend of mine. Do you know him?"

"Don't think so. I don't get out that much."

Dave completely missed the tone of sarcasm. "Great guy. You'd like him. Anyway, we were looking for some female companionship and decided to go to the River Palace."

—

The River Palace was also known as a local hang out for prostitutes, who plied their trade to Western businessmen. Unlike other places in the world, Ukraine's prostitutes were not unstable or drug-addicted. For the most part, they were well-educated and literate women. Prostitution simply offered them a better standard of living and a way to support their children. As the *Kyiv Post* put it, *"Pity the nation that can make streetwalking sound attractive to so many of its daughters."*

—

Dave was far from finished and continued to elaborate on the events of the evening. "When we got there, I spotted this tall, thin, lanky thing in the *discotheque*. I didn't think she was that good-looking at first, but it was getting late. So, I went up and offered her a hundred bucks to do both me and Carl. At first she refused, but like I said, it was getting late and most of the clientele were leaving. I kept after her and finally she agreed. We grabbed a taxi and went to Carl's place. He's got a great apartment. It overlooks Kreschatik Boulevard."

"So, what about this office space?" Rhett was looking out the window, bur Dave wasn't listening.

He was too busy elaborating on the night before. "Man, for a hundred bucks, this chick was a great piece of ass! Carl and I took turns with her 'til dawn. I did her first and then, while Carl was screwing her, I had her give me a blowjob. Christ Almighty! She must have been a nymphomaniac, because once she got started, the bitch wouldn't stop. She wore Carl out and was still working on me in the cab when I dropped her off this morning."

―

Suddenly, Boris pulled to an abrupt halt in front of a building across the street from Hotel Ukraine.

Salom and his men were waiting to ushered the two into an office where they were introduced to the Ukrainian director of the Red Cross who called for an interpreter. Salom told him that Dave was involved in a project to build a Western medical center in the heart of Kyiv. The director wanted to know more and made sure to mention that the Red Cross was building warehouses that could house any supplies and equipment the center might need.

Once the meeting was over, Dave filled Rhett in on all the details as Boris drove them to the bar. "Do you know what that was all about?"

"Not really."

"Salom is interested, because those warehouses are near Boryspol Airport. Humanitarian supplies are stored under much more lax conditions than other imports into Ukraine. To Salom's way of thinking, if he can get access to that warehouse space, he can use it for smuggling contraband to sell on the Black Market. After all, I've offered him my services as a front man. See? I told you he needs me."

Rhett continued looking out the car window. He knew most everything in Kyiv had become corrupted, even the Red Cross. Why else would they be associated with the likes of Salom and his Mafia? Plus, the pharmacies were beginning to have difficulties finding medicine. As a result, there was always a black-market peddler standing outside the door willing to sell anything for the right price which was right down Salom's alley.

For the most part, everything that was happening was beyond Rhett. He was becoming numb to the corruption and didn't really give a shit about the details. All he knew was that they needed an office he didn't care where it came from.

———

As it turned out Dave didn't need Salom's connections, because the following week he found an office on his own. It was above a supermarket called *The LA Express* and controlled by a repatriated Jewish businessman named Rudy. The floor above the supermarket had been refurbished to

Western standards. It was clean, spacious and unlike most offices which were decorated with busy, gaudy Soviet-style wallpaper that never seemed to match anything, its walls were white.

Rudy had immigrated to California at the end of the seventies building up a few businesses in the L.A. area. When the Soviet Union broke up, like many expatriates, he figured he could return and get in on the ground floor of the rubble of the U.S.S.R. Being a native, he had already established the connections he needed. He was a savvy businessman to boot.

When he returned to Kyiv, he established a number successful dental clinics, a few supermarkets, controlled several pieces of prime real estate, and who knows what else.

Dave struck a deal with him offering to get tenants to rent office space in exchange for reduced rent for himself.

However, Rudy made a point of telling Dave about his previous tenants. "The son of bitches were Italians. They did not pay rent for the six months. I finally had them evicted by my chief of security. He is former officer of the KGB. They also stick me with thousands of dollars for the phone bill."

Dave assured him he had everything under control. "You know me, Rudy. I won't do that. Hey, I'm on a roll. I know a lot of Western businessmen. Trust me, I'll make the place work and have this space rented out in no time. No *problema.*"

Still, Rudy continued to drive his point home. "I expect people to pay and pay on time. Those fucking Italians! They burn me and I don't want it to happen again. I am a tough businessman and do not like for anyone to bullshit me."

"Don't worry," Dave assured him, "I'll handle everything. I've got it covered."

Just then, a burly man appeared in the doorway. Rudy introduced him as his security chief, Alexei. He was a friendly sort with a gold front tooth that shone every time he smiled. Rudy turned to him, explained the deal in Russian then excused himself and left.

Alexei already knew about the Kowboy Bar and wanted to be of service. In broken English, he told Dave he worked for a security company that could protect him from any interference from the Mafia once the bar was open.

Dave pulled Alexei close and smiled. "No *problema*. I have roof . . . *krusha. Tipaneemayesh?* You understand? My partners — Chechen Mafia." He laughed, patting Alexei on the back.

Alexei simply smiled, looked in Rhett's direction and excused himself.

Rhett couldn't believe what he had just heard and wondered why Dave was telling a member of the former KGB about his partnership with the Chechen Mafia.

Nevertheless, he was happy to finally have an office, until Dave told him that he and Igor would be moving in with the Chechens at one of their offices.

"I can't afford to have Salom or his men hanging out in Rudy's offices. I want you and Igor to work out of their offices and keep an eye on what Salom's up to." The very last thing Rhett wanted to do was to spy for Dave on Salom and his Chechens.

Luckily, a few days later, the deal fell through on Salom's offices and Rhett was much happier to be working out of Rudy's place. Keeping an eye on what Salom and his gang was not exactly Rhett's idea of public relations.

Still, Dave had office space to rent. As a result, he began contacting all his friends and business connections. Unfortunately, he had no takers. Most everyone he talked to were content to work out of their apartments. Many Ukrainian firms did the same. Therefore, most Western companies figured while in Rome… Not having to shell out the cost of operating like a legitimate business like they did in the West saved them money. Besides, many were already paying outrageous rents to Dave for their apartments and most were doing anything they could to save a buck.

All of those business contacts who were Dave's bosom buddies when he was buying them drinks at night, had sobered up in the morning when it came down to the bottom line.

XI

A Mouthful of Much Obliged

After years of government regulation and anti-smoking campaigns the U.S. tobacco industry was on its last gasp. As a result, Phillip Morris and R. J Reynolds were looking for new markets and the former Soviet Union was known for having some of the heaviest smokers in the world.

Not that they didn't have their own brands like Stolichnaya, to Kazbek and Apollo-Soyuz, the post-Soviet love affair with anything American meant that once favorite cigarette brands were losing ground to American brands. At first, cigarette manufacturers tried creating new brands of cigarettes such as President, Hollywood and even Cowboy, they were no match for likes of Marlboro and Camel. Besides, like every other industry in the former Soviet Union, the factories were outdated. In addition, they simply were no match for Western advertising.

Plus, like every other industry that was Western flooding into the country eager to pick over the remains of the former Soviet Union, tobacco was no different.

—

After the blowout at the Kowboy, Dave had caught the attention of two of the biggest tobacco companies in America and both saw the value of linking their brands to the dance hall and saloon — especially Marlboro. What better way to turn Ukraine to *Marlboro Country* than by hooking up with The Kowboy Dance Hall & Saloon? In fact, Marlboro was offering to cover the cost of putting up billboard all over the city. Consequently, Dave told Rhett's to track down Kyiv's billboard companies and set up a meeting with the country representative of Phillip Morris.

And that's how Rhett found himself sitting in the offices of Phillip Morris to meet with the country's director. Basil was a Brit and recognized the potential and upped the ante. He had worked on similar promotions in other parts of the world and offered to help out by promoting a Battle of the Bands on Sunday nights. Phillip Morris would give the bar everything they wanted and even more. Rhett was elated. There was only one catch — they wanted exclusive sponsorship.

Basil knew that Dave had also been talking with R.J. Reynolds and explained that Marlboro didn't want to compete with Camel in the bar. Rhett could see his point and agreed to sort things out with Dave.

Basil informed him that the marketing director for Phillip Morris in Europe, would be flying in from Zurich and had instruct her to contact him when she arrived. At that time, she would work out details concerning the placement of a Marlboro billboard inside the bar. It was something Rhett desperately wanted.

Rhett wasted no time in getting back to the office to tell Dave the good news.

"So how did it go with Marlboro?" Dave asked.

"Holy shit, Dave!" Rhett could barely contain his excitement. "These guys are ready to give us everything we want and more! I can't believe it! They're willing to provide the bar with posters, ashtrays, lighters, T-shirts. And not only that, they're even going to give us money to help with the promotions. And most importantly, they're going to put a Marlboro billboard that covers an entire wall. They're willing to do all this in exchange for one thing."

"What's that?"

"They want to be the exclusive cigarette sponsor in the bar."

"Can't do it," Dave replied.

"What the f—?"

"I said, I don't think I can do that."

"What are you talking about? This is exactly what you wanted. You said that everyone was going to pay you to advertise. Well, this is it. They're going to pay for The Kowboy's advertising."

"It's not enough. Last night at the Arizona I got this great idea. I'm going to have a 'war.' A war of the sponsors."

It was a phrase that Rhett would come to hate, when associated with Dave Seigal and The Kowboy Dance Hall & Saloon.

Dave was beginning to fall into a habit of coming up with a bunch of "brilliant" ideas during those meditative drinking hours between one and four in the morning.

He was also being wooed by Pepsi and Coca-Cola. Everyone who was a competitor had begun to aggressively compete with one another for an upper hand in the Ukrainian marketplace. They were willing to do just about anything for Dave, short of blowing him, to be the sponsors of The Kowboy.

Unfortunately, Dave was like an ugly duckling that had never been asked to the dance. He couldn't make up his mind on whom he wanted to waltz with and whose offer to decline — hence, Dave Seigal's battle of the sponsors, to be fought over on the glorious battlefield of The Kowboy Dance Hall and Saloon.

"Look, I'm going to go down in the annals marketing history as the man who introduced the big fellows to marketing warfare. Rhett, one day they're going to write about this in marketing books. The battle of the competing sponsors." It was as if he had invented the concept.

It didn't seem to Rhett that Dave had much use for history. "Look, I don't know if you heard, but the "Cola Wars" started about twenty years ago."

"I've got it all figured out. To my way of thinking, since the club is going have a Mexican Cantina and a Texas-style bar, I'll give each sponsor their own territory. Marlboro and Coca-Cola can occupy The Kowboy, and Camel and Pepsi will deploy their forces in The Cantina."

Rhett interrupted Dave's train of thought. "Listen Dave, that's all fine and dandy, but Marlboro and Coke ought to be our natural sponsors. And if they want to be exclusive, I say give it to them. No matter what anybody says, they are the big kids on the block."

Frantic, he tried to make his point. "Look, Marlboro's ready to cover a whole wall with a cowboy billboard. That alone is worth a few grand. They fit the image of the bar and they've got a lot more money and promotional products behind them. They're more in line with the image. It's that simple. They can help us promote the place. They'll put money into the promotions, and we need that money. You don't have enough money to promote the place like they can. It just makes sense."

Rhett knew that business was ego-oriented. He also knew that to be successful, business sense and ego had to be delicately balanced. Unfortunately, Dave's business sense was losing ground to his ego. He liked the sound of his "war" and wasn't about to give it up in the name of common sense.

"I'm going to make them both fight for the right to be in my bar. They need me. I don't need them. They are going to have to pay me. I'll go with whoever offers me the most. Don't worry, you'll see. I'm right about this. I've got it all under control."

"Look, I know it's your bar and I can only make suggestions. But just remember, the sun don't shine on the same dog's ass every day. Just think about it. That's all I'm asking."

"Okay, I'll think about it."

To make matters worse, Rhett could plainly see that being around Salom was making Dave feel like a "wise guy." He liked to brag to anyone who cared to listen that he had the toughest roof in town.

—

And just like that, Dave changed his mind. Although he originally maintained he didn't need advertising, all of a sudden, he was promising everyone he was going to advertise with them. The only problem was, he didn't have the vaguest idea how much advertising cost. As a result, trying to keep up with his whims proved to be a daunting task, because what he might want in the morning could change by the afternoon.

Unfortunately, Dave had a habit of making those deals of fantasy based on how much he had to drink and whoever he happened to be talking to at the moment.

One night when he ran into an ad executive of a trendy society magazine called *LOOKS International*. He told her that the bar was going to do a lot of advertising with the magazine and his advertising director would be calling her to work out the details.

After that, he ran into a young American who was the advertising sales manager of a media company called Perekhid Media, owner of a weekly rag called Dosier Dosuga, which covered Kyiv's nightlife. Of course, that would be the perfect place to promote The Kowboy Dance Hall & Saloon

Then there was a radio station called Super Nova owned and operated by a young Middle Easterner. He made promises him a lot too.

In other words, Dave was offering everyone a handful of gimme and a mouthful of much obliged.

—

While Dave made the contacts at night, details were left to Rhett to clear up in the mornings. After all, he was the ad guy.

Fortunately, a lot of media companies wanted the club to be successful, because that meant more advertising revenue for them. In fact, they were even willing to give him a break until the club got on its feet offering to extend him credit, which was almost unheard of in the media market of Kyiv

Unfortunately, Dave wasn't big on dealing with budgets either. So, when almost every advertising proposal came to around ten grand, Rhett took every one and cut them to the bone, which disappointed many an ad rep. Consequently, he had to explain to them that they would be much happier getting paid less, rather than having a lot of money owed to them that they would not be able to collect.

Since Rhett would be the one who would be working with the media, he shot straight with all of them and proceeded with caution. The last thing he wanted was for the club wind up owing a lot of money it couldn't afford to pay. He knew if that happened, everybody would be looking for someone to blame. And in all probability, that would be the ad guy.

He knew The Kowboy was going to need their support and didn't want some bill collector dogging him for money. He wanted to keep them on the bar's side

—

Rhett was turning into Dave's wake-up service. Since nothing rolled while Dave was asleep, which wasn't often, everything had to wait until he was up and running.

On one particular morning, when he didn't answer his phone, Rhett thought he must be asleep or had yet to come in from the night before. He hung up and tried again, letting the phone ring. Still, there was no answer. Not knowing what else to do, he sat down and waited.

Soon the phone rang. It was Dave's gravelly whisky voice. "You just call?"

"Yeah, did you just get in?"

"No, been home a few hours. I couldn't get to the phone. It's in Toby's room and he has some chick in there with him. I had to wait until they were finished fucking." He laughed.

"OK. Then, other than Toby, what's up?"

"Come over to my apartment. Boris ought to be here in about an hour. I want to tell you all about some people I met last night."

—

Toby answered the door in his underwear. He took one look at Rhett, then turned around and walked back into the bedroom scratching his ass and slamming the door behind him. Rhett found Dave on the couch in the living room, trying to shake off the cobwebs.

"Are you going to make it?" Rhett asked.

"Yeah. I was out a little late last night."

"For a change?" It was supposed to be a joke, but Dave didn't quite catch the humor.

"I'm just a little tired, that's all."

"So, tell me, who were these people you met last night?"

"I met this lady, an American from New Jersey. She's the Executive Director of The Children of Chernobyl Relief Fund. Her name's Nadia

Makivsky, Matkowsky, or something like that. I can't remember. I was kinda drunk. I've got her card around here somewhere. Anyway, I ran into her at the Arizona and she told me that she was looking for a place to hold an after-party for all of the VIP's who would be flying to Ukraine for the tenth anniversary commemoration of Chernobyl."

"Really? That sounds pretty good. What's that got to do with us?"

"Well, Jack Palance is going to be there, along with Steven Spielberg, the group Yes, as well as, Vangelis and Robert DeNiro. What's that got to do with us? I offered her The Kowboy for an after-party after the ceremony."

"Wait — What? Are you serious? Jack Palance and Robert DeNiro? Are you absolutely sure about that?"

"That's what she told me last night. It seems that Jack Palance is Ukrainian and he's going to be the honorary chairman for the event."

"Are you sure the bar will be ready by then?"

"No problem, I intend on having this bar ready for the grand opening on April fifteenth, anyway. That's Tax Day. I've decided I want to have a party every year on Tax Day."

Dave was off on another of those visionary moments of his.

"It'll be for all the ex-pats. If you're living out of the States, you get an automatic extension. I figure it'll be a great time to have a party. Everybody can come down to The Kowboy and celebrate not having to pay their taxes."

"Okay. Sure, fine. Sounds good to me, but we missed the February opening and have postponed the opening several times already."

"I know, but this place has to be open by April fifteenth, come hell or high water. I've got a lot of money going out and not much coming back in. If I don't get that place open soon, I'm going to be in some serious shit."

"Well, if we can do it, it's going to be some great public relations for the bar. There's bound to be a lot of news coverage."

"Oh, yeah. CBS, NBC, ABC, CNN, they're all going to be here that week. And get this. I also met a couple of reporters from CNN International. They're interested in doing a story on Toby and The Kowboy."

"Do you have any idea what that's going to do for the bar? Can you imagine what it would cost to advertise on CNN for one minute? We could never afford that kind of publicity."

"And they'll probably do a story from the bar at the after-party."

"Jack Palance and Robert DeNiro at The Kowboy? Are you absolutely sure about this?"

"Of course, I'm sure. Plus, Nadia told me that if we hold this party, she'll have Palance come in for a personal appearance a few days earlier. He arrives in Kyiv on a Monday. I can't believe it. Jack Palance is actually coming to my bar."

Even though Dave was tired, he was ecstatic. "Look, I'm not going to have a chance to meet her before I leave. Oh, here it is. I've found her card." He handed Rhett a crumpled card. "Here, you handle the details."

"What did you offer her?"

"Anything she wants. We'll provide the bar, the booze and all the food.

"Then that's all the more reason to have the restaurant ready. That's a lot of people to feed. How many are going to be there?"

"She told me about two hundred. But it doesn't matter if the kitchen's ready. We'll get someone to cater the food."

"Like who? Do you know someone?"

"Don't worry, we'll find someone. How about Western Foods? I heard they're catering events at the embassy."

"Yeah, okay. I know those guys. I'll give them a call. Maybe they'll be interested in running the restaurant. It would solve one more headache if we just contracted it out to somebody who's already in the business."

"OK, call them. But don't promise them anything. I eventually want to offer that place to Taco Bell. Pepsi owns them and I heard they're looking for locations around Kyiv. I don't want to give anything away too soon."

"But you know how slow Pepsi works in this market. They were supposed to open two hundred Pizza Huts here over two years ago, but that deal never happened."

"Just call Western Foods and set up a meeting, down at the bar."

—

When Dave and Rhett arrived at the Kowboy, they began taking inventory. There was still much to do and so little time to do it. However, between the booze and bragging, Dave was beginning to think he could accomplish just about anything.

"Look, Dave," Rhett warned, "I gotta tell you, if were not ready for this, we're going to look really bad. We could be looking at a potential disaster. Not only in Kyiv, but on an international scale. If those people with the media show up, it's either going to be a public relations coup or a public relations nightmare. Do you understand?"

"Don't worry," Dave assured him, "I've got it under control. We've got two months to get everything ready. You just set up that meeting with

Nadia while I'm in California and tell her she can have anything she wants."

"That I can do."

"And call Coca-Cola, Pepsi and call that guy from Sauza Tequila."

"What guy?"

"His name's Joe something or other. Didn't I tell you about him?" It was evident Dave was not thinking too clearly. "I got his card somewhere. I'll find it and give it to you."

"Okay."

"I also want you and Lena to go down to Obolon and order all the beer taps and mugs. We've got to get things going."

—

Rhett returned to the office and immediately got on the phone contacting everybody he could. Dave was still exhausted, hungover and beginning to wane. He looked like a whipped puppy as he told Lena he was going back to his apartment to take a power nap.

Although Dave kept telling everyone he had everything under control, Rhett was under no such illusion.

Even Sergei, his original partner in The Kowboy, was trying to justify Dave's involvement with Salom as being a deal between Dave and the Chechens. He kept telling himself it wasn't any of his business. Dave could pay them out of his share. Sergei would merely turn his head, look the other way and hope that the didn't try to invade what had originally been the Moscow Mafia's territory.

Rhett was on the phone when Salom appeared at the doorway flanked by two of his henchmen. He told that Lena he had a deal he wanted Dave to look at.

Lena told them that Dave had gone to his apartment to rest. Evidently, it was something that couldn't wait.

She left with Salom to go and find Dave.

—

A few days later, Rhett saw him again. It was the Ukrainian cowboy, wearing the same outfit. He smiled at Rhett as he stepped onto the subway. He got off at the next stop.

A few days later, he saw the Ukrainian cowboy, wearing the same outfit. He nodded at Rhett as he stepped onto the subway car in the Metro. Then, he got off at the next stop.

Fifteen minutes later, he saw him again. This time, it was on the trolleybus. Rhett imagined the Ukrainian was just as curious about him as he was about this mysterious cowboy. They acknowledged each other slightly.

A few stops later, the cowboy got to step off the trolleybus, but just before he did, he turned, placed his finger on the brim of his cowboy hat and tipped it. Rhett did the same. All in all, it was a bit surreal to the point of an all-out buckaroo bonzai bizarro moment.

XII

Promises Made, Promises Alleged

Dave was scrambling all around Kyiv trying to collect money from his rental properties. The German Embassy owed him $20,000 dollars, but informed him it would be another week before the money could be wired from Bonn.

Unfortunately, Dave couldn't wait because he was to returning to California and desperately needed money to keep the construction on the bar moving forward.

He had promised to hold the benefit for Chernobyl. No longer could he postpone the opening as he had so many times in the past. He had finally committed himself to something and it was too late for him to turn back.

Frantically, he instructed Lena to place a call to Salom. After all, Salom was his partner and surely, he could float him a loan for the few weeks it would take to collect the rent from the Germans. Lena was told to ask Salom for twenty grand until he returned to Kyiv.

Moments later, as he paced back and forth the phone rang, but the call was from Phillip Morris for Rhett. They had the sponsorship agreement ready and were eager for Dave to sign.

Rhett informed the representative that Dave would be leaving for America in a few hours. If Phillip Morris wanted a signed agreement signed, they would have to step on it in order to catch him.

Within the hour, a young man showed up with the agreement. Of course, it contained the exclusivity clause.

As Dave read it, he came to the paragraph about exclusivity. He looked at Rhett and then at the young man. "I don't think I can sign this. There's a clause in here giving you exclusive rights in my bar. The problem is, Camel is willing to give me a lot of support too."

"I understand." The young man replied, "however, we feel that our company can give you so much more in terms of support for your club. We are willing to offer you free souvenirs and other promotions, as well as pay to have a billboard installed in your club. We are prepared to provide you with almost anything you need to promote The Kowboy."

"I just don't think I'm ready to do that." Dave replied, "However, I'll tell you what I will do. I'll give you exclusive rights in the cowboy section of my bar. But Camel gets the Cantina. It's part of my strategy to have a war between the sponsors. Coke and Marlboro can have the Texas side of the bar; Pepsi and Camel get the Mexican side. Nobody has ever done anything like this. Not until now."

Rhett's eyes rolled back in his head.

"I am terribly sorry, but I do not think my director will agree to that," The young man replied. "We have found, from past experience, that when two sponsors are in the same club, the promotional materials always get mixed together and it dilutes the effectiveness of both."

"Just a minute." Dave walked over to Rhett and whispered. "We have to make a management decision here."

Rhett took it to mean that Dave was asking his opinion as Dave motioned him over to the corner of the room.

"Look, Dave," he whispered, "these guys are willing to give you so much more than Camel can ever give you. Like I said, Marlboro is the perfect fit for The Kowboy's image. If you want to play hard to get, fine. What I'm saying is, if you need them to kiss you first, by all means let them kiss you before you get in bed with them. But when it's all said and done, get in bed with these guys. To hell with this war of the sponsors. It's not worth giving up what they're offering you."

Dave looked at Rhett for a moment then suddenly turned and walked back to the rep.

"Okay. I don't think I can sign your agreement."

Rhett simply closed his eyes and muttered, "So much for my opinion."

"Go back and tell your director that I will sign this agreement, but you only get exclusivity in the cowboy section." Then he marked through the exclusivity clause. "People are going to have to pay me to advertise in my bar."

"I do not think he will accept your conditions, but I will give him your offer. If he accepts your proposal, will you give us your gentleman's agreement that no Camel material will cross over to the cowboy section?"

"You have my gentleman's agreement." Dave shook his hand and the Marlboro representative left.

Rhett appealed to him once more. "Dave, I hope you know what you're doing. If they don't go for your deal, we could be out quite a lot of merchandise, promotions and, most of all that billboard on the wall."

Suddenly, the alcohol and lack of sleep, compounded by his financial worries made him explode. "Goddamnit! I don't have time to get into this right now! I've got other things to worry about!"

"I'm not arguing. I'm merely stating my opinion. Jeezus! I thought that's why you asked me in the first place."

"Don't worry about it! I've got everything covered. You'll see. I'm right about this"

"Okay. Fine." He let the matter drop.

In the meantime, Lena had been on the phone with Salom. As she hung up she looked at Dave. "Salom has agreed. He will loan you the money."

"Thank God!" He then turned to Lena giving out his final instructions. "Pay the work crew, pay for some materials and give Rhett a couple of hundred dollars to tide him over. Rhett, contact our suppliers, that lady from Chernobyl, and keep things moving until I get back. I'm outta here!"

He then grabbed his bag and walked out in a whirlwind of commotion.

———

A few days later Salom gave Lena some money, but it was only half of what Dave had asked for. The money was gone in no time and she still needed the remaining ten thousand. Whenever Rhett asked her if Salom had come up with the rest of the money, she would merely shrug and smile. He took that to mean it was highly doubtful that Dave would get any more out of Salom.

As a result, he decided not to press Lena for his money. She had enough problems on her hands. Besides, two hundred would not going to make or break him.

———

Rhett called the Director of The Children of Chernobyl Relief Fund and arranged to meet with her on the *Passazh*. He told her it would be easy to find him. He would be the only cowboy standing in the street.

As it turned out, there would be two cowboys. Igor had gone full tilt cowboy on him and showed up wearing the cowboy hat Dave had given him, as well as the duster that Rhett had presented him at the now infamous after-party.

Curious to see the place she had been offered for the reception, Nadia agreed to meet him on *The Passazh* at eleven o'clock the next morning.

They waited over an hour out in the cold, until she finally arrived in a red minivan apologizing and explaining that she had been with the president's committee for most of the morning.

Rhett escorted her through the alley to the workmen's entrance at the back of the building and down the stairs.

As soon as she was inside, she looked around. "Are you sure this place is going to be ready by next month?"

He sensed her reservations and really couldn't blame her. "That's what Dave told me. Besides, we really have accomplished a lot recently."

"I certainly hope so, because there are going to be a lot of important people attending this affair."

"Dave has assured me that everything will be ready. We have crews working day and night. Now, Dave told me to give you anything you want. So, exactly what you are going to need?"

As he hurriedly scribbled, Nadia dictated what she expected. "I want hot dogs, spareribs and, of course, we need to have a variety of traditional Ukrainian dishes. You know what? I think it would be nice to have some authentic Wester food like barbeque, or tacos, or ..."

"Well, I used to compete in a few chili cook-offs back home. So, I could whip up a mean batch of chili ..."

"Yeah — yeah. Chili sounds fine."

"No problem. In fact, all my Ukrainian friends seem to love my chi ..."

But Nadia was far from finished. "I also wanted a guarantee in writing saying that Dave Seigal will be responsible for providing all the food and drinks for the party and that this place will, in fact, be ready on April 26th for the party. I'm not going to take any chances. This is far too important an event to rely on some backroom bar agreement."

"I'll tell him you said so. I also understand that Jack Palance, Steven Spielberg and Robert DeNiro are going to be in attendance, along with Yes and Vangelis. Is that correct?"

"Well, Jack will be there and Jon Anderson of the group Yes. But I don't know anything about Vangelis. Who is he? And I thought Dave was going to get us Robert DeNiro."

"Dave said he was going to get Robert DeNiro?"

"Well, I told him that I would like to get someone as famous as DeNiro. He's known internationally and his appearance would really get us a lot of international attention. Besides there is a famous Ukrainian actor who resembles DeNiro. I thought it would be good to have them both together at the event. Spielberg was another one I wanted. Dave said he was going back to California and would arrange it."

"Christ Almighty!" he muttered. If Dave was out drinking and promised her DeNiro —

But that's the way Dave did business and a lot can get promised when everybody's out drinking. It was just one more thing that made Rhett uneasy about those wonderful deals Dave would make when he was out boozing at the bars.

"Frankly, I'm not sure what you all talked about or if he has connections with DeNiro or Spielberg. But, let me talk with him and I'll get back to you on that. Okay?"

Rhett promised that he would get everything straightened out as to what Dave could and could not do.

Nadia thanked him and took one more look at the place. "I really hope you can get this ready in time. I can't stress enough how important this is going to be. Not only for us, but for Dave and his bar." Then she excused herself, explaining she had to go to another meeting.

It was good too, because she had given him enough to worry about what exactly it was Dave had promised her. He sat for a moment stunned by the conversation he'd just had. All he could do was hope that Dave knew what he was doing.

—

When Rhett walked into the office, Toby was talking to somebody on the phone.

"Is that Dave? Let me talk to that son-of-a bitch!"

Toby handed him the phone.

After his meeting with Nadia, Rhett had more than a few questions. "Dave, I've just come from the meeting with Nadia."

"So, how did it go?"

"I'm not really sure. Did you promise her DeNiro?"

"Did she tell you that?"

"Yeah."

He could hear Dave laughing on the other end of the line. "Well, we were both pretty drunk when we talked. Don't worry about it."

"Jesus Christ Dave! She wants an awful lot and she's worried about the place being ready."

"What did you tell her?"

"I told her you said she can have anything she wants."

"Good. So, what does she want?"

"Like I said, she wants a lot. I told her I could make chili, but if I'm going to do that, you're going to have to bring back a shitload of chili seasoning."

"No problem, but I don't have time to worry about that now. I just got through talking with the folks at CNN. They told me they talked with the head of CNN and he was real hot on the idea about doing a story about Toby."

"You mean Ted Turner?"

"Yeah. He thinks it's a great story."

"Ted Turner? Are you sure?" Rhett's eyes rolled back.

"Of course, I'm sure."

"Okay, then if you're absolutely sure then you know what that's going to mean for us, don't you?"

"Yeah, yeah. I know, but I don't have a lot of time to talk. My phone bill is completely out of control. I don't know how I'm going to pay for it. So listen to me. I want you to give them a call."

Dave gave him the phone number of the CNN correspondents in Kyiv. "It's a woman and a man. His name is Phillipe or something like that. I think he's French. I can't remember the other one's name. Call 'em and set up a meeting and arrange for them to do the story on Toby."

"Okay, but I'm telling you one more time. This party is either going to be a public relations dream or a public relations nightmare. I hope you realize that. If we're not ready. . . . . ."

"Don't worry about it. Everything's going to be all right. I've got it all under control. Just give them a call and set everything up."

"OK, but just remember I'm telling you this."

"I've got to go now. Just do it. Good-bye." Before he could say anything else, the line went dead.

He dialed the number Dave had given him. A woman answered in Ukrainian. He asked for Phillipe. Moments later, a man was on the phone. Rhett told him he was handling the publicity for The Kowboy. They agreed to meet the following day on *The Passazh*.

—

Meanwhile, the Marlboro rep had also arrived in Kyiv from Zurich and called Rhett to set up a meeting down in the club. When she arrived, Rhett showed her around the bar, pointing out the wall where he wanted the Marlboro billboard. She also offered to provide the bar with anything it needed or Dave desired.

Then she added, "Of course, there *is* the exclusivity issue."

"Look, if The Kowboy were my bar, you would already have exclusive sponsorship, but unfortunately, it's not. Dave's the owner, so I have to abide by his decision. However, I continue to push the issue and eventually I think I can persuade him to change his mind."

"I hope so," she replied, "because we are prepared not only to provide you with the one billboard, we may even pay to have it changed every few months. It would give your bar a fresh look from time to time. We even

100

might custom-design a billboard specifically linking The Kowboy's theme with Marlboro. Are you sure there is no way you can change Dave's mind?"

"Not at the moment, but as I said, I continue to try."

"I'll tell you what I will do. I will go ahead and authorize for the billboard be installed and I think after he sees what we can do for this bar, he will eventually become convinced that we are far more capable of supporting the success of this place than anyone else."

"You definitely have my support, for whatever that's worth."

"Okay, I'll get everything rolling. It should be up in around ten days. I have to go back to Switzerland, but I plan on being here for the Chernobyl reception. Maybe I can talk to Dave then."

"You're more than welcome to be my guest."

"However, I will be with some very important representatives from Phillip Morris at that party. I hope you realize that having our competition's items in the bar will present me with a very sensitive situation."

"I understand."

"I will only ask one thing of you at this point. I want you to give me your guarantee that no competitor's promotional material will find its way into the cowboy section of this bar."

"Dave has already given his gentleman's agreement to your local representative."

The term "gentleman's agreement" in conjunction with Dave's name seemed to amuse her. She grinned. "Yeah. Well, I hope so."

—

As soon as the Marlboro rep left, Rhett looked at his watch then quickly ran up to the street and onto *The Passazh*.

As soon as he rounded the corner, he saw a man and a petite blonde walking toward him. "You must be the one we're looking for."

"How did you guess?" He quipped.

This is my colleague, Natalya. I'm Phillipe. We're from CNN."

Rhett held out his hand to greet her. "And you must be the one who answered the phone yesterday."

"Yes, I am." Her English was perfect.

You sound American, but when you answered the phone yesterday you spoke in Ukrainian. Are you Diaspora?"

"Right again."

Rhett was aware that Ukraine had a complex relationship when it came to the Western Diaspora. Most of them were the descendants of Ukrainians who had fled Communism during the twenties. Over the decades, the two cultures had evolved quite differently and while some embraced them, others saw them as naïve arrogant intruders. As a result, he said nothing else about the subject.

"So, where can we go to talk about this cowboy singer of yours?" Phillipe asked.

"We can go to the Carambol. It's right up the street."

Natalya declined the invitation. "Thank you, but unfortunately, we are very busy coordinating the filming during the week of the Chernobyl commemoration. However, we met him the other night at the Arizona, but we've been unable to reach him by phone."

"That's odd. There must be something wrong with that phone. Tell you what, when I talk to Toby, I'll tell him to get in touch with you. In the meantime, if there is anything else I can do, just call me at the office."

———

The construction continued to roll along, even though at times it seemed to roll along at a snail's pace. Still, the Kowboy Dance Hall & Saloon was slowly, but surely coming together. Rhett just hoped and prayed it would be ready by April 26th.

On occasion, he would catch a glimpse of the Ukrainian cowboy walking through the streets of Kiev. Rhett still couldn't figure out exactly what his story was. It was all so mysterious. Nevertheless, it had piqued his curiosity.

XIII

The Trouble with Texas

"Fuck Boris!" Toby exclaimed as he stormed into the office.

Lena looked at him, clearly taken aback by his sudden outburst. "Is there a problem with Boris?" Lena asked.

"I don't like him. He's been late several times to pick me up to take me to practice."

"You understand, Boris has many things to do." She replied, defending Boris. "He has other tasks. I understand he might occasionally be late, but I am sure he tries his best."

"I don't care. All I know is Dave gave him to me to get me around where I want and when I want." It was evident Toby thought Boris was supposed to be his personal chauffeur.

"Was he late today?" Rhett asked.

"No, today he was on time, but then he acted like he wanted me to be grateful. When he picked me up this afternoon he said, 'See, today I pick you up at right time. I no late,'" mocking Boris' broken English. "Like I was supposed to thank him or something."

A smile came over Toby's face. "So I looked at him and said, 'Yeah, so?'"

All Boris wanted was a simple thank you, but to Toby's way of thinking, he was fishing for a compliment. And he, for damn sure wasn't about to give him one. "I know he wanted me to tell him that he had done good, but I wasn't going to do it," he declare in a cocky west Texas accent.

"Why not?"

"Because I hate it when somebody tries to get a compliment."

"Would it have hurt you to tell him 'Thank You?' Lena told you, Boris has a lot to do and he really tries to do his best for everyone."

"I don't care. That's just the way I am. I don't give out compliments, especially when someone is sitting there begging me to give them one."

Rhett thought for a nineteen-year-old, Toby was awfully opinionated, if not a total asshole.

He changed the subject. "Did you know the people from CNN have been trying to contact you?"

"Yeah, I already gave them a call this morning."

"Is everything set then?"

"I guess so. They said they want to do a story on me when the bar gets open. I said, 'That's if the bar ever gets open.'" He didn't seem at all concerned that he was about to get an opportunity to be featured on international television.

He sat down and was trying to get his computer hooked into America Online when Todd appeared in the doorway. "Toby! Haven't seen you since you knocked the shit out of that disk jockey at the Super Nova kick-boxing match."

"I did nail him pretty good, didn't I?" Toby wasn't only bragging about it, he was laughing in a mean-spirited way.

Rhett turned to Todd. "Did he really hit someone from Super Nova?"

"Yeah, but the guy kind of had him coming to him."

"What do you mean, 'the guy kind of had it coming to him'? I've got to work with those people. Besides, we've even offered to give Toby his own radio program in order to promote the bar. Does anybody seem to realize that the radio station is giving the bar a lot of free publicity? Do you have any idea how much that's worth to us?"

"Well, you weren't there, Rhett. The guy was getting a little excited about the Ukrainians winning and he pushed Toby a little too hard."

"I don't give a flying fuck. It's not good for the bar to have our fine young American cowboy going around knocking the shit out of Ukrainians acting like some redneck."

"Yeah, whatever," Toby interjected.

"Relax, Rhett. You don't even know what you're talking about."

Although he wasn't happy with Toby, Rhett was also surprised at Todd's reaction. He was an investor in The Kowboy and had been living in Ukraine long enough to know better. He didn't like it from either of them.

Toby was becoming a far cry from the polite kid that Rhett had met at the Carambol not so long ago. It was beginning to seem that he was not the nice young American boy he wanted everybody to think he was either. From that moment on, Rhett started to pay closer attention to Toby.

———

The next morning, as Rhett sat in Boris' car waiting to pick up Toby and take him to his rehearsal, Boris turned to him. "Rhett, answer me something. Just between you and me."

"Sure. What?"

"Why is Toby such a schmuck?"

"What? Is 'schmuck' a Russian word?"

"No, it is English. You know what this word is, 'schmuck'?"

"Yes, I know. It means *mudak*. Why do you ask?"

"You know, I work very hard. I try to take everybody everywhere. But Toby, he no treat me like a man."

"What do you mean?"

"He tell me pick up this, pick up that. I am driver. I no Toby's boy."

Boris was a man in his mid-thirties and he was saying that Toby, a nineteen-year-old kid, was treating him like his own personal a baggage boy.

"Maybe he doesn't mean it."

"No. He mean it. I try to be nice. You know that. You always say thank you to me. Toby, he no say nothing."

106

"Well, I am a bit older and I've lived here for a while. Maybe it's because he's young and doesn't know any better."

"Maybe. But I no like."

"Well, sometimes Americans tend to have a bad habit of treating people in other countries without respect." Still, Rhett didn't like the idea of some wet-nosed pup treating Boris in such a manner. "Would you like me to talk to Toby? Perhaps that would help."

"No. I no want to cause trouble."

Obviously, Toby hadn't been around that much, but to Rhett's way of thinking, it wasn't a reason for him to be treating a grown man with such disrespect.

———

A week before Dave returned, he called. "Hey, I found a manager for the bar. His name's John. He's an old cowboy who's had a lot of experience in the bar business. He told me he owned a bar called … now get this … Cowboys in Tulsa. I told him that's where you were from. Anyway, he told me that he could help me get an electric bull. He knows someone who manufactures them. I think you'll like him. I've told him all about you."

"Oh, yeah? Just exactly what did you tell him?"

"I told him you were from Oklahoma and that you've been handling everything while I'm in California. I said that I could never afford to pay you what you're worth."

"Well, thanks for that. What's he like? How did you find him?"

"He's the guy who's been printing my T-shirts in Hemet, California. I was in his shop the other day and he was asking me what I was doing over in Russia."

"Did you tell him that you were in Ukraine, not Russia?"

"It's all the same to him. Anyway, I told him about the bar and he got real interested. So when I asked him if he would like to manage the bar, he jumped at the offer."

"Great, what else?"

"He can manage the bar when I'm not in Kyiv and I'll manage it while I'm there. We'll trade off and you can help as assistant manager. It's perfect."

"Fine. When do I meet him?"

"He's coming to Kyiv just before the opening. Is Lena there?"

"Yeah, she's standing right here."

"Put her on." He handed the phone to Lena.

Rhett listened as Dave asked her if the Germans had paid yet. Lena told him they had not.

He then asked if she had received the loan from Salom. "Yes, but he gave only half of the money." She replied. "No, the money's already gone and the phone is not working at your apartment. The bill has not been paid and I haven't paid Boris either . . . Yes, I understand."

Dave told her not to worry. When he returned, he would take care of everything. Then he hung up.

Rhett could see the strain beginning to show on Lena's face, even though she tried not to show it. She was trying to hold everything together during his many absences, but it was becoming increasingly difficult. Everyone was hounding her for money.

Nevertheless, she believed in Dave and always tried to remain optimistic.

He thought of how Toby had been treating Boris and despite not being paid, he continued to work for Dave. Even Lena, his most faithful employee, had not been paid in months.

Rhett hoped Dave realized how lucky he was to have so many people who were loyal to him.

Toby, on the other hand, was a different story. Even though Dave had given him money to live on, he continued to dine out at Kyiv's finest restaurants. He was beginning to run short too and starting to complain.

If it wasn't Anton or Boris, it was money or Dave. Toby was constantly bitching that his phone wasn't working and came to the office every day to make phone calls to the States. He apparently had no idea, nor did he seem concerned about anyone else. Even though everyone was barely hanging on, doing without, it wasn't his problem.

In the meantime, Rhett was paying Igor his meager salary out of his pocket.

However, he had not realized how bad Boris' situation had become, until Igor told him. Boris' wife hadn't eaten in days.

As a result, it was the first thing he brought up the day Dave returned.

"Have you paid Boris yet?"

"I paid him this morning. He's gone to buy some food at the gastronome to take home to his wife." Then with a mournful look, he feigned concern, "Did you know that she hadn't eaten for two days?"

"Yeah, I just heard it this morning. That's why I was asking you. You've got a good man in Boris," Rhett added. "I hope you realize that, Dave. You have no idea what he has been putting up with."

"What do you mean?"

Dave didn't act cognizant of the fact that the reason Boris and wife hadn't eaten was because of him. However, since Boris had asked Rhett not to say anything about his problem with Toby, he simply replied, "I'll tell you later."

———

Dave was hoping that the Germans had come up with his rent money. They had not.

After paying off a few bills, Dave found himself in the same situation he had been in before he left.

At first he went to Salom to ask for the balance of the twenty thousand loan, but Salom told him that his ship had not returned from Africa and he was in a money crunch too. It had been months since Salom's slow boat had sailed. Rhett was beginning to wonder just how long it was going to take for Salom's ship to come in.

Dave was asking anyone he could think of to float him a loan, the American business community, Rudy, even the landladies whose apartments he leased and wasn't paying. Between trying to collect from the Germans, meetings with Salom, trying to raise money and drinking all night, he had little time for anything else. He put the word out that he needed a short-term loan and would be willing to pay as high as twenty percent in interest. That's when a friend put him in touch with a man named Oleg.

Dave and Rhett were sitting in the downstairs coffee shop, when he arrived carrying a sports bag over his shoulder. Oleg was thick, burley and tough looking, but he was always smiling and seemed to be in a good mood. He had some extra cash and was looking for something he could invest in. And when he heard twenty-percent interest. Well, that sounded good to him.

Having no desire to be a part of another shady negotiation, Rhett excused himself and went upstairs to the office. Twenty minutes later, Dave came rushing in. He sat down at the computer, quickly typed Oleg's name on a blank loan agreement using the bar as collateral, and printed it out. Grabbing the contract and a bag he quickly walked out of the office. Within minutes, he returned with a bag full of Oleg's cash and grinning from ear to ear. It appeared Dave was back in business.

XIV

Duck Holiday

Rhett and Igor huddled in a freezing alley waiting for Dave. They had been scheduled to do an interview, but as usual, he was running late. When he did arrived, he was with a diminutive young lady cradled closely underneath his arm. He introduced her as Svetlana.

They smiled and politely tipped their hats. Then Dave kissed her good-bye and slapped her on the ass. She disappeared down the street and around the corner.

Rhett said nothing. It wasn't his business. However, whenever Dave had a wild night, he didn't need to be asked.

"I ran into her at an embassy party last night. She took one look at me, I looked at her and we thought there was something familiar about each other We met about a year ago and had a real good time. Sveta's a good fuck too, but goddamn, she's a screamer." He laughed. "Once she gets going, you'd think someone was killing her. I remember the first night I got her to my apartment. The neighbors were ready to call the police. Christ! I finally had to put my hand over her mouth, just to keep her quiet."

"That's fine by me. After all, a man is only a guy. But some pictures were published in *LOOKS International* magazine of you playing grab-ass with models at a party. Personally, I don't give a damn what you do. I figure it's your business. But if you plan on bringing your wife over ..." Rhett stopped in mid-sentence then he continued. "You know how people talk in this town. It's a fish bowl with the foreign community. I'm just telling you, cover your ass."

"Don't worry about it. Kathy's seen those photos and she believes whatever I tell her. It's cool. I told you I got a great wife." He laughed.

—

When they arrived to the radio station, an announcer was waiting. It was the same DJ that Toby had punched at the kick-boxing match. However, there was no mention their altercation.

"Do you know where is Toby?" He asked. "We've been waiting for him to come and record his radio show."

"Toby hasn't been doing his radio program?" The way Toby had been acting lately, Rhett wasn't too surprised. He simply shook his head and sighed.

"No, we have not heard from him. Is he going to do his show?"

"Of course he is," Rhett replied. "I'll talk to him. That's if you still want to continue with the program."

"Surely. We are always ready anytime he is."

"I'll have him call you then." More and more, Toby's veneer was beginning to crack. He pulled Dave to one side. "Do you have any idea how important that radio show is for the bar? I mean, I'm doing all I can to promote the place, but Toby's show is like having an hour of free advertising every week. We need all the airtime we can muster. What's that kid's problem, anyway?"

"I don't think he really likes doing it," Dave replied as he was eyeing an attractive blonde walking by.

Rhett was furious. "Fuck what that kid likes or doesn't like. I was under the impression he was working for you. You're paying his bills, for Christ sake! Tell him to do the goddamned show."

"It's not really that big of a deal. He doesn't like the DJ anyway. I heard they had some problems"

"Who does he like? For Christ's sake, Toby punched the guy. Did you know that? He's treating all the Ukrainians like shit. He even treats Boris like his personal baggage boy and I don't like it. If you don't want to say something, I'll by God, say something."

"Okay, okay. Settle down. I'll have a talk with him."

For a moment, Rhett wondered if he had said too much about Boris.

"Listen, Dave. The way this kid's acting is really beginning to bug the hell out of me,. He's getting a little too big for his britches if you ask me. But then again, you didn't ask me."

"Don't worry about it. Let me fill you in on something about Toby. Remember when I told you he was discharged from that flight school for an ulcer?"

"Yeah."

"Well, that's only part of the story. They did discharge him for that and that's what it says on his papers. Truth is, Toby couldn't take the pressure and he was beginning to crack. He confided this to me one night. The ulcer discharge was just a polite way to avoid him having a psych discharge on his record."

"Look, I don't have anything against the kid personally. It's just that I don't like the way he's behaving around the Ukrainians."

"I know, I know. I've been hearing a few things from other people too. All this attention he's been getting is starting to go to his head. It's the main reason Tim left. Toby wouldn't let him play and kept telling him to go and sit in the corner. I had to tell him I didn't pay a lot of money to have Tim sitting in some corner.

"Well, he's going to turn out to be a real pain in the ass if you don't do something about it pretty fast."

"Don't worry about it. Musicians like Toby are a dime a dozen. Hell, do you know that he never played before a real audience before he came here? He told me so. The real talent is the band. He's just the front man. The main reason he's here is to train them how to play country music. After that I plan to send him home and bring over other singers."

"Well, that makes me feel a lot better. Eventually, people will get tired of him playing the same old songs every night, anyway."

"That's the plan. But you're the only one who knows this, so I'd appreciate it if you didn't tell anybody else."

"Don't worry, I won't. Remember, I've got a stake in this too."

"I've been thinking. Why not mix up the music? We can have jazz on Sundays and Super Nova's wants to sponsor a Battle of the Bands. Besides not every foreigner here is going to like country music. It'll give us some variety."

"Sounds fine by me. That's also what Marlboro was proposing. I like it."

"Good! It's a done deal then. Just wait 'til John gets here. He'll know how to manage everything, including Toby."

"Well, I certainly hope so. I just hope the problems with Toby don't to get any worse."

"Listen, Rhett, I'm an entrepreneur. And there's something you need to understand about entrepreneurs. We put the people together to do the job. I don't have the time to take care of all of the details. That's why I'm bringing John here. I've got everything under control. You just do your job."

The announcer stuck his head out of the door and signaled he was ready to do the interview. Dave and Rhett followed him into the sound booth. Due to Dave's inability to speak Ukrainian, the interview would be done in English. The announcer would translate Dave's responses, while Rhett would answer in his strange Ukrainian dialect.

Rhett looked on in amazement as Dave described what the bar was going to look like, from the electric bull to elaborate arcade games that he was flying in from America.

Then he proclaimed that everyone working at The Kowboy would be called by the names of famous American gunfighters. He was going to be called Billy the Kid and Rhett would be known as Doc Holliday. It was the first time that he had heard about it.

Understandably, the announcer wasn't familiar with many famous characters of the American West and misunderstood the name Doc. He asked Dave to clarify who Doc Holliday was. Dave tried to explain, but it only confused the announcer who didn't quite catch the gist of what he was trying to say. Consequently, when he translated Doc Holliday, he translated it as *Utka Prazdnika.*" Rhett looked at the announcer then looked at Igor who was laughing from outside the booth. He had just been dubbed as the famous American gunslinger who went by the moniker "Duck" Holliday.

———

The next three weeks flew by quickly. Even though the bar wasn't ready, Dave was preparing to return to California again.

He was in the bar when Salom came to pick him and Lena up and take them to the airport. The Germans still hadn't paid, nor had he rented out any of Rudy's office space. He had been covering his expenses with the money from the loan Oleg had floated him.

Rhett thought it was a hell of a way to do business, but Dave wasn't the kind of person to listen to anyone else's opinion. After all, it was the way he did business — fast and loose. As fare as he was concerned, he had everything under control as the cars sped away to take him to Boryspol Airport.

A few hours later, when Lena returned to the bar, he asked, "Did Dave leave you any money this time?"

"No,"

"But what about the money he got from Oleg?"

"He gave it to Salom."

"He gave it to Salom?!" Rhett couldn't believe what he was hearing.

"Yes, Salom told him he wanted his money back, so Dave had to give him what remained from Oleg's loan."

"Wait. Now, let me get this straight. Are you telling me that Dave gave Salom eight grand?"

"Yes, but Salom was not happy."

Lena began to explain that Dave had been carrying the eight grand in a bag when he went to the airport with Salom. As usual, he was planning on taking those eight thousand tax-free simoleons back with him back and repatriate them to their home in America.

Unfortunately, on the way to the airport Dave discovered that Salom had other plans for that money. He wanted the ten grand he had lent Dave back and was demanding payment on the spot. Dave had no choice; he forked over everything he had. Despite his bravado, when push came to shove, Salom scared the shit out of him.

Even though Salom was supposed to be his partner, the idea of investment was an alien concept. Waiting for a return from the profits of the bar was completely out of the question. This time, Dave's — or rather *Oleg's* — money stayed with Salom. Those Ben Franklins would never see America again.

By the time Dave boarded the airplane, his baggage had been relieved of a few kilograms of a green leafy substance called money. When he landed in Amsterdam, there would not be a hot time in the old town tonight.

Still, Salom wasn't at all happy being shorted. Compared to ten, eight was like being French-kissed by your grandmother. Needless to say, Salom was not pleased.

XV

Big Bad John

A week before he returned, Dave phoned Lena and told her to type out a letter. Rhett overheard, as she repeated what he was dictating over the phone.

The letter was to be addressed to him and have "Children of Chernobyl" on the top. It was an invitation and a letter of gratitude in Ukrainian stating everything he was bringing into the country was a donation to the organization. Then he told Lena was to forge the name of the director of the organization at the bottom of the document and fax it to him.

Once he arrived back in Ukraine, Dave would present the forged document to customs officials in order to avoid paying import duties and smuggle boxes of cowboy hats and souvenirs into the country.

As soon as Lena hung up the phone, Rhett looked at her. "Is he serious? He actually wants you to send him a phony letter just to get a bunch of souvenirs past customs? Does he realize what could happen if anyone find out about this?"

Lena shrugged in embarrassment, but she worked for Dave and didn't have much of a choice. She was in no position to take the high ground over the issue. She simply typed the letter and faxed it.

Rhett simply shook his head. Even for Dave, it was low.

———

Toby strode into the office and picked up the phone and dialed a number back in the states. "Hello, darlin'. I just wanted to hear your voice….What have I been doing? Nothing much. I just go home at night and fall asleep thinking of you. I miss you so much." He was on the phone for over an hour talking as if he were placing a call across town..

When he hung up, Rhett looked at him. "Why don't you give the people at Super Nova a call. They've been waiting to hear from you."

"I'm not really into doing that radio program anymore. It's not my style. I was thinking maybe I'll have you do those radio programs for me instead."

Then, without another word, he grabbed his bags and like a banty rooster strutted out of the office.

Rhett turned and looked a Lena. "Americans! Maybe I've been here too long, but I'm beginning to hate them."

———

It was the middle of the night when the phone rang in Rhett's apartment. As soon as he picked up the phone, he heard Dave's voice on the other end "Hey! What are you doing Friday night?"

"Wait a minute. Let me check my social calendar to see if I'm busy. Nope. Nothing here. Of course there's nothing here, you asshole!"

"Well, leave Friday night open. Kathy and I will be arriving in Kyiv. We're going to have dinner at the Arizona and I want her to meet you. What time is it there?"

"Get a watch!" Rhett slammed down the receiver.

———

Dave was beginning to change apartments like a man would change a cheap suit and when he returned, he immediately moved his wife into a larger apartment located in one of the most prestigious areas of Kiev. He needed to have a place where his wife wouldn't run into his and Toby's revolving door of female admirers.

Rhett rang the doorbell and waited. A moderately attractive woman answered. It was Dave's wife, Kathy. She was wearing blue jeans, her hair cut short and if it weren't for the hips, she might have been mistaken for a boy.

"Good evening, ma'am." He quipped, "I'm Doc Holiday and I've come to pick you all up for dinner. Boris is waiting downstairs."

"Come on in, Doc." She laughed. "Dave's told me all about you. We're almost ready."

He followed her just as Dave was coming out of the bedroom "Almost ready. Did you see what I brought back for the bar?"

"Not yet." Rhett followed Dave into the living room. Where he saw stacks of cowboy hats and a bunch of cheap Mexican souvenirs lying about everywhere.

"Got your chili seasoning and I even brought some spurs for you."

For a moment he was excited, until he saw the toy spurs. Nevertheless, he put them on, trying not to show his disappointment telling himself that in all probability, no one would know the difference.

"Aren't these cool?" Dave was laughing like a little boy as he played with a couple of cap pistols,

"Let's go, boys," Kathy interrupted. "Boris is waiting and I'm hungry."

As they entered the lift, Dave turned to Rhett. "John and his wife are flying in on Sunday. Can't wait for you to meet them. They're great people."

The lift stopped on the first floor as three walked out into the night, climbed into the car and sped away to the Arizona.

When they arrived, Toby was waiting at a corner table with his arm around a young woman. She was the new receptionist Dave had hired that afternoon.

After he had heard Toby sweet talking his fiancé a few days earlier Rhett thought maybe she was there as a new member of the company. Either way, he didn't really care and didn't give it a second thought.

When he opened the menu, he took one look and exclaimed, "Christ Almighty! Twelve dollars for a hamburger, twenty dollars for a pitcher of beer, five dollars for french fries, and eight bucks for a mixed drink!"

The prices were steep by anyone's standards. Nevertheless, the place was packed with highly-paid Western advisors and the nouveau riche of Kyiv ready and willing to shell out the money for an evening that would make them forget they were living in the post-Soviet Union.

"Don't worry. I'm paying. Order anything you want. It's on me." With what Dave was not paying him, Rhett more than ready to take him up on his offer.

Rhett leaned over to Dave. "Just look at these prices. If we charge half of that, we're gonna make out like bandits. People will be flocking to The Kowboy."

"Don't worry, they will," He laughed.

Rhett looked up to see a couple of young American executives approaching their table. "Well, the cowboys are here tonight. When's everything going to be ready?"

"Soon," Dave replied. "We're going to have a party next Friday and you guys are invited. So, make sure you're there?'

"Wouldn't miss it for the world," one of them answered.

"I decided to wait until Friday to open. I know that Tax Day's on Monday, but people have to go to work the next day. So, that's not a good day for us to throw a party. Besides, that gives me a few more days to get the bar ready."

Rhett was relieved. For once, he happy to agree with one of Dave's decisions. After the months of hard work, he was hoping he was seeing the light at the end tunnel.

After dinner, Dave and Rhett walked into the game room where he immediately ordered a couple shots of Tequila.

He looked over his shoulder to see if his wife was watching. "I don't want Kathy to see me. She doesn't approve because I've got this problem with my liver."

Rhett didn't have that problem, or at least he didn't think so — at least not yet. Finally, he was enjoying himself for the first time in a long while. He could almost smell the success. Despite everything, The Kowboy Dance Hall & Saloon was about to happen.

However, truth be told, Dave's back was up against the wall. He had wasted a lot of money high-rolling around Kyiv and even though he had returned cash-poor with only a few grand in his pockets he was still spending like there was no tomorrow.

He owed a lot of money, made too many promises and needed to get The Kowboy open as soon as possible. He needed money, and he needed it fast.

—

A few days later, Big John Hamilton and his wife Casey arrived in Kyiv. When Dave offered to take them to their apartment to rest up, but they would hear nothing of it. Even though they had been travelling over twenty-four hours, they both were thrilled to be in Eastern Europe for the first time — excited about the adventure of it all. They were ready and raring to go.

They couldn't wait to meet everybody and everyone had been waiting for them. The two came walking into The Kowboy for the first time. Both were wearing a lot of jewelry.

John was a stocky, boisterous man with a silver Abe Lincoln beard. He wore a cowboy hat, boots, jeans, and an Oakland Raiders windbreaker.

His wife Casey was a formidable attractive woman in her late forties, sporting a rhinestone outfit. She was busty, had bleached-blonde hair and though some might think that she was wearing a bit too much make-up, it was easy to see that in her younger years she had been a stunningly beautiful woman.

Rhett was the first to walk up. "Howdy, I'm Rhett. So what do you think about the place?"

"I love what I've seen so far." John laughed as he looked around. "I can't believe that I'm actually seeing a cowboy saloon in the middle of Russia."

"Ukraine." Rhett replied.

"What?"

"Kyiv's in Ukraine."

"Right. So, tell me, how did you wind up in Eastern Europe?"

123

Rhett gave him some background on his days with the Peace Corps and how he had been intrigued with the city ever since he first laid eyes on Kyiv.

"I initially came over with two other Americans. Back when it was part of the Soviet Union. One was my business partner. He was one of those typical good ole' boys from Oklahoma, and a boisterous bullshit artist."

"So what happened?" John asked curiously.

"Well, we landed in Moscow, were given a quick tour of Red Square. Then we were hustled off to a train station where we boarded an overnight train to Kyiv. The next morning, as we crossed the Dnieper River, I saw this stainless-steel statue of a woman standing with her sword pointing skyward shining brightly in the morning sun. She was truly a sight to behold.

"Anyway, the Soviets were gracious hosts. We were treated to banquet after banquet. We toasted each other, talking about our dreams of mutual cooperation and future successes. Then it all turned to shit."

"How's that?" John asked.

"Greed, pure and simple"

"What do you mean?"

"The two men I came with thought we were the only Americans to ever visit the Soviet Union and just like that they were going be millionaires."

"Sounds like you had a lot of opportunities."

"I guess so. But they reckoned they could hustle the "Russkies," and unfortunately that's when the lies began. One side promised the sun while the other side promised the moon and it turned out being one hell of a fiasco."

"Did you get a lawyer?" he asked

"Hell, one of those sons-a-bitches was a lawyer." Rhett laughed bitterly. "He was a fat, sweaty pig of a man, whose only international experience had been in the whorehouses of Tijuana and his only legal expertise was defending drug dealers back in Oklahoma."

"Why'd you bring him along?" John asked.

"I thought he was supposed to be looking after my best interests. Boy, was I wrong. He was along for the ride and to see what he could glean for himself."

"Did you try to sue them?"

"Did you ever try to get a lawyer to sue another lawyer? Besides, in Oklahoma the only thing worse than a lawyer is a child molester. By the time it was all over, I had lost my business and didn't have enough money left to take them to court."

"Did you report him to the bar association?"

"That's a joke." Rhett scoffed. "Here, they've got the Communist party and the Mafia. In Oklahoma, they've got the good ole' boys' network and the Oklahoma Bar Association. They're as corrupt as anything you'll find in this country."

"You got that right!" Casey chimed in. "I've never been anywhere as corrupt as Oklahoma!"

John laughed. "Sorry, but Casey hates Oklahoma."

"Don't worry. I completely understand. After all, I've lived there all my life."

However, Casey wasn't finished. "Well, John, you've got to admit, when we lived in Tulsa, we were always having to pay off one son of a bitch or another to keep that bar open."

John was still laughing. "Casey finally gave me an ultimatum. I could either leave Oklahoma with her, or she was going to leave without me."

"Goddamned Okies! I hated that place!"

"Believe me, I have no great desire to go back there either," Rhett replied. "So, have you ever been to Muskogee?"

"Oh, God!" Casey's eyes rolled back in her head. "Now, there's a place that's got a Mafia. And the drugs they've got in that town …"

Rhett was beginning to smile. "Yeah. Every time I hear Merle Haggard's 'Okie from Muskogee' it cracks me up. 'Don't smoke marijuana' my ass."

"That was called the most corrupt city in America a few years back. You remember, John? Where did we read that?"

"OK, dear. Settle down. We don't live there anymore and we're far away from there now." John was laughing.

But Casey was hot. "I know, I know, but every time I think about that damned place —"

Rhett started laughing too. "A friend of mine once told me, 'We don't have any industry in Oklahoma. We just steal from each other.'"

"I can certainly believe that!" Then Casey began to laugh.

"Well," Rhett sighed, "I guess we've said pretty much what we had to say about Oklahoma. Boy, I can really tell Casey's not too fond of the place."

"Oh, you can see that, can you?" John replied "No, not at all."

As Casey walked away, she could still be heard cursing and mumbling something about Oklahoma.

John continued. "Well, my attorney is F. Lee Bailey,"

"F. Lee Bailey?" Rhett stared at him. "Doesn't he cost a hell of a lot of money?"

"Yeah, but if I ever get into serious trouble, and believe me I have several times, I want to have the best lawyer that money can buy."

Rhett thought for a moment "Well, he sure as hell helped get O.J. off."

"I threw a guy through a window at my bar one night, because the dumb son of a bitch wouldn't quit fuckin' with me."

"Did he learn his lesson?"

"Sure did. When he went through the window the glass severed a vein in his neck. It cost me a lot of money to get off that murder charge. Almost lost the bar. Even though I've never met the man, it's why I've got him on retainer."

John was turning out to be an interesting character, if not a complete bullshit artist.

—

Later that evening, Rhett offered to show John how to get to his apartment should he ever had to walk there. He didn't think it was that far, but he had become used to walking. John wasn't. It turned out to be a forty-minute trek.

As they walked through the darkened streets of Kyiv, Rhett began to show him some of the landmarks.

Suddenly, something large darted out in front of them and over their feet.

"Holy shit!" It startled John and he stepped back. "What was that?"

"A rat."

"A Rat! But did you see the size of it?"

"Yeah. Get used to them. Kyiv's an old city. They got rats as big as dogs here. Hell, the cats won't even fuck with them."

"I hate those things." He shuddered, but Rhett was unfazed.

"So, John, tell me some more about yourself.

"My dad was a preacher."

"You're a religious man?"

"Yep, son of a preacher man. But not that organized religion shit! What about you?"

"I don't know. I suppose I believe in a bit of everything — a little bit of nothing."

"You know, Rhett? I've been around religion all my life and most of 'em are nothin' but a bunch of damned hypocrites."

"Yeah, I know what you mean. I was raised by a bunch of self-sanctimonious Southern Baptists and what I can't seem to wrap my head around is the idea of why the hell would I want to spend eternity surrounded by a bunch of assholes.

"I mean you ought to see some of the missionaries over here. They really piss me off. screamin' that these people are all damned for being born in the Soviet Union, that Chernobyl is God's retribution. It's the last thing these people need and a wonder they get any converts."

"My old man was like that. All it ever did was make me want to raise hell. I remember this kid when I was growing up. He was a fat little fucker, always picking on me on the church bus. I was only twelve at the time and when I told my dad, all that bible thumper did was wail the tar out of me and tell me to quit cryin.' When he got through, I looked him square in the eye and told him 'That's the last time you'll ever see me cry.' And by God, it was."

"And what about the fat kid?"

"Well, after the old man beat me black and blue, I went and got my baseball bat. The bus would drop off the kids at the church for choir practice and that fat little fuck always had to take a piss as soon as he got off. So, I went to the toilet at my Dad's church, hid in one of the stalls and waited for him to come in and take a leak. He didn't know what hit him. And I kept hitting him 'til there was blood all over the place, all over the bat and all over me. Then I took that bat and gave it to my old man. You should have seen the look on his face."

"What did he do?"

"Nothin'— not a goddam thing, but to call the cops. They took me and put me in the Chino correctional institute until I was fourteen. That place only made me meaner and I gave 'em more than enough reason to keep me in there until I was sixteen."

"What about the fat kid?"

"Him? Well, he never completely recovered. About a year later, he died of a brain embolism. I guess it had been such a long time, they didn't think about tryin' me for killin' that fat pissant. But I knew it was the beating I gave him that caused it. I laughed my ass off when I heard. It was one of the happiest days in my life."

"By God, man, you're an ill-tempered son of a bitch!" Rhett chuckled.

"Yeah. It's one of the reasons why Casey doesn't let me drink anymore."

"So, what brought you here?"

"I was getting bored in America and needed a little adventure. I've been just about everywhere, but I've never been to Russia."

"Ukraine."

"Yeah, whatever." Then John continued. "So, when Dave offered me a chance to manage this bar, I asked Casey what she thought and here we are. I didn't always run a T-shirt shop. I bought it for my son." Then John changed the conversation. "So, tell me Rhett, whatever happened with those partners of yours back in Oklahoma?"

"Well, a few months after Kyiv, we returned to Moscow to participate on a business cruise up the Volga River. By that time, the greed had driven them into a frenzy. They were pissed off because I wouldn't lie to the Soviets and back their bullshit story. One night, the lawyer even tried to push me over the side of the boat. Then, when we got back to Oklahoma, it was my partner Claude who told me he was the "swingin' Dave" in the deal and threatened to kill me if I didn't back away."

"Was he serious?

"Hell yes, he was serious. When it came down to friendship or money, Claude always chose money. In fact, he always bragged about being a greedy son of a bitch. He also owned the local gun show in Oklahoma City. You ever see the kind of people who go to gun shows? Most of them look like a bunch of inbreds from 'Deliverance.'"

"Did you contact the police?"

"They took a report but said without proof they couldn't do anything. Besides, half of them worked his gun show. So, unless I actually showed up shot or dead, the police wouldn't make a move. After that, the goddamn lawyer talked my business partner into changing the locks to the business. They even stole my passport. Basically, I was screwed."

"Did you ever do anything to them?" John asked.

"Boy, you don't know just how bad I wanted to, but what could I do? Everything I tried legally turned out to be shit. I had already lost my business, not to mention a butt-load of money. The only thing left was to shoot them, and that wouldn't have gotten me anywhere except prison."

"Why the Peace Corps?" John asked.

"It was a way to get back to Kyiv."

"Well, that's one hell of a story. Ever think about getting some payback?"

"Every fucking day."

"Maybe I might be able to help you out."

"How's that?"

"I still know some people back in Oklahoma. Maybe I could arrange for them to pay those guys a visit."

"Yeah? Then what?"

"Basically, whatever you'd like. A broken arm or leg — an accident of some sort."

It was not altogether an unappealing offer. "Let me think about it and I'll get back to you."

John was becoming more interesting by the moment.

"Goddamn, Rhett! How far are we going to walk? My boots are killing me."

"Sorry about that," Rhett laughed. "I guess it was further than I thought."

"Well, you might be used to this walking shit, but I'm sure the hell not. Remind me not to go walking around with you again."

131

"You'll get used to it."

"You don't seem to get my point. I don't have any intention of getting used to it."

"We're almost there. It's right down that street." Rhett pointed to a light at the end of a dark street.

As they approached the apartment building, John tripped over something. "What was that? Was that . . .?"

"No. That's just a drunk." Rhett answered as he stepped over a man lying in his own piss and vomit.

John looked down. "Is that shit common here?"

"Get used to it. You'll probably see a lot more of it here than you're used to."

Rhett left him at the apartment with Dave, Kathy and Casey. As the door to the lift closed, he could hear John cursing him for making him walk over half of Kyiv. He simply smiled.

XVI

Samahon Sunset

The following morning, Rhett arrived at The Kowboy to find John and Casey going over price lists with the liquor supplier. They couldn't believe their eyes and were appalled by the prices.

"Damn! No wonder the clubs are so expensive around here," John exclaimed. "With prices like these, I'm surprised that anybody can stay in the bar business. A bottle of Absolut Vodka costs fifty dollars and a half-gallon of Paul Masson is thirty-five. And that's wholesale!"

Casey nodded. "This is absolutely ridiculous. Can you imagine how much it's going to cost to stock this bar?"

"It's because you're looking at imports," Rhett commented. "Was there any Stolichnaya on that list?"

"No, I only saw imports," Casey looked skeptical.

"Well, there you have it. You're looking at the imports and with the import taxes here, the prices are going to be outrageous. Why not serve the local stuff?"

"Is it any good?" Casey asked.

"It's Stolichnaya, for Christ's sake. How much is Stoli back in the States? It's considered the top of the line and it's expensive, right?"

"Right."

"That's because it's an import in the States. Here, it's the local brand and you can buy it retail for about a buck."

John and Casey looked at him. Then they looked at each other.

Still, Rhett wasn't sure if they were quite getting his drift. "Look, this is the way I look at it. When I'm in Mexico, I drink tequila. When I'm in Scotland, I drink the scotch. When I'm in Germany, I drink the beer. When I'm in England, I drink gin. When I'm in France, I drink the wine. And when I'm in the former Soviet Union, I drink the damn vodka. Hell, they invented it! You would think they'd have the process down by now."

"But will the customers buy it?" Casey still wasn't convinced.

"Look, most of the customers are going to order mixed drinks anyway. What did you serve in your bar in Tulsa? Stoli? I bet you served them something cheap like Tvarsky unless they asked for a call drink. Right?"

"Hell, I didn't even serve them anything that nice," He responded. "I served McCormick."

"Well, there you go. Anyone that orders a call drink that's mixed is an idiot in the first place. Have a few of those imports for the dipshit who thinks he's a connoisseur and charge him out the ass for it. Anyway, most people aren't going to even ask. Vodka is basically vodka, and I'd rather spend a dollar on a bottle of the local Stolichnaya than eight dollars on a screwdriver with Smirnoff, which is considered shit in America anyway. Besides, look at the difference in the profit margin."

"But what about wine?" Still, Casey wasn't convinced.

"Listen, these folks have been drinking for centuries, long before there even was the good ole U.S. of A. Hell, the Indians didn't have alcohol until the Europeans brought it over and got 'em all fucked up. Since I've been here, I've been drinking Crimean and Moldovan cabernets and chardonnays and they're not bad. In fact, they're pretty good."

"They have those here?" Casey asked. "Why haven't we seen them?"

"Of course they do, and you've probably seen them. You just didn't know it, because you can't read the labels. Anyone can find them right across the street in the local gastronome for two to three bucks. Can you imagine how cheap it is if you can get it wholesale? And the Soviet champagne is famous for its quality, not to mention the cognacs and brandies. If you ask me? I say fuck the French."

"Then why aren't we buying those?" John asked.

"I have no idea."

"But where can we get the local brands?"

"Look, there's a winery not two blocks from the office. They make all kinds of wine. I'm sure if you go to the director of that plant and offer to buy a shitload of wine, he'll be more than happy to sell you all you want. Besides, you'll be supporting the local brands, which I guaran-damn-tee you is going to make the government happy. And that'll be very good for our business."

John and Casey looked at each other then asked in unison, "Why didn't Dave tell us about this?"

"Because he can't read Russian and he drinks at the high rollers' places. I'm the one who's been living here on a hundred and fifty bucks a month."

"Can you take us to that place?" Casey asked.

"Sure. When you come over to the office this afternoon, we'll drive over and you can look at their wine selection. I'll even translate for you. Dave got one thing right though and that's when he decided to sell Obolon beer at the bar. It's locally brewed here in Kyiv. Hell, France even imports it because it's cheap."

John and Casey looked completely dumbfounded.

But Rhett wasn't finished. "Not only that, Obolon sells pre-made gin & tonics and rum & colas. I can buy them for about forty cents a bottle at the local kiosks. You can sell that shit all night long and you don't even have to worry about mixing the drinks. I've tried them and after about four, I got a decent buzz. And face it, ninety percent of your customers just want to come in and have a good time, listen to music, get shit-faced and get laid." Rhett hoped he had made his point and left.

—

135

The next day when John and Casey came breezing through the office, they told Rhett they didn't have time to go to the winery. Instead, they would do it at another time. Although, it was normal for most Americans to want to see the sites the first time they came to Kyiv, Rhett couldn't tell if they had come to manage the bar or were simply tourists. But.

They seemed completely enamored with city and impressed with Dave's "entrepreneurship." However, they seemed content to overlook the multitude of little details that were missing.

Even so, it seemed to John that there were so many opportunities with all people willing to help him establish a business in Ukraine. Almost every day, it seemed that he got one offer or another.

"None of this is as easy as it sounds or looks," Rhett warned him. "Some have tried it and have been successful. Others merely wound up losing their shirts dealing with either government regulations or the Mafia."

"Well, there's so much they need here. There has to be a way."

That statement gave Rhett an idea. "Look, John, I know you're not a drinking man, but there's something the locals make here. It's called *Samahon*. I have a bottle and if you would like, I'll bring some in and you can sample it."

"Samawhat? What the hell is that?"

"*Samahon*. I'm not really sure, but I think it's the Ukrainian version of moonshine. However, there's one thing I do know and that is it has one hell of a kick to it. I think it would go over really big in America if it was marketed properly."

"But moonshine's illegal."

136

"I know that, but it didn't stop some distillery making something like it and selling it to liquor stores in mason jars."

"Well, you're right about that. I've seen them," John replied.

"And no matter what America wants the rest of the world to believe, we've got a hell of a lot of people over there who like to get shit-faced. That's why the liquor and bar business is so good."

"Well, just what is this *Samahon*?"

"Ukrainians are famous for it. Back in the eighties when Gorbachev was on his anti-drinking crusade, a lot of distilleries got shut down. However, that didn't stop people from drinking. They just made their own hooch. Besides, there are a lot of people who are having a hard time making ends meet. So it's cheaper for them to make it rather than buy it. The process varies depending on who's making it, but I know a man who has a particularly good recipe. Look, I'll bring some tomorrow. If you want to, you can have a little taste and tell me what you think."

"Well, even though I don't drink, I will have a little taste and tell you what I think."

"That's all I'm asking. If you don't like it, just tell me and that will be that."

—

No sooner had they walked out the door when Toby came walking into the office.

Rhett leaned back in his chair and jokingly welcomed him. "Ah, if it isn't our young red-necked little peckerwood."

"What the hell is that supposed to mean?"

"It was supposed to mean it's a joke."

"Oh." Evidently, Toby didn't seem to have much of a sense of humor.

Sitting down, he picked up the phone and dialed his fiancée in States again.

Rhett wondered if Toby was aware how much international rates cost, because he didn't seem too concerned about it. After all, it wasn't his phone or his phone bill.

"Hi, sweetheart . . . Yeah, I miss you too. Every night I just lay there thinking about you."

After twenty minutes Rhett looked at his watch. Then he heard Toby say, "And I'll be thinking of you tonight when I go to bed, sweetheart. I love you too." Then he hung up. Once again, it was all sounding much too good to be true.

Rhett already knew about Toby from that morning at Dave's apartment and he still couldn't figure out what the deal was with Toby and the receptionist. But Toby was a healthy young nineteen-year-old, who was far from home, and anyway Rhett figured he had more important things to do than to be concerning himself with Toby's love life.

———

The following morning Rhett found John working behind the bar. When Rhett arrived at The Kowboy He walked up, pulled out a flask with a small skull on the front and placed it on the counter.

John took one look and burst into laughter. "Is that supposed to mean something?"

"Just pull a couple of shot glasses from out behind that bar and try some of this."

He reached down and pulled out two glasses. Rhett filled them both with *Samahon*, downing his in one shot.

John took a small sip His eyes widened. "Damn. I can feel that burn all the way down," John exclaimed, his eyes getting big.

"Just give it a few moments and you'll begin to feel it."

"Hell, I already feel it. You forget, I don't drink and I feel this a lot quicker than most. But you're right, it is smooth." He looked at the half-filled glass and finished it. "Whoa!"

A smile came across Rhett's face. "Tastes a little like tequila, don't it?"

"Yeah, sorta, only better."

"Now, listen to the reasons why I think this could go over in America."

John was listening, waiting for the full effect of the *Samahon* to hit him.

Rhett continued. "Basically, a lot of Americans are fad drinkers. Take tequila, for example. Not too many Americans drank it before it became popular in the sixties. Then it was like everybody was taking a lemon and putting salt on their hands. After that came "Urban Cowboy," *Mezcal* and the worm. That was in the late seventies. I've also developed a drink for those who don't like to drink their liquor straight up. Since *Samahon* tastes a bit like tequila, I came up with a variant of the Tequila Sunrise. I make it the same way . . . call it *Samahonskye Zaxhid Sonsa*."

"What's that mean?" John asked.

"*Samahon* Sunset. I've made it for the Ukrainians and they seem to love it. Do you know what Jägermeister is?"

"Damn right I do! Sold a ton of that shit at my bar in Tulsa."

"Okay, when that came along, they told everyone it was the closest thing to absinthe you could buy. When some congressman heard the rumor he tried to get it banned, but that only made it more popular. Then Jägermeister did an ad campaign with people smiling and saying 'It's All True.' And boom! Before you knew it, everybody was trying Jägermeister."

"So, what's your plan?"

"Okay. First off, everybody here thinks I'm crazy when I tell 'em they should make *Samahon* for export. Sure, it's the same as moonshine, but somebody had the idea of marketing that name. That's what we do. Most of the distilleries here will make anything if they think there's a buck in it. That's why Obolon beer is manufacturing gin & tonics and rum & cokes."

John looked intrigued. "Go on."

"Now, Dave says he has excellent contacts with Obolon. So I suggest we have them manufacture some samples of this stuff. I'll design the labels and do the marketing plan. All we have to do is find an importer to handle it. If it's made in a legal distillery, there shouldn't be a problem. Right?"

"Sounds good to me," John replied.

"Plus, it has its own ceremony that goes with it, like the lemon and salt thing with the tequila."

"What's that?"

"Well, here, they take a pickle. After they down the shot of *Samahon*, they take a bite out of the pickle and sniff their hand."

"What's that supposed to do?"

"I have absolutely no idea. I never figured that one out. But I've been doing it for three years."

"So how do we market it?"

"The same way *Mezcal* was marketed. Their advertising campaign said 'Bite the Worm.' Now, most Americans wouldn't think of eating a worm. Yet, they do it anyway. *Mezcal's* strategy was to create a market for those who thought that they were tougher than everyone else. After that, all those swingin' dicks started drinking *Mezcal.*" Anyway, this stuff is a hell of a lot better.

"You're right, it does, and I know some liquor distributors in the States." It was all that Rhett was waiting for. "Well, there you have it. Now we know that everyone thinks that Russian vodka is high quality. That's where the advertising campaign comes in."

He put his hands up as if to signify a headline. *"Anyone Can Drink Vodka, But Not Everyone Can Drink Samahon."*

"I like it!" John responded.

"And we use the Cossack image to sell it."

"Sounds like you've got everything figured out."

"Look, I know that everybody thinks I'm a little eccentric, but that don't mean I'm stupid."

"Never said you were"

"What are you all talking about?" The turned around to see Casey who had walked up behind them.

"Honey, he just brought me some of this stuff to try. They call it *Samahon.* Boy, it's something else."

"You had a drink?" Casey looked disapprovingly at John. She didn't look at Rhett too kindly either.

"Well, just one, honey. I wanted to see what it was like."

—

The day flew by quickly as John and Casey prepared The Kowboy for its first "official" party. Everything was under their supervision and even though there was no local wine or vodka, Casey had taken Rhett's advice and ordered the pre-mixed gin & tonics and rum & colas.

The restaurant wasn't finished, but a caterer was working in a small kitchen area checking to see if he had what was needed to serve the customers.

The "bull room" wasn't finished either and the mechanical bull had yet to arrive. Still, enough was finished to have a party and since everything was supposed to be free, nobody would have much to bitch about. Dave's wife Kathy was busy hiding all the bar's imperfections by tacking up the cheap, gaudy souvenirs he had purchased in Mexico.

Rhett had held off on the advertising, keeping it to ads that merely said, "The Cowboys Are Coming."

Nobody paid much attention to the fact that Dave and Lena were out for most of the day, travelling back and forth between those mysterious meetings with Salom. Nobody cared. They were all too busy getting the bar ready.

Early in the evening, Todd appeared with another American. He introduced him as Mike, a good looking, swarthy young man in his mid-twenties who was doing business in Kyiv. However, he was unclear about just exactly what it was.

Every American seemed to have their own view of what was going on in the city and it seemed that everyone had their own connections, most of whom they would never talk about. Mike was no different. He was vague about his connections. But he made it clear that he knew who he needed to know in order to do whatever it was he was doing. It was the way a lot of foreigners did business in Ukraine — very fast and very loose.

When Dave walked into the bar Todd introduced him. "Dave. I want you to meet Mike. He's volunteered to bartend for us tomorrow night."

"Great! I need all the help I can get."

"I figure it'll be a lot of fun. If for nothing else, I figure I can meet some chicks," Mike added.

Mike was intrigued about The Kowboy and wanted to get to know Dave better. He immediately started asking him about his connections in Kyiv and seemed to be particularly interested in Dave's *"krusha."*

"Todd says you've got a pretty strong roof."

Dave had already been drinking. And as usual, he was more than willing to tell anyone who wanted to know that the Chechens were his "roof." In fact, he was proud of it.

"Aren't you afraid of the authorities knowing about who you're doing business with?" Mike asked curiously, "There's a lot of talk about the former KGB cracking down on the Mafias in the city."

"Let me tell you something about the KGB," Dave answered. "They're the biggest fucking Mafia in this city."

"Really?" Mike replied. "You're not worried about them then?"

"Fuck them, they're all a bunch of pussies!"

"You really think so?"

"I said they're a bunch of pussies," Dave repeated. "My roof pisses on them."

Mike seemed surprised by his arrogance, as well as his confidence in his "roof."

"So what do you mean? Are the KGB like the FBI?" John chimed in. "If that's the case, those guys couldn't find their own ass. Even if you handed it to them"

Dave laughed. "Exactly,"

"You really think so?" Mike repeated.

"Let me tell you something about the FBI," John interjected. "They've been trying to pin something on my ass forever and they haven't been able to do a damn thing."

Rhett simply downed a vodka and tried to look like he knew what everyone was talking about. Besides, he really didn't have anything to add and, for the most part, it was all sounding interesting as hell to him.

"What do you know about the Kennedy assassination?" John asked.

"Well, I've read a lot about it," Mike replied. "It was before my time, but I knew a girl whose parents said they knew all about what really happened."

"Let me tell you, Lee Harvey Oswald was a patsy. I was Jack Ruby's partner in that strip joint back in Dallas. Oswald didn't have a damned thing to do with that assassination. He didn't know anything. He was set up to take the fall. Jack Ruby knew he had cancer and the Mafia paid him a lot of money to take the fall and get rid of Oswald."

"That's interesting," Mike said. "That's kind of what I was told."

"Listen, my wife is John Gotti's niece and I can tell you a lot of stories about the Mafia. When I married her, they took me in and helped me get started in the business. I had been in a lot of trouble as a kid and they helped straighten me out."

The conversation went on like that for about an hour. From the Chechens, to their involvement in the bar, to the KGB, to Giancana's connection to Kennedy, Gotti, who killed Castellano and even where Jimmy Hoffa's body was really buried. According to John, he had even been running prostitutes out of Vegas and Jimmy Swaggert had been on his yacht.

Dave and John were coming forth with the most amazing revelations. It impossible to tell if anyone was really telling the truth or simply bullshitting. Everything was beginning to sound like something out of an Oliver Stone screenplay.

It was all way too deep for Rhett, but he was having a good time listening to it all. But that's the way it always was when a few people started to drink. The only thing was, John didn't drink.

Eventually, it was getting late. Mike thanked Dave and John for the interesting evening and then he left.

As Dave watched him leave, he turned around and started laughing, but John wasn't laughing.

"Does anybody know who that kid is?" he asked.

"No, he's just some friend of Todd's. He brought him in to bartend."

But John was starting to sound concerned. "Do you realize what we just told him tonight and we don't even know who the fuck he really is or what he does."

Dave looked at him and smirked. "Hell, it was mostly bullshit anyway."

"I wasn't bullshitting!" John snapped. "We just told this kid a lot of information and we don't even know who the hell he really is."

"What do you mean?" Dave asked.

"Listen, that kid could be anybody, for all we know. Has the FBI opened up an office here yet?"

"Yeah, as a matter of fact, they just did recently."

"Why did they open one here?"

"To help the authorities combat the Mafia problem here." Rhett finally chimed in, downing another vodka without looking up. "The more that they can help them with the Mafia in this country, the less problems they're going to have with them back in the States."

"Well, all I know is that kid was asking too many questions," John replied.

"Yeah. As a matter of fact, he was asking a lot of questions about the Mafia, wasn't he?" The subject was starting to sober Dave up and started him thinking.

"We just gave that guy any information he wanted. Dave, you'd better ask Todd just how well he knows him." The more John thought about the situation, the more he didn't like it.

Rhett lit a cigarette and poured himself another drink. "Well, hell. I'm only sorry I didn't have anything to contribute to the conversation."

"I'm, by God, serious!" John continued. "If the FBI wanted to know what you are doing over here, what better way than to send in a man undercover to work at the bar."

"I'll find out who he is from Todd," Dave replied. "And if I have to, I'll have Salom and his guys take care of him."

Great! Rhett thought. Mike had asked too many questions and now Dave was talking about having him whacked. He may have been drunk, but he was half-serious about it too.

It was late when they closed up the bar. As they walked down *The Passazh,* Dave and John continued to talk about silencing Mike. Rhett simply listened.

As the three men approached the Metro, Dave put his arm around Rhett and looked at John. "You know the one who really knows what's going on with this bar is Rhett here. Maybe we ought to think about killing him."

"Yeah, right. Kill me," Rhett shrugged Dave's arm off his shoulder. "I'm probably the one honest son of a bitch that either of you guys know."

Dave laughed, slapping him on the back. "Just kidding. See you tomorrow."

Rhett left the two men standing on *Kreschatik* Boulevard and disappeared through the doors that led down to the Metro.

HELL OR HIGH WATER

"If you're going through hell, keep going."

Winston Churchill

I

The Rattlesnake Queens

Friday, April 19th finally arrived. The bar had been prepared as best it could. Although it wasn't anywhere near ready, Dave was resolute.

John and Casey put on their best face. Dave had invited everyone he knew from the ex-pat community, as well as his Ukrainian friends. It was going to be his "Hell or High Water Grand Opening." Do or die, he was bound and determined to open The Kowboy Dance Hall & Saloon. And, well ... by God, it was going to happen.

The construction of the front to the club had yet to be started. In its place, hung a wooden sign bearing the likeness of the club's cartoon cowboy mascot. It had originally been designed to hang on the wall behind the stage, but Dave had hastily nailed it to the top of the door to the entrance to the saloon. It was hanging at a slant.

148

With a handlebar mustache and resembling like something that had just stepped out of a Remington painting, Rhett looked pretty damned authentic. At least for a cowboy in Kyiv. A he rounded the corner *of The Passazh* he saw a long line standing outside the entrance to the bar.

Rhett quickly walked past them and went down into the bar putting on his chaps and those "Toys Are Us" spurs.

Looked around at the condition of the bar, he could see that it was a nightmare waiting to happen. The lighting fixtures weren't finished and hanging precariously from the ceiling. Only half of the barstools had been finished. The mirrors for the walls hadn't arrived. Dave had covered them with anything that he could nail on the particleboard backing, from Polaroids of the bar under construction, to his homemade drawings of the floorplans, Marlboro posters, and a mishmash of Coca-Cola signs that had been brought to the bar by the distributor. Some matched the cowboy image. Most did not.

Only two of the signs for the facade of the western town had been completed. Even they were at a slant hanging above the storefronts behind the bar.

Although Kyrill had finished the painting of "Kowboys of Kyiv," since Dave hadn't paid the crew of carpenters to build a frame, it was conspicuously absent.

The "bull room" was not only without its fabled bull, the floor had yet to be installed. It was nothing but concrete and dust. However, the Marlboro billboard covered a wall and looked impressive in its own right.

Fortunately, the bathrooms were almost complete and to some extent, were in working order. Although few toilets had been installed, the bathrooms were nowhere near enough to handle a large crowd. Similarly, only half the wash bins had running water.

The Cantina was in worse shape. There was no restaurant equipment, its murals hadn't been finished and only the table stands were built.

It would have made a wonderful movie set if Dave were filming a movie but the simple fact of the matter, that was all it really was. Other than being a facade, it really wasn't a functioning bar at all.

Half of the staff were Ukrainian. The other half were young American businessmen and advisors who had volunteered to be bartenders for the fun of it and to meet some women.

Everything was hanging together by a thread. In that aspect, one could say it was an authentic representation of a nineteenth century Wild West saloon.

As Rhett stood there looking at this unfinished canvas, he couldn't help remembering how Dave would say, "My theory is to keep it simple/stupid." Maybe he had heard it someplace and to a certain extent he was right to a certain extent, he was right. Even though he believed that all of the money would be made in liquor sales, Rhett understood that people had to eat. It was the food that would bring them in, the music would encourage them to stay and after that they would drink.

—

Dave had sent an invitation to the mayor of Kyiv to attend a pre-opening ceremony. Instead, Yuri Nikotenko, the deputy mayor, showed up to do the honors along with the president of Kyiv's American Chamber of Commerce who represented the American business community.

Somewhere, Dave found a piece of red ribbon and threw together an impromptu ribbon cutting ceremony. He instructed Toby and Rhett to hold each end, as Lena translated Yuri's speech into English. Yuri told the crowd how honored the city of Kyiv was to have a little piece of Americana opening on *the Passazh* for everyone, both American and Ukrainian, to enjoy.

Then Dave gave a speech. "This moment is the culmination of a dream come true. Ever since my arrival to Kyiv, I've wanted to open this bar. I want to welcome everyone and say, 'The Cowboys have come to Kyiv and Kyiv will never be the same.'"

Boy, was he right!

Then, he ceremoniously handed over the scissors to Yuri, who cut the ribbon. And with that, everyone descended down into "The Kowboy Dance Hall & Saloon."

—

As more people began arriving, Dave had a little change of mind. A small detour, so to speak. Although he had given everyone the impression that everything would be free at his pre-opening party, suddenly he could smell the opportunity to make a buck. He quickly ordered some makeshift signs that said, "Welcome to The Kowboy — Ten Dollars Admission Please." Although the late arrivals weren't too happy, they paid anyway, but not without a few complaints.

Then Dave's wife came up with a brilliant idea. As long as people were willing to pay admission, why not start selling Kowboy T-shirts for twenty dollars a pop and the cowboy hats for forty? After all, this was the new capitalism. So, why not make a few bucks even though they paid only four bucks for the hats in Mexico.

All in all, Dave was going to make out like a bandit as he ordered even more signs.

—

The Rockland Ladies took the stage and Dave was right. They were like a Ukrainian female version of the Stray Cats, except with cowboy hats. They came to life in front of the crowd and sounded better than they ever had in rehearsal. It was a sight to behold as everyone was rockin' to the ladies' rockabilly style as the evening's events began to unfold.

The staff adjusted from moment to moment, depending on Dave's whims. Soon the trickle turned into a flood as people began pouring in. Within an hour's time, the crowd swelled into a seething mass of partygoin' lunatics — and more were coming. The good thing was that the growing mass of people hid the unfinished details of the bar.

Surrounded by so many English-speakers, Dave's partner Sergei appeared uneasy. He wished Dave good luck and quickly left. As it turned out, he had other reasons for feeling uneasy.

No sooner had he walked out of the saloon than Salom and his entourage appeared. Five bodyguards, thick, burley and tough-looking, surrounded him. All of them were smartly dressed in expensive suits and full-length Mafia-style overcoats.

Most of the crowd was too busy having fun listening to the music to notice. After all, this was Kyiv and mobsters were a relatively common sight.

Salom greeted Rhett with a smile, shaking his hand and looking around. He was obviously pleased with what he saw. Then he asked *"Gdye Dave? (Where's Dave?)"*

That's when Dave came winding through the crowd. He looked content, proud and happy with what was surely going to be a successful night and an even more lucrative business venture.

Dave took Salom by the arm, escorting him through the crowd, laughing and muttering something in English spiced with the few words of the Russian that he knew. He signaled Andrei to come over and interpret for him. Then he escorted Salom and his entourage to the end of the bar, in front of the stage and seating the gangsters where they could better observe what was going on.

Before long, Dave seemed to be everywhere, greeting and welcoming everyone to his Kowboy Dance Hall and Saloon.

—

A contingency of Coca-Cola executives arrived, thrilled to see their signs displayed so prominently throughout the saloon. One was a young well-dressed young man who was accompanied by an older East German wearing a bright red blazer, signifying that he was truly a company man. He was Günter and he was the director of Coca-Cola's Eastern European operations.

Rhett walked over, welcomed them and introduced himself as the director of advertising and public relations. The younger man was polite and cordial, unlike the older man, who was obnoxious, overbearing and full of insults.

"So why are you working here?" Günter asked. "Couldn't you find a decent job in the West?"

For a moment, Rhett was taken aback. Then he answered politely. "I like it here. It's interesting for me."

"You must be very desperate." He snapped back. "Do you have any experience working for anyone that is worth anything?"

"I've worked for several corporations, including your competition."

"They're nobody. We sell ten times the product they sell."

"Well, I also worked with the U.S. Olympic festival."

"Why did they fire you?" It appeared that Günter wasn't about to let up.

Rhett turned to the young man, who quietly apologized. "I'm sorry, but he is my boss."

"Well, I hope you enjoy yourselves." Rhett replied and then walked away.

Despite the old man's cynicism and lack of manners, the rest of the Coke representatives were impressed and eager to enter into a business relationship with the bar. They could sense that the place was going be popular.

Before long, John came over to Rhett. "One of the reps is willing to write us an open check to help promote The Kowboy. However, like Marlboro, they want to have exclusive rights for distribution too. They're willing to do just about anything to get Pepsi out of the place."

"Does Dave know about this?"

"Yeah, he was there when they made the offer."

"What did he say?"

"He told them that he wanted them to pay for the facade."

"And ….?"

"They agreed. He said he would think about it."

"Shit!!" Once again, Rhett thought that Dave for allowing his ego to get the best of his business sense.

As they talked, a tall, sultry Ukrainian beauty walked by. John's neck snapped back in her direction.

"Damn, Rhett," John exclaimed. "I can't believe the women here. Every other one is a knockout."

The scores of beautiful Ukrainian women who were filing into the bar were certainly getting his attention. They were too hard to ignore. In fact, they were impossible not to notice them.

"I thought you were a married man," Rhett replied.

"I might be married, but I'm not blind"

"There's no doubt about that." Rhett laughed.

Beer, premixed bottles of gin and tonic, rum and cola, straight shots of tequila and, of course, plenty of vodka were flowing freely over the bar and quickly down the throats of the clientele.

Rhett chose to stay with the premixed gin and tonics, a much less potent mixture than the straight vodka or cognac he had been accustomed to over the years of hard drinking in Ukraine. It was a safer bet and he was tense, not knowing what to expect. It was obviously going to be a very long night. He wanted to be loose but stay somewhat alert or, better yet, semi-cognizant just in case anything unexpected might happen. In other words, he wanted to have some of his wits about him but enough liquor in him should he need it for a little courage or painkiller. Whatever the case may be someone decided to get into a brawl, which was not entirely unlikely.

The evening seemed to be on the road to success. Within three hours, the place was packed with a legion of hard drinking revelers.

—

Around eleven o'clock, the dance troupe arrived, five tall beautiful Ukrainian women, two of whom were the twins. They were dressed head to toe in cowgirl hats and makeshift cowgirl regalia.

Toby and The Cowboy Bar Band were in full swing on stage. This night, everybody was a cowboy, whether they were American, East Coast or West, English, Scottish, Irish, German, or Ukrainian. Whatever nationality, it made no difference. It was loosely controlled pandemonium hanging by a thread.

Nikotenko, the mayor's assistant, was standing at the bar hugging, kissing and toasting Dave, John, Casey and just about anybody and everybody he could get his hands on. He was accompanied by his wife, a tastefully dressed graceful woman, and very much a lady. It appeared that she had quickly developed an immediate affection for John's wife, Casey.

In the meantime, Salom and his gang seemed to be content to sit quietly at the bar in front of the stage. They observed everything, not missing much. From the look on his face, Salom was beginning to smell money too.

—

John and Rhett walked through the crowd, mingling and joking with the clientele and keeping their eyes open.

Dave was bouncing around everywhere drinking, dancing, posing for photographs and slapping everybody on the back. And the booze kept coming like there was no tomorrow.

The dance troupe gathered at the entrance to the bar at the opposite end of the stage. Rhett worked his way through the crowd to find Dave and inform him that the next act had arrived. He told him, as owner of the saloon, it should be his honor to introduce them to the crowd.

At the end of the band's number, Dave jumped up onto the stage and grabbed the microphone. Then a pre-recorded tape began to play "Introducing The Kowboy Dance Hall & Saloon. Kyiv's newest and without a doubt, most unique night spot." A roar rose up from the crowd.

Then, with much ado, Dave got the crowd's attention. "Hi, everybody! I think most of you here tonight know me. I'm Dave Seigal and this is my bar. So, I want to welcome you all to the first in a series of great evenings and entertainment at The Kowboy Dance Hall & Saloon!"

The crowd let out a cheer and everyone applauded.

"But first, I would like to introduce the star of our show. He's a young man by the name of Toby Smith who has come all the way from Texas. You're gonna' be hearing a lot about him in the near future. Next, I want to introduce everybody to our very own Kowboy Bar Band. To listen to them, you would think that they're straight out of Nashville, but they're not, they're Ukrainian."

Dave introduced everybody from the manager to the bartenders, telling everyone to tip "because that's all they're getting paid tonight." Then he said, "I also want to introduce you to the original Cowboy of Kyiv. You've probably seen him walking the streets of Kyiv for the past three years and most of you probably thought that he's been here making the longest movie in history. But now he's in charge of my advertising and public relations. So pretty soon you're going to be seeing a lot of billboards and advertisements all over Kyiv." With that said and done, Rhett's introduction was complete.

Dave continued, as the dancers worked their way through the crowd, "And now, we have something very special for you tonight. We have our own group of country line dancers. However, I want you to know these beautiful young ladies are also Ukrainian. So, for your entertainment, may I now introduce you to The Kowboy Dance Hall & Saloon's very own Rattlesnake Queens!"

And with that, Toby and the band kicked in with a rousing rendition of "Adelaide" as the young Ukrainians began line dancing in sync. The crowd went wild.

However, the show was far from over. After the line dancers finished, a fifteen-year-old girl named Yanna took center stage.

"Stand back everyone." Dave warned the crowd. "Give this little lady plenty of room."

People were surging toward the front of the stage to catch a glimpse of what was going to happen next. Finally, when the mob was pushed back sufficiently to give Yanna enough room, the music started again. At that point, she began to twirl a lasso, jumping in and out of the hoop just as if it were a real Wild West Show. And boy howdy, was it ever.

The crowd was beside itself and the more they cheered, the more incredible her lasso act became. She was performing backbends and splits while all the time the lasso twirled furiously in one hand above her head.

As if that weren't enough, she threw her lasso aside grabbing a bullwhip, cracking it only inches from the noses of those who were standing precariously in the front. They tried to push the others behind them back, but the crowd kept pushing forward to get a better glimpse of what was happening. Could this really be occurring in Kyiv? Damn straight it was! The crowd surged forward again. They still could not believe what they were seeing. She then turned the fury of her whip upwards into the air at the wagon wheel light fixture barely hanging from the ceiling. Spurred on by the crowd she began to flick one of the light bulbs on and off with the tip of her whip.

Although Rhett had seen her act before, at this point he couldn't believe his eyes either. The only thing he could think of was "Holy Shit! I hope that wagon wheel doesn't fall down on those bunch of screaming lunatics!"

It was truly a sight to behold. And the crowd? Damn! By this time, they had gone beyond the frenzy stage. They had gone absolutely eyeballs-a-poppin' wild! Yep! Things were looking mighty good at The Kowboy Dance Hall & Saloon.

———

As soon as she finished her act, Dave took the stage again. Only this time, he was carrying one of the short baseball bats that were kept behind the bar. It had a bottle opener attached to one end.

Rhett was standing behind the bar. He was still in a state of jubilation from the crowd's acceptance of the previous acts and wasn't paying a whole lot of attention. However, the euphoria began to wear off quickly as he realized what Dave was saying.

"Now, I want everyone here tonight to know how things are going to be run at the Kowboy. First off, I'm the owner of this bar and you should know this is an American bar, run by Americans, with an American staff.

Now, I'm going to lay down some ground rules. If you start getting a little out of control or if you get too drunk, one of our bartenders is going to come over and tell you to settle down, and you'd better listen because if you don't, you're going to be asked to leave. Now, see this bat I'm holding? It has two purposes. One is for opening beer bottles. I think you can figure out what the other use is for yourselves. So, if you don't listen when you're told to settle down, then one of the bartenders is going to yell out, 'Yo Rinnie!' At that time, all of our bartenders are going to come flying over the bar with these baseball bats, and believe me, they know how to use them. But before you're thrown out into the street, we're going to take your picture, it's going to be put up at the entrance to the bar and you're permanently banned. Now, if that isn't enough, I'm going to tell you a little something else. I want everyone here to know that I've got the baddest "roof" in Kyiv. I'm telling you now because you don't want these guys on your ass and you damn sure don't want them coming after you. Now, I want everybody to have a good time. And let's all welcome back Toby Smith and the Kowboy Bar Band."

It wasn't quite the nicest welcoming speech anyone ever delivered, and the customers didn't really need to hear that Dave was involved with the Mafia, not to mention, from a public relations standpoint, it was about as dumb a speech a business owner could deliver on his opening night. But Dave was drunk and as he usually did when he had his fill of "loudmouth soup," he was letting his mouth overload his ass.

Nevertheless, the band began to play as the drinking and dancing resumed. Todd and the other bartenders were pouring drinks as fast as they could. Before long, everybody seemed to have forgotten Dave's little speech.

Yuri was still standing at the center of the bar. He was hugging and kissing everyone, telling John and Casey if they needed anything, to call him and he would take care of any problem. He was as big and burly as John and he was as strong as an ox. However, it appeared that his wife had decided he had enough to drink and was gently coaxing him to leave, reminding him he had to go to work early in the morning. She was the perfect complement to his brutish demeanor, thanking everyone for inviting them and giving her husband a moment to unwind from his grueling schedule at the mayor's office. They excused themselves as she guided him reluctantly towards the door.

It was getting close to midnight.

———

Dave returned to the festivities and began working his way through the crowd again. Before long, Valerie came walking through the door. She looked pleased to see that everything was going so well. After all, she had invested $25,000. She was holding a beer in her hand content to stand in the corner of the entrance and watch the festivities.

Moments later, Rhett caught something out of the corner of his eye. It was Dave. He was in a shoving match with a drunk and he was signaling for help.

"Rhett, goddamnit! Can't anyone see I've got a situation over here! I need some backup! Now!"

Rhett moved quickly through the crowd placing himself between the two men and grabbing the drunk by his shoulders. His eyes couldn't focus, he could hardly stand up and he was completely incoherent. He was an Irishman and he was mumbling something, but his speech was so slurred it was unintelligible.

Todd was close behind, taking hold of the drunk as they separated both men. It seemed that nobody really knew what was happening, but Rhett could tell that things were beginning to turn ugly.

Rhett turned to Dave as he yelled, "What the hell happened?!"

Dave was furious and Rhett was finding it was much harder trying to control Dave than it was the drunk.

Dave was screaming at everyone, demanding an apology from the drunk. "This is my bar, you motherfucker! You apologize to me right now or you're a dead man! You'll be floating face down in the Dnieper River by morning! You hear me? You're dead!"

"Jeezus! Calm down, Dave," Rhett said. "This guy's really drunk and beyond the point of being dangerous to anyone."

It didn't matter. Dave was beside himself. He was now screaming at Rhett. "This son of a bitch came up to me and grabbed me. He started pushing me backwards saying 'Are you a man? C'mon be a real man.' He was going to sucker-punch me when I called for help! Where were you guys?! Where was my backup?! This motherfucker is dead!" He then pointed his finger at the drunk and screamed "You hear me?! You're a dead man! You know who I am? This is my bar! You apologize right fucking now or my roof is going to fucking kill you! You understand?"

Todd moved in and tried to settle him down. "Everything's under control. Relax, Dave." But Dave was too far gone to listen to anybody.

The Irishman held out his hand as if he wanted to shake hands with Dave, but Dave wouldn't have any of it, slapping it away. He was too busy yelling at the drunk telling him how badly he had fucked up.

"Don't worry." Todd said. "Just go back to your guests. We'll take care of everything."

But Dave had already rushed off into the crowd, saying something about getting Salom and his men.

Todd turned to the Irishman. "You gotta go now, man."

The Irishman was still trying to apologize. "I'm shorry, man. I'm jusht really drunk."

"I know," replied Todd, "but that was the owner of the bar and you just fucked with the wrong person. That's it. Now, come on. Just leave now. I'm sorry, that's the way it is. Now go."

The Irishman was beyond comprehension, saying, "I jusht need to get my coat and then I'll go."

"Okay. Where is it?" Todd asked.

He pointed behind the bar.

"Ohh, Man!" Todd replied looking at the stacks of coats behind the bar.

It was a problem, because Dave hadn't bothered to complete the coat check room As a result, the Irishman's coat was somewhere underneath a large stack of coats that had been thrown behind the bar.

"Okay." Todd said, "We'll get your coat and then you go."

That's when Rhett saw the crowd part. It was Dave coming for the Irishman, bringing along Salom and his henchman. He was going to make an example out of this poor bastard. He pointed in the direction of the drunk as Salom and his men moved quickly toward him.

Rhett put his arms around the drunk, motioning Salom and his thugs away. *"On prosta peeyani, nyet problema."* (He's simply drunk. No problem.)

They stopped. Then Salom smiled, disappearing with his crew back into the crowd and returning to their positions at the end of the bar.

The next thing Rhett and Todd heard was a loud crack coming from the bar behind them. Reeling around, they saw Dave standing on top of the bar with a bat in his hand. Drunk and screaming, he pointed at the drunk. The bat came crashing down on the bar again, breaking in half sending splinters flying everywhere.

"You get that son of a bitch out of my bar now! You understand me? Right fuckin' now! He's a dead man!"

Valerie was still standing over in the corner with a look of horror on her face staring up incredulously at Dave.

Dave jumped off the bar and walked in Salom's direction. Todd returned behind the bar and began pouring beers for the crowd of thirsty people. And just like some cowboy movie, someone yelled "Yeeehaw!" The crowd immediately forgot what had just occurred and the partying began anew.

John arrived on the scene. grabbing the drunk and began moving him toward the exit. The Irishman kept asking for his coat behind the bar, but it was impossible to find it in the mountain of discarded clothing.

Rhett followed as John escorted the drunk up the stairway and outside. Two women followed, saying they were friends of the poor bastard. They took him by the arm, saying they would take care of him.

The Irishman was still apologizing as they all disappeared around the corner into the darkness behind *The Passazh*. It was cold and beginning to rain.

———

For a moment, John and Rhett simply stood looking at each other, shaking their heads and taking in the cold night air.

Rhett lit a cigarette and broke into laughter. "Jeezus H. Christ! What's next?"

Then they descended the stairway and back down into Kyiv's wild and woolly Kowboy Dance Hall & Saloon.

As they came through the swinging bar doors at the bottom of the steps, Rhett looked at Valerie. She still had the look of absolute shock on her face.

Rhett looked at her. "We don't need that kind of shit happening,"

"No screaming shit!" was her reply.

That's when Dave walked up bragging, "I'm glad it happened. I couldn't have planned it better myself. In fact, I was going to stage a scene just like that, so everyone could see what would happen if they caused trouble in my bar. He just saved me the trouble. I couldn't be happier if I had arranged it myself. Did anybody know who he was? I'll find out, and when I do, I'll have Salom and his boys pay him a visit. He's history in this town. He has no idea who the hell he just fucked with."

Rhett leaned over to Valerie. "Yep, poor son of a bitch was just unlucky to be at the wrong place at the wrong time."

Then he grabbed another drink and took a position at the top of the stairs. He stood looking down into the seething mob of people. There were no signs of the party letting up. The crowd wasn't going anywhere until it drank everything it could get its hand on. You could hear the country music all the way down *The Passazh*. It was well after one o'clock.

II

The Young Hooligans

Rhett was beginning to have the uneasy feeling that the night was beginning to unravel when he looked up and saw a group of tough-looking young hooligans come swaggering down the stairs. They looked cocksure of themselves, moving past Rhett and down into the bar. He thought they looked like trouble, and that's exactly what they were.

They began by arguing with the doorman about paying to get in. Rhett stood at the top of the stairs behind them, not knowing what was going to happen next. But he knew from the look of things that it wasn't going to be anything good. The only thing he could be thankful for was if there was going to be a fight, he was drunk enough to numb any blows that might be coming his way.

He watched as Salom moved toward the entrance flanked by his men. Rhett could feel the tension beginning to mount as the two groups faced off. Meanwhile, the Westerners were too busy enjoying the music and the dancers to notice much of anything.

Fortunately, Dave and his mouth were nowhere to be seen.

Salom and his Chechens quietly began to move with the young toughs up the stairs and out to the entrance on the street. Rhett followed behind them.

After several minutes of arguing and then calming, the two groups began moving down the street, through a passageway and into a darkened alleyway. The arguing continued. Rhett lit a cigarette, stationing himself at the entrance to the alleyway. He was trying to follow the gist of what was being said, not understanding much and not knowing what was going to happen next.

That's when from the entrance to The Kowboy, he heard someone call his name. It was John. "What's going on? I saw Salom and his men leave and came outside to see what's happening."

Rhett moved up the street to meet him before he came down too far.

"So, what's going on here?" John asked. "Where did Salom go?"

"I'm not really sure, but something's going down."

"What's happening?" John and Rhett looked down into The Kowboy only to see Dave walking up the stairs.

Then they looked at each other as he approached them.

"Nothing!" They said in unison.

"We're just getting some fresh air," Rhett answered, "that's all."

"Just go back inside and take care of your customers," added John.

Neither of them wanted Dave around in case something happened. Anyway, he was too drunk to be of much help.

"Where's Salom? Have any of you guys seen him?"

"Nope. I think he's probably downstairs," Rhett answered quickly. "Why don't you go back down and see if you can find him."

With that, Dave shrugged, turned around and walked back down into the bar. The two men watched him disappear into the saloon.

As soon as he was out of sight, John turned to Rhett. "Okay, tell me. What's going on?"

"To tell you the truth, I'm not really sure. But Salom and his people were arguing with some tough-looking young punks who didn't want to pay Dave's cover charge. They all walked down there into that alley. So, I don't know if something is going down or not."

"Well, you'll find that I'm a pretty good backup if you need it." John replied.

—

Salom and his men had been lured into the alley. It was dark, but the numbers slightly favored the hooligans.

"Why should we pay to go into that place? "This is our street."

"It is not your bar." Salom replied.

"So whose bar is it, those fucking Americans'? They should pay us."

"It is my bar and if I say you pay, you pay."

"And who the fuck are you?" The leader smirked. "This is not your territory."

"*Malchik!* (Boy!) Watch your mouth or I will shut it for you!" Salom's men moved toward the gang.

"*Yob Bani Vrot!*" The young hooligan looked Salom defiantly in the eye. "Fuck you in the Mouth!"

Salom was taken aback by the insolence of these young boys, but before he could react a dozen more came out of the shadows.

Suddenly, a gang member's arm swung a bottle from behind his back. It shattered on the side of Salom's head.

The trap had been sprung. From every direction they descended on Salom and his men with bricks, bottles, lead pipes, knives and axes.

Salom's men had not been carrying weapons. They were caught completely off guard by the attack.

As one man fell to the ground, his jaw broken by an ax handle, Salom caught a glimpse of flashing steel and felt a sharp pain in his side. One of his bodyguards, a champion kick-boxer, reacted quickly, kicking the knife out of the attacker's hand, then with a blinding speed, rendered two more thugs unconscious.

Even though the attackers outnumbered Salom and his men by three to one, they were no match for the more experienced men. Six more were already lying in the alley. The attackers disappeared as quickly as they had attacked, scattering in every direction.

Rhett and John had heard the shouting coming from the alleyway, halfway down the street. Two of the hooligans came running out of the alleyway, crossing the street and running past Rhett. They disappeared into the darkness of the archway at the end of *The Passazh*.

There was no sign of Salom or anyone else coming from the alleyway. They looked at each other, and then Rhett began to walk quickly down the street. Before he reached the alley, Salom came running out of the alley with one of his men. He was holding his side, and blood was pouring down one side of his face.

As Rhett moved toward him, Salom motioned him away and jumped into a Mercedes. With the tires screeching, the car sped past Rhett and John, disappearing behind *The Passazh*.

One of Salom's men stepped out of the darkness, appearing in the archway behind them. He was furiously punching the buttons on a mobile phone, trying to establish contact with someone. He tried several times.

"V chem Problema? (What's the problem?)*"* Rhett asked. *"Vy slushily ot Salom? Vse poryadke?"* (Have you heard from Salom? Is everything all right?)

"Ne znayu (Don't know),*"* came the answer.

Not knowing what was going to happen next, John and Rhett moved back to cover the front door of the bar. With no cover, no protection, they were on their own. The Kowboy had lost its "roof."

As both gangs disappeared into the night, neither knew the status of Salom or his men.

Then two members of the *Militsia* appeared on the street and began walking towards the bar. When they reached Rhett, he greeted them. One asked him for his identification. He obliged.

Rhett explained to the officer there was a private party and asked them if they would like to come inside. Truth be told, he welcomed the presence of the *Militsia*. No matter what one might have said about the police; at least they were the law. It had been a fact that Rhett had repeatedly pointed out to Dave — a fact he had repeatedly ignored.

Rhett escorted the policemen downstairs into the bar where Dave met them at the lower entrance.

"What's the problem? What do these guys want?" he asked.

"They're just curious," Rhett answered. "Show them around."

Unaware of what had just occurred, Dave waived them on in. He was still looking for Salom and his security.

Rhett returned up the stairway and nervously stood vigil.

A few drunks were beginning to slowly flow out of the bar. Some had drunk enough and were staggering home; others just wanted some fresh air and were milling about. The *Militsia* emerged and seemed to be satisfied that everything was in order with the possible exception of an extremely large group of foreigners down inside, who were completely smashed, having a good time and listening to some god-awful American music.

Dave emerged with Valerie. After what she had witnessed inside the bar, she must have decided to join the festivities and try to forget about Dave's little performance. Her mood had definitely improved. It was about three o'clock, she was relaxed and fairly intoxicated. However, she was evidently wise enough to know when it was time to call it an evening.

Dave helped her to the only car and driver he had hired to take people home. Although, he had promised that there would be enough cars and drivers on hand to transport anybody home who might need it, as usual, Dave only thought of the "Big Picture." Details weren't exactly his long suit.

She looked happy as a clam as Dave poured her into the taxi. It immediately sped away, taking Valerie safely home to sleep it off.

Then Dave turned and approached Rhett. "John told me about Salom. What the hell happened up here? Have you heard anything else?

"I don't know for sure, but it appeared that Salom was attacked in the alley."

"Well, find me if you hear anything more."

"Okay. If I hear anything, I will."

Dave turned and walked back inside as Rhett leaned against the doorway and lit another cigarette. "I'm getting way too old for this shit." He muttered.

——

One of the dancers emerged from the bar. She asked Rhett to escort her down to Kreschatik and help her find a cab. It was late, she was tired and ready to leave.

As they walked down into the darkness that enveloped *The Passazh*, Rhett's eyes darted back and forth, checking out every corner, not knowing what might be waiting in the dark. His ears listened for any sound.

When they arrived on the city's main street, the streetlights illuminated the few taxis still parked on the street. Everything was quiet as Rhett put the dancer in one and watched it drive away.

It must have been a strange sight, a cowboy in a duster, chaps and spurs standing alone in the center of Kyiv in the middle of the night.

Rhett turned and began walking back into the blackness of *The Passazh*, where The Kowboy Dance Hall & Saloon was still going strong.

Halfway up the street, he saw a dark figure staggering towards him. It was the Irishman, still drunk, looking lonely, humiliated and desolate. He had staggered back into the bar, looking for his coat. If he thought everything would have been forgotten, he was wrong.

Todd was the first to see him, standing at the end of the bar with a stupid smile on his face. He tried to warn him to leave, but Dave had laid eyes on him too and sent John to assist him in his exit. That's exactly what John did, except this time it was with a lot more emphasis. Grabbing him by the back of the neck, John proceeded to bounce him off the walls, all the way up the stairs and kicking him out into the street.

By the time Rhett met him halfway down *The Passazh* he could hardly walk. However, he wanted no more trouble and kept saying, "I'm sorry, I'm real sorry. I didn't mean anything. I'm not a hooligan. I'm sorry."

Rhett laughed it off. "Go on home and sleep it off. Come back some other time when you're in better shape." He patted him on the back and sent him on his way. The Irishman kept mumbling how sorry he was as he disappeared into the dark streets of Kyiv.

By the time Rhett reached the door of The Kowboy, John sent another incoherent drunk flying past him. This time it was a Ukrainian, who had been wildly dancing in front of Toby. Unfortunately, he had made the mistake of bumping into the microphone stand causing it to hit Toby in the mouth.

Thinking he had hit Toby, John came flying across the bar and cold-cocked him. The kid didn't know what hit him and still didn't know by the time John sent him stumbling out of the saloon.

Even though John laughed a lot, that bad temper could make him dangerous at the flick of a moment.

Fortunately, he two female companions who were ready to come to his aid. Taking charge of the hapless drunk, they escorted him off into the night.

Rhett and John returned down into The Kowboy walking together through the crowd looking for any more signs of potential troublemakers.

The bar still had well over two hundred die-hard drunks, drinking, dancing and having one hell of a good time. No one had any intention of leaving while there was still something to drink and country music to listen to.

It was almost four in the morning and the place truly looked like an old Wild West Saloon after a bunch of saddle weary cowboys had finished wrecking it.

Rhett looked up to see a Scotsman snake dancing with a slinky Ukrainian woman on top of the bar. He recognized him. It was the same Scotsman who had broken Rhett's finger during the beer bottle fiasco weeks earlier. However, it was late and he decided to let them go at it. As far as Rhett could see, no one seemed too offended.

—

Despite the misgivings John and Dave had about Mike, he had been working behind the bar. With a smile on his face, he walked over to Rhett and pointed to a young Ukrainian sitting at a table in the corner. "I want you to meet somebody. That guy over there's been talking about you and said he wants to meet the cowboy."

Mike was grinning from ear to ear, as he followed Rhett. When Rhett held out his hand to shake hands, he noticed the young Ukrainian's grip was like a vice.

Still wearing a shit-eating grin, Mike interjected. "He wants to know if you're a real cowboy,"

"Well, what do you think?" Rhett asked the Ukrainian, who still hadn't let go of his hand and was looking him straight in the eye.

"I think he wants to arm wrestle you." Rhett looked at Mike, realizing he had set been up.

Evidently, the Ukrainian must have seen a lot of westerns, because he wanted to prove his manhood by defeating a rough-and-tough cowboy in an arm-wrestling contest in order to impress the young lady sitting at his side.

Rhett politely declined acquiescing to the young man's strength and prowess. "I'm much too old and I can see that you're a strong and healthy young man. It would be no contest."

Rhett started to walk away, but quickly realized he wasn't going anywhere. The young Ukrainian wanted to show off for his girlfriend and wasn't about to let go.

Being from California, Mike was just as curious as the Ukrainian and was getting immense pleasure out of the situation.

As for Rhett, he was just happy that people didn't settle these foolish tests of manhood with guns anymore.

Nevertheless, he could plainly see there was no way to get out without arm wrestling the young man. As a result, he sat down as a crowd began gathering around the table.

As Mike counted to three, Rhett arm immediately went down, practically pulling the Ukrainian's arm down with him, letting him win quickly . . . perhaps a little too quickly.

Once again, Rhett turned to walk away, but the Ukrainian wouldn't let go of his hand. He had proven nothing to his companions or his lady and insisted that Rhett do it one more time.

"Okay. One last time and no more," Rhett replied. "Is that clear?"

The Ukrainian nodded his agreement.

What was a guy to do in a situation like this? The young man was at least fifteen years younger and obviously in better shape. Rhett hadn't worked out in years and probably couldn't beat the lady who was sitting at his side.

He could see that this young Ukrainian was confidant — perhaps a little too confidant. Then for some reason the phrase "the quick and the dead" came to mind. The only thing Rhett had over the young man was experience and that was exactly how he would play it.

The two brought their arms together as Rhett put enough tension in his arm to let him know what little power he had was there. As they set themselves. Rhett relaxed his arm ever so slightly so the Ukrainian could feel it. Then he looked him straight in his eyes.

Rhett looked at the young woman at his opponent's side. He could tell she was getting hot. She was absolutely moist with anticipation watching her man prove to her what he would obviously prove to her later in the bedroom. The Ukrainian was a little too eager to claim his victory and whatever rewards of ego that came with it.

Rhett turned his head to the side and waited as Mike began to count.

"One. . ."

Rhett closed his eyes and concentrated.

"Two. . ."

He took a deep breath.

"Three!"

Rhett moved quicker than the young Ukrainian expected. In his over confidence, the young man had failed to set himself properly. Before he could recover, Rhett had pushed his arm backwards a full eighty percent of the distance to the top of the table and unexpectedly found himself in the awkward position of having to play defense.

Rhett could feel the Ukrainian's strength weaken as he tried to regain the advantage he had so foolishly given away. Unfortunately, he was at a disadvantage from which he would not recover. Rhett took a deep breath. His arm was aching from years of idleness and neglect. Whatever strength he had left, he used. There was nothing the young Ukrainian could do as the back of his hand slammed down on the table.

Unable to believe what had just happened the young man appeared to be in shock Rhett had won and he had lost. He couldn't. Neither could Rhett. As he quickly pulled his hand away. The Ukrainian tried to grab it again, but Rhett backed away in a hurry. His hands went up, as he proclaimed in Ukrainian, "That's all. It's over."

Rhett pointed to his head. "Sometimes it's here." It was the brains combined with what little brawn he had left that had won as he realized he had pulled the muscles in his arm.

Rhett looked over at Mike, who couldn't believe what had just happened either. He wanted to see Rhett beaten, as much as the Ukrainian. The crowd began to cry foul, saying the young Ukrainian had been caught off guard. And that he had, but it was his own fault.

Everyone, including Mike, demanded another rematch, but Rhett politely refused. They had agreed to only one match and already he had given them two. Besides, there was no power left in his arm and he knew there would be hell to pay the next morning.

The old gringo simply walked away with whatever dignity he had intact.

But the young Ukrainian had lost face. He had disappointed his lady. As she walked away in disgust, it was clear he wasn't going to get any kind of reward this night.

Sitting at the table and fuming over his loss, he glared at Rhett. Whatever sportsmanship he thought he had was lost along with his woman.

As Rhett walked away, turned back and looked at the young man. "Relax. It was only a game."

"Anyway," Rhett thought to himself, "it serves all these little motherfuckers right, picking on an old man." Mike included.

But Mike wasn't about to let it go. He followed Rhett saying, "You really pissed that guy off."

"Why? I won fair and square."

"But you didn't give him a chance to get set."

"So what? I gave him two chances. He just blew it, that's all."

"Yeah, but you embarrassed him in front of his lady. Now he wants to beat the hell out of you."

"Oh, it was all right if he beat me in front of all his friends. That was okay, but now that I've won, he wants to beat the hell out of me?"

"Look at him. He's not happy with you at all. I think he really wants to kick your ass." Mike was having too much fun with the situation. It was evident that Mike still wanted Rhett to prove that he was a real cowboy.

"Are you serious?"

"Yeah. Just look at him."

Mike was right, the young man was obviously pissed off.

"That's all I need tonight. After all that's happened, now I have to worry about some macho Ukrainian dickhead wanting to fight. Well, fuck him and fuck you too. Thanks a lot Mike. Now, get out of my face."

"It's not my fault. You're the one who beat him."

"Bullshit! You're the one who got me into this. If something happens, I'll expect your ass to back me up."

"I'm just yanking your chain," Mike laughed.

"Good, then you go over and tell him that." Rhett turned away and disappeared into the crowd.

———

Rhett grabbed a bottle from behind the bar and poured himself a drink. No sooner had he downed it than he found himself face to face with Dave.

"Now, tell me. What happened with Salom tonight? What did you see?

"Look, Dave, all I know was that everybody was arguing about something and before I knew it, all hell was breaking loose."

"It was a setup! Somebody was trying to set the bar up with an incident that would close us down. That's why the *Militsia* was swarming all around the street. It was a setup pure and simple, but it failed and somebody's going to pay!"

Rhett just looked at him as if he were some kind of rambling lunatic and poured himself another drink.

Dave continued, "I've gotten word that Salom is safe. I'll find out more by tomorrow. Those who did this are dead men! It was the head of the Mafia that controls this street, they arranged all of this. They wanted to show me and the Chechens that this was their street and they were in control.

Rhett rolled his eyes, but Dave wasn't finished.

"Salom and his guys are going to find everyone involved in this, and I guarantee you, those punks who jumped him are going to regret this for the rest of their lives, which won't be long. They have no idea who they messed with tonight. There's going to be war, a fucking war!"

"A fucking war?" There was more than a tone of sarcasm in Rhett's voice.

"That's right, a fucking war. Now, I'm going to leave for a while and meet with Salom. You and John hold down the fort. I'll be back in a half-hour. Now, let's start closing this place up."

Rhett turned back to the bar and poured another drink.

Dave walked over to the stage, instructed Toby to announce that the party was over and to start moving people toward the door. He then left with one of Salom's men.

It was almost five in the morning when John made the decision to close. Dave hadn't returned, the bartenders and waitresses were milling about, ready to leave and Toby had gone.

Rhett ascended the stairs and walked out onto the street. He heard the door lock as it closed behind him. He slowly walked down *The Passazh* toward Kreschatik Boulevard.

Hard-core partyers were flagging down taxis to take them to the all-night casinos and discotheques that were still open in the various regions of the city.

Rhett flagged one down and fell into the back. With half closed his eyes, the scenery was blurred and surrealistic as the cab traveled quickly through the dimly lit streets of Kyiv.

Finally, the taxi dropped him off on Prospekt Pobedy, the expansive boulevard in front of the apartments where Rhett lived. He stood there numbed, looking at the sun slowly rising over the rows of stark grey high-rise buildings.

III

Aftermath of a Hard Night

"BLYAD!" The pain shot through Rhett's arm, jolting him out of an uneasy sleep. He could barely move it and it was a reminder of his dubious moment of glory from the night before. In the only two nights The Kowboy had been open, he had come away with a broken finger and pulled tendons in his right arm. At that rate, he didn't know how long he was going to last. However, he was living up to the cowboy image.

Rhett poured himself a coffee, laced it with cognac, then he quickly dressed and was out the door.

He took the Metro into Kyiv's Center. When he arrived at the bar, the front door was locked. A crudely made, handwritten cardboard sign in English and Russian was nailed to the door. It read:

Due to Plumbing Problems,
The Cowboy will be Temporarily
Closed until Monday at 6PM.

He knocked on the door, but nobody answered. After the events of the previous night, Rhett wondered what it meant. He was also wondering why no one had bothered to call him.

Determined to find out, he walked around back to check the entrance in the alleyway. As he came to the spot where Salom and the others were attacked, he looked around the alleyway for signs of a struggle. Other than a few spots of dried blood, there was nothing to indicate what had occurred the night before.

When he found the back door unlocked, Rhett descended the darkened staircase, not knowing what to expect. As he rounded the corner of the corridor, he noticed a peculiar putrid odor. The place smelled like shit. And that's exactly what it was.

As Rhett walked past by the bathrooms, he could see workmen knee deep in raw sewage frantically trying to get the toilets working.

He saw John and Dave sitting at the bar.

Walking behind the bar, Rhett pointed in the direction of the toilets. "What's going on there?"

"The pump was installed backwards." Dave scowled. "Everything that was deposited into it last night has backed up."

Rhett opened his mouth as if to speak, but Dave stopped him. "Before you say anything, I don't want to hear about that goddamned Irishman! I've already had to set Valerie straight over the phone this morning."

"Okay, fine." Then Rhett finished what he was going to say. "How much money did you pull in last night?"

"About fifteen hundred, which is not bad considering technically, we haven't even opened yet." Dave laughed. "Anyway, I'm glad you're here.

I've called a meeting between Val, Todd, Mike and all the other bartenders. I told them all to be here around noon."

When Dave got up to see how the workmen were coming along, John looked at Rhett. "For God's sake, don't say anything about Dave about that damned Irishman. He's been railing about it for hours, ever since Valerie called him this morning. Jeezus, I don't know what she said, but he went off like a rocket and was screaming at her over the phone."

"Don't worry, I won't," Rhett answered, "but I'll tell you this. Dave's got to understand that this is a place for people to come and have fun. He's acting like he's been watching too many cowboy movies. The only problem is, Dave doesn't seem to realize that in the cowboy movies, when someone gets the shit kicked out of them, or shot, the director calls cut. Then everybody gets up, dust themselves off, get their paychecks, and go home."

"I know. You're right," John agreed. "But right now it's a real sore spot with him. He's blown this whole thing completely out of proportion. I think he knows he was wrong, but at this point he doesn't want to admit it. So, I don't want anybody getting him started."

"Fine, I won't. But I'm telling you, people don't want to come into this bar and get the shit kicked out of them. Especially by the owner and his "roof." If those Chechens had done what Dave wanted them to do last night, everybody in Kyiv would know about it by now. Hell, the drunk wasn't the problem. Dave was the problem. This place should be more like *Frontierland* not *Westworld*. And customers for damn sure don't want to hear about Dave and his Mafia connections."

"I know that and you know that," John answered. "But right now, I don't know if Dave knows it."

"Look, John, do you realize what the American Embassy would do if they find out about this kind of shit happening here? They'll put this place off limits to all American personnel. They've done it before and they can do it again. Then there go all the customers that Dave needs to make this place profitable. He's got to realize this isn't some kind of James Bond movie. This is our asses!"

"Right. But in his mood right now, there's no sense in going into it any further. Anyway, Dave told me this morning he and Kathy were flying out to California tomorrow to go to some balloon festival in Santa Fe."

"What the f —?" Rhett was trying not to be too loud. "Is he fucking crazy?" he whispered. "You know we're supposed to host that Chernobyl party next week. What the hell does he think he's doing, leaving at a time like this?"

"Listen, Rhett. It might be just as well. We don't need him going off again at that party. It'll probably be better to have him six thousand miles away in New Mexico."

"I suppose it makes sense. Maybe it would be better to have Dave as far away as possible. There was no telling what he was liable to do." Rhett paused for a moment. "Listen, John. Dave said he pulled in about fifteen hundred dollars last night. Did he really pull in that much?"

Rhett figured that Dave had given him a low estimate, since he had never been the type to give accurate information to anyone.

"I'm sure he pulled in a lot more than that. I saw him with a bag full of money, but he didn't really tell me how much was in there. So I didn't ask. I figure it's his bar and if he wants to tell me, then he will."

"Well, at least we can pay off some of the bills we owe." Rhett was trying to be optimistic, but he really didn't feel it. "He's been given a lot of credit from a lot of people and I don't want to get too deep with our suppliers …"

John interrupted. "Shhh! Here he comes."

Dave walked in their direction shaking his head, pissed off about the plumbing, ranting again about Valerie and the drunk Irishman. Then he looked up at John and Rhett. "We're going to establish a few rules here."

"That's a laugh!" Rhett whispered under his breath.

"That damned Valerie! She thinks she knows everything, but she doesn't know shit! That son of a bitch was going to sucker-punch me last night, and where was my backup?"

He looked at Rhett. "Where were you guys? If it hadn't been for Salom and his boys, there's no telling what would have happened. But I'm glad it happened. I couldn't have planned it better than if I had planned it myself! I have my example now and I know exactly who that was. He's some accountant who just started working for a British accounting firm. I know who he is and where he works. I'm going to have Salom and his boys pay him a little visit. I'm going to make sure that little shit is run out of Kyiv. "

It was the same song, second verse. The unlucky Irishman was going to be Dave's scapegoat and he had decided to make a "by God Dave Seigal" example out of him.

John and Rhett simply looked at each other and kept quiet.

185

Then Rhett asked, "What about Salom?"

"Don't worry, everything is under control. Salom was already here before you arrived."

"Yeah, he had a bandage on his forehead." John added, "I could tell that he was definitely in pain. One of his men had two black eyes and his head had been completely wrapped in a bandage."

"The whole thing was planned," Dave chimed in. "Salom and his men were purposely baited to leave the bar. That gang was supposed to lead them down into the alleyway."

The only thing that had saved Salom's life was his long trench coat. It had deflected the knife of his attacker as he came at him slashing away at his midsection.

Dave continued, "Salom told me the Chechens have already captured the gang that jumped him. They're holding them at their compound located somewhere outside of Kyiv. They'll get all the information out of them about who was behind this attack."

—

No one really knew for sure if the attack had been staged to make a point to the Chechens. Was it a message, or was it an assassination attempt upon Salom?

In any event, Dave's partner Sergei seemed concerned. "Sergei appeared really nervous when he came by my apartment this morning. Apparently, he was aware of what had happened last night and wanted to get a gun that he had given me."

"Are you serious?" Rhett wouldn't have believed the conversation if it hadn't been for what he had witnessed the night before.

"Absolutely," Dave replied. "He wanted to have a gun in case there's any more trouble. He's not taking any chances and is getting his family out of Kyiv. But, I'm telling you this. If Salom finds out that Sergei had any part of what went down last night, he's a dead man and I won't be able to help him."

It was Dave's final comment that made Rhett realize that Dave was beginning to abandon any loyalty he once had toward Sergei.

Dave looked at his watch. "I need to go and unlocked the door."

Rhett and John looked at each other as Dave turned and walked upstairs

Toby was the first to arrive, followed by Lena and her husband. About twenty minutes later Todd and Valerie came walking in followed by Mike and the other bartenders.

As Dave greeted the staff, Rhett walked over to caution Valerie to avoid mentioning anything about Dave and the Irishman.

"Don't worry," she said, "Dave already bit my head off over the phone this morning. Believe me, I have no intention of saying anything."

As everyone gathered around the bar as Dave began his meeting. "Okay, after last night we need to establish some rules, develop some policies and systems on how this bar is going to be run. But first, I want to talk about the incident that happened last night…."

Dave was off and railing again. It made no difference that no one was going to bring the incident up. Dave wanted to talk about it and this time, he wanted to do it in front of everyone. He was out on a limb and was determined to make his point.

Then to everyone's amazement he made an announcement, "Kathy and I are flying to California tomorrow. Now, I know it's only a few days before the Chernobyl event, but that's why I hired John and Casey. They'll be in charge in my absence."

The meeting adjourned and Dave went to his apartment to pack for California. He was beginning to fall apart and knew he had promised the Moon to the Chernobyl committee. As a result, his only solution was to run, to get out of town and leaving everyone else holding the bag. What he didn't say was that he was taking the bag along with all the bars money with him.

Valerie too, had elected to leave the country in favor of a weekend holiday in Budapest. Rhett couldn't really blame her in light of what she had seen happen the night before.

IV

Chechen Judgment

Alosha opened his eyes. He couldn't tell how long he had been unconscious, but he remembered the brutal beating he had suffered at the hands of the Chechens.

He looked to his right and saw his friend Givey. He almost didn't recognize him. His left eye was swollen and barely hanging in its socket as blood streamed down the side of his face. Alosha noticed how grotesque Givey's arm looked. It was clearly dislocated and hanging limply to his side. His hands were bound behind him, as were the hands of a half dozen of his comrades.

Alosha surveyed his surroundings. He was sitting in the center of a large room that had once been a kitchen of a large industrial Soviet complex.

The adjacent room, which evidently was an old factory cafeteria, had blades of grass coming out of the cracks in the floor. It was dirty and tiles were falling off the walls or coming up off the floor. Old symbols of the Soviet era were still hanging on the walls, but there was no longer any furniture. His captors were standing in the middle of that room talking with one another. Alosha noticed that three of them had reddish hair.

The kitchen itself was a little cleaner. Abandoned cookers, food processors, huge cooking apparatuses that easily weighed over a thousand pounds each filled the room. Almost all of the equipment was industrial size. It was a truly desolate-looking and the last place Alosha wanted to be.

A man, smartly dressed, enter the room. Alosha recognized him from the night before. He was the leader of the group they had attacked. A bandage on his forehead that partially covered his reddish hair. He was followed by three other men. One's head was wrapped in a bandage and he had two black eyes. The man looked straight at him, then walked to the adjacent room to confer with the others.

Alosha heard a low moan next to him. It was Givey beginning to regain consciousness. The Chechens had been particularly brutal with him, for it was Givey who had slashed the man in the camel hair trench coat.

When the Chechens heard Givey they walked into the kitchen. One addressed Alosha. "Who hired you?"

"I don't know. It was a man who came up to us at the kiosk under Maidan Nezalezhnosti. I don't know his name. He gave us a hundred dollars apiece and told us to take care of the men who guarded the American bar on *The Passazh.*"

"One hundred dollars apiece?" The man asked.

"Yes, sir."

"That was cheap for my brother's life."

"I am sorry, sir. We did not know who you were. If we had, we …."

"What was the man's name?"

"I don't know. Honestly. If I did, I would tell you."

"And this is the man who tried to kill my brother?" The man looked at Givey. He was barely conscious and didn't know what was happening.

"Please forgive us," Alosha pleaded. We are simply a bunch of hooligans. We are young. We didn't know any better."

Alosha saw the man hand something to his brother, who then walked behind Givey. Alosha was trembling.

He leaned over Givey's shoulder and whispered loudly into his ear. *"Yob tvoya mat!* (Fuck your mother.)" Grabbing Givey by the hair and pulling his head back, the man brought a straight razor to his neck, slowly and methodically slitting his throat. Givey gave out a gurgling sound as his eyes opened. Blood gushed out of his mouth and spurted outward from his neck. Then Givey's eyes rolled back in his head and he was silent.

Alosha and his friends gasped in unison. Then they began crying and screaming, begging for mercy.

"Now, I will ask you again. Who hired you?"

Tears were streaming down Alosha's face. "I swear to you. I do not know. Don't you think I would tell you? Please, forgive us. We were foolish."

"Malchat!" Alosha's interrogator was losing his patience. "Shut up! Do you recognize this man?"

One of the Chechen's stepped forward. It was the one whose head was in a bandage. He had a tire iron in his right hand."

"Which one did this to you?" The interrogator asked.

The Chechen stared directly at one of the captives. The interrogator nodded.

The Chechen stepped forward and with all his force brought the tire iron down on the boy's head. There was a dull thud as blood splattered on the Chechen. He brought his arm back to strike again and kept striking him until there was nothing left but a bloody pulp of tissue and bone where once there was a head.

Alosha and the others could not stop shaking.

The interrogator shouted at all of them. "Do you think for one minute I will not gut you like the pigs you are?"

He grabbed a large knife from the table and plunged it into the gut of another, disemboweling him as he ripped him open from his sternum to his chest. The hapless victim looked down screaming as he watched his insides spill forth into his lap and onto the floor with a sickening splat. Then he fell silent.

"Now answer me, you pigs!" The interrogator screamed. "Who was it that paid you to kill my brother!?"

The room fell silent, except for the whimpering and sobbing of the Chechen's captives. Although, Alosha and his young comrades could be ruthless, this was a level of brutality that he had not encountered .... A butchery that was beyond his worst nightmares.

The captors adjourned to the adjoining room leaving the survivors in the midst of the bloody carnage to contemplate their fates. Alosha could hear one of his friends repeat *"Oh, Bozh. Oh, Bozh. Oh, Bozh."* over and over pleading for God to save him. But God could not hear.

For what seemed like an eternity the remnants of the street gang sat waiting for what would happen next.

Finally, the Chechens returned. Once more, it was the interrogator who spoke. "I will ask you once more and I want you to think. Who paid you to do this?"

Alosha was sobbing. "I don't know. Please, I am telling you the truth. If I did know, don't you think I would tell you? Give me a name, anything. Maybe we can help you find the people you want."

"Then I am truly sorry for you," the interrogator responded as he nodded his head in the direction of one of the industrial food processing machines. One of the Chechens pulled a switch and the gigantic machine started up with a loud whirring sound as the blades began to rotate.

Two others grabbed another one of the prisoners and began to drag him screaming in the direction of the machine.

Alosha closed his eyes as the screaming reached a crescendo. And then he heard the sound of flesh and bone being ground. He tried to cover his ears, tried to shield his senses from the horrors that were going on only a few feet away, but he could not. His hands were tied. For the first time in his life, Alosha began to pray.

V

Habla Español?

Rhett thought it was about time to show John around and invited him to join him up om the streets of Kyiv. John really liked the place, but why shouldn't he? He and Casey were little more than tourists. All they had seen of Kyiv was from the back seat of a car. Dave would take them to the most popular and expensive restaurants every night. And when it came to impressing someone, Dave was really good at putting on the dog.

Rhett led John down into the Metro, where they boarded the subway going to Volodomirsky Market. Although Kyiv had begun to build supermarkets, they were nothing like the monolithic supermarkets of America. They were smaller versions, built for foreigners, the nouveau riche and the city's elite.

John hadn't seen the real markets of Kyiv … the places where Rhett had learned to shop from his days in the Peace Corps. A place where he would find fresh vegetables and fruit, home-canned salads or pickles, cheeses, butter, fresh honey or sauces and on occasion caviar. It was here where one could also purchase fresh beef, pork or poultry, but you had to have a stout heart to shop in these sections of the market. Everything that was edible from slaughter was for sale. Cows and pig's heads, as well as tongues, brains, intestines and even jars of blood sat on the tables next to slabs of raw meat.

John was amazed as they made their way through the seething mass of people lined up in what seemed like endless rows of humanity selling just about anything and everything. Some were holding up only a pair of socks, desperately hoping for a buyer. Many had been engineers, teachers, doctors or even scientists, but the state of the economy was in shambles, leaving them with no other way to earn a decent living.

These markets would usually grow up and around one of Kyiv's food markets and to John it seemed like one gigantic flea market. Some items such as fur coats or alligator shoes were a bargain. Others, like plastic sets of salt and peppershakers or bottles of ketchup, were not. If one looked very carefully, they could usually find what they needed. It was the crazy economics of Ukraine spawned by the Shadow Economy and ruled by the Mafia.

It was at Volodomirsky, away from the bar, where the two cowboys that they could discuss things freely, speaking in a language that few, if any, could understand.

"You know?" John said, "I just can't figure out why Dave is leaving like this."

Rhett was surprised after what John had said earlier. "But I thought you said it was probably just as well."

"Yes, I know I did. But that's not the point. The point is, it's his bar. He's got the most to lose. Why in God's name he would just go flying off to some damn balloon festival is beyond me."

"I think he's lost it," Rhett answered.

"What do you mean?"

"I mean, I think he's had a nervous breakdown or something very close to it."

"You really think so?"

"I can't say for sure. I'm no psychiatrist, but ya gotta admit, he's been acting pretty goddamned strange."

As Rhett stuffed everything into a backpack slung over his shoulder, he began to point out what would be needed to make the restaurant a working business.

"This is where that we can buy the supplies we'll need for the cantina. That is, of course, if we ever get around to building the kitchen. In the meantime, I'm going to need to find a place where I can cook the chili for the Chernobyl event next week."

That's already covered." John replied. "Dave told me that Salom found a place with a kitchen. Plus, he's even agreed to donate the meat."

"Really?" Rhet was surprised. "Well, that's odd. Salom doesn't really strike me as a charitable soul."

"So, answer me this, Rhett What about Dave's connections with the Chechens? Can he trust them?"

"Of course not, Listen, that's Dave's bar only as long as they want it to be Dave's bar. Anytime they decide they want the bar, it's theirs. And there's not a damned thing that he can do about it."

"Then why is he partners with them?"

"I have no idea. Look, Dave has made his deal with the devil and his only hope is to convince them that he's indispensable, that the bar can't operate without him and his Americans. After all, we're the cowboys and we're supposed to know how to make the saloon operate in a Western manner. It's the only ace that Dave can play, but even that might not be enough in the end."

John frowned. "Why wouldn't they be safe as partners then, if we're the ones that can make the bar work?"

"Greed. Pure and simple. It makes no difference how much money we can make for them by working together. Once these guys smell money, they'll want it all. It's the way they think."

"But it doesn't make sense."

"It doesn't have to," Rhett explained. "That's the way things are around here. Dave thinks these people are his friends, but he's playing a dangerous game. The main point to remember is we're the foreigners here and it's their country. No matter how Western they may seem to us, they think different from us. Don't ever forget that."

"Well, I don't give a fuck who they are." The anger in John's voice began to rise. "I'm not afraid of them. There may be more of them than me and I may go down fighting, but I guaran-goddamn-tee you, I'll take some of those son's a bitches down with me."

"Spoken like a true cowboy, John. But look around you. Do you see any cowboys around here? We're in the land of the Ukrainians and there's a hell of a lot more of them than us. It's basically the same as being in Indian Territory a hundred years ago. It don't make a rat's ass how bad you are. The reality is we're outnumbered. Remember your history, John. Custer thought he was a badass too and see where that got him. Besides, we don't speak Ukrainian any better than Custer spoke Sioux."

"Well, what about Sergei? What's the deal with him?"

"What do you mean? Sergei's Dave's partner in the bar. Dave talked Sergei into giving him that place to build The Kowboy."

"Well, this morning, I overheard Dave talking to Kathy. Salom wants Sergei out of the bar. He was obviously concerned about it too, because he was telling her that Sergei had been his friend ever since he came to Kyiv and he didn't want to screw him around like that."

"See what I mean?" Rhett exclaimed gesturing angrily with his hands. "Shit! It's already started. That place was Sergei's to begin with and it's in one of the best locations in Kyiv. That's why Salom wants it. But I'll tell you this — if Dave does what Salom wants, if he caves in to Salom's demands, that will be the beginning of the end, because it won't stop there. We'll all be screwed. Salom won't want to share anything with anybody. He will want it all. Just remember I told you this."

John looked confused. "Then why in the hell did Dave bring Salom in on this deal?"

"Beats the hell out of me. He was asking for trouble when he did that. Mark my words. If Dave puts the screws to Sergei, we're all fucked."

"How come you have such a different view of things from Dave?"

"Look, John, I've been living with the Ukrainians, living the Ukrainian lifestyle as much as any American can, while Dave's been living high on the hog. He may have a lot of experience in the Western business community, but there are some things about living in this country that Dave doesn't understand. It's one of the things that can make me valuable to Dave, if he would only listen."

As they continued talking on their way back to The Kowboy, they began to hear strange music coming from the entrance to *The Passazh.*.

"What is that? What's that music?" John couldn't figure out why they were walking on the streets of Eastern Europe and it sounded like they were in the middle of a Sergio Leone movie.

"It's a group of Peruvian students. They travel around the streets of Kyiv playing Andean music."

"Peruvians, eh? Why don't we talk to them about playing in the Cantina restaurant?"

"I'll ask." Rhett approached the musicians. "Any of you guys speak English?"

"No habla Inglés. Habla Español?" One responded. He could not.

Rhett thought for a moment. *"Vwe govareeti Po-ruski?(You speak Russian)"*

"Da. Kaneshnya" was the answer. (Yes, of course)

"Oh! Slova Bog! Otlichnya! (Oh! Thank God! Excellent!) And just like that, they were back in business.

Then as John looked on completely dumbfounded, they began to communicate in the only way they could …. in Russian as the surrounding Ukrainians broke into laughter.

The scene looked as if it were some sort of bizarre combination of a dubbed Borscht/Spaghetti Western complete with an Ennio Morricone soundtrack.

VI

Peter the Great

The following Monday morning, Dave dropped by the bar one last time before he and Kathy flew off to Amsterdam. He was planning to stay a couple days before continuing on to California.

As usual, Salom was driving him to the airport.

The decision had been made to keep the bar closed until Friday, when it would re-open for the Chernobyl after-party. To some extent, it was a relief. There was a lot to do and the bar was still a long way from finished. Dave had promised the moon and was leaving it to those he left behind to deliver.

Once again, Rhett reminded Dave that it would either be an international success or an international humiliation, based on how well the party was presented and how well it was received. However, Dave was looking for any excuse to cancel the event and his attitude was quickly changing toward Nadia and her organization.

"If she doesn't like my bar, then she can take her precious guests somewhere else."

It was at that moment when Nadia unexpectedly arrived, walking into The Kowboy flanked by two committee members.

She looked around trying to maintain a certain degree of dignity, but it was obvious by the look on her face that she was deeply concerned. "Are you sure this place is going to be ready by Friday night?" She asked, looking around at the unfinished walls and the aftermath of the pre-opening party.

That was all Dave needed. He quickly walked over to Nadia and curtly replied, "If you don't think my bar is good enough for you, you are certainly welcome to take your party elsewhere."

Clearly taken aback by Dave's statement she replied, "I want you to know, we had offers from the River Palace, the Studio and many places. They all would have gladly offered their establishments to host the reception Friday night. However, I was assured this place would be ready! It's too late to change the party now, we've already sent out the invitations. We have no choice!"

John quickly moved in between them. Laughing in his amiable manner, he sought to reassure Nadia, "Don't worry, it looks unfinished now, but by next Friday you won't even recognize this place."

Dave walked away, content to leave John to handle the situation.

Rhett quickly turned to her startled companions. "After all, it is Ukraine. Surely you understood the problems encountered in trying to undertake a project of this magnitude." They smiled and nodded in agreement. "Besides, it's really unbelievable what we've accomplished so far. Of course, it's going to take a lot of work, but I have faith that we're going to have everything ready by Friday."

John went behind the bar and pulled out a stack of white straw cowboy hats asking Nadia to try a few on.

"Oh! These are wonderful! We don't have many in New York. Turning to her companions she asked, "What do you think? Do I look like a real cowgirl?" Like a child on Christmas morning, she tried one after another as they gleefully encouraged her.

When Nadia found one that suited her. John ceremoniously presented it to her.

"Save it for me. I'm on my way to meet with the President's committee, I don't think it would be proper to stroll into the meeting wearing a cowboy hat."

As John continued flattering her, Dave sat at the end of the bar, arms folded and watching like a surly little brat.

John placed the hat under the bar. "Don't worry darlin', we'll keep it in a special place right here and you can pick it up Friday night."

With that, she excused herself, sounding a little more relieved. However, as she was leaving, she turned around one last time to take one more look. Raising her eyes towards heaven, she looked as if she were saying a tiny little prayer that everything indeed would be ready come Frida night. Once again, The Kowboy Dance Hall & Saloon had dodged another bullet.

Moments later, two representatives from R.J. Reynolds arrived. They wanted to look over the bar and were interested to see just exactly what they had been given in the Cantina.

Dave's mood quickly improved as he escorted them through the saloon and into the Cantina area while re-elaborating on his vision of creating marketing history by having competing sponsors battling it out for the hearts and minds of the Ukrainian consumer.

"Years from now, this battle of the sponsors will go down in the annals of marketing history." He boasted, while being oblivious to the fact that his idea was far from an earth-shattering revelation.

Nevertheless, the Camel representatives seemed happy to be there. Having the opportunity to rub their competition's nose in a place that was a natural for Marlboro sponsorship was fine by them.

Rhett simply rolled his eyes.

By the time Salom arrived to take Dave to the airport, Rhett was happy to see him go. More and more found himself agreeing with John's logic. Nobody wanted him going off and insulting some VIP. In his present state of mind, the farther away Dave would be from the Chernobyl after-party the better.

———

By the time Rhett arrived at the office the phones were already ringing. It was Marlboro's representative calling for Zurich. She wanted to know how things were progressing. Had the billboard been installed yet? Rhett told her it had and that it looked great. She also wanted to make sure that no Camel merchandise would be infringing into Marlboro territory, reiterating that she would be accompanied by important representatives from Phillip Morris. Rhett reassured her that everything was under control and gave her his word that he would make sure it didn't happen. He was beginning to sound like Dave.

Before she hung up, she had one last question. "This really isn't my business and you don't have to say anything if you don't want to."

Rhett held his breath, closed his eyes, and waited for her next sentence, hoping it wasn't going to be what he feared it would …. it was.

"Is there any truth to the rumors about 'third parties' moving in and taking control of the bar?" In less than two days the rumors had begun and traveled all the way to Switzerland.

Rhett put his hand over the phone, took a deep breath, then answered, "What do you mean?"

"It's just that I heard a few things and I wanted to know before Phillip Morris gets involved any further. We've already invested a lot in terms of the billboard and merchandise and we would like to know if the bar is having any difficulties."

"Well Vera, I was down at the bar this morning. Dave was there. His manager John was there too. Considering this is Ukraine, everything seems fairly normal to me."

Surprisingly, Rhett's flimsy statement seemed to satisfy her, because she replied, "I just wanted to keep apprised on the situation. Just in case something was going on. I hope you understand my concern."

Rhett was glad she was in Zurich, out of range of the stench that was beginning to permeate The Kowboy and spilling out onto the streets of Kyiv …. figuratively and literally.

No sooner had he hung the phone up than it rang again. This time it was a call from the editor of Dossier Dosuga. She too, was wondering about the rumors and why Dave had left so suddenly.

Soon the phone calls were like bullets, coming faster, with more frequency, and like long range missiles, some were coming from a greater distance than he had expected.

Before the day had ended, Rhett had received more than a half-dozen such phone calls. Considering the rumors contained a lot of truth, Rhett fielded them the best he could. However, it didn't help matters that Dave had been so proud of his Mafia connections.

From that day on, rumors would become a constant companion to The Kowboy Dance Hall & Saloon.

—

Later that afternoon, when Rhett returned to the bar, he found John and Casey working with the construction crew while Lena and Andrei tried to keep up with interpreting their instructions.

Rhett greeted them all. "What would you call someone who has just deserted his troops in the face of the enemy?"

"I don't know," Casey answered. "A coward?"

"Close — Dave Seigal."

In reality, the joke wasn't that funny. Nonetheless, as it quickly made its way around the bar everyone seemed to like it.

Rhett pulled John aside to tell him about all the inquiries as John signaled Casey to come over and listen. "Listen, John. You're the manager and I figure the more you know the better you can do your job. So, I'm going to tell you everything that I know or hear about. Now, I know this is Dave's bar, but I've been here every day for the last six months. Dave comes and goes every few weeks. I see things that he doesn't. I just figure it's better if you know as much as possible. Okay?"

John agreed. "I appreciate it and I'll tell you everything that I know. I'm going to count on your experience. Dave told me about you in California. He said he had a guy here that he was lucky to have helping him and probably couldn't afford."

"I would call that an understatement." Rhett scoffed.

"So, what exactly is your deal with Dave?"

"I told him that I would back his play for a percentage of the action if he's successful. In the meantime, he's supposed to take care of my apartment and give me some money to live on. Look, John, I'm really good at what I do and I'm not afraid of the work. I told Dave he needs an organization behind him if he's going to pull this thing off. I figure that's where you and I come in."

"Well, Dave told me that he couldn't do all of this without you. He told me if it's successful, you won't have anything to worry about."

"I certainly hope so." Rhett sighed. "Anyway, I'm in way too deep to turn back now."

Then John turned the subject to Sergei. "Do you remember telling me what you thought about the situation between Sergei and Salom yesterday?'

"Yeah?'

"Well, it started this morning."

"What started?" Rhett asked.

"This morning before Dave left, I went with him, Salom and Sergei to the lawyer' office. They went down to sign some papers. Salom now owns thirty percent of the bar."

"What about Sergei?"

"He wound up with less than fifteen percent."

"Are you sure?"

"I was there. I saw the whole thing happen."

"What did Sergei think about it? After all this was his place to begin with."

"What would you think if you just got fucked?"

"Dammit!" Rhett exclaimed. "It's happening faster than I thought."

"Well, it's Dave's bar." John shrugged. "He can do whatever he wants. I'm just doing this for him as a favor. But if those Chechens think I'm going to work for them, they've got another thing coming. Right now, I'm going to concentrate on making this party happen. I gave that lady from Chernobyl my word and I aim to keep it."

"Well," Rhett replied, "at least we've got the money from the other night to pay for the party's food and drinks."

"What money are you talking about?"

"What do you mean, 'what money'? I thought you said that Dave had a bag full of cash from the other night."

"He did, but he didn't give any to me. Far as I know, he took it with him."

"He what!?"

"He took it with him."

"He took it with him?" Rhett slapped his forehead. "So, how are we supposed to pay for the food and drinks!?"

"Well, I brought some money with me. My guess is that the rest of the stuff, we'll just have to get donated or something."

"John, this isn't really the kind of society that goes around donating to worthy causes."

"I don't have time to think about that right now. We'll take it as it comes. I just hope we don't have any more of this Mafia shit to deal with."

"If we don't, we're going to be real lucky," Rhett answered.

"Well, anyway, Salom told me he would contribute the meat for the chili and he has a kitchen."

"Okay, if you say so."

It was getting late and John decided everything that could have been done for the day had been done. "I'm bushed. I think we're going to call it a day and go to the apartment. Rhett, I'll meet you at the office tomorrow morning. We have to send a fax to our son. If Dave needs some money to get that bull, maybe John Jr. can float him a loan."

Rhett thought John and Casey might be cutting Dave a lot more slack than he deserved. However, John was having an adventure and still thought he might be able to find a way to make some money out of this mess.

As soon as Rhett walked into his apartment, he opened a bottle of vodka. There was a pain in his chest and his left side was numb. The years of drinking like a Russian was beginning to take its toll. Nevertheless, he figured if he drank enough, he wouldn't worry about the bar, the party, or the pain.

As he sat in the dark, Rhett couldn't help but think there always seems to be a point when the line between doing something good or becoming someone bad stands right before you. Everyone tends to walk a little over it from time to time. But, when Dave neglected to tell anyone he was taking the bag will all the money, he had just waltzed a little too far over that line to make it back.

———

The following morning when John and Casey came walking into the office, Casey appeared angry. John was laughing, but it was more out of disbelief and disgust than anything.

"What? What is it?" Rhett couldn't figure out what had happened.

"Go ahead, Casey." John smiled. "Go ahead and tell him." John said smiling. "You're not going to believe this. Go on, Casey, tell him about your conversation with Peter the Great this morning."

"What? What does Peter the Great have to do with anything?"

Casey began to relate the conversation she'd just had with Dave. "Oh, you're going to love this one. I just got off the phone with Dave a little while ago. He wanted to call and tell us what a wonderful time he and Kathy were having in Amsterdam. They wanted us all to know that they had spent a romantic evening floating down the canals last night and they were doing just fine!" Her eyes rolled back in her head.

"I told him 'That's just great Dave. We're all so glad that you and Kathy are having such a wonderful time. You've only left everyone here to do all of the work with no money. Thanks a lot!' And you know what? That son of a bitch didn't even catch on I was being sarcastic. Do you know what he had the audacity to say?"

Rhett was grinning. "Nope, but I'm sure you're going to tell me."

"He told me" Her voice mimicking Dave. "Oh, you'll pull it off. I have confidence that you can do it. That's why I brought you and John to Kyiv. Don't worry, I have faith in you.' So, I tell him, 'Thanks a lot, Dave. You have no idea how good that makes me feel!' Then he tells me, Don't mention it." Casey was flabbergasted.

"And that's not all! He then starts telling me about an old run-down building that he and Kathy had found in Amsterdam. He tells me it had been owned by Peter the Great and that Kathy thinks that they should buy it and refurbish it because .... and get this!" She paused for a moment then took a deep breath.. " Kathy thinks they should buy it, 'because, after all,

Dave, you really are the reincarnation of Peter the Great.' So Dave tells me they've decided to buy it. At that point, I was so beside myself I couldn't even think of a reply!" Casey put her finger down her throat as if to make herself throw up.

At first, Rhett looked over at John. After that little tidbit, he knew Dave had completely lost touch with reality and his batshit wife wasn't too far behind.

Rhett then turned back to Casey. "Did he really say that?"

"Yes!" Casey snapped back.

"You know," Rhett answered, "I think she's got this Peter the Great thing mixed up with someone who's acting like a total Dave! I guess, once a Dave, always a Dave."

Casey wasn't finished either. "Then he tells me, 'Well, our plane is leaving for California in about an hour. So, I'll call you from California. Bye.' But before he could hang up, I said, 'Oh, by the way, Dave, who deserts his troops?' He didn't know. So I told him! He didn't seem to think that was so funny, but before he could say anything else, I said, 'You all just have a wonderful time!' Then I hung up on him."

"Rhett, tell Casey what you told me the other day about Dave," John added.

"What was that?"

"About his mental state. Casey, Rhett told me he thought Dave was having a nervous breakdown."

"Well, you have to admit it is a possibility." Rhett surmised, "Especially after that Peter the Great story."

"Nervous breakdown my ass! He's fucking nuts!" Casey replied.

VII

The Chicago Tribune

That night, Sergei walked into The Kowboy accompanied by a gang of young men. John, Rhett and Toby looked up surprised to see him. Even though John told Rhett that Sergei had left the city, it was apparent he had returned to Kyiv.

Apparently, after Dave signed the agreement giving Salom a huge chunk of the business, Sergei decided to call a summit meeting. He wanted to set down some ground rules before Salom moved into a more secure position of power.

Suddenly, Salom appeared at the doorway. Not wanting a repeat performance of what had happened over the weekend, he too had brought along his gang for protection.

He still had a bandage on his forehead and some of his men looked like they had been through a cement mixer. However, this time he had more than enough backup, should they be needed.

The two gangs moved in fast, walking past the Americans. A few greeted John and Rhett, shaking hands as they quickly passed by on their way the back of the bar

John immediately turned to Casey. "You need to go to the apartment right now. Don't worry. Everything will be all right. I'll call you when it's all over."

Having no way of knowing what might happen, the three cowboys gathered behind the bar. Toby grabbed a bat while Andrei stood close by, should he be needed to interpret.

The Americans were faced with a dilemma. If things should get out of hand and violence did erupt, what would they do? Whose side would they take? Both sides were Dave's partners. If they supported one side, how would the other side react? There was really nothing the three cowboys could do. They just sat and watched . . . and waited.

It had been a long time since there were any serious outbreaks between rival Mafias in Kyiv. Each had their own territory and respected the others' dominions …. until now.

Dave's alliance with the Chechens changed the complexion of things in Kyiv. He had offered Salom a piece of something in a territory that was clearly not his to give. It threatened the unofficial peace which had existed in Kyiv over the years. It was a partnership that could very possibly start a Mafia war.

They could hear the gangs arguing as the gangs attempted to iron out their differences. Things would begin to heat up and then they would die down. Finally, they heard a loud clasping of hands. It appeared that Sergei and Salom reached some sort of agreement. As quickly as they had descended on The Kowboy, they were gone.

Only Sergei remained.

He walked over to Andrei and instructed him to tell John that everything was okay. If Salom had a deal with Dave, he would respect it. Whatever Dave had agreed to with Salom would be between Dave and Salom, but Salom and his men would not be in charge of the bar.

From that day forward, a different group of young hoodlums would come walking through the bar. Most of the time, there was no way of telling who they were, whether they were

—

The next day, Rhett received a call from a man who identified himself as a reporter from the *Chicago Tribune*. He wanted to do a story on Dave, The Kowboy and what it was like doing business in Kyiv, especially the issue of having to deal with the Mafia.

"I'm sorry." Rhett apologized, "Dave's out of town and won't be back until next week." Nevertheless, the reporter was persistent. He still wanted to see the bar, so Rhett agreed to meet him that evening.

Slamming down the phone receiver, Rhett shouted, "Fucking Great!"

—

When Rhett arrived at The Kowboy, he found Toby and John sitting at the bar.

"I got a call from a reporter from the *Chicago Tribune* this afternoon. He was trying to find Dave and wants to do a story on the bar and how it's functioning in terms of Mafia interference."

"What did you tell him?" John asked.

Rhett sat down. "I acted naive about the Mafia thing. I thought the best idea was to invite him to come down to the bar. He should be arriving any minute. I figure if we're careful about what we say, we can dance around the Mafia story and at the same time get some good press for the . . ."

"What do you mean 'we,' white man?" John interrupted. "You're the public relations guy."

Before Rhett could respond, a tall, thin man walked into the bar. He was smiled as he extended his hand the Rhett. "Hello, I'm Tom Hundley of the *Chicago Tribune*."

He looked around, seemingly amused by what he saw. "This is certainly not what I expected to find sitting right in the middle of Kyiv."

Rhett offered him a beer as Tom sat down at the bar. "You don't mind if I ask you some questions, do you?"

"Certainly not. What do you want to know?"

"Listen, you guys," John interrupted. "Toby and I are going to get something to eat. Soooo . . . you look like you can handle this Rhett. We'll just go on now and I'll talk to you later."

Rhett watched as they walked out of the bar, leaving him alone with the reporter. Thanks a lot . . . assholes!" he muttered.

Rhett turned back to the reporter. "Well then, how can I help you?"

Tom started off slowly, talking about how it was so interesting to see a western-style saloon in Kyiv. "How is it walking around Kyiv dressed as a cowboy? What do the locals think?"

"Well, for one thing," Rhett replied "they can definitely tell we're from out of town."

Tom smiled.

Rhett gave him a few stories about being a cowboy in Eastern Europe. It was like a chess game. Tom would ask his questions, trying to get Rhett to open up more and more, while Rhett waited for the one question he knew would be coming — and then it came.

"So tell me, what about the Mafia?"

"What about them?" It was like an episode of *Ukrainian Jeopardy*.

"Well, don't you have problems with the Mafia wanting protection money?"

"Look, this is Eastern Europe there's Mafia everywhere," Rhett answered. "You just take it as it comes. Personally, I haven't had any trouble with them and I've been here for a while. In fact, they usually act like they like me. They're always asking me to sit down to have a drink with them. I guess they've all seen the Chuck Norris and Clint Eastwood movies. They're very popular over here. It seems to me that they kind of like the image. You know, the cowboy thing."

"They are?"

"Sure. I suppose it's because the American cowboy symbolizes freedom and these people are just experiencing that."

"Really?"

"What's the one thing about America that appeals to everyone?" Rhett leaned back against the bar. "Cowboys, of course."

Tom smiled, jotting something down on his note pad. "So, you don't have to worry about the Mafia?'

"I didn't say that. Sure, there's a problem with the Mafia, but you go to any major city in the world, including America, they all have some kind of criminal activity going on. Where are you from?"

"Chicago."

"See? Now don't tell me there isn't any Mafia in the city that gave birth to Al Capone."

"I see what you mean."

"It's like this," Rhett continued, "the Soviet Union was a police state. Everything was controlled, so there didn't seem like there was much crime. The streets were safer then. However, when it broke up, the government wasn't in as much control as it had previously been. So of course, crime increased, but it still has a long way to go to catch up with any major American city. I'm just saying that we just take it one day at a time and see what happens."

Tom figured that was as about as far as he was going to get on the Mafia issue and Rhett, for damn sure, wasn't about to bring it up again.

"But this cowboy thing, why here?" Tom asked.

"Where else can a grown man go and play at being a cowboy? One thing for damned sure, I sure as hell can't go back to Oklahoma. They're all trying to be sophisticates there."

"Really?"

"Let me show you an example. See this cowboy hat?" Rhett took his hat off to show him a burn on the brim. "You know where that happened?"

"Where?"

"Back in Oklahoma."

"They did that to your hat in Oklahoma?"

"Yeah, at an art show. You would have thought I was a leper, the way they reacted to this hat. Some tragically hip son of a bitch thought it would be funny if he placed his lit cigarette on the brim. I didn't discover it until later."

"That's an interesting story."

"Yeah, well, that's when I realized, we're all bigots in our own way. It's all a matter of what kind of tribes we're in and whom we choose to hate. Look at what's happening in America today. Once we didn't have the Soviet Union as our enemy, we had to find someone else to hate. So, we started hating each other. Americans just can't get along without hating someone. It's the American way. Hell, it was an American that bombed that building in Oklahoma City."

"Interesting. I never thought about it quite like that before."

"Well, I'll tell you one thing. I've been walking around this city for years and I've felt safer here than if I had been walking around dressed like this in Detroit. You've got to admit, I'd be one dead son of a bitch if I was foolish enough to do something like that there."

"You're probably right." Tom looked at his watch. "Well, it's getting late. I have to go back the hotel."

"Dave should be back next week. I'm sure he's going to be awfully disappointed he didn't get a chance to talk with you."

"Me too, but I've got a deadline and I have to return to Warsaw. I may try to call him next week."

"If you're interested, you're more than welcome to come by in the morning to hear the Kowboy Bar Band rehearse. You could talk to Toby and John, get their angles on what it's like to be here."

"Thanks, I might take you up on that." Then Tom left.

The interview was over.

Rhett was relieved, he knew Dave was playing one card short of a full deck and too damned proud of his Mafia connections not to talk about it. He was relieved that Dave was gone, because the stories were spreading through the Western community like wildfire. Hundley could have talked to any number of people who had heard them. He probably had already.

Nevertheless, Dave's unexpected trip back to America hadn't made things look any better either. Rhett hoped Hundley never got a chance to talk to Dave.

However, everyone knew Dave was a big bullshitter, though nobody really knew for sure. It was the one thing that the bar had going in its favor. Fortunately, a lot of people who wanted to see The Kowboy succeed were giving Dave a lot more leeway than he deserved.

Rhett was alone, stressed out and mentally exhausted. He thought about John and Toby. "What do I care if they shoot their mouths off about the Mafia. What do I really know anyway?"

Rhett lit a cigarette, reached under the bar, pulled out a bottle and poured himself a drink.

—

Rhett couldn't sleep that night. No matter how much he drank, he was too wired. His mind was racing when he woke up at three o'clock in the morning. He didn't know if it was from the drinking and smoking, or the stress. He figured the pain in his chest was simply some sort of karmic test he was being put through. Several times a day, he became dizzy. He shook it off by purchasing some Soviet tranquilizers at the *Apteka,* the local pharmacy. He ate them like candy to keep himself relaxed. They seemed to help, but it was like putting a band-aid on an open wound.

At 4:00, he knew he wasn't going to fall asleep again. He got up, put some coffee on the stove, and started to get ready for what surely would be another long, grueling day.

That's when the phone rang.

When he picked it up he heard a familiar voice. The woman he had left behind in Oklahoma. The love of his life. She was calling to tell him she could no longer wait. That she had met a good man and was getting married. It was a short call and he really could not blame her. After all, he was the one who left to embark on his Quixotic quest.

Even though the sun had yet to rise, he sat down and poured himself a drink.

He felt like he was living in some kind of hell on earth. Perhaps he was, but it only made him more determined, but he had to get through the day somehow. He had things to do, even if it killed him. He walked out the door and locked it behind him.

As he rode the Metro, he thought about where life had led him, about the decisions he made and thinking there was still so much left to be done. It was one day before the Chernobyl commemoration.

His train of thought was suddenly interrupted when the Ukrainian Cowboy stepped into the car at the Universität Metro station. At that moment, it was a welcome diversion. Rhett smiled and tipped his hat — he responded with a tip of his own. Their fleeting acquaintance had yet to developed into conversation. All the same, he was curious and thought, "Just who in the hell is this guy?"

—

When Rhett arrived at the bar Casey had an update. "Dave called this morning to tell me that he had spent a relaxing day on the beach and they were getting ready to leave for a leisurely afternoon boat trip to Catalina. Afterwards, they will be traveling to the balloon festival in Santa Fe. He just wanted to let everyone know that he is doing just fine. The trip is giving him a chance to relax and get his head together."

"Like, I really give a shit!" Rhett muttered.

However, Casey did have a bit of good news. "I was able to persuade Yuri Nikotenko's wife to donate the bread for the party. It seems that due to her husband's political position, she owns just about every bakery in the city."

"Well, at least that's something." Rhett commented. "Now we have bread and chili. Anything else?"

"We found a caterer who has volunteered his services, but he needs for someone to come up with the cash to pay for the supplies."

"That's okay." John chimed in. "I've got enough cash to cover the rest. So, let's just concentrate on getting this place ready for the party tomorrow."

Nevertheless, Rhett knew it would take a Herculean effort if they were to have any chance of success.

He looked over at Toby who seemed content to sit on his butt while watching everyone else do the work. Even though he was only a nineteen-year-old kid, with all the attention he had been receiving since his arrival, it seemed as if everything was going to his head.

By this time, he had been screwing so many girls that he was beginning to think he was God's gift to the women of Ukraine and strutted around as if he really were Garth Brooks. However, a few of them had been talking among each other and were beginning to realize Toby was sleeping with more than just one.

Eventually, the band arrived and Toby had something to do. They were still rehearsing when Tom Hundley arrived to finish his story. While he waited to interview Toby, John poured him a beer. As he sat down to enjoy the music, one could tell that Tom liked what he was hearing, because he was grinning ear to ear. He couldn't believe he was actually listening to country music in the middle of the former Soviet Union. He was also beginning to become more fascinated with the cowboy angle of his story. The one about how a group of cowboys were faring in the Wild East.

As soon as Toby finished rehearsing, Rhett introduced Tom to the young country musician and at the ripe old age of nineteen, Toby seemed to be the acting expert on country music, Ukraine and just about anything that the reporter cared to ask him.

Toby did get one thing right though and that was the band was truly amazing. These conservatory-trained musicians could play country music . . . and how they could play. For that matter, they could play just about anything they chose to put their minds to. And unlike Toby, they could read the music. Tom was rightfully impressed.

When the dance troupe arrived, Toby was in the middle of an interview and far too important to be bothered. The only possible thing that Rhett could think of to resolve the situation was to tell the dancers, "You really don't need to have Toby in order to practice. Practice with the band. They're the real stars."

After all, it was Dave's Circus with John was the ringmaster and Rhett as the clown — and Toby? Well, he was the monkey, always content as long as he had someone with whom he could grind his organ.

Tom was getting his story. Maybe it wasn't the one he had come for, but it was turning out to be a good story all the same. However, Tom was still trying to dig up some dirt on the Mafia connection and more than a little suspicious by Dave's absence.

After Tom finished with Toby, he went to John to get another angle and to ask more questions about the Mafia. John was only too happy to oblige. And boy howdy, how he liked to talk. He had taken a quick read of the place and had it all figured out. With all the expertise that one would gain after being in a foreign country for less than two weeks John filled Tom in on the scoop of what was happening at The Kowboy Dance Hall and Saloon.

Eventually, Hundley left and seemed fairly pleased with what information he had been able to pick up.

As he was leaving, the advertising manager for IntelNews' *Economic Review* arrived proudly holding up its latest issue. Since it was an English-language weekly business magazine which was distributed to all of the embassies and top international companies operating in Ukraine it was great publicity for the bar. Its readers were just the type of clientele The Kowboy needed.

Over all, the article was positive, but most of it was based more on Dave's dreams rather than reality . . . and Dave had a lot of dreams. Among other things, the article promised 200 new jobs to local Ukrainians and several production outlets for the Ukrainian manufacturing industry.

It also said The Kowboy would feature live Country and Western music, a mechanical bull, video games, old cowboy movies and an American-style Tex-Mex restaurant

Not only that, the article elaborated on Dave's plans to establish a chain of similar bars in Warsaw, Budapest and Prague. He was also quoted as saying he was planning to establish manufacturing outlets in Ukraine to produce Western products and souvenirs that would be hawked throughout Eastern Europe.

It even quoted the city's Deputy Mayor Yuri Nikotenko saying that "Seigal's venture was representative of Ukraine's warming relationship with the West, which had led to the establishment of a bit of Americana in a corner of Kyiv."

The article went on to say that the club would provide a venue for local talent playing a wide variety of music for a variety of patrons. It even mentioned Dave's vision of the competition that would pit sponsors against one another between the saloon and the cantina.

In addition, Dave was quoted as saying the start-up investment costs were approximately $250,000. However, Rhett remembered that Dave had told him he would be able to build the bar for less than half of the amount. Still, no one could really verify what kind of money had actually gone into the bar, because Dave operated, more or less, on a cash basis. Only he knew how much money was being spent. And besides, Dave liked to talk big, because he always had everything under control.

Nevertheless, Rhett knew that Dave had received over a hundred grand from different people, either as investors or as loans. What few of them knew was Dave had begun to use percentages in The Kowboy for additional collateral whenever he needed money.

Dave also declined to name Sergei as his local partner in the article, claiming himself alone as the chief investor.

But it was the final line in the article that was truly ironic. "At this time, The Kowboy Bar faces no competition in Kyiv, though Seigal predicts the competition will increase within two years," The irony being that the competition had started from within. The battle for the control of The Kowboy Dance Hall & Saloon had already begun.

VIII

A Cowboy Meltdown

Bearing a striking resemblance to his famous father, it was midday when Cody Palance walked into the bar. He had been scheduled to sing at the Chernobyl after-party and was arriving to rehearse with the Kowboy Bar Band. His appearance at least gave Rhett some assurance that his famous father was somewhere in Kiev. However, there had been no word about whether or not De Niro had been sighted anywhere in the city.

Rhett walked up and introduced himself asking, "So, what are you going to perform tomorrow night?"

"Stairway to Heaven," Cody answered in a raspy whiskey voice.

"Really?" Rhett wondered if he was up to the task considering Cody looked as if he had been through a rough night and perhaps not in the best of shape to attempt such a feat. It wasn't as if he had chosen anything too difficult. Hell no! Of all the songs one would choose to perform, Cody had chosen a heavy metal anthem with one of the most difficult vocals in rock history.

Nevertheless, Cody appeared determined to perform in front of an audience that would include Jon Anderson of Yes, a vocalist who had been dubbed "The Voice" by the some of the best rock musicians in the music world.

\Rhett had to give the guy credit. He had either a lot of guts or just plain audacity. It was one or the other and Rhett was damned if he knew which one it was.

While Cody was rehearsing, Toby paced back to and fro complaining how he hated rock and roll. He had taken an instant dislike to him and even though he was out of earshot, Toby was making his opinions known. "Shit! He's nothing more than a drugged out daddy's boy, riding on his daddy's coattails."

While Toby's observations may or may not have been true, Rhett kept thinking, "Who the hell is this kid and why would anybody consider him to be a connoisseur of rock music?" More and more, Rhett was regarding him as a little wanna-be cowboy star, who had no room to be criticizing anyone.

Once Cody was finished rehearsing everyone got back to the business of getting the bar ready. It was beginning to look as if by the following evening The Kowboy might look like a real saloon.

—

Everything was moving forward, until John mentioned that a representative from Coca-Cola had been to the bar and were complaining that someone had moved their signs to locations in the bar than where they had originally placed them. As it turned out, Dave had created yet another problem by moving their signs to hide the fact that his bar was anywhere but complete

Although Rhett assured John he had already worked out the situation with the top executives of Coca-Cola and that everything was fine John was still concerned. "All I know is the representative was really pissed off when he saw that those signs had been moved and was threatening to pull out all of Coke's promotional materials."

"Don't worry, John," Rhett reassured him, "everything's fine. After all, This is supposed to look like an authentic saloon, not an advertisement for Coca-Cola."

Toby had been listening to the conversation and felt it was time to put in his two cents worth. "Yeah!" He barked. "Why'd we take them signs down? I liked 'em there!"

Up until that moment, Rhett had remained somewhat in control, but it was more than he could take. "Listen you impudent pup, what the fuck do you know? I'll be damned if I'm going to start taking any shit off of you! That's it!" he snapped.

Then he turned to John and Casey. "Who does this kid think he is anyway and why in the hell is he telling me how to do my job?"

For a moment, everyone was quiet. John and Casey were taken aback by Rhett's sudden outburst. Up until that moment, Rhett always remained somewhat in control and they were surprised to see him losing his composure. It was a meltdown they weren't expecting.

Rhett walked halfway up the stairway where he stopped, trying to regain his composure. He blew it and he knew it. After a few moments and some deep breaths, he got himself together and walked back down into the saloon.

"Okay . . . okay. Sorry, I apologize." Rhett thought if he talked calmly, everything could be put back into perspective. "Let's start this all over. Okay, Toby. To begin with, I'm a lot older than you and . . ."

Toby interrupted him. "Don't give me that shit. I don't care if you're a thousand years old. I don't give a fuck who you are!"

"Okay, fine." Rhett threw up his hands and laughed. He took one look at John and walked out of the bar.

——

Rhett was outside cooling off, as he watching as a man took down the cowboy sign Dave had so haphazardly nailed to the front of the building, when he felt a hand on his shoulder. It was John along with Casey and Andrei the interpreter. "Relax. Don't worry about it. Toby's just a little prick. That's all."

Together they strolled down the street and were met by the owner of the Bon-Bon, Kyiv's answer to Baskin-Robbins. After some small talk and a few jokes, translated with Andrei's assistance, the owner invited them to sample his ice cream.

The group sat down as the owner ordered dishes of ice cream with large bowls of whipped cream on the side. It was one of those little oddities of Eastern Europe. Just when you think they're catching on to how things are done in the West, they do little things to remind you that you're not in Kansas anymore.

The owner told them to enjoy themselves, then politely excused himself. That's when John did something that struck Rhett as a little odd. He reverently bowed his head and began to say grace over their ice cream. It would have been okay with Rhett, but he had never seen John say any prayers over anything, much less over a dish of ice cream. It was the damnedest, weirdest thing to be happening at that moment. Fine, lunch or dinner, he could understand that, but a moment of worship over the ice cream was just a bit surreal. His eyes went from John to Cory and then to Andrei. They were all sitting with their heads bowed in reverence. Rhett would never be able to figure that scene out. It was just another one of those strange moments in a cacophony of strange moments that had become the daily occurrences that made up his life.

As soon as John finished saying grace, Andrei dove into his ice cream and started packing it away like there was no tomorrow, attacking it as if he had been never tasted ice cream before.

Rhett simply sat there watching his dish of ice cream melt down before him.

—

Toby and the band had just finished rehearsing when the mayor's deputy, Nikotenko, walked in accompanied by two men. One was his assistant administrator, the other was the Chief of Police and Yuri's personal bodyguard. Yuri had had been talking to them about a cowboy bar in the center of Kyiv and wanted to introduce them to his newfound cowboy friends, especially John . . . he really liked John.

As Andrei interpreted, Yuri explained he had just been chosen to be a candidate in the upcoming mayoral elections. As a result. he and his colleagues wanted to do a little celebrating and listen to this thing called country music.

"Pour them all a few beers," John ordered. But being vodka drinkers, they were looking for something stronger. Rhett reached under the bar and brought out a bottle of vodka with some shot glasses. He poured everybody a round, but John, being a non-drinker, politely refused. Consequently, Rhett pulled out a beer mug Rhett and poured him a 7-Up. Then they all toasted to Yuri's future success.

Yuri turned to Rhett and asked if he would have the band play a few songs for his friends.

At that moment, it was the last thing Rhett wanted to do. He had no desire to go over and ask Toby to do anything, except maybe to kiss his ass. But this was the deputy mayor of Kyiv, and obviously an important man. Rhett did what he was asked and walked over to Toby. "Those men over there want to hear you guys play something."

Toby curtly replied, "We're done rehearsing!"

"That's fine with me Toby, but I'm not the one who's asking. It's those swinging Dave over there." Rhett pointed to Yuri and his friends. "They're from the mayor's office. If you don't want to play, you go tell them."

Toby got the band together.

Rhett walked back to the bar as the men toasted several more rounds while listening to Yuri's command performance by Toby and the Kowboy Bar Band. Every time Toby finished a song, he began to leave the stage. But every time he tried to, Yuri would send Rhett back over to have him play another and another — and another. Each time it happened, Toby became more and more irate. However, he at least had the good sense not to piss off an influential city official by refusing to play.

The drinking continued throughout the morning until midday when Yuri invited John and Casey to join him for lunch across the street. Although they initially declined, Yuri was persistent and wouldn't take no for an answer. Hard-pressed to refuse, they followed the Yuri out of the bar with Andrei in tow as a translator.

As soon as they walked out of the bar Toby left the stage and grabbed a bat from behind the bar. Pacing back and forth, bringing the bat up and down in his hand, acting as if he wanted to use it on someone, Rhett had a pretty good idea who that somebody probably was. However, he really didn't care and continued working, choosing to ignore him.

Moments later the Rockland Ladies arrived for rehearsal and after a half-hour of ear-splitting music, Rhett was relieved to finally get a little peace and quiet.

He was surprised to see Yuri came walking back in without John and Casey. As he sat down, he took notice one of the Rockland Ladies standing at the end of the bar. Calling her over, he signaled Rhett to pour him a beer and a vodka for himself and the young woman. As she politely tried to fend off his huge groping hands, it became apparent when Yuri drank, he had an eye for the ladies.

Diplomatically, it was awkward for Rhett as he tried to engage Yuri in conversation which only served to frustrate him. Nevertheless, it gave the young woman enough time to excuse herself and leave. It was a small relief for Rhett, because the last thing he wanted to do was make Yuri angry by interfering with his amorous intentions. The situation didn't get any better when A few minutes later, two tall, thin, beautiful models came in and sat down at the bar.

As Yuri eyed them over, he instructed Rhett to pour more drinks turning his attentions in their direction. Fortunately, the models were much more experienced and defter at handling his overtures while at the same time being somewhat polite.

That's when Todd came bouncing into the bar. "Hey, Rhett. Thought I'd drop by and see how things are going?"

"Don't ask."

Todd took one look at Yuri stroking the long blonde hair of one of the models. "Oh, yeah. Yuri gets a bit flirtatious when he's had a few. It can make for an awkward situation, but seems you have everything under control. Well, gotta bounce. See you later." And with that, Todd was out the door as quickly as he had arrived.

"*Gde John i Casey* (Where's John and Casey)*?*"

As soon as Rhett mentioned them, Yuri remembered he had left them waiting at the restaurant across the street and motioned for Rhett to follow him.

Rhett smiled at the models and glanced in the direction of Toby who was still pacing and was cursing under his breathe at God knows who.

—

Rhett followed Yuri across the street to a little French restaurant called Lyon, where he found the John and Casey sitting at a table staring down at some kind of fish that had been served with the head and tail intact. They were pushing the catch of the day around on their plates, occasionally taking a bite in hopes of making it look like they were eating more than they actually were. Rhett hated fish. Evidently, from the looks on their faces, so did John and Casey. It bore little resemblance to what Rhett remebered French Cuisine looked like.

On the other hand, Andrei was scarfing down his meal like a starving refugee. Rhett was amazed watching him eat while he continued to interpret, bits of fish spewing out of his mouth between bites. He was like a bottomless pit and there seemed to be no limit to the amount of food he could pack away at one sitting.

Yuri called for another menu, but Rhett shook his head. *"Dyakuyu, aley ya ne golodni* (Thank you, but I'm not hungry)."

When Yuri's deputy heard him answer in Ukrainian, he asked Rhett why he was not speaking in Russian. It was an example of the ongoing identity crisis that had plagued Ukraine since the fall of the Soviet Union. Half of the country considered themselves Ukrainian, while the other half identified more with Russia.

The Chief of Police told his deputy to relax. He was amused with the idea of a cowboy trying to speak in Ukrainian . . . and he should have been. The way Rhett spoke Ukrainian was pretty damned funny.

After a few toasts of cognac, the Chief of Police excused himself saying he and his deputy needed to get back to work. As they were leaving, Rhett turned to John and smiled. "I should get back too, so I'll leave you all to finish this wonderful lunch."

John quickly stood up. "Maybe I should join you."

Leaving Casey behind with the bottomless pit that was Andrei, and Yuri who was getting drunker by the moment, the two hastily made their exit.

Once on the street Rhett saw Toby emerge from The Kowboy still carrying the bat. As he watched him walking down *The Passazh*, Rhett leaned over to John. "Take a look at that. Where does he think he's going with that damned bat? Doesn't he realize he's a foreigner? Besides, he doesn't speak the language and this for damn sure ain't in Texas"

However, John's attention had been diverted by two women as passed by. "Jeezus Christ, I can hardly stand this. The women here are absolutely stunning."

"That they are John . . . that they are." Rhett laughed.

Watching some of the most beautiful ladies in the world was one thing that was wonderful about springtime in Ukraine. And their beauty was all the more devastating when they wore short skirts and skimpy, revealing tops. As they walked up and down the streets of Kiev it was obvious that Ukrainian women had no problem with their femininity.

While John was busy looking at women, Rhett noticed that Yuri had exited the restaurant and was trying to prop himself up against a post from the restaurant's awning. He was ogling women too, until his attention was diverted by a young member of the *Berkuyt* who was inspecting his automobile.

The *Berkuyt* were an elite military police force that patrolled the streets of Kiev. They were always recognizable in their trademark red berets, military fatigues and the Kalashnikov automatic weapons slung over their shoulders.

Yuri walked over to the officer and began to berate the young man belligerently telling the officer who he was and, in no uncertain terms, to get the hell away from his car.

Moments later, Casey emerged dragging Andrei — who was still eating — behind her.

As Yuri argued with the *Berkuyt*, Rhett turned to John. "C'mon, we've got a lot of work to do and I think it's about to get real ugly out here."

IX

The Berkuyt

When the *Berkuyt* began removing tags from the automobiles, Yuri warned a young officer not to touch his car. After a heated discussion, Yuri hauled off and cold-cocked the young man, laying him out flat on the street. As the other officers came running to assist their fallen comrade, Yuri quickly ran into the Kowboy Dance Hall & Saloon in hopes of finding refuge.

Rhett was talking to John when he looked up to Yuri come flying down the staircase, his momentum sending his stocky frame crashing into a wall. He frantically shouted John's name saying something in Russian. John simply stood there, confused as Yuri grabbed him by the shoulders. He couldn't understand a word of what Yuri was saying, but Rhett could. He was pleading with John, "Help me! Help me!"

Everyone was dumbfounded, because they had not witnessed the incident that had just happened on the *The Passazh*. Then they saw the *Berkuyt*. Four of them, charging down the stairs and into the bar. They went for Yuri, who kept shouting for somebody to help him. Andrei stood there, speechless, frozen, dazed and confused. No one knew what the hell was happening or what to do.

The four officers tried to grab Yuri, but having been an athlete during the Soviet era, he built like an ox and wasn't about to go along peaceably. A struggle ensued as Yuri tried to escape their grip. The officers threw Yuri to the ground as they fought to handcuff him.

"Andrei! What the hell's happening?" John shouted, but Andrei was in a complete state of shock and didn't know what to say. Everyone was yelling as Yuri kicked up at the Berkuyt from the floor. One fell to the ground as the others tried to sit on Yuri. Another managed to get a chokehold on him and together, they managed to cuff his hands behind his back.

Rhett shouted to the *Berkuyt* in Russian. "Relax! Do you know who this man is?"

John turned to Andrei and yelled, "Snap out of it! Say something dammit!"

Finally, Andrei began shouting, "Guys, guys. Do you know who you are beating? Listen to me! This is the mayor's deputy. Please, relax! Do *not* do this, please!"

It was complete chaos. For the life of him, Rhett couldn't remember Yuri's last name. Then he suddenly remembered the "Economic Review." Vaulting over the bar, Rhett picked up the journal, frantically flipping through the pages. He finally found the article that had mentioned Yuri's name and began shouting "Nikotenko! Yuri Nikotenko! Do you know who that is?!"

Unfortunately for Yuri, the officers weren't up on the names of the members of the mayor's cabinet. And they damned sure weren't listening to Rhett. He turned to Andrei. "For Chrissake, Andrei! Tell them who in the hell they're beating the shit out of!"

Yuri was like a raging bull as the *Berkuyt* brought him back to his feet. He slammed them with his body and head, kicking them and cursing, calling them every name in the book. *"BLYAD! SUKIN SIN! YOB TVOYU MAT!"* He screamed. "Whores! Son of a bitches! Fuck your mothers!"

John was trying to calm everyone down as Andrei explained to the *Berkuyt* who they were dealing with. Even though they were still angry, they were beginning to listen. It was beginning to dawn on them just who Yuri was.

Rhett came from behind the bar and put his arms around Yuri, placing himself between Yuri and the *Berkuyt*. "Yuri, Yuri!" he kept saying. "It's me, Rhett. Look at me. Do you know who I am? I'm the cowvboyskie. Do you remember me? Calm down, please!"

Tears of rage and humiliation were pouring from Yuri's eyes. He focused his eyes for a moment, seemingly cognizant of whom Rhett was.

As Rhett turned around, he found himself looking down at the muzzle of a Kalashnikov pointed squarely at the middle of his chest. "Jeezus Fucking Christ!" he muttered to himself. He held his arms apart and gestured to the *Berkuyt* as if to say "What the hell you want to do now?"

He looked at the officer. *"Spokoyna, Vse Periatke.* (Relax, everything's all right)."

The other *Berkuyt* were explaining to Andrei, who in turn was translating to John and Casey. They were telling them that Yuri was drunk and had just assaulted an officer.

John turned to Rhett. "See if you can take Yuri to the back while I talk to these guys."

The officer lowered the Kalashnikov from Rhett's chest as he let out a sigh of relief.

Rhett turned back to Yuri, speaking to him in Russian. "Yuri, come with me. Relax. Everything will be all right. Do you understand?' Yuri nodded. His face was purple. His eyes had a sad glazed drunken look to them. Tears were still rolling down his cheeks.

Rhett took Yuri by the arm and led him away to the back of the Cantina while John and Andrei tried to sort things out with the *Berkuyt*.

Yuri was still furious. They had cuffed him too tightly, cutting of the circulation to his hands. Rhett tried to humor him and looked at him, saying, "*Chort Vismete Yuri! Vwe kak Beek!* (Goddamn, Yuri! You're like a bull!)" He looked at Rhett, finally realizing that the cowboy had been speaking to him in Russian. He hadn't expected such gems of obscenity to come from Rhett's mouth and for a moment began to laugh.

Yuri asked Rhett about the cuffs and when one of the *Berkuyt* took Yuri by the arm, Rhett pointed to the cuffs telling him they were hurting Yuri. Still, Rhett stayed close to Yuri, fearing that he would become angry again. He didn't want the *Berkuyt* to get any more pissed off than they already were.

Rhett mentioned the cuffs to Andrei. But the *Berkuyt* were afraid to take them off. Nevertheless, they were beginning to comprehend they had arrested a man who could make their lives very difficult. However, they didn't want another fight with him either.

Meanwhile, Yuri was slowly gaining his composure and was thinking of how he would exact his revenge on his attackers. He began cursing them once again. It was fairly obvious that Yuri was telling them exactly who they had screwed with and that they would regret this day for what they had done to him.

Yuri's hands were turning blue. The cuffs had cut off the circulation, causing him even more pain as the *Berkuyt* led him up the stairs, pulling him by his arms. Rhett complained again, showing the *Berkuyt* Yuri's hands. At the same time, Yuri was talking to the officer. It was the same officer who Yuri had decked earlier. His face was still red from the blow. The young officer asked Yuri if he would behave himself should he remove the handcuffs.

Yuri only laughed. He had a sardonic, sadistic look on his face. Rhett knew it and the young officer knew it too. He was going to pay dearly. Although he couldn't catch it all, it was all seemingly very Russian to Rhett.

Suddenly, the Chief of Police appeared at the top of the stairs. Flashing his identification, he demanded an explanation.

After a few words, the officer removed the handcuffs. Yuri rubbed the dark red and blue marks on his wrists where the cuffs had been. However, he didn't take his eyes off the young officer, who was now trying to explain his actions to the Chief of Police. The Chief said something to him in Russian as he took Yuri by the arm and escorted him up the stairs as John followed them out the door.

Rhett walked back down into the saloon and grabbed a bottle from behind the bar and poured a drink. Everything that had just occurred seemed like a scene from a movie; it was all so unreal. Rhett had to think a moment. "Did what just happened really happen? Was I really stared down point-blank into a Kalashnikov? Yep, it sure as shit that was a Kalashnikov. He poured another and quickly downed it.

Looking up he saw John walking down the stairs shaking his head in disbelief and laughing. Before Rhett could say anything, he said, "God, you're not going to believe what happened just now."

"What? What?" Rhett poured another drink

John was still laughing. "I was following Yuri, the Police Chief and those *Berkuyt* officers upstairs. As soon as Yuri got to the top, he turned around and decked that cop again. I mean, he laid him out flat on the sidewalk for the second time."

"Good God!" Rhett closed his eyes. "I'm in a horror movie that has no ending."

——

An hour later, the Chief of Police returned with Yuri's wife. It was plain to see that she was mortified. She wanted to hear what had really happened from John and Casey.

John tried to make her feel at ease. "We were just concerned about Yuri. Is he okay? That's all we're worried about."

"No. No. My husband's all right. He's at home. I put him to bed. I just wanted to apologize to you for putting you to all this trouble."

"Don't worry about us. We're just fine."

"You should know, my husband was a very famous sportsman in the Soviet Union. It's just sometimes when he drinks he gets a little crazy. I want to thank you all for what you did for him this afternoon. I promise you; we will not forget it."

Then her voice began to sound angry. "But those men who did this today, they will regret what they have done. My husband is a very powerful man and they will be punished. They will regret the day they were ever born. They want to live by the gun; they will die by the gun. I promise you this."

The Chief nodded in agreement.

"If there's anything we can do for you . . ." She continued.

"You have already done so much for us by donating the bread for tomorrow night." Casey interjected, "You and your husband will be coming tomorrow night, won't you?"

In light of the incident with the *Berkuyt*, Yuri's wife had wisely opted to take Yuri outside of Kyiv for a few days. "No, no. Tomorrow we will leave Kyiv for our summer home. After this afternoon, my husband needs to have some rest."

"We understand," Casey replied. "We'll miss having you here."

"When we return, if there's anything else you need. If you have any troubles, please, you call Yuri or me. You now have friends in Kyiv."

She thanked John and Casey again and left with the Chief of Police. The Americans had done well, protecting Yuri as best they could. They now had a trump card to play should they ever need it.

All Rhett could think of was how much shit was going to hit the fan when those four guys in the *Berkuyt* got called in on the carpet for beating the hell out of the Mayor's Deputy.

At that moment, Todd came bounding down the steps. "Hey, guys, what's happening? Did I miss anything exciting?"

John and Rhett simply turned and looked at each other.

X

Cowboyskie Chili

She was a stout, bleach-blonde New Yorker in her fifties and royally pissed off. "My name is Victoria and I'm from the Chernobyl Committee. I've come to see if this place is going to be ready for tonight."

In contrast, her husband, who was thin compared to her, stayed a few paces behind her saying little or nothing.

Victoria inspected every corner of the bar thoroughly from the bar area to the Cantina, to the toilets, complaining, giving out orders every step of the way while trying to sound as threatening as possible. "From what I've seen so far, it's absolutely disgraceful."

"I know that it looks a little rough right now, but I can assure you that everything will be ready by this evening." Casey was trying to be as charming as she could be. "You won't recognize the place by the time the guests start arriving."

"It had better be!" Victoria snapped as she tripped over a step on the way out. "There's a lawsuit waiting to happen and I want you to know that my husband's a lawyer too!"

"Oh, shut up!" It was the only thing her husband had to say as they left the bar.

———

Lena was busy arguing with the workmen, trying to convince them of the importance of having everything ready by the evening. On the verge of tears, she was uncharacteristically furious and screaming at them.

However, the workmen were beginning to doubt Dave's ability to pay for them and one of was arguing back.

At one point, as the worker began raising his voice, that's when John stepped in. "I can't understand a word of what he's saying, but I don't like the tone he's using with you. But you tell him I'm ready to kick the hell out of someone and if he doesn't change his tune, I'll be happy to start with him." Then John instructed her to translate.

The man quickly apologized.

"He says he needs money to buy the materials to finish the tables." Lena translated.

"In other words, he's telling you he hasn't even started on the tables yet?" John asked.

"Yes, I believe that is so."

"Tell him he's fired and he can go. Tell him to get the hell outa here"

John started to look around. Spotting several pieces of particleboard stacked up against a wall. He had Lena instruct a couple of the workmen to bring him one, along with an octagonal light fixture, a pencil and a power saw.

Within moments, he had traced around the light fixture and told the workmen to saw out the pattern.

"There you go. There's our tabletops. Ask them if they get the point." They did and immediately began tracing and cutting out tabletops mounting them on the wrought iron table stands. Casey threw some red checkered tablecloths over them and voila! Suddenly, the bar had tables.

While Dave was off enjoying himself at some balloon festival in Santa Fe, the more determined John and Casey became. They would be damned before they let the party turn into a disaster.

—

Rhett didn't have time to think about Dave either. He had to cook up a batch of chili for two hundred guests. He left the bar and was on his way to meet the caterer at the metro station at Kontraktova Ploscha, with the most important ingredient in his knapsack, a five-pound container of Williams Chili Seasoning.

As soon as he exited the metro, he saw the caterer waiting to drive him to someplace where he could make his cowboyskie chili. Rhett jumped in the front seat and they drove off, traveling over a bridge and crossing the Dnieper River to the left bank to a dirty industrial section on the edge of the city.

The car pulled up in front of a typical Soviet building, big, industrial and dismal. Rhett followed the caterer inside through a series of winding grey corridors until they reached the kitchen.

"Jeezus! This place looks like something right out of an apocalypse movie!" Blades of grass were growing out of the cracks in the floor that had once been a kitchen of a large Soviet complex. Old symbols from the Soviet era were still hanging on the walls and tiles were falling off. It was truly a dirty and desolate looking place.

Abandoned cookers, food processors, huge cooking apparatuses that easily weighed over a thousand pounds each filled the room. Almost all of the equipment was industrial size. It was truly a dirty and desolate looking place.

In one corner of the kitchen, helpers were peeling buckets of onions, garlic, tomatoes and peppers.

Rhett immediately instructed the caterer to send his driver for more provisions and tried to act as normal as he could under the circumstances.

He walked into the adjacent abandoned cafeteria and popped a few more Soviet tranquilizers, washed them down with an open bottle of wine and lit a cigarette. He had to devise a game plan.

"Okay." He told himself, "Chili's not exactly rocket science or brain surgery or anything like that. Is it? Nope it's not. So, nooo *problema*."

He finished his cigarette and sauntered back into the kitchen area.

"All right, let's have a look at that meat. How much is there?"

"About twenty kilograms." The caterer replied.

"Hmmm, twenty kilograms, that's two point two kilos to the . . . yeah, yeah that's about forty-four pounds divided by two hundred . . ."

Rhett took one look at the meat. It was a suspicious color of grey and didn't look all that appetizing. "In the States our meat looks a lot fresher." He was still talking to himself. "That's it, our meat just looks better. Okay, it's probably safe enough. Anyway, this isn't America and people here eat things that we never would eat and nobody's dying from the food. They're dying from radiation. That's what this party's all about anyway. Right? Right."

He told himself that it was very fortunate that none of the guests would ever see where or how their food was being prepared. "Chili's basically a dish of questionable origin anyway. So, what's the big deal? If people get sick, it's probably because of the radiation." He muttered although no one could understand a word he was saying.

An assistant brought over an apron. Rhett put it on over his cowboy hat thinking it would give him the look of authority in terms of cowboy cuisine. After all, at that moment, he was the authority.

He began looking for a large pot where he could prepare the chili. The caterer pointed him in the direction of a huge machine that looked more like a diving bell than it did a cooking apparatus. But that's what it was. A monstrous industrial cooker the size of a Volvo that must have weighed a ton. He'd never seen anything like it, with the possible exception of those old versions of "Industry on Parade" he used to see on black and white television when he was a kid.

He was then taken to another gargantuan contraption that turned out to be, quite possibly, the world's biggest food processor.

"How many kilograms of vegetables are here?" he asked. He assessed the amounts and asked for someone to start the beast up. The whirring nearly scared the hell out of him. Standing a few feet back, Rhett began throwing in vegetables.

The Ukrainians eyed him suspiciously, for they had no idea of what he was doing or even what the hell chili was. Neither did the caterer. Although he was a chef, he was a Finnish chef and had no practical experience in the art of chili cooking. Most likely, the only thing he knew about chili was whatever he had read in a cookbook, which made Rhett the chili expert of the moment.

With thoughtful expressions and theatrical gestures, he tossed in handfuls of onions and peppers, then some garlic and the occasional tomato here and there, until the monstrous machine had fully processed about forty pounds of the concoction.

He instructed one of the cooks to unplug the machine, because there was no way he was going to put his hands into the jaws of the metallic monster while it was running. Then he signaled one of the prep cooks to bring the ingredients over to the colossal cauldron.

Opening a couple of bottles of red wine, he poured them in figuring that between the garlic and alcohol, it would kill anything that might be dangerous for human consumption.

As the Ukrainians looked on, he tipped his hat just for effect.

Rhett then asked for the questionable looking meat. As he threw bits of it into the cauldron, he noticed something shiny. Putting his hand into the greyish ground meat, he pulled out something that looked like a man's mangled ring. Rhett looked at it for a moment, then threw it over his shoulder.

Then he commenced to the process of making the chili, adding the chili seasoning by the cupful. There was no sense in keeping to a recipe at that point. It was all smell and after that, it would come the tasting.

The aroma began to fill the room piquing the Ukrainians' curiosity. However, the caterer and the Ukrainians weren't going to put anything in their mouths until Rhett tasted it first.

Before long, it was beginning to smell familiar and Rhett thought it might be safe enough to give it a try. It wasn't bad, but it wasn't quite there. It still had an odd aftertaste.

At that point, Rhett ordered everything opened. A half a bottle of wine here, a bottle of tomato sauce there. It was beginning to smell better, so he persuaded the caterer to sample it. After a moment, he gave Rhett a thumb's-up then encouraged the Ukrainians to give it a try too. Despite the mystery meat, Rhett had successfully prepared a batch of down-home Soviet styled version of Cowboyskie Chili." He thanked God, Jerry Jeff Walker and the Terlingua Chili Cook-Off for the basic characteristics of old-fashioned chili.

Satisfied it was finished, Rhett wiped his hands, tossed off the apron, tipped the cowboy hat to his new comrades and sashayed out of the building. It smelled like victory.

———

Rhett could not believe his eyes as he walked into The Kowboy. It was as if a miracle had occurred.

For the first time, it looked like an actual saloon and dance hall.

The mirrors had been installed, serving tables were covered with tablecloths and John was overseeing the workmen as they completed the final installation of the dimmer switches for the light fixtures. John and Casey had also persuaded the Seagram's company to donate enough cases of gin, vodka, wine and whatever else it took to get them through the night. The bread had arrived and there were dozens of marvelous baguettes, croissants, Italian loaves and more. Plus, the caterer's crew was beginning to arrive with the rest of the food, including the Cowboyskie Chili.

Lena had contacted the representatives from Panasonic convincing them that it would benefit them greatly if they could provide a wide-screen television and a video cassette player to enhance the evening's entertainment. She told them a lot of important people would be attending the party and it would be an excellent public relations ploy if their products were on hand to show their support for such an important occasion.

John and Casey were rightfully proud of what they had accomplished. It looked as if The Kowboy Dance Hall & Saloon we going to make it after all.

Rhett took the metro home and quickly changed into a pair of knee-high black leather boots, an old double-breasted tuxedo jacket, ruffled shirt, string tie and his new long black leather duster that had been custom made for him by an unemployed arms manufacturer. He popped a few more Soviet tranquilizers and was out the door.

On the way, he stopped off at a local kiosk, tossing down a hundred grams of vodka. It went down hard.

XI

Ten Years After Chernobyl

When Rhett arrived at the bar, the presidential security had already made a sweep of the place. Sergei and Salom were conspicuously absent.

Miraculously, John and Casey's efforts had succeeded and as Rhett walked by them, John greeted him with a "Hi, Doc. How's it goin'?" Rhett acknowledged with a smile. The combination of the vodka and Soviet tranquilizers were beginning to take effect. He was relaxed and the numbness didn't seem important anymore.

Even though Kyrill's "Kowboys of Kyiv" painting had been finished it was still sitting in his studio. In its place hung banners of the evening's sponsors and one for the Children of Chernobyl Committee. Since Pepsi had secured sponsorship for the event, their promotional pieces were everywhere stretching out of their territory in the Cantina and invading

Coca-Cola's realm. However, Coca-Cola had seen the opportunity to upstage them by putting their logo on the new facade outside.

A large-screen TV had been delivered as promised, along with a bright blue fluorescent Panasonic sign. Even charity came with a price and they wanted to make sure that everyone was aware of their presence.

A neon Sauza Tequila sign hung between the saloon and the cantina, courtesy of the country representative for Sauza who had donated the only two bottles of Sauza Tequila in Kyiv.

Rhett commandeered Lucy to be the official Sauza girl and wear a Sauza waitress outfit complete with a gun belt that had been designed to carry the bottles with places for shot glasses instead of bullets. Even though she was an investor, she seemed complimented by the attention and more than happy to oblige. Besides, Rhett thought she was as attractive as any of the models, with the possible exception she wasn't as tall.

However, Andrei had arranged for a bevy of Ukrainian models to act as hostesses and serve drinks while Todd was insisting on using one of the models. Rhett really didn't care and told Todd to explain it to Lucy, because he sure as hell couldn't figure it out.

As a result, Todd gave the job to a tall leggy brunette. She put the two bottles of Sauza in the gun belt as Todd instructed her on the finer points of lick, bite and shoot technique of Tequila drinking.

However, as beautiful as the models were, grace and brains were not their long suit and as Rhett walked away, he heard a crash. The model had dropped one of the bottles of Sauza. Rhett simply shook his head and thought if it had been Lucy, the bottle wouldn't have had near as far to fall.

A temporary bar was situated on the imaginary border, between the "Texas" and "Mexico" territories. Rhett walked over and ordered a vodka from the drop-dead gorgeous bartender. Over her shoulder was the neon Sauza Tequila sign. He gave it a toast, downed the vodka and asked for another.

Everyone took their places and waited. The atmosphere was near perfect. By the Grace of God, the Devil or whatever, the Kowboy Dance Hall & Saloon was ready.

As the first guests began arriving, they looked truly surprised to see a cowboy saloon in the middle of downtown Kyiv. Another evening was about to begin.

—

A dignified looking gentleman in his eighties with a full head of white hair entered the bar followed by an entourage. Rhett didn't recognize him at first, but then it dawned on him. It was Jack Palance.

Being born of Ukrainian parents who had immigrated in the early part of the century, Palance was the guest of honor. Not many people in Ukraine had ever seen any of his movies, nor had any idea of who he was, let alone being the legendary actor who had done one armed push-ups on the stage of the Academy Awards. But Rhett knew for damn sure who he was and, by God, he was going to meet him.

He looked tired and a bit disoriented as he looked around the saloon and then he saw the television. The movie *Shane* was playing and he had arrived at just the moment his character appeared in the movie. He watched intently, seeing himself as a young actor, a half- century earlier. Palance looked up as Rhett approached him, toy spurs jingling with every step. "Mr. Palance, welcome to The Kowboy." Palance's eyebrows came down on his forehead turning his face into a puzzled frown.

Then when Rhett began to speak in Ukrainian, Palance looked surprised to hear an American cowboy speaking to him in the language that his mother had taught him as a child. They spoke to each other, exchanging small pleasantries as a young Ukrainian woman, standing at his side seemed delighted by the exchange.

Suddenly, another gentleman abruptly interrupted in English. "Where is Mr. Palance's table? We'd like to sit down if you don't mind." Rhett took that as his queue to shut up. He looked around for a table he thought they might like, escorted them to it and excused himself. Then he went back to the bar. The encounter had jangled his nerves a bit and he downed another drink.

As more people arrived, elegantly dressed in formal attire, Toby and his Kowboy Bar Band took the stage.

Members of the Chernobyl committee were accepting $100 donations at the door, ensuring that only the highest of rollers would be allowed, keeping the party exclusive and the rougher elements out.

The serving tables had been elegantly laid out and arranged with various Ukrainian dishes. People were lining up and eagerly digging in to the evening's bill of fare.

Jon Anderson of the musical group Yes walked in the saloon. He was surrounded by the traditional groupies and other musicians who had been performing with him at the concert.

Soon the bar was packed with VIP's roaming through The Kowboy Dance Hall & Saloon soaking up the American atmosphere.

Executives from every type of international company were mingling with one another; friends and competitors alike touched elbows with each other. You name it, if they were the heavy players in the market, they were there.

A group of Scottish businessmen arrived, standing together at the bar in full Scottish regalia, kilts and all. It added an even more international flair to the evening's celebration. It looked like The Kowboy was finally getting the right kind of exposure it needed to be a success.

John and Casey worked their way through the crowd, shaking hands and making sure that everybody felt at home. Those who had been left holding the bag had accomplished the impossible.

For once, Dave and his Chechens were the furthermost things from everyone's mind.

———

After the dust-up with Toby, Rhett avoided him like the plague. Nevertheless, everyone seemed to be doing their jobs and the evening was going like clockwork.

Between sets, Toby strutted back and forth like a banty rooster acting every bit the part of the country music star. Dave had created a monster who believed the only thing that mattered was Toby. He hated foreigners but wasn't cognizant of the fact it was he who was the foreigner. His lack of language skills left him with little more than a few grunts or a "I don't speak that language" as he dismissed the locals he didn't want to talk to, which included just about everybody, unless she was young and beautiful.

When the dance troupe arrived and asked Toby when they could begin their performance. he curtly brushed them off. "Sorry, already did those songs last set and I don't change my sets around for nobody."

Rhett knew that no matter what was said to him, Toby was going to do what he was going to do — and that was that. He was furious, but things were going too well to risk a confrontation in front of this group of dignitaries.

As Toby and the band began their next set, Rhett walked over to John and told him what Toby had just said to the dancers. After all, John was the manager and it was his job to make sure things ran smoothly.

John just turned to Rhett and replied, "Yeah? So, what do you want me to do about it?"

Rhett walked away trying to figure it all out when all he really wanted to do was to walk over and jerk Toby off the stage and slap the living shit out of him. However, everyone was enjoying themselves and Rhett knew it was neither the time nor the place. All he would accomplish would be to make an ass out of himself.

He walked past the table where Palance and his party were seated. "Is there anything I can do for you gentlemen?" he asked.

Palance courteously replied, "No, thank you." However, the curt gentleman sitting next to him interrupted. "What would we want from an ugly son of a bitch like you?"

Rhett took it as a feeble attempt at humor and answered, "I have no idea, whatsoever." He kept his mouth shut, turned around and walked away.

He walked out of the bar, went to a kiosk down the street and ordered another 100 grams of vodka and slammed it down. Rhett stood there, trying to regain his composure. After another straight vodka, he walked back toward The Kowboy Dance Hall & Saloon.

As he descended the stairs, he could see the dance troupe was performing to a receptive crowd as the Kowboy Bar Band played George Strait's "Adelida."

Rhett walked over to John. "What did you say to Toby?"

"I just convinced him during the break that the people were here to see the whole show and not just Toby Smith."

"Look, John, I'm sorry, but goddamn it, that kid's turning out to be one big pain in the ass."

"Don't worry about it." he replied. "He'll be okay. He's just a little bit uptight. That's all."

Rhett thought he'd try to be diplomatic. "Well, he's young. Maybe he's just high-strung because his fiancée is back in Texas."

"Bullshit!" John laughed. "He kept Casey and me up all night. He had four of those models in his bedroom. We barely got any sleep."

"I was just trying to give him the benefit of the doubt."

"Well, there ain't no doubt about it. I can tell you, that's not his problem."

At that moment, they were interrupted by Igor, Rhett's young assistant. He had a concerned look on his face. "Mr. Palance."

"What about him?"

"I've just seen him walk out of the bar alone."

Considering what had been happening around the saloon and *The Passazh*, he quickly ran upstairs with Igor following close behind.

They found Palance wandering around outside searching for his limousine, but it was nowhere in sight. He looked tired, a little dazed and was ready to go back to his hotel.

Rhett introduced Igor and as the two spoke to each other in Ukrainian, he tried to find a car. That's when a sleek black limo pulled into the rear archway of *The Passazh*. Rhett flagged it down and helped Palance into the back seat. He thanked them and the car drove him away to his hotel. Rhett told Igor he had done well, but then again, he always did.

Moments later, they were joined by Cody Palance. He had yet to perform his song and was looking for his father. He looked disappointed when Rhett told him that his father had already left.

Rhett couldn't really tell if he was drunk or not. He was the kind of guy who always had that strung-out look about him. Although he had his father's features, he had nowhere near the stamina his father possessed in his early years. It wasn't entirely Cody's fault, but what does a son do growing up in his father's shadow? It was obvious he loved and respected him. He even bragged about his father doing his famous one-handed push-ups at a restaurant the night before.

Rhett looked at him wondering if his decision to perform "Stairway to Heaven" was his way of showing his father that he could accomplish something difficult too.

With a shrug, Cody went down to perform. He wasn't all that bad of a guy. Rhett kept thinking of how Toby had cut him down behind his back . . . out of earshot. From the street, Rhett could hear him perform and thought his father would have been proud, because the young man sounded great and didn't miss a note.

After his performance, Cody came back up on the street. He was looking for a taxi to take him back to his hotel or wherever. Rhett watched as he walked away disappearing into the darkness looking like a lost and lonely solitary figure.

As Cody disappeared around the corner, the man who had been with Palance inside the bar came outside. Looking around for his limo, he barked at Rhett. "Where's my Limo! What did you do with my limo? Do you have any idea who I am?"

He was just the kind of a man that one takes an instant disliking to.

"Nope. Can't say that I do"

"Well, I'm Palance's manager. I own him and I'm a rich man. See this Rolex? It's worth ten thousand dollars. Now, where the hell's my limo? I need for someone to take me to my hotel."

Rhett half-heartedly apologized for not having a car ready and offered to get him a taxi, because the man was starting to seem nervous and didn't want to walk too far into the night. He was in a tux and wearing a lot of jewelry. The perfect person waiting to be mugged.

The best place to get a taxi was Kreschatik Boulevard at the other end of the street. The nearest street with any traffic was behind them at the rear of *The Passazh* where it was dark. Rhett went out onto the street and flagged down a car asking the couple inside if they would mind driving the old man to his hotel.

"*Skilky?* (How much?)" the driver asked.

"*Skilky vwe khotite?* (How much do you want?)" Rhett answered.

The driver asked for an outrageous sum. To his surprise, Rhett agreed. Anyway, it wasn't his money and the old bastard looked like he could afford it. After all, he said he was a rich man and he was wearing a Rolex.

Rhett walked over to Palance's manager who was holding a handful of cash. He took it him by the arm and escorted him to the car. Opening the rear door, he gently pushed the man into the back seat. The manager looked a little nervous. It wasn't a regular taxi. He was getting into a strange car with strange people who didn't even speak his language.

"Uh, how safe do you think this is?" he asked. "You don't think they're going to rob me or anything like that do you?"

"Of course not. They look like honest folks to me. Now, just hand me one of those bills you have there in your hand and I'll pay them. Don't worry, everything will be all right."

Rhett couldn't keep from chuckling as he waved good-bye to the car disappearing into the darkness The look on the man's face was enough for having to put up with his attitude . . . and anyway, they really did look like honest people.

———

With that bit of business finished Rhett turned around and descended back down into the saloon where things seemed fairly normal. The guests were digging into the delights of the cowboy chili. Consequently, Rhett figured it was about time to get really relaxed. Everybody else was. Once more, he bellied up to bar once.

The Chernobyl committee members were beginning to change their tune about The Kowboy. Everything was forgotten in the merriment. Not to mention, they were being very well fed and had a few drinks in them too. It appeared to have changed their opinion as they were now congratulating John and Casey for organizing the best party in memory.

Rhett simply leaned against the bar, thinking about the days earlier, "when they were ready to hang his nuts hung out to dry. What a glorious evening it was turning out to be and everybody was just lovin' the livin' shit out of one another

"In fact, the liquor was flowing so freely, it seemed that everyone had forgotten the evening's earlier somber event. Loosened ties, unbuttoned tuxedo jackets and cowboy hats had become the proper attire of the moment as everything was taking a backseat to the good ole' boy party in The Kowboy Dance Hall & Saloon. Altogether, it was a not an unpleasant sight.

Nadia was on top of the bar dancing, strutting her stuff in exchange for a $10,000 check from the director of Pepsi to be donated to her foundation. It was a bit more dignified than the Scotsman and his snake dancer's version that had been performed on the bar a week earlier.

As soon as Nadia was back on the floor, looking as if she were having a high old time dancing and laughing in the crowd, Rhett walked over to her. "Would you like to meet our dancers?" he asked.

Nadia turned and bluntly replied, "Why?"

Rhett had to stop himself from rolling his eyes. "Well, Nadia, for one thing, they're Ukrainian."

Her friends had heard the exchange and for once it wasn't Rhett with the egg on his face. She had put herself on the spot and was looking to save face by appearing to be a gracious lady . . . even if just for a moment.

"Oh . . . well, then . . . uh, okay. Of course, why not?"

"Fine." Rhett made the polite introductions then walked away, shaking his head as she exchanged her superficial pleasantries with the dancers. He wanted another drink.

It was all quickly forgotten when the head of Pepsi called Nadia and John to join him on stage. If Pepsi was going to donate $10,000 to The Children of Chernobyl, he was going to make sure everybody knew it.

When John was introduced as the owner/manager of the Kowboy, Rhett's eyes caught his for a moment. Then they thanked John and Casey for being such wonderful hosts. They should have. They had been quite hospitable and deserved the credit a lot more than "Crazy" Dave Seigal.

Then with much ado, Pepsi presented the ten grand to Nadia.

Rhett leaned against the bar, content to just watch. Oh, well, drunks are drunks," he told himself. "Except tonight, these drunks are all a little higher class. At least tonight they're acting a bit more civilized."

Despite everything they had dodged another bullet and averted another catastrophe. Once again, things were looking good for The Kowboy Dance Hall & Saloon.

—

At four o'clock, John closed the bar, locking the door behind Rhett. He was wrung out and exhausted, both physically and emotionally as he walked down *The Passazh* to Kreschatik to find a taxi. It felt like he had been on his feet days and his boots were killing him. He could barely walk for the pain.

Rhett crossed through a darkened passageway under the boulevard. When he reached the other side, he sat down on the side of the stairwell leading back up to the street.

He heard someone say something, but he was too tired to listen. Out of the corner of his eyes, he could see two officers of the *Militsia* approaching. He knew the drill. They asked him for his identification papers. What he was doing out so late. Was he drunk?

"*Ya prosta ustalla* (I'm simply tired.)" Rhett told them he worked at The Kowboy club and started taking off the toy spurs.

The *Militsia* seemed as bored as he was and probably figured it was as good a sport as any to hassle him a bit. Besides, when did they ever have a chance to ask a cowboy in the middle of the night for his passport?

He reached inside his duster and pulled it out. After a few moments they let him go.

Rhett hailed a cab and climbed into the back. It sped off, disappearing into the darkness.

It had been another night in what was becoming the ongoing saga of The Kowboy Dance Hall & Saloon.

"Tomorrow night," he whispered to himself, "we'll finally open for business," . . . or so he thought.

XII

Cause It's The Tax Man

It seemed he had just fallen to sleep when the midday sun came gleaming through the window. He lay there, completely exhausted, wondering about the future of The Kowboy. Eventually, he dragged himself off the sofa and poured a cup of coffee once again it was liberally laced with cognac.

Although he still tired, but he needed to go see what was happening at the bar.

When he arrived, he found Even the band and a line of employees standing outside. Working his way through the crowd Rhett began pounding on the door. Eventually, he heard the lock open. It was Andrei. Quickly whisking past him and down the stairs he found John and Casey sitting at a table near the bar.

"Okay, what's the problem this time? Why's the bar closed and why didn't anybody call me?"

Frustrated, John replied angrily. "We can't open tonight. Salom's bookkeeper said she had been tipped off that the tax people were coming for an inspection. Evidently, we still don't have all our licenses and they would have closed us down."

"What?" Rhett exclaimed. "You mean we've been open all of this time and nobody's thought of making sure if we have all our licenses or not? You mean to tell me that Dave hasn't handled this yet?"

"Obviously not. Evidently, Sergei was supposed to handle it."

Rhett was beside himself. "Hell, even I know that you're supposed to have a license to operate a bar. Christ Almighty! Even in the States, you have to have a license."

"I know, but I was told they don't have them all yet."

"Then I suggest that we get them or copies of them in our hands and keep them here at the bar . . . just in case this ever happens again. So exactly when in the Sam Hill *are* we going to open?"

"Don't worry." John reassured him, "As far as I'm concerned, everything will be up and running by tomorrow night! That's if there aren't any other problems. But who knows? "I wish I could figure out what the hell is going on with this place. If somebody understood what was going on, they could make a lot of money."

Rhett simply shrugged his shoulders. "It's possible, but it's not easy and working with the Mafia makes this all a shaky deal, no matter what Dave says."

"Then, why is he working with them?" John snapped. It was a question that kept coming up — again and again.

Suddenly, John exploded. Son of a bitch! I'm just trying to figure out why the hell anybody would do business in this goddamned country! No one seems to be able to get a straight answer on anything and I'm getting sick and tired of all this bullshit!"

It was beginning to become apparent to Rhett That John and Casy's earlier exuberance finally wearing thin and they were increasingly becoming frustrated dealing with Sergei and Salom. They couldn't figure out who to listen to, or why they were having to deal with the seemingly simple problems that were constantly arising.

"So, what's Dave spending on advertising?" John asked.

"Not much. I've been trying to keep the expenditures down," Rhett answered. "So far, we've only committed to two publications. One is Dossier Dosuga, which costs about a hundred dollars every time we run an ad."

"What's the other?"

"*LOOKS International*. It's a glossy magazine for Kyiv's jet set."

"How much does that cost?"

"It comes out quarterly and a quarter page runs around two thousand dollars."

"Why is Dave spending that kind of money on advertising when we don't have enough money to keep the bar running? What kind of damn advertising professional are you?"

Rhett was stunned by his anger. "I really don't have an answer to that. It was Dave's deal. The decision was made when Dave had high expectations for the bar. He was the one who agreed to advertise with *LOOKS*. At the time, I was under the impression that Dave had the money to support an advertising budget, but you do have a point. That's the best answer I got."

"What in the hell was Dave thinking, to go off to some a balloon festival when his place is in this shape?"

"I honestly don't know what to tell you, but as anyone will tell you, it's Dave's bar. He's the one who keeps saying he's got everything under control and he's going to do what he wants to do no matter what. You try telling him different."

"Well, all I can say is, it's one hell of a way to run a business."

Rhett looked around the bar. "So, where's Toby?"

"He's gone to the Arizona. Did you know that Toby's decided to go back to the States?"

"No, I didn't. But Toby and I really don't talk too much these days."

"He told me last night. Seems he's trashed his old apartment and the phone's been disconnected due to an unpaid phone bill. It's why he opted to move out of his flat and moved in with Casey."

"I don't think Dave's going to be too happy with that deal."

"Well, Toby's not too happy about his deal with Dave either. Evidently, Dave hasn't been paying him what he promised"

"Hell, I can't say that I blame him. Dave hasn't paid anybody what he's promised them. So, what did you tell Toby?"

"I told him he would be a fool to go back now. He's spent all this time getting ready for the bar to open. Everything's just getting started. If he goes back this early in the game, he's going to regret it. Here, he's somebody, but if he goes back to Texas, he's just going to be another little redneck pecker-head."

"Well, I can't say that's going to break me up," Rhett replied.

"If he goes back, I give him about six weeks to change his attitude. After shoveling shit on the farm for a while, he'll be begging to come back."

"Maybe, that's not such a bad idea after all. Maybe he needs to shovel a little shit to put him back in his place. Anyway, I'm going to the office if you need me — See ya later."

And with that Rhett got up and walked out of the bar, leaving John cursing to himself.

XIII

A Couple of Old Comrades

When the phone rang, Rhett heard a voice he hadn't heard since he had first arrived in Ukraine. It was Sasha Yablonsky, an old friend from his old Peace Corps days at a sanatorium outside Kyiv called *Puscha-Voditsa*. It was during those early days that they spent long nights talking, drinking and dreaming of opening a cowboy restaurant.

Sasha had since moved to St. Petersburg, but had returned to Kyiv for a brief visit. He had heard about The Kowboy Dance Hall & Saloon from a mutual friend and told Rhett he couldn't wait to see the place. Rhett was looking forward to showing him that the dream, even if it was turning out to be a nightmare. They arranged to meet on *The Passazh*.

—

No sooner had Rhett exited the Metro when someone tapped him on the shoulder. He turned around to see Sasha's face grinning from ear to ear.

As they walked to The Kowboy, Rhett began to tell him about the bar, but when they arrived the door was locked again.

"*Blyad!* What's the fucking problem this time?" Cursed Rhett as he pounded on the door.

After a few moments, he heard the door being unlocked. Once again it was Andrei. He started to enter, but Andrei stopped him. "I'm sorry, the bar is closed. No one is allowed in."

"What the hell do you mean 'No one's allowed in.'?" Rhett snapped back. "My friend has come all the way from St. Petersburg and I want to show him the fucking bar! Now, let me in."

"I'm sorry. You'll have to call John. He's gone back to the apartment," Andrei replied, pushing Rhett back, shutting the door and locking it. Rhett was livid as his face turned purple with rage.

Sasha followed him as he crossed the street to a public phone and placed a call to John's apartment. There was no answer.

They returned to the front of the bar, but the door was still locked.

"That son of a bitch had the audacity to lock me out!" Rhett exploded, kicking the door and cursing in fluent Russian. Still, the door remained locked.

Sasha was amazed. "Your language has improved incredibly," he laughed.

Every Russian obscenity that Rhett could think of came pouring out of his mouth. About a half-dozen Ukrainians nearby seemed amused at the sight of a cowboy standing in the middle of the street displaying such linguistic skill.

Once more, Rhett found himself taking a deep breath and trying to gather his composure. Sasha was still laughing.

This time, he spoke in Russian. "*Molodetz, Rhett. Vwe govoreeti paruskie ochen horosho* (Well done, Rhett. You speak Russian very well)."

Rhett turned to him. "Let's go have a drink."

They went to a kiosk in the passageway underneath *Kreschatik* and ordered a couple of vodkas as Rhett apologized. "I'm really sorry about this Sasha, but ever since the place opened it's been one problem after another. It's been a nightmare ever since the owner took on the Mafia as partners."

"His partners are the Mafia?"

"Stupid, huh? Plus, he's brought in a manager from California who doesn't know a word of the language. In other words, the whole thing's been a goddamned Chinese fire drill."

"Don't worry about it." Sasha reassured him. "What's important is we got to see each other."

"When do you go back to St. Petersburg?"

"Tomorrow. I'm taking the morning train to Moscow."

"You got any place to stay?"

"I'm staying with my wife's family."

"What are you doing tonight? You want to go back to my place and I'll make us up some cowboyskie chili. I've got some *Samahon* too. But I gotta warn you. This stuff is so strong it'll knock your Dave right in the dirt."

"Not *Samahon*!" Sasha exclaimed.

"C'mon. It'll be like old times. Just so long as you don't *'blyuviyatt'* on my floor like you used to at *Puscha-Voditsa*."

"Oh, God! You still remember that?" he laughed, surprised that Rhett remembered the Russian word for vomit.

———

Over the evening, Rhett filled Sasha in on all that was happening at The Kowboy, from Dave's scene with the bat to Salom's stabbing, Yuri's beating, the Kalashnikov in his chest and the trouble with the ballistic Texas troubadour.

Sasha sat listening incredulously. "I cannot believe this is all true. It sounds like a movie. Why would this owner be stupid enough to make partners of the Mafia in the first place?"

"Well, I'll tell you Sasha, after what I've been through, I've decided to write it all down in a book. No one would ever believe me back home and if I hadn't been through all this shit, I wouldn't believe it myself. Every time I tell myself it can't get any worse, it does."

When the *Samahon* was gone and Sasha had his fill of Rhett's cowboyskie chili, he staggered off into the night to find his in-law's home.

He was feeling no pain and Rhett could only hope that he would make his train to St. Petersburg the following morning.

XIV

Dossier Dosuga

The following night, despite a sign that said the bar was closed Rhett found the door was unlocked. Quickly going inside and down the stairs, he found John and Casey sitting at the bar trying to talk with Sergei without an interpreter.

"Now, what's the problem?"

"It's this goddamned greaseball," Casey snapped, pointing at Sergei. "He's the problem. I think he's saying that he's taking over the bar!"

"Are you absolutely sure about that?"

Before she could reply, Todd came walking into the bar. He immediately, sensed there was some sort of problem and offered to interpret for Sergei.

"So ask him, Todd," John instructed. "Is he taking this bar over from Dave or what? Because if he is, I'm out of here. I'll give him the keys right now if that's the case. Tell him I work for Dave and no one else." John held out the keys to Sergei, who looked perplexed.

Todd interpreted what John said.

"No, no!" Sergei replied, and turned to Todd speaking in Ukrainian.

"He says Dave is still his partner and he still wants you and Casey to run the bar." Then Todd interjected, "I don't think he was trying to take over anything. He was merely saying things need to be organized, the licenses need to be in order. He just wants the bar to be run as a business."

"And what about Salom?" John asked.

Todd translated as Sergei spoke. "As far as Sergei's concerned, Dave's deal is with Salom. He says it doesn't concern him, but if Salom is to be Dave's silent partner, it's between Dave and Salom."

"Well, who am I supposed to be talking to?" John asked.

Todd interpreted. "Sergei apologizes and says everything will be all right. You are in control. That's why Dave brought you here. He just wants the bar to be successful. That's all."

Sergei then shook John's hand and left.

Todd turned to John and Casey. "I think everything is all right."

However, John and Casey were still frustrated. They were at the end of their ropes. They didn't know who was whose partner. But one thing they did know, they didn't like Sergei.

At that point, John walked over to Rhett. "I've had just about enough of this shit. Fuck Sergei, fuck Salom and fuck that shithead Dave! I'm just about ready to kick everybody's ass and I don't care if they're Mafia or not!"

Rhett gestured for John to calm down. "I know how you feel, John. Just remember what I told you about Custer and the Indians. Ya gotta remember we're the ones outnumbered here"

"Right now, I don't care what or who they are!"

"Well, I really believe Sergei is just trying to get things back to normal. I know he looks like a greaseball. Quite frankly, I don't know what he did with his hair. When I first met him he didn't look that way. He looked a lot nicer. I swear."

"I don't know who is who! All I know is I'm tired of all this bullshit! What am I doing here anyway? This is Dave's bar! Where the hell is he?"

"Listen, just calm down. This is basically all of Dave's doing. He's the one who's always talking about some goddamned 'war.' I've never heard that word unless it was coming out of Dave's mouth."

"Well, I'm about ready for one!"

"Look at it this way. What if you and I were both in California right now and we both knew some fast-talking Korean. Let's just say the guy was a real good talker and he had this business deal that was going to make you a lot of money. Then you find out that I own the business that he sold to you. You'd be pissed off at me, right?"

"Yeah, so what's the point?"

"Just stay with me on this one. Okay?"

"Okay. What are you trying to say?"

"What I'm saying is, this Korean has just sold us both the same business, but he doesn't speak English all that well. However. both you and I speak English. Now, before we start killing each other, we're going to start talking with each other, because we speak the same language. Right?"

"Yeah?"

"Well, we find out that we're not trying to cheat each other. It's that damned Korean that sold the business twice. That's the situation that Dave's has gotten himself into along with us. Now these guys have already had a summit. So, obviously they've been to talking to each other."

"Right. So?"

"So if you and I found out some Korean was screwing us both around, who would you be pissed off at, me or that damned Korean?"

"What in the fuck are you talking about?"

"All right. I can see that I'm getting a little too stream of consciousness here. But my point is, Dave is screwing over everybody. That's the problem. We're all totally confused about what's actually going on. But I guarantee you that sooner or later, if they haven't done it already, these guys are going to start talking to each other. And when they do, they're going to come to the conclusion that Dave is cheating them both. Then you and I are going to be up shit creek, paddling right along with Dave. Dave's the one who's got everybody so confused right now. Nobody knows what the fuck is going on. Do you understand what I'm trying to tell you?"

"Uh, I think so."

"Well, good! I'm glad because I've just totally confused myself."

"Have you been drinking?" John asked.

"Not yet, but now that you mention it, maybe that's not a bad idea. Where's the vodka?'

Rhett reached behind the bar, grabbing a shot glass and a bottle, he muttered to himself, "I think I'm mad. I must be mad. I *know* I'm mad." He poured a drink and tossed it back.

—

The following week, an article was published in the *Kyiv Post*. It reported that four policemen had been executed by the government for criminal activities. The details were vague, but Rhett wondered if it might have been the young officers with the Berkuyt. the ones upon whom Yuri had sworn vengeance.

Two weeks later, *Dossier Dosuga* magazine featured a photograph of three cowboys on the front cover with a headline that said, ***ARE THE COWBOYS COMING?***

The true flavor of the southwest is tempting the tastebuds of Kyiv's partying crowd . . . finally. And we're not talking Odessa here, we're talking Texas! The long-awaited grand opening of Dave Seigal's dream bar came and went, pretty much.

Amidst rumors of a Mafia takeover, problems with the plumbing and controversial comics about the bar, The Kowboy has held private parties for a month now and recently began opening its doors daily. "We've been working every day this week," Seigal said Saturday. "And we'll be open every day from here on out.'

Not a small feat, but then he's got a super staff composed of friends, foreign and local. These sidekicks have stuck with the project, from helping on the construction to tending bar. And with major start-up costs, he said he's very grateful to be surrounded by people willing to take on practically volunteer night shifts.

"Be sure to tip the bartenders, 'cause that's the only money they're making tonight." Seigal shouts throughout the evening in between sets of Texas born and bred Toby Smith, who sings with the local band he trained to play Country & Western Music, and the Kyiv cult Rock-a-Billy group The Rockland Ladies.

Add to this a wild girl lassoist and dancing cowgirls, and you might as well be in Dallas.

Being a musician himself as well as a social butterfly, Seigal said a driving force behind pursuing The Kowboy was to provide his

271

friends a cozy place to listen to live down-home music and drink lots of beer.

Apparently, he has done just that, because the little underground town with paintings by local artists, neon signs, cheap beers, tequila shots and beef jerky is really packing them in!

Despite Salom's stabbing and the mention of a Mafia takeover, it turned out that Dave and the club still had its supporters. So, in the overall scheme of things, the article turned out to be fairly positive publicity for The Kowboy Dance Hall & Saloon.

THE RETURN OF "CRAZY" DAVE SEIGAL

"I may be crazy, but it keeps me from going insane."

Waylon Jennings

I

A Teetotalin' Cowboy

Kyrill's *"Kowboys of Kyiv"* painting hung at the entrance to the bar. Its sheer size made it impressive. As Rhett stood before the gargantuan painting of the three cowboys standing before of a panorama of a Kyiv in flames, he couldn't help but notice the irony of the calamitous birth of the Kowboy Dance Hall & Saloon.

It was the night before the official fifth and "final" grand opening when Dave strode into the bar like a conquering hero. "I'm back, got my head together and I'm ready to straighten out all of the problems and make a lot of money."

"Peter the Great" had returned.

Acting upbeat, John and Casey were laughing and joking as if nothing had happened during Dave's sabbatical. Everything's ready to go. We've just been waiting on you,"

As John and Casey filled him in on the success of the Chernobyl party, Dave looked around. "Look at this place. I can hardly believe my eyes. Everything looks just great.

"We were just holding down the fort for you while you were in California." Casey's voice virtually dripped with honey.

"Well, all I can say is you all did one hell of a job!" Dave proclaimed. "I knew you could pull it off. So, where's Toby?"

Toby was conspicuously absent. "I think he went to the Arizona Barbeque to have dinner." John replied.

Dave turned to Rhett sitting at the bar. "So, how are you doing cowboy? John told me you were about at the end of your rope."

Rhett shrugged. "Well, things could be a lot better, but I really don't want to go into it right now. I just want is to get this place up and running."

Dave's concern lasted about as long as a heartbeat. Sauntering behind the bar, he pulled out a bottle of tequila and a couple of glasses sliding one over in Rhett's direction. Then he turned back to listen to John and Casey's glorious account of how well things were going.

Rhett could not believe they were the same people who had been cursing Dave only a few hours before his arrival. He simply looked into his glass, shook his head and downed the tequila.

As Dave poured more shots, Casey excused herself to go back to the apartment. Dave continued drinking and talking to John until the bottle was gone, then announced it was time to go to the Arizona and find Toby.

Rhett was wondering why John had said nothing about Toby's decision to go back to the States. He got up and walked over to John, who anticipated what he was about to say. "I know, I know, but I'll talk to him about Toby later. He's just gotten back to Kyiv and I don't want to get into anything just now."

Rhett turned around, walked back to the bar and downed his final shot of tequila.

He opted out of the Arizona and so did John. No one wanted to spend the evening watching Dave get shitfaced and telling everyone how he had everything under control.

As they walked down *The Passazh*, Dave turned to Rhett and put his arm around his shoulders. "So, tell me. How are you doing?"

"To be honest, not that great." Rhett's arm was numb again.

"Look, I've known you've been through a lot these past few weeks. John's told me all about it and I want you to know I appreciate it. You've stuck with me through this whole thing. Just hang in there. I promise you, things are going to get a lot better from here on out."

"I sure as shit hope so. They can't get much worse." Rhett couldn't tell if he was being sincere or if it was just the liquor talking.

"Tomorrow, we'll talk about everything. You're the only one who really knows what's going on here. You've been with me from the beginning. Hey, you're my best friend." When Dave hugged him, Rhett knew it was liquor.

"Yeah, sure. Okay, I'll see you all tomorrow." Rhett left them on Kreschatik Street and headed for the Metro. Even though his head was spinning, at this point he was in too deep. There was nothing else to do. but to play out his hand to the end and hope things would work out.

—

The following morning, when Dave arrived at the bar he was hung over. It was obvious that he had spent all night drinking again. Rhett could tell he had been on another bender and it had done serious damage. This time he looked different. He was pale and had a bad case of the shakes. Dave looked as if he had been poisoned and he was scared.

"John, I've come to a decision. I'm going to stop drinking." He held his head in both hands.

"Are you serious about that?" John asked.

"Yeah, after last night. I can't keep this up any longer. My liver won't take it. I've got to quit." He then turned to Rhett. "I knew that this was coming. After last night — that was it for me. I've decided to quit drinking."

"Okay, fine." Rhett answered.

"Listen, why don't you join me and we'll quit drinking together. You help me and I'll help you. Besides we don't need to be drinking in this bar.

"Sure, Dave. If you want to quit drinking, I won't drink with you."

He shook Rhett's hand. "It's a deal then."

Dave slowly got up and went behind the bar. As he pulled a 7-Up from the cooler, Rhett turned to John. "So, what's the deal? Did he hurt himself a little too much last night and in the light of day he's swearing off the booze?"

"He sounds like he's serious. I think he's really going to try to stop drinking. What do you think?"

"Well, I've heard that sometimes you can teach an old dog new tricks. He's just gotta want to learn. So, we'll see. Maybe, if he can get his head right we can get to the business of running this damned bar."

"I sure hope so. And what about you Rhett? Were you serious? Are you going to quit too?"

"I don't figure I'm as bad off as Dave. Not quite yet. But I told him if he wanted to quit drinking, I wouldn't drink with him, and I won't. When he's around me, I won't drink."

Rhett thought it was a good thing too. The last thing the Kowboy needed was a repeat performance of Dave standing on the bar with a bat and howling like a rabid monkey.

Dave returned nursing his soft drink. "Look, Rhett. John told me how hard you've been working. So, why don't you take off tonight?"

"What? But tonight's the grand opening."

"That's OK. John and I'll handle everything. Just take the night off and relax. You've earned it."

Rhett was put off at the suggestion. Without a word he stood up, turned around and walked out of The Kowboy Dance Hall & Saloon.

—

That night, Rhett sat alone in a darkened apartment, a pack of cigarettes and a bottle of brandy at his side. He didn't get much sleep that night.

The next day, when Rhett hadn't heard from anyone, he telephoned John's apartment. No one answered. He telephoned Dave — same thing. Then he went to the bar only to find the doors locked. It wasn't right for anyone not to be at either their apartment or the bar.

He called for two days until John finally answered his phone.

"Where the hell have you guys been?"

"Oh, Salom took us down to Yalta. He wanted us to meet some people that he wants us to do business with. I met some guy by the name of

Lazarenko. He must have been really important, because everyone was really was sucking up to him — even Salom. I'm not really sure, but I think Salom may even work for this guy."

"Thanks for letting me know. After all that's happened, I didn't know what the hell to think."

"We left so early in the morning, nobody thought to give you a call."

"Well, fuck you very much, John"

"Sorry about that. Somebody should have called you."

"Ya think? So, why Yalta? What was happening there?"

"It was a zoo. When we got there, they presented Casey with a ram. Then they slit its throat and gutting it on the spot. It didn't bother her, though, She grew up on a farm and she's seen it all before. Then we spent the day roasting the goat over an open fire while everyone proposed toasts, got drunk, shot off their guns, and kissed this Lazarenko guy's ass all day long."

"Was Dave drinking?" Rhett asked.

"Not that I saw."

"So, what about the grand opening?"

"It all went off without a hitch. A lot of people came in, but to be honest, it wasn't all that grand."

"What about tonight?"

"It's all in Dave's hands. Casey and I are flying back to California this afternoon. I've got to take care of some business. I've got some oil investments in Nigeria and I need to see what's going on. I haven't heard from my partner in several weeks. We should be back in about three weeks."

Rhett didn't know what to think. For the first time, Dave would be in full charge of the bar. "Peter the Great" was on his own.

II

The Rodeo of Rock & Roll

It was billed as The Rodeo of Rock & Roll and the sound was deafening as it exploded with ferocity past Rhett as it blasted out onto the streets of *The Passazh*. He was almost knocked backwards by the sheer force erupting out of The Kowboy Dance Hall & Saloon

As he descended the staircase, Rhett could see Dave standing in the bar with a look of shock and sheer horror. Glasses were literally shaking on the shelves and for a moment, Rhett thought the mirrors were going to shatter.

"Jeezus H. Christ, Dave! You can hear that all the way down the street. People are going to think that Chernobyl has blown again. You think these guys can turn down the volume a bit? You're for damn sure going to get some complaints from the neighborhood. Not to mention they're going to blow your complete sound system to hell."

"I know! I know!" Dave screamed.

"What?" Rhett could hardly hear him. "What? Who are these guys anyway?"

"I don't know. I had Anton book a couple of bands to play for tonight's Battle of the Bands!"

Not only was Anton the manager for that Kowboy Bar Band, he also handled several punk rock and heavy metal bands.

279

"It sounds like you have a war going on down here!" Rhett was trying not to laugh.

Rhett followed as Dave made a beeline for Anton who was rockin' out to the sounds of Nokturnal Mortum. "Hey, Anton! Anton! I can't afford to have them play that loud!"

"But it is the kind of music they play!" Anton explained. "Their fans like it!"

"I don't care! Tell them to go home!" Dave shouted.,

Anton looked confused. "But I hired them to come all the way from Kharkiv! We will still have to pay!"

Dave was beside himself. "No problem! I'll pay them not to play!"

"Not to play?" Anton seemed even more confused.

"Yeah, I'll pay them! Now tell them to go!"

"But I have already put the handbills all around Kyiv. There will be many people."

"I don't care how many people there are! Just tell them to go! I'm sorry, but I can't afford to get into trouble with the city administration!"

Andrei was already at the door trying to reason with residents of nearby apartments who were already complaining about the noise.

Dave was panicking. "I'm just going to close the bar! I'm sorry. I have no choice!"

Rhett looked over to see Toby shaking his head. It was obvious this was not his scene, nor his brand of music. He was already making his way toward the exit.

Dave had been in control of the bar for less than a day, and he was already getting a crash course in the Bar Management School of Hard Knocks.

"I guess you won't need me tonight then! So, I think I'll just go on home now."

Rhett could hardly contain his amusement and was grinning as he followed Toby out the door. *"Spravadlivoc (Justice)!"* Rhett chuckled to himself.

Dave was right behind him with the keys, hoping to lock the doors behind him. But, before he could, fans began pouring past him and down into the lower depths of the bar.

The bar had no phone, so calling for help was out of the question. Dave knew he had a potential riot on his hands if he tried to close the bar. He had no backups either. John and Casey were on a plane, Toby was most likely on his way to the Arizona Barbeque and he could only watch as Rhett disappeared down *The Passazh.*

As The Kowboy Dance Hall & Saloon quickly filled with punk rockers and heavy metal fans, Dave knew he had a potential riot on his hands if he tried to close the bar. In addition, it was a markedly different crowd, because most of them didn't have any money to spend. Dave could only watch as the punk rock band took the stage and blasted away for two hours.

The band was finishing its final number when the CNN film crew came walking through the door looking to do the story on Toby, but Toby was nowhere to be found.

———

The following day Dave was still recuperating, when Salom walked into the office with a coarse-looking bleached-blonde woman in her mid-thirties. He introduced Tatiana as his bookkeeper and explained through Lena that she was experienced in keeping books for restaurants and wanted her to handle the books for the bar . . . just to make sure that everything was handled in Dave and Salom's interests. He also wanted Tatiana's husband to be in charge of the restaurant.

At first Dave declined the husband's services, but he did want a bookkeeper who could handle two sets of books. One set for him and Salom, another to show anyone else. As Lena translated, Tatiana said it was possible.

"Lena, tell Salom I trust his judgement. Tatiana will be fine."

Lena translated and Salom nodded.

"And tell Salom that as far as the bar is concerned, I want Salom and Salom alone to be my partner . . . if Salom understands what I mean."

Salom indicated he knew exactly what Dave meant. It meant things didn't look too good for Sergei.

"And tell Salom this is only to be kept between us." Again, Salom nodded in agreement. They shook hands and Salom left with the bookkeeper.

During the entire time, Rhett had been working at the computer and although he acted oblivious to the conversation, he was listening to everything. It was just like he told John, Dave had made the decision to squeeze out his long-time friend and one-time business partner Sergei.

—

A few evenings later, CNN returned to the bar to film the story on the kid from Texas playing country music in the former Soviet Union. Just as they were ready to start shooting, Toby stepped off the stage. "What story?" He told them. "I'm going back to Texas. As far as I'm concerned, there ain't no story."

The crew looked stunned.

However, Dave was more than stunned. He was absolutely flabbergasted It was the first he heard of Toby's intention to quit. He quickly called Toby to the back of the bar. "What in the hell do you think you're doing?"

"I just told them the truth. There ain't no story. I'm leavin'."

Toby's revelation hit Dave like a bombshell. But Toby wasn't finished. "I've been talking to the group and I've gotten us some bookings back in the States. I'm taking 'em back with me.

Dave was speechless as he watched Toby walk out of the bar. He had made this kid a star and now the impudent pup had the audacity to not only screw him, but screw him in front of an international news organization. By the time Dave returned to the CNN crew, they were already packing their equipment to leave. As far as they were concerned, they weren't about to waste their time on some bogus story. There would be no story about the young cowboy musician — or a cowboy club in the former Soviet Union.

Not only had Toby had blown a priceless chance for The Kowboy, he also blew a chance to grab a lot of international publicity for himself. Now, nobody would know Toby Smith and he only had himself to blame.

After that, it was obvious that things would only go downhill between Dave and Toby.

—

Dave was in the office when he received a fax from California. John had located a mechanical bull that was supposedly the same one that John Travolta had ridden in Urban Cowboy, complete with papers of authentication. He had also purchased some arcade games to the tune of twenty-eight thousand dollars. All Dave had to do was send him the money to pay for the equipment and its shipping to Ukraine.

Unfortunately for John, Dave was in debt way over his head and didn't have anywhere close that kind of money.

Then he then received a call from his wife who told him that Casey had been in contact with her. It appeared that John's investments in Nigeria weren't panning out and she was pressuring his wife for money too.

In addition, the German Embassy was continuing to stall him on the twenty grand they owed. He was placing calls to the Consulate General every day and was constantly assured that the money had been wired from Bonn. However, it had yet to arrive.

Todd was also starting to run short of cash to the point of being unable to pay the rent on his own apartment and began pressuring Dave to pay him back the money he had invested in The Kowboy. The bar's problems had become seemingly insurmountable and he no longer cared about doubling his money. He was simply wanted out and would satisfied if he could just break even.

Desperate, Dave went to Valerie and somehow convinced her to write him a check for another thirteen thousand dollars. He told her it was so he could buy the bull from John and have it shipped to Kyiv. After that, he said it was for an air-conditioning unit for the bar. Despite the fact that he kept changing his story, she wrote him a check anyway and was now into The Kowboy Dance Hall & Saloon for close to forty grand.

The strain of running the bar compounded by the fact that he had been sober for a week was beginning to wear on Dave. He placed a call to John and told him he needed him back earlier than expected. Unfortunately, since Dave was running short on cash, he couldn't pay for John's airplane ticket. As a result, John was forced to come up with the money out of his own pocket and pay full price for a one-way airfare to Kyiv.

It was as if everyone was having a run of bad luck, yet desperately hoping against hope that everything would work out. Still, Rhett couldn't figure out while everyone seemed to be short of cash, it appeared they were all spending it quite freely.

Meanwhile, Dave was still being pressured by Salom to turn over the operations of the restaurant to Tatiana's husband. It didn't seem to matter that he knew absolutely nothing about Tex-Mex cuisine. Consequently, it was beginning to look like the bill of fare at the cantina was going to be *Cowboyskie Borsch.*

III

Rootin', Tootin' Pardners

Everyone turned their heads when Dave and Rhett strolled into the American Chamber of Commerce wearing cowboy hats.

As they looked for seats in the back of the auditorium.one lady leaned over to another and whispered, "Are those guys for real?"

"Yes." Her friend laughed. "And it's rumored that they're doing very well."

The meeting had already started and the subject on this particular evening was about the Mafia and the issue of bribes. "Most reputable companies operating in Kyiv do not pay bribes to do business," the speaker said, "and technically, it's against U.S. law."

Dave leaned over to Rhett, "That's a bunch of bullshit. I can see two people sitting up there right now that I know for a fact have paid bribes."

One of the Commercial Officers with the American Consul walked by and slipped something into Rhett's hands. "You're famous," he whispered.

It was a fax about a news story that ran in an American newspaper. The headline read, *FOREIGN INVESTMENT COMES SLOWLY AS UKRAINE EMERGES, FAST AND LOOSE.* It had four paragraphs that were of particular interest to Rhett:

One foreign businessman who recently opened a restaurant in Kyiv covered his bets by taking in a Moscow crime syndicate as a partner and then paying a rival outfit for protection.

Rhett Avery, a 47-year-old former ad executive from Oklahoma, has another approach. He takes the Wild West metaphor literally. He and a passel of American "pardners" have opened Kyiv's first Cowboy bar. He dresses the part, from the black Resistol cowboy hat down to the Nocona boots.

"The cowboy image seems to work here. They respect us. We're not men in suits." Avery said.

Rhett leaned over to show the article to Dave. "You lucky son of a bitch! My name is mentioned in the paragraph right after the one about some fool who hired a Moscow crime syndicate and paying a rival Mafia for protection. Now I'm going to be the one who goes down in history as that idiot." Dave laughed.

—

The next day, Rhett saw another fax that contained an article in the *Chicago Tribune*:

LETTER FROM KYIV

U.S. entrepreneurs are out to turn Kyiv into the cowboy Capital of the East, Tribune correspondent Tom Hundley finds.

Rootin', tootin' pardners

KYIV - They looked like they stepped out of a Louis L'Amour novel, three hombres in black hat, black suits and black boots, heading up Kyiv's main street with the slightly bow-legged gait that comes from too long in the saddle or too many John Wayne movies.

These gents mean business, American-style business in the Wild East of Ukraine.

Rhett Avery, 47, an Oklahoma City advertising executive turned Peace Corps volunteer-turned entrepreneur, Western hat by Resistol, boots by Nocona.

John Hamilton, 52, a Texan who recently sold out his share of a successful nightclub in Oxnard, Calif., and headed East. Hat and boots of uncertain pedigree.

Igor Gunia, 19, a greenhorn from Kyiv, but learning fast. His hat is a Resistol hand me down from Avery. Still saving up for that first pair of real cowboy boots.

"Crazy cowboys," think the locals. Crazy like an armadillo, say the Americans.

"What's the one thing about America that appeals to everyone!" asks Avery, striking his best Marlboro pose. *"Cowboys, of course."*

So Avery, who first came to Ukraine on a Peace Corps project in 1992, planted the seed with Dave Seigal, a California real estate developer seeking business opportunities in Kyiv. The seed finally blossomed in one of the most improbable business ventures this side of the Dnieper: a cowboy bar in the heart of the Ukrainian capital.

It's called, plain and simple, The Kowboy Bar, and looks like the genuine article. At least it looks like the genuine article when I first saw John Travolta playing an urban cowboy named Bud, and Debra Winger rode a mechanical bucking bull.

Hamilton, who manages the place, assures me that even in Texas I'd have to look far and wide to find a cowboy bar that measures up to Kyiv's.

The grand opening was last month. The mechanical bull, imported from Dallas, failed to clear customs in time, but that hardly mattered when actor Jack Palance, the original Ukrainian cowboy, showed up instead. He was in town for a Chernobyl benefit.

But the real star of this cowboy bar is a 19-year-old singer and guitar picker named Toby Smith.

Smith, from Odessa, Texas, played football at Permian High, which Texans understand to be the next best thing to playing for the Dallas Cowboys. He also studied classical piano for 12 years.

A few months ago, Smith was in Levelland, Texas, wondering what might be out there beyond South Plains Junior College, where he was enrolled in the school's commercial music program.

The answer came in the form of an Internet job posting that found its way onto the department's bulletin board. Some Kyiv cowboys were looking for a musician who could put together a country and western band.

"I'm your man." Smith replied, and was offered the job on the spot.

Kyiv is loaded with talented musicians, none of whom had heard of Merle Haggard or Garth Brooks until Smith arrived with a suitcase full of tapes.

He quickly found his drummer, guitarist, bass player and keyboard man. All of them conservatory musicians playing with local rock bands.

Finding a fiddler was harder. "I auditioned about 15 fiddle players before I found the one I liked," said Smith. His name is Dimitri and in real life he is a violinist with one of Kyiv's major orchestras.

Smith doesn't speak Russian. The band members don't speak English. Their common language is music, and after four months of playing together, they sound like they tumbled out of a Nashville recording studio.

It's too early to tell if Kyiv's Kowboy Bar will be a commercial success. But doing business in this country is definitely not for city slickers, which pleases Avery.

"I reckon this is the last place on earth where I can truly be a cowboy." he says. I sure can't go back to Oklahoma and do it. Folks there all want to be New Yorkers."

Tom Hundley is the Tribune's Eastern Europe correspondent based in Warsaw.

The article was great publicity and even more importantly, the Mafia was not mentioned. It was picked up by the AP wire service and ran in papers throughout the United States.

IV

Banty Roosters

When John arrived back on the scene, Rhett found him sitting at the end of the bar. Casey's brief love affair with Kiev had reached its conclusion and she had chosen to remain home in California.

John motioned to him. "Rhett, come over here. I want to show you something."

Opening his briefcase, John pulled out a photograph. "Here's the mechanical bull I bought in the States. It came with papers and everything, confirming that it came from Gilley's and was the one ridden by Debra Winger in Urban Cowboy."

"So, when's it going to be shipped?" Rhett asked.

"As soon as Dave comes up with the money."

"That makes sense, but when's that going to be?"

"I guess when the bar starts making money."

John was shaking his head as he turned to Rhett, "I just hope he doesn't screw up like he did in the states."

"What do you mean?"

"His daughter is a friend of my daughter. That's how I met Dave in the first place."

"Dave has a daughter?"

"Yeah, from a previous marriage. He doesn't admit it. I didn't know until she came in and asked me how her father's business was doing in Kyiv."

"What did you tell her?"

"I didn't have to tell her anything. She knows how her dad does business. She said that she hoped he didn't screw up in Kyiv, like he had done twice in America."

"He screwed up in America?"

"Yeah. According to her, before he came to Kyiv, he had gone bankrupt twice, once in Minnesota and the last time in California. He had to leave the states, because he was in trouble over workman's comp or something. It was one of the reasons he's over here."

It wasn't exactly how Dave had been portrayed in the Wall Street Journal, but then again, it was becoming evident that Dave had a habit of misrepresenting a lot of things.

Rhett was beginning to wonder if that mechanical bull would ever find its way to Kyiv and The Kowboy Dance Hall and Saloon.

"So, how have things been going at the club?" John asked.

"Pretty normal so far. The crowds have been okay, but not anything like they were in the beginning. The restaurant still needs to be built, Salom wants his bookkeeper's husband to take over the restaurant and the place still doesn't have a phone. To make matters worse, these damn Mafia stories are beginning to circulate all over the place. It's not helping things."

"And how's Dave been acting? Is he drinking?"

"Not as far as I know. But the main point is, if we can't shake all these stories and put them behind us, the American community won't come here in the numbers they used to. Besides, the Embassy can still put us off limits. You need to have a come to Jesus conversation with Dave."

"Don't worry, I will. What have you been doing?" John asked

"I spend most of my time working at the office during the day and here at night, but I really can't keep working both day and night."

"Don't worry, we'll get it all back on track again," John was attempting to reassure him, but Rhett didn't particularly feel all that reassured.

"On the positive side, I found a lead on a supply of excellent vodka. It's called Ancient Kyiv and it makes Stolichnaya look like horse piss. I know someone who works at the distillery and has connections with its director. She told me she can get us all that we need."

"Well, let's get it then."

"It's only a matter of cash, and Dave's credit is pretty much shot."

"Listen, Rhett, I'm counting on you to help me out. So, what's happening with Toby?"

"As far as I know, he's out of here in a few weeks. Did you hear about the CNN fiasco?"

"Boy, is that kid stupid." John laughed. "I tried to tell him but the little peckerwood just

wouldn't listen."

"Well, Dave moved him back into his old place after that little stunt with CNN."

—

Still, Toby didn't know when to back off. Dave had made him a star and, by God, that's how he wanted to be treated. When he showed up for the evening's show, he walked up to Dave and boldly announced, "I'm moving back in over at John's"

"No, you're not," Dave replied.

"I've got to have a place where I can call my folks.'

"That's your problem. You've already run up a three-thousand-dollar phone bill. Do you want to pay it?"

That's when Toby thought he would give Dave an ultimatum. "Then I won't play tonight."

"So what! You think I need you that bad? Listen, I could put a howling dog in front of that band and they could make him sound good."

"Well, I'm moving in with John and that's that!" Toby snapped back.

Once again, Toby bit the hand that fed him not realizing that Dave had the power to kick him out in the street without a pot to piss in. And that's precisely what Dave did. He fired him on the spot, exactly the way he hired him. "Pack your things and get out. You're on your own."

Toby was suddenly taken aback. He hadn't counted on being left homeless smack dab in the middle of Eastern Europe.

Still, Toby thought he had one last trump card to play, because a few hours later he came strutting into the bar. John saw him first and he was holding one of those bar bats. He simply sat back, closed his eyes and waited for it to happen.

Toby stood at the end of the bar and laid his bat over the counter, acting like a banty rooster, making all those chicken-necking moves that a rooster does. Then he glared in Dave's direction. It turned out to be a bad move on Toby's part, because if he thought he could intimidate Dave into backing down, he was wrong.

Dave took one look at the bat and then at the nineteen-year-old kid. "Did you bring that bat in this bar to use on me? Am I supposed to be scared?" His voice began to rise, until everyone in the bar could hear him.

"Why, you little punk! Come on!" Dave screamed. "Pick up that bat and try to use it, if you think you're man enough! Go ahead, pick it up! I'll take that bat and shove it so far up your ass, you'll look like a fucking popsicle!"

No one knew what Toby expected Dave to say, but that for damned sure wasn't it. He was visibly shaken by Dave's outburst. After all, he was a boy trying to play a man's game and his bluff had just been called.

"Now get the hell out of my bar and take that bat with you! Go pack your shit and get out of my apartment too! You've got twenty-four hours before I send Salom and his boys to kick down that door and throw your sorry ass out in the street!"

Toby didn't say a word. He simply picked up his bat and quietly left.

—

When Rhett arrived, he saw Dave on stage performing in his whiskey voice and loving every minute of it. As he had so bluntly pointed out to Toby, "they could make a howling dog sound good," and that's exactly what they were doing.

"What the hell is Dave doing up there" he asked. "Where's Toby?"

John explained to a dumbstruck Rhett what had transpired between Dave and Toby.

"So, now we have 'Howlin' Dave Seigal' as our headliner. What's going to happen next?"

"You did know Dave's going back to the states next week."

"What?" Rhett couldn't believe his ears. "He's leaving again?"

"Yep!"

Great, just great — and with Kiev Day only a week away. One of the biggest holiday weekends of the year." Rhett shook his head in disgust, walked out of the bar to one of the kiosks and ordered a shot of vodka.

—

It wasn't until the following night that Toby dared to show his face. He quietly walked back into the bar and asked John if he could have a word with him.

John quickly took Toby aside. "I tried to warn you kid, but you wouldn't listen."

"I know." Toby looked like he was on the verge of tears. "Look, I know I was out of line, but I really need a place to stay. My plane doesn't leave for two weeks and I don't have any place to go. Could you talk to Dave . . . Please?" Toby was finally getting a taste of humble pie.

John took pity on him. After all, he was only a kid. "Look, just go back to the apartment and don't let Dave see you come back in this bar tonight. I'll talk to him. We'll get something straightened out. Come by tomorrow and we'll talk about it."

"Okay. I would really appreciate it." A bit of that original humility had returned to his voice. Toby left as quietly as he had come in.

Although Dave had his fill of Toby's antics, John appealed to him to give the kid another chance. He persisted until he convinced Dave that Kyiv Day weekend was too important not to have Toby playing.

Eventually, Dave acquiesced. "Okay, okay. Toby can play until his plane leaves, but I don't want to see his piece-of-shit face in this bar unless he's on stage playing music. As long as he keeps his mouth shut, you can do with him whatever you want."

V

Kiosks & Currency Exchanges

A hard currency is issued by a nation that is considered politically and economically stable. Unfortunately, when Ukraine declared its independence from the Soviet Union and moved away from the ruble zone it had to create its own currency which would ultimately be called the Hryvnia.

A few months after the collapse of the Soviet Union, I traveled to Kyiv to discuss the possibilities of creating a cowboy-themed restaurant. So, I booked a flight to Kyiv to meet some man I had never met.

As I walked through customs at Boryspol Airport, I was met by Aleksander, who drove me to the studio of a designer by the name of Vasyl Lopata. As soon as we arrived, I was shown the original pen and ink drawings that would eventually be used for the new Ukrainian Hryvnia.

A few days later, Aleksander informed me that the Mafia had been monitoring our movements because they were the ones who actually owned the restaurant to be converted into a cowboy bar. Reluctantly, I passed on the deal, because after what I had learned in London a few years earlier, but that was another story. Nevertheless, the last thing I wanted to do was get involved with a Mafia in Eastern Europe.

Instead, I joined the Peace Corps as a business advisor and traveled back to Ukraine to pursue a lifelong dream of experiencing a world that lay beyond the narrowly defined borders of Oklahoma.

As for the Hryvnia, the government decided to delay its rollout until 1996 and issued an interim currency called Karbovanets, otherwise known as coupons, instead. What resulted was hyperinflation, where Karbovanets were losing their value so fast that people were literally throwing stacks of banknotes out of their windows in disgust. Consequently, Ukrainian currency was worthless outside of Ukraine.

—

Eventually, Dave finally got his money from the German Embassy. However, they paid him in German Deutsche Marks and not in American dollars. Dave wasn't too happy about it either, because he was trying to figure out how on earth he was going to spend those Marks when he got back to America.

As a result, he began by paying everyone off in German banknotes. Todd got his share of in Deutche Marks, but Dave didn't pay him near enough to cover the twenty-five grand that he had sunk into the bar. In fact, he convinced Todd to return some of the money, explaining that he needed it to pay John for the electric bull.

Rhett got his rent in Deutche Marks too. There must have been something about the face of Benjamin Franklin that people just trusted, because his landlady wanted dollars too.

Obmin is a word that expresses an action, *Valuta* is the agreed exchange value of a currency. As a result, there were Currency Exchanges all over Ukraine where one could exchange Ukrainian Karbovanets for hard currency, which was why Rhett went down to the currency exchange on the first floor of the LA Express, but he was too late. Dave had already cleaned them out of every last greenback they had. Not only that, Dave was going around to every *Obmin Valuta* in Kyiv trying to unload as many of these Deutsche Marks for dollars as fast he could.

———

The night before he was to depart for California, Dave was sitting with John and Rhett across the street from The Kowboy having dinner in the Lyon restaurant.

"I want to know," Dave asked, "who it is that's spreading all of these rumors around town about the bar and the Mafia?"

"Well, it sure as hell isn't me," Rhett answered. "I don't have the money to get out much."

"It's not me either," added John.

"It's probably that lying little prick Toby! He's been hanging out at the Arizona, shooting his mouth off to those damned Marines."

It never occurred to Dave that he had been the one who had been bragging about his "roof" all over Kyiv.

John appeared to be supportive of Dave's position too. "That little shit has a big mouth. You can't trust him or believe a thing he says. We'll just use him until Kyiv Day. After that, we'll dump him "

"I can't stand a liar. I may exaggerate a lot, but I don't tell lies." Then Dave looked around the restaurant. "You know, the Mafia's moved in on this place. It was open only a few weeks before they walked in one night and took over. That's why the food and service is so bad here now."

Even though Dave liked to talk about the Mafia, he refused to recognize that he was in a dangerously similar situation. Nevertheless, there was one thing he had failed to realize, and that was if Salom really wanted him out of The Kowboy, there would be little or nothing that he could do about it.

—

Later that evening as Dave was packing for California, he began stuffing dollars along with the Deutsche Marks into the lining of his bag, ready to smuggle the cash past customs and back to America.

When Dave flew out of Boryspol, he was carrying all the money along with Valerie's check for thirteen grand with him. Once more, he was leaving John with nothing, expecting him to run the bar out of the daily profits.

—

Tuesday morning, a man walked into a California bank carrying a satchel. As he sat down across the table from the bank representative, he asked if it was possible to exchange eighteen thousand dollars' worth of Deutsche Marks for American dollars.

"It's highly unusual, sir." The woman replied. "We're a small branch and we're not really prepared to make such a large transaction involving a foreign currency. If you don't mind, may I ask why you have such a large amount of Deutche Marks?'

Dave explained that he operated a cowboy bar in Eastern Europe and had been unable to convert the currency into American dollars before he left Kyiv.

"Oh! You must know John and Casey then. Her daughter works here."

Really?" Dave replied. A thin bead of sweat began to form on his forehead.

"Casey's an old friend of mine and she told me all about that place. Listen, as I said, it *is* highly unusual, but seeing as you're a friend and all, let me talk to our manager. I'm sure we can do something." Then the woman excused herself.

Moments later, she returned. "Well, sir, I've asked our manager and . . ." When she looked up, she found that she was speaking to an empty chair. The woman looked around the bank, but Dave was nowhere to be found.

That same week, a man walked into Jeep dealership, laying down a pile of cash for a new Jeep Cherokee.

—

As soon as Dave was gone, Toby moved back in with John and immediately began telephoning the States. The way he saw it, Dave had screwed him over and he didn't care how much of a bill he ran up before he left. In a way, he was right. Dave had set a bad example and Toby was just following what he had learned from Dave.

Even though Toby was playing at the bar again, his heart was clearly not in it. One night after his first set he told John, "I'm taking off early and going to the Arizona to have dinner."

"Whoa right there, kid!" John snapped, "The night's not over and I don't care much if you're hungry or not. I convinced Dave not to throw your butt out into the streets. So, get back on that stage before I kick the shit out of you!"

In a rare moment of wisdom, Toby returned to the stage and picked up his guitar.

VI

When the Roof Collapses

The night before Kiev Day, Rhett found John, standing outside the bar along with the rest of the employees. He wasn't looking too happy either.

"Why is everybody standing out here?" Rhett asked.

"Salom's bookkeeper told Andrei that the bar would have to be closed again. According to her something still isn't in order and apparently, a tax inspector had arrived and ordered everyone out of the bar.

John was clearly upset and turned to Andrei "So, when will we be able to open?"

Andrei shrugged. "After the weekend, I am told,"

John grabbed Andrei by the collar, dragging him down inside to confront the tax inspector. "Andrei, you tell this son of a bitch that this bar is going to be open. If he wants to close us, then he's going to have to put a chain around the entire street."

Andrei translated and the man answered.

"What did he say?" John snapped.

Andrei looked back at John. "He said, 'No problem.'"

It appeared that Tatiana had been less than truthful and was still angling to get control of the restaurant for her husband. Nevertheless, it was obvious that someone wanted to see the bar closed, only John couldn't figure out just who.

—

The following morning, it was quiet in The Kowboy, because most of the Ukrainians were outside enjoying the carnival-like atmosphere as the entire city was making preparations for its Kyiv Day celebration. As a result, it was clear there wouldn't be much of a crowd until later in the day.

That's when John pulled Rhett aside. "You know I don't drink, but I do have one vice and after dealing with that bitch Tatiana, I could use something to relax. You wouldn't know where I could a joint, would you?"

"Really?" Rhett smiled and immediately the Chesire Cat came to mind. "As a matter of fact, I might just know someone who could help you out."

John followed Rhett up to *The Passazh* where he placed a call to Kyrill. Then he turned to John. "Kyrill won't be here with your joint for a couple of hours." So, while we're waiting, would you like to go out onto Kreschatik and watch the crowd at Maidan Nezolezhnosti? It would be a shame for you to miss what's happening during one of Kyiv's biggest holidays of the year."

There was already a huge crowd gathering in the center of the city. Music was blaring from a massive stage that had been erected. Every act who was anybody in Kyiv would be performing for the masses of people in the city's main square, with the possible exception of one — Toby Smith and his Kowboy Bar Band.

Obviously, the sight of two cowboys standing in the middle of the crowd drew a lot of attention. Especially, from an attractive young lady who looked intrigued by the way they were dressed. "Are you really cowboys?" She asked

Rhett answered her in Ukrainian. She seemed delighted to hear a cowboy address her in her native language. Russian was one thing, but not many foreigners spoke Ukrainian.

The young woman asked Rhett if he was Ukrainian by descent. "Nope, I'm just a cowboy who lives in Kyiv."

Then he introduced her to John. "Rhett, tell her that she is a very pretty young lady," She blushed and thanked him.

For a few moments, Rhett spoke to her in Ukrainian, then asked if she would speak in English so John could understand. It was obvious by the way he was looking at her that he was dying to get in on the conversation.

She charmed the socks off of John as she spoke in her polite English. As the strolled down Kreschatik Boulevard Rhett couldn't help but notice how she delighted him with her rosy cheeks, healthy young body and blonde hair. He was completely enamored.

"John, it's time to go back and meet Kyrill."

But John wasn't listening. "You go on ahead. I'll meet you at the bar."

Rhett found Kyrill waiting outside The Kowboy and asked him to wait so he could find John. However, John was nowhere to be found. Even with his cowboy hat, it was impossible to find him anywhere. In a crowd that had swollen to over ten thousand and growing by the moment, John had gone MIA. Rhett quickly came to the conclusion that John had wandered off the reservation following that pretty little filly around. So, he went back where Kyrill was waiting.

While it would have been more convenient to smoke the joint in the club, with all of the trouble that the club had experienced, getting busted in the bar was the last thing Rhett wanted to see or the bar needed.

Passing several members of the *Militsia*, Kyrill led him down *The Passazh* to a little park located around the back of a nearby apartment building where he lit up a joint

"When will Dave be returning to Kyiv?" Kyrill asked.

"I'm not really sure. Did he pay you for the painting?"

"No, not yet. I am not concerned though. If I let it bother me every time someone does not pay me," he said, "my life would be miserable. So, I simply prefer to enjoy life."

The way things were going, Rhett hoped he wasn't going to have to wait too long.

Since Dave had persuaded Kyrill to take out half the amount in trade, Rhett asked if he had taken advantage of it yet. He hadn't.

"I'll wait until Dave is up on his feet. In the meantime, I can pay for my own drinks."

Unlike everyone else who Dave owed money, Kyrill was an artist and cool about the whole affair. He had a lot of experience getting stiffed by "businessmen." Neither was he blind. He knew that Dave was having problems with the Mafia.

As the pot began to have its effect, all those unpleasant little feelings of paranoia returned. To top it off, in essence Ukraine was still a police state and since it was a holiday, there were a lot more *Militsia* in the center of the city.

Kyrill took one look at him and knew. "Don't worry, relax. Enjoy the *kife*"

"I know," Rhett laughed. "However, just because I'm paranoid it don't mean they're not watching."

Kyrill smiled and put out the joint. "Come, let us go and try to find John."

When they returned to the bar there was still no sign of John.

"I'm sorry, Kyrill." Rhett apologized. The last time I saw him, he was totally enamored with some young girl and I don't know where he could be."

Kyrill just gave Rhett that Cheshire smile of his. "Ah, spring. *Ces't la vie*."

———

Eventually, John did return and as evening approached, Salom's security guards entered the saloon. A heavyset one said something to Lena who turned to John. "He wants me to inform you that they have not been paid."

"Okay, so ask him who pays them."

Lena translated. "He said he doesn't know. It is a problem between Salom and his chief."

"So what's he saying, Salom hasn't paid him?"

"He says there will be no security for you this weekend."

"Well, tell him I'll just go ahead and pay him."

Lena kept translating. "He says he's sorry, but it is an issue for Salom to settle."

John was beginning to get angry. "Well, let's call Salom then."

With no phone in the bar, Lena left to go up on *The Passazh* to place a call to Salom. When she returned, she told John she had gotten no reply from any of the numbers he had given her. Apparently, when Salom did not want to be found, he was conveniently impossible to locate.

John was livid. Once again, it was obvious that someone wanted to see the bar closed.

Rhett and Todd had walked up and been listening to the conversation. "What are we going to do without security?" Todd asked.

Rhett looked at Todd and then back at John. "What's with all this bullshit? Call Yuri Nikotenko. He and his wife told us if we had any problems, to contact —"

"I'm not too sure," Todd interrupted. "It would mean that we would be bucking Salom's authority, and Salom is Dave's partner. What's Dave going to say if —"

"Fuck Dave!" Rhett exclaimed. "He's not here Todd. John's the manager. As far as I'm concerned, it's his call."

Rhett turned back to John, but he was talking to the security again. However, nothing he said seemed to work. They were still refusing his offer to pay them directly. All they kept saying was it was a problem for Salom to handle with their director.

"Hey, John!" Rhett shouted, "To hell with these guys! So far, our security hasn't been worth a shit anyway! I say let's call Yuri and get some actual police down here. Remember what I said. They are the law and they have the legal right to do whatever's necessary. It's what I been telling Dave all along. But we have to hurry if we're going to get in contact with Yuri. It's getting late and it's a holiday."

John looked at Rhett, thought for a moment. Then he turned to Lena. "Call Yuri."

"Yesss!!!" Rhett Gave a quick fist bump. Finally, the bar would have some legal and, for once, decent security.

Unfortunately, his joy was short-lived. Lena came back with the word that Yuri had already left the office for the holiday and wouldn't be back until after the weekend.

"Shit! Shit, shit, shit, shit, shit . . . *shit!*" Rhett walked away, kicking at the air. It seemed like he couldn't win for losing. "So John, how do you want to play this?"

Looking at Rhett, John replied, "To hell with them. We'll open without Salom's damned security."

The security men were surprised by John's decision. As they left the bar, one of them turned to John. In broken English, he said, "You no have protection now."

"Fuck you!" John replied, giving him the finger. "I'm all the security that I need."

John could see that Lena was exhausted, drained and distraught. It showed in her face. "You've done enough already. Go Home. It's the holidays; you should be with your family. Andrei can be my interpreter."

She refused at first, but eventually John convinced her that everything would be okay. Reluctantly, she agreed and left.

John then walked over to Rhett. "Well, I guess you and I are it. We'll have to be the security tonight. Are you ready to back me?"

Rhett didn't particularly like the situation. He had done security before, when he'd been much younger. He also figured Todd wouldn't be much help either. He didn't like the odds if he and John had to face another group of hooligans, but he was equally as pissed off as John.

He thought about it for a minute, then answered, "I guess you got it then. Just let me go home and get a few things. I'll be back in an hour."

—

Rhett's adrenaline was pumping all the way to his apartment. As soon as he arrived, he went directly to a drawer and pulled out a box. He didn't know why he had decided to bring them to Ukraine, but at that moment he was glad he had. He pulled out a pair of spiked leather gauntlets. If nothing else, they looked imposing and he figured they could do some damage if he had to use them. He began to stuff everything in his backpack.

He walked over to the cabinet and pulled out the bottle of *Samahon*. Call it what you want, liquid courage or painkiller, he was going to have a few shots before he returned to the bar.

He put a pot of *borscht* on the stove and sat down to relax for a moment, getting himself in a mind-set for another long and unpredictable night.

Rhett quickly finished the *borscht* and a few more shots of *Samahon*. He took a few deep breaths, one final shot of *Samahon* and grabbing his gear was out the door determined to be ready for anything.

He didn't know where it was coming from, but he could almost swear he was hearing the theme from High Noon playing in his head as he rode the Metro to Kreshchatik Boulevard and The Kowboy Dance Hall & Saloon.

VII

The Ukrainian Cowboy

Todd watched as Rhett strapped on the series of spiked leather arm pieces. They wrapped from his knuckles and extended up the length of his forearm. If nothing else, the gauntlets looked imposing.

"Damn, Rhett!" Todd gasped. "What the hell are you going to use those for?"

John laughed when he saw them. "Well, I guess those ought to do the trick."

Todd just shook his head and walked away. He always thought Rhett was a little crazy.

Before long, people were pouring into The Kowboy. Some had been there before. Others were new faces. As the band began to play, John and Rhett moved through the crowd greeting customers and watching for troublemakers.

All in all, everyone seemed to be having a good time and everything appeared to be normal. Then again, it was still early.

Salom's bookkeeper sat behind the cash register, watching everything like a hawk.

Later in the evening, Rhett noticed John talking to the young girl he had met earlier that morning. He walked over to greet her. "So, how do you like the place?"

"Oh, it is so interesting. I never would have dreamed that such a place existed in Kyiv. I am having such a wonderful time. Thank you."

John still looked as enamored as he had been when he met her. "I'm going to show her around the place and I'll catch up with you later."

"Good, enjoy yourself." He gave John a wink and turned around to notice someone who looked familiar. It was the mysterious Ukrainian cowboy he had seen on the streets of Kyiv.

When the young man looked up and saw Rhett, a broad grin appeared on his face. As Rhett walked toward him the Ukrainian cowboy extended his arm to greet him with one of

those overhanded manly handclasps and introduced himself as Alexey.

"Preevyat, Kak Dila? (Hello, how are you doing). What do you think of the Kowboy Dance Hall & Saloon?"" The Ukrainian gave it a "two thumbs up." It appeared he had found the bar of his dreams and then he introduced his friend. "I want you to meet my friend Andrew."

"Doozhe Priemno (Very pleased)," Rhett greeted him.

His friend looked a bit surprised. "Oh, you speak Ukrainian?"

"Troxhkey (A little)."

"I see you."

"Yeah, I see you too." Rhett answered.

"No. I mean, I see you around Kyiv. You always walk with your cowboy hat. Everybody know you here. You real cowboy, no?"

"What do you think?"

"I think you real cowboy. My name Andrew."

"Yeah, I heard that. Pleased to meet you, Andrew. My name's Rhett."

"What?"

It was hard to hear with the music playing so loudly. "Rhett!" He repeated it a little louder.

"Oh, pleased to meet you." His hand reached upwards toward Rhett's hat.

"No, no, no." Rhett laughed as he quickly backed away. "Don't be touching the hat."

Noticing the gauntlets, he held up his hands and took a step backwards. "Oh, sorry. No problems. I want cowboy hat too. I mean, I want to buy cowboy hat."

"Well, wait a little while. I think we'll be selling them here soon."

"Like that." Andrew pointed at Rhett's hat, his finger waiving back and forth. It was apparent that he was having trouble standing.

"Well, probably not like this one, but —"

"No, I want cowboy hat like that. How much cost?"

"This one?" Rhett touched the brim of his hat. "About two hundred dollars."

"Ohhhh. I'm sorry. I'm little bit drunk."

"That's okay. Just have a good time, no problems. I have to go now." Rhett patted him on the shoulder. "See you later."

Andrew saluted and staggered out on the dance floor, dancing like a whirling dervish in front of the band. He was bouncing all over the place and could barely keep his balance

Rhett continued walking through the saloon as Andrew began.

John had been watching the encounter and walked over to Rhett. "What's his problem?"

"Oh, him? He's not a problem. He's just three sheets to the wind. Besides, it seems that all the Ukrainian men dance like that. What can I say, they're white guys"

"Well, he'd better not cause any problems. I'm not in the best of moods tonight and I don't feel like putting up with any shit."

"Don't worry about him. He's just having a good time He's harmless."

"Damn! These people sure do like to drink, don't they?"

"Yep! They surely do that John . . . they surely do. It's the culture. Now, you get back to that pretty little filly over there before she gets lonely." Rhett tossed back a drink.

It was around ten o'clock when the Chechens walked in the bar. As Salom walked past Rhett, he quickly took note of the gauntlets strapped on his arm. Speaking through Andrei, he asked to meet with John in the back office.

When they returned, Rhett could see Salom talking with his bookkeeper behind the bar. Then he headed for the door, with his henchmen following closely behind him.

Rhett turned to John. "So tell me, what was the deal with Salom?"

"Oh, he wanted to apologize for the problem with the security. He said he would get everything straightened out tomorrow.

Rhett rolled his eyes. "Yeah, right!"

Looking around, Rhett noticed the young girl John had been talking to was nowhere to be seen. "Hey, what happened to that pretty little prairie chicken?"

"I gave her some money for a cab home. Look, I knew I wasn't going to score with her, but I just enjoyed having her around. When she left, she told me this was the most fun she ever had in her life."

—

It was almost midnight when two men appeared behind the bar and began talking to Tatiana. Rhett didn't think much about it. He figured they were Salom's men. However, he noticed that one was carrying a satchel.

John noticed it too. He watched as Tatiana stuffed the night's proceeds into the bag. He walked over to Rhett as the man passed him walking out the door.

"Did you see that?" John asked.

"You mean the guy with the bag?"

"Yeah. He just walked behind the bar and Tatiana filled it with money,"

"You think we should do something about it?"

"What the hell can we do? He's already gone. Besides, Tatiana works for Salom and she's like a pit bull with lipstick guarding that cash register. Anyway, Salom's supposed to be Dave's partner. If these guys are going to steal from each other, that's their problem. We'll just wait — but I guarantee you, I'll know before the night's over.. If money's missing at the end of the evening, that's when I'll catch her"

Rhett figured John knew what he was doing. After all, he was the manager.

———

The bar closed at around three in the morning as everyone started to clean up and get ready to go home for the night.

Tatiana sat down with John and counted up the proceeds. She counted out the money and told him that the night's total came to thirteen hundred dollars. She looked at John and instructed Andrei to tell him that the bar had done well, but John wasn't buying it. He made her count the money again. It still came to thirteen hundred. Although she tried not to show it, she knew that John was on to her.

"Andrei, tell her that according to my calculations, the total should be closer to around five thousand." Tatiana tried to act shocked and confused.

John continued. "Tell her she can say whatever she wants, but I've owned bars for over twenty years and I know just how many kegs of beer and how much alcohol we've gone through tonight. She's short more three thousand dollars. Now, where is it?"

John refused to budge, and neither did Tatiana. John had called her on it and told Andrei to inform her that her services would no longer be needed. She acted insulted that John would have the audacity to accuse her of stealing and stormed out of the bar.

John looked at Rhett. "I'll place a call to Dave tonight and tell him about Tatiana. But as far as I'm concerned, she's fired."

John knew she was a thief, but he didn't know for sure if she was doing it for Salom or herself. It was just the way business was done when dealing with the Mafia. Everybody stole from everybody.

VIII

St. Andrews Descent

John was already in the bar counting the empty bottles and kegs by the time Rhett arrived the following morning. He knew his calculations were correct and was determined to have the proof by the time Dave returned in Kyiv. Besides, he and Rhett had both witnessed the bagman take the money out of the bar.

"John, I've got a friend I'd like you to meet." Rhett was hoping John was listening. "He's with the Ministry of Foreign Relations and would be a good man to know if you're planning on doing any business in Kiev. He can also fill you in on the truth about the Mafia here, the former KGB and the Ukrainian Secret Service."

John agreed to the meeting and Rhett led him to the historical district of Podil and the Foreign Ministry building where Volodomir was waiting to meet them.

"Volodomir, this is John. He's the manager of The Kowboy." Then Rhett turned to John. "I want you to talk to Volodomir. about the problems we've been having. He's a friend of mine. I trust him and you can be straight with him"

Volodomir was accompanied by his wife, a French businessman who was an associate of his wife and a German diplomat. Once the introductions were made the group began to walk down Andriyivskyy Spusk, one of the oldest streets in the city.

As they descended the steep cobblestone street, it all seemed very international to John, because there were alternate conversations in Ukrainian, Russian, French, German and English, depending on who was talking to whom.

"Rhett has asked me to meet with you and since we are friends, tell me what is it I can do for you." Volodomir asked.

John began with the trouble when Salom's security had walked out the night before. Volodomir asked who had hired them and John informed him that Dave's partners had been in charge of that responsibility.

Volodomir shrugged. "Then what was the problem?"

That's when the subject of the Chechens and the Mafia came up. "We've had been having trouble with both of Dave's partners, the Chechens and

Sergei," John confessed. "Dave told me everyone in Kyiv needs to have a roof to do business, but they keep interfering with the activities of the bar."

As soon as Volodomir heard the term roof, he stopped. "If I may, let me offer you some advice." Suddenly, he became serious and in a stern tone he turned and pointed directly at John. "Anytime the Mafia is involved, they will try to move in and take control. It doesn't matter to them if a business is successful or not. If you have a good business, they will always run it into the ground. They are greedy and don't understand that sometimes it is better to wait for their share of the profits. They always want all the money and take so much out of a company, it cannot survive for long. This is the main reason that businesses come and go in Kyiv on a daily basis."

Then Volodomir turned and continued walking down the street, but he was far from finished. "I want to make it very clear that any business openly involved with the Mafia is asking for trouble. It will eventually come under the scrutiny of the police and our government security service. And no matter what anyone tells you, they are the law." He was echoing exactly what Rhett had been telling John. "They have the legal power to close any business if they choose do so . . . for any reason."

"But Dave told me his roof is a very powerful group with contacts high up in the government." Then John repeated Dave's assertion that the former KGB was nothing more than a Mafia group itself and a weak one at that.

Volodomir scoffed at the notion. "This may be true, but almost everyone in Ukraine will tell you they are connected with government officials. More times than not, this isn't true. It is simply a way of cheating naïve foreigners out of money. In any event, the Mafia are not businessmen; they are criminals. Besides, this is Ukraine now, not the Soviet Union, we now have our own security services. Never forget this point."

"Well, I'm just the manager." John answered. "It's Dave's business, but I appreciate you taking the time to talk to me."

"Rhett and I have been friends ever since he arrived in Ukraine," Volodomir added. "As a favor to him, I will make some phone calls to my friends in the SBU. They are our main government security agency. They will provide you with the security you need and you won't have to worry about dealing with the Mafia." Then he looked straight at John and re-emphasized his words. "No matter what anyone tells you, they are the law."

As they continued walking down Andriyivskyy Spusk, they came to a little side street where they ran into the head of the American Chamber of Commerce. Seeing the cowboys, he walked over to greet the group. "So, hey there cowboys. How's the bar going? Oh, by the way Rhett. I met with an artist friend of yours from Oklahoma City named Christine."

"Boy, it sure is a small world, ain't it? How did you meet her?"

"She was visiting with my mother in law in Chicago and asked me how you were doing."

Volodomir laughed. "Everybody knows about Ukraine's cowboy. He is famous here."

"*Samahon* anyone?" Rhett pulled out a small flask from his duster. When everyone saw what he was holding, they all broke into laughter.

"What do you say Volodomir? Shell we have a toast?"

Volodomir turned to John. "Ukrainian's very famous for tour *Samahon*. Do you know what it is?"

"Rhett's already introduced us." John laughed.

Somebody produced some cups and Rhett poured a round for everyone.

"I usually don't drink," John said, "but I'll have one just this once."

Speaking in Ukrainian, Rhett made a toast to success, the future of Ukraine and its economic reform.

Volodomir smiled at him and told him well done. *"Molodetz, Rhett . . . Molodetz."*

They had only walked down about a third of the street when John turned to Rhett. "I don't have time for this. I'm not a good tourist, my feet are killing me and I hate crowds. Anyway, I have a lot of things to do and need to get back to the bar."

Unfortunately for John, they were in the middle of a crowd of thousands.

"Okay, but it's going to take a little while to get us out of this," Rhett told him. "Give me a minute and I'll show you back to the bar. But first, I have to tell Volodomir and make arrangements to meet up with him later."

Rhett turned to Volodomir and explained that he had to help John make his way back to the bar.

Volodomir seemed disappointed. "It is a pity. I had planned for us all to have lunch together at the Arizona Barbeque. I also wanted to talk more with John about your problems with the Mafia"

"I'm sorry," Rhett replied, "but John has a lot of work to do. I'll catch up with you later and we can talk about it"

Rhett moved quickly down the steeply inclined street, followed by John, who was complaining about his feet all the way down. "Damn you Rhett, and your walking everywhere! I don't know how I'm going to do it, but I swear I'm going to get even with you for doing this to me. Somewhere, sometime, I'm going to pay you back for this."

Rhett couldn't help but laugh as they descended Andriyivskyy. When they reached the bottom, John suddenly stopped. "That's it! I've had enough! I'm not walking one step further! Get me a damn cab to take me back to the bar!"

———

Later that afternoon, over dinner at the Arizona Barbeque, Volodomir turned to Rhett. "So, tell me, what John said about the bar . . . is it true?" Reluctantly, Rhett had to admit that it was.

"Well, I hope that he listened to what I told him. I told you before that Dave was a fool to have the Chechen Mafia as partners. I only hope that he changes his way of doing business. He is asking for a disaster. And Rhett, be careful — watch yourself."

"Thanks. Don't worry, I will."

Then Volodomir dropped the subject.

After the dinner, everyone said their good-byes and with a final warning from Volodomir, Rhett left and returned to the bar. He only hoped that John had been smart enough to listen to Volodomir's advice.

———

When he walked into the saloon, Rhett was surprised to see Tatiana sitting behind the cash register. Glaring at her as he passed by, he walked straight to the back room and knocked on the door. When Lena opened it, he could see John with Salom and several of his henchmen.

"Is there anything you need me to do?" Rhett asked.

"Just watch the bar and I'll be with you as soon as I finish with Salom."

Rhett waited for the meeting to end and about a half hour later, John walked up to him. "Thanks for showing up when you did. It was beginning to get a bit tense in there. Salom asked me if you were my backup."

"What did you tell him?"

"Damn straight! I told him that you were here to watch my back and that you were very good at it." He laughed.

Rhett then looked at Tatiana "What's that thieving bitch doing sitting behind the bar? I thought you fired her last night."

"I know. I did," he answered, "but Salom brought her back and insisted that she be here tonight. There wasn't really much I could do about it."

"Well, you know exactly what she's going to do. She's going to steal more money!"

"I know. We'll just have to keep an eye on her and see what happens. After all, Salom is supposed to be Dave's partner. So, if Salom says she stays . . . she stays. He also wants me to turn the restaurant over to her husband, too. As far as I'm concerned, it's all between Dave and Salom now."

—

The night was as crowded as the night before. People packed the place and the dancing troupe wowed them again.

As usual, there was a bevy of beautiful Ukrainian ladies wondering who they would have to screw in order to be rescued from their post-Soviet dystopian nightmare. It was either that or getting trafficked to the brothels of the Middle East or somewhere even worse.

Once again, the bar had no security — John and Rhett were on their own.

As they kept moving, looking for signs of trouble, here wasn't any except for Tatiana. She was still behind the bar skimming money and after John's meeting, it was obvious that she was doing it for Salom.

As Rhett passed John and Andrei, he noticed them talking to a group of Ukrainians by the door. John stopped him. "Rhett, this gentleman wants to know if you know how to use those," pointing to the gauntlets.

"What do you think?" Andrei translated. The men broke into laughter, telling him in Ukrainian *"Molodetz"* (Well done)."

"Do you know who this gentleman is?" John asked.

"Nope! No idea."

"He's the sheriff of Kyiv."

Rhett shook his hand. *"Ochin Pryatna Posna Komitsa"* (Very pleased to meet you)."

The sheriff and he laughed even harder. He leaned over and said something to Andrei. "The gentleman would like to know how you would like it if he made you a deputy sheriff of Kyiv."

"Can he do that?" Rhett asked.

"Certainly. He's the sheriff and said he will give you a badge for a souvenir."

Rhett looked at the sheriff. "Then tell him I'm not looking for a souvenir. If he wants to make me a deputy, then I want to be a real deputy with full powers. If he's serious, then so am I."

Andrei translated. The sheriff grinned and nodded his approval.

Rhett then looked at John. "I'm not kidding. I'm as serious as a heart attack. I'm ready to rack some ass." John laughed too and patted him on the back.

Then Rhett turned around and continued to work his way through the crowd.

Everything was kept down to a dull roar and eventually the evening ended without an incident.

—

Once more, John found himself confronted with Tatiana, but it was no use. Even though they went around and around over the evening's take, the difference was this time she was more confidant. Salom had brought her back and it was becoming evident that whatever John had to say about the matter was irrelevant. She had been given a license to steal and almost had a dismissive attitude toward him.

Just as Volodomir had warned him, it made no difference to Salom that the bar was in debt. John was only given enough cash to replenish the stock on a day-by-day basis. The only thing he could do was wait and hope that when Dave returned, he would straighten out the mess he created. Meanwhile, few if any employees were getting paid.

All that mattered was, every night Salom could line his pockets with anywhere from two to three grand. For that amount of money, Dave was paying quite a premium for Salom's partnership and protection. The sad truth of the matter was, it was The Kowboy that needed to have protection from Salom and his Mafia, more than anyone else in Kiev. For a man who hadn't put any money in the bar, it was turning out to be quite a lucrative partnership for Salom.

IX

The Cat & the Mouse

Walking down Dimitrova Street on his way to Republikansky Metro station, Rhett was on his way from the office to The Kowboy when he noticed a black car pulling up slowly behind him.

He walked a few paces before he turned around. That's when he saw Rudy's security chief, Alexei, grinning from ear to ear, his gold front tooth sparkling.

Rhett turned to greet him. *"Priviet."*

"Gde poyiditey (Where you going)?" Alexei asked.

"Doe Kovboi (To The Kowboy)."

Alexei pointed to his driver's seat indicating he was offering to give him a ride, something he had never done before. But he had always been friendly and Rhett was getting tired of walking everywhere feet. So, as long as Alexei was offering — Why not?" He got into the car.

They tried to converse with each other, but everything was basically limited to small talk. Alexei spoke less English than Rhett spoke Ukrainian.

When Alexei asked how everything was going at the bar Rhett answered, *"Ne pohano* (Not bad),"

Then the conversation turned to the Mafia. Although Rhett couldn't catch every word, he could understand that Alexei wanted to know if he was aware of the big problem between the Mafias and the businesses in Kyiv.

Rhett began thinking about that first afternoon in the office, when Dave was bragging to Alexei about having the biggest, baddest Mafia in Kiev as his "roof."

He was also thinking about Volodomir's advice to John when Alexei's car made a turn that wasn't in the direction of the bar. He said something about taking Rhett to his firm to meet his director. Alexei assured him it wasn't far and it wouldn't take long.

Rhett already knew it was the former KGB that had set up Alexei's security service and that it most likely still had close ties with Ukraine's new government security service.

Rhett looked at him. "*Chomu* beni (Why not)?" There wasn't really much he could do about it anyway.

And with that, the car sped off in the direction where Rhett had never been before. It was farther than he thought and seemed to take forever, but eventually Alexei pulled through a pair of large gates of a compound and into a courtyard in front a brick building.

Armed uniformed men with large Dobermans guarded the entryway. Rhett knew the property rates in Kyiv were sky high. So, it was obvious the company was either very wealthy, very well connected . . . or both.

He also doubted seriously that he had brought to this place just for grins. Alexei wanted something more than just the pleasure of his company.

He wondered what John or Dave would think about this interesting little side trip if it had been one of them.

Alexei led him into the building and said something to the guard at the front desk then signaled Rhett to follow him.

Alexei took him to the second floor and it was obvious whoever owned the place knew the importance of good office space. As he walked down a long corridor, he noticed the expensive deco-style lighting fixtures. The walls were covered with a new deep violet velour and black metallic wallpaper that was popular with the nouveau-riche business class. The doors were painted in a glossy black enamel. As Rhett looked into the side offices, he could see that even by Soviet standards, the place was immaculate and elegant.

Alexei led him to a reception area where a secretary was sitting and said something to her, then opened a door to an inner office.

He motioned for Rhett to sit down on the sofa, excused himself, then left. As he looked at the surroundings, everything had the unmistakable feel of old-style Soviet mentality. Rhett sat wondering what would happen next. He didn't have to wait long.

When Alexei reappeared, he was accompanied by a with a younger man with a stocky build dressed in a tailored black pinstriped business suit. Alexei introduced him as Mikhail, his director. One could easily tell by the way he dressed, by the way he carried himself this was a very important man.

Rhett greeted him in Ukrainian. He returned the greeting in English. "Pleased to meet you, and it is okay to address me in English."

His tone was polite and cordial. "What do you think of our offices? Would you like a tour?"

"Of course," Rhett answered. "I've been very impressed by everything I've seen so far."

Mikhail seemed pleased by the compliment. "You will have to forgive me. Our equipment and furniture have yet to be delivered."

"Still, it's very impressive. In fact, I wouldn't mind working here myself." Mikhail looked at Alexei and translated. They both laughed.

"How long have you been in Kyiv? What has brought you here?"

Rhett told him. He had nothing to hide.

"I am curious. Tell me, what is your involvement with The Kowboy?" Mikhail was taking over where Alexei left off.

"I'm the director of public relations." Rhett was hoping that with everything that was happening at the bar the irony of that statement wasn't too obvious.

"You do know, the Mafia is a big problem in Kyiv." It was becoming apparent there was nothing Rhett could tell him about Dave's involvement that he didn't already know.

For the next hour, Mikhail remained vague, talking in generalities. Then he posed a hypothetical question to Rhett. "What would you think the government authorities would do if they found that a bar had connections with the Mafia? Do you know how much disdain they have for the Mafia and what they are doing to our country?"

"I absolutely agree with you. The Mafia is a big problem. I know it's been giving all of Eastern Europe a bad reputation."

Mikhail liked his answer. Then he asked point-blank, "What will you do when the government comes and takes away your business and you lose all your money?"

Rhett thought for a moment. Then he smiled. "I have no idea. It's not my business and I certainly wouldn't risk my money in it."

Mikhail and Alexei both laughed.

Then Mikhail patted Rhett on the shoulder. "You seem to be an honest man. I think I like you."

It felt like a scene straight out of a James Bond movie. It was a classic game of cat and mouse and Rhett had no delusions as to who the mouse was. It was, he thought . . . pretty cool. Rhett was beginning to like him too.

If nothing else, he thought Mikhail was asking a lot better questions than that reporter from the *Chicago Tribune*.

After a couple of hours, the director looked at his watch. "I am very sorry, but I have an important meeting to attend and I must leave. I have enjoyed our conversation and am very pleased to have met you."

He extended his hand. Rhett shook it saying, "Me too — *Duzhe Pryyemno* (My pleasure)."

Mikhail smiled then excused himself and left.

And with that, Alexei took Rhett back down to the car and as they sped away, Rhett looked back at the compound, then at Alexei. "From what I heard that the former KGB was a very professional organization."

Alexei nodded.

"I've also heard during the Cold War you outsmarted the CIA many times."

He broke out into a broad grin and nodded again.

Eventually, the car came to a stop on the street behind *The Passazh.*

"*Duzhe dyakuyu* (Thank you very much)." Rhett said, shaking Alexei's hand. "*Vse Naykrashche. Doe pobachennya* (All the best, see you later)."

As he watched Alexei drive away, Rhett took a deep breath and sighed a bit of relief. He thought a moment, then laughed and said to himself "Okay, Rhett. Now you've been questioned by the former KGB. What's next on the agenda?"

As he turned, he saw John, Todd and Mike standing outside and walked toward them. "What are you guys doing out here? What the hell's going on now?"

John grimaced. "The tax inspectors are back and we all have to wait outside until they're finished taking inventory. Where have you been?"

"Funny you should ask. I've just spent the last afternoon being questioned by the former KGB."

Nobody was listening. Nobody was interested. Instead, they were preoccupied with the subject of how important a figure Salom was and how powerful his Mafia was in Kiev.

"I don't think Salom is as big as Dave thinks he is," Mike asserted, "but I heard he has a brother named Saiyid. He's supposed to be the heavy-duty one.

John nodded. "If Salom was as bad a Dave says he is, one would have thought there would have been a lot more retribution for that stabbing incident."

They agreed with Dave's assertion that the KGB was nothing but a bunch of pussies.

However, all of the talk on how big Salom was or wasn't was beginning to bore Rhett. He simply shook his head as he walked away over to a kiosk and ordered a hundred grams of vodka.

It was amazing to Rhett, with all the crap they were going through over licenses just to sell overpriced cheap American liquor, all he had to do was to walk a few feet across the damn street and get a shot of Stolichnaya for the equivalent of approximately thirty cents.

When he walked back, he noticed they had been joined by Salom. Until that moment, Rhett had always seen Salom with a smile on his face. He had always seemed friendly and jovial, but this time something seemed different. Salom appeared deep in thought. Something was clearly on his mind. His brow furrowed, he was frowning as he paced back and forth.

Rhett tugged at John. "Look over there. Have you ever seen Salom like that?"

John turned around. "What do you mean?"

"Well, just look at him. He's thinking about something. Do you know what it is?"

"No. What?"

"He's trying to figure out how he can get his hands in your pocket too."

"I'm not sure what the hell is going on," John replied. "But I do know this; there's still a lot of bad blood between Salom and Sergei."

"What do you mean?"

"According to Lena, Salom told Sergei that the stabbing incident was not forgotten and this thing between them was far from over."

Nonetheless, even though John was well aware of the problems that existed between Dave's two partners, he had little idea what Salom had in store for him.

X

The Chechen Sports Club

The smell of sweat, smoke and canvas permeated the air. The place was dark, musky and dank as John entered the expansive room. Andrei followed closely behind. He could make out the shadowed figures of men sparring. Some were kickboxing, while others were lifting weights or punching bags hanging from the ceiling. It reminded John of the gyms he used to visit when he was being groomed to be an enforcer for the Gotti crime family.

"Andrei, what the hell are we doing here?" John asked.

"Salom sent word that he wanted us to meet him here."

"What for?"

"I do not know. He just sent the car and I was instructed to bring you. That is all I know."

"Then where is Salom?"

Before Andrei could respond, a voice came from a darkened corner of the room. "John! *Privyit John. Dobro pozhalovat' v moy sportzal!* (Greetings. Welcome to my gym.)" John recognized the voice.

Out of the darkness stepped Salom, flanked by his men. All of them were wearing their long black business coats.

John greeted him, shaking everyone's hand. He then turned to Andrei. "Ask him, why we are here? I really need to be back at the bar. I've got a lot of work to do there."

Andrei translated and Salom responded.

"He apologizes, but he wanted to show you the gymnasium. It is one of his businesses and he understands that gymnasiums are popular in the United States. He said you look like a sportsman and was wondering if you could help him find a partner for this business."

"Well, I'm stocky, but I wouldn't exactly call myself a sportsman. But I'll tell you, what's popular in the States is the health and fitness clubs." John responded. "And they are quite different from your average sports gym."

Andrei interpreted, "Salom wants to know what is the difference."

"To begin with, they are a lot cleaner, the exercise equipment is more modern and health clubs aren't as dark as this place."

Andrei continued to translate. "He says he understands and has asked me, perhaps you could find him an investor to help make this gymnasium more acceptable by Western standards."

"Why does he need investors? He's a businessman. Isn't he capable of modernizing this place himself?"

"He says, yes, of course he is, but he needs a partner with Western know-how. Someone who can make this place as popular as The Kowboy."

"Tell him that when I go back to the States, I'll see what I can do."

"Spaceba John."

"He says, 'Thank you.'"

"Now, tell him I need to get back to the bar."

But Salom was far from finished. "He's asked me if you would like to see a match between his champion and an opponent. You remember his champion, do you not, John? He is one of Salom's bodyguards. I think it would be polite."

"Okay, but just for a moment. Explain to him I need to get back to the bar."

"He says certainly. He understands you are very busy and promises not keep you long."

Salom signaled to the two men standing in the ring and the match began.

His champion was sleek, quick and merciless. Within minutes, he had dispatched his opponent to the mat with a roundhouse kick to the side of the head. As the boxer struggled to get back to his feet, his nose bleeding, Salom's champion quickly came down with his elbow to the back of his neck. He went down again. It was obvious the match was over; the man would not be getting up. The bout had lasted less than a minute.

"Excellent. I'm very impressed," John replied. "Now if you will excuse me, like I said, I need to get back to work."

But Salom wasn't quite finished yet. He said something to Andrei, who was clearly taken aback.

"What did he say?" John asked.

"He has asked me to ask you if perhaps you would not care to spar with his champion. It will be a friendly match, just for sport."

John looked at Andrei and then to Salom, who was looking back at him with a crocodile smile. It was evident that he was being set up. It was a show of force. A challenge that John knew he would not be allowed to refuse.

Salom's champion was leaning on the ropes smiling down at John.

John looked at the kickboxer. He looked back at Salom. He thought for a moment, then quickly responded. "Sure, why not! But just a friendly sparring match. And after that, I've got to get back to the bar."

Andrei was clearly nervous when he responded for Salom. "He says certainly, but of course."

Compared to Salom's kickboxer, John looked portly. But like Yuri, he was as solid as a bull. He climbed into the ring and was offered gloves.

"That won't be necessary," John replied. "It's only a friendly little sparring match."

Andrei translated as Salom nodded. His smile broadened to a grin.

The others in the gym dropped whatever they were doing and gathered around the ring to see what was about to happen.

John planted his feet solidly on the mat and braced himself. The kickboxer bounced up and down lithely, stretching his neck, his head going from side to side as he brought his gloves repeatedly together. Then he moved in on John.

But before the kickboxer could lay a hand on him, John slammed his fist squarely in the middle of his opponent's face, cold-cocking him. The boxer's head snapped back as he fell backwards, landing flat on his back in the middle of the mat. He never knew what hit him. He lay there . . . out cold.

Salom's eyes widened and his jaw dropped.

"Okay, that's it!" John quickly said as he climbed out of the ring. "Thanks for the workout. I've gotta go now."

Andrei couldn't believe his eyes either. John had knocked out Salom's champion so quickly that those who were watching barely saw it happen. The gym fell completely silent.

"John," Andrei interjected, "I'm not sure, but I don't think it is very polite to have knocked out Salom's champion with such brutality."

"Really?" John replied. "What the fuck do you think he was going to do to me? Huh? Now, let's get out of here. I got work to do."

The midday sun lit up the inside of the gym as John walked out the door. He was followed by Andrei, who kept looking back at the motionless figure still lying on the mat.

XI

Lone Wolf

Toby was finishing his final week before returning to the States. Ironically, he was onstage singing Clint Black's *A Bad Goodbye.*

John and Rhett were working the crowd when Rhett noticed Volodomir and Olga sitting at the bar. Walking over, he greeted them in Ukrainian. *"Privyit moi druzi. Yak spravee?* (Hello my friends. How are you?)"

"After our conversation, I curious about how things were going here and Olga was in the mood for some Tex-Mex food. So, I told her why not come to The Kowboy and try your Mexican restaurant." Volodomir replied.

Rhett apologized. "I'm sorry, the kitchen isn't up and operating yet. Let me get you a couple of drinks."

When the drinks arrived, the bartender asked for money. "It's on the house." Rhett told her. However, she refused to hand over the drinks saying someone would have to pay.

Rhett looked over at Tatiana. She sat behind the cash register with a smirk on her face. It was obvious she was letting him know who was really in charge. him to know who was really in charge.

334

Rhett looked at Volodomir and Olga who appeared somewhat surprised. Hastily, he pulled out a handful of *karbovenets*.

Volodomir thanked him saying, "It's okay. We will pay for our drinks."

"No, no, I won't hear of it." Rhett felt embarrassed and humiliated. "It's okay. There's just some confusion, that's all."

He looked around and saw John talking to someone at the door. Excusing himself and Rhett walked over. "John, can I talk to you a minute?"

"Can it wait a minute? I'm busy right now."

"Do what? No, I don't think it will wait!" Rhett snapped. "I just had smoke blown up my ass by Tatiana. When I tried to comp a couple of drinks for some very important people, I was told in front of them that I would have to pay."

"Just a minute. I'm busy right now. I'll get back with you."

By the time Rhett returned to the bar, it was too late, Volodomir and Olga had already left.

It was the final straw. He slammed some money down on the counter and ordered a drink. As far as he was concerned, he was off the clock.

———

The following day, John tried to reinstate his authority as he negotiated with Salom, through either Lena or Andrei. He didn't want Tatiana behind the cash register and he damn sure wasn't going to turn over the restaurant operations to her husband.

Unfortunately, John had become a mere ornament to convince the foreign community that the saloon was managed by Westerners. Other than that, he was irrelevant and little more than a figurehead.

Unaware of John's problems with Salom when Sergei walked to the saloon and began to complain about the way the bar was being run. He knew that the bar was attracting crowds and it must have been making something. It was more than John could take. He had finally reached the end of his rope and handed the keys to Sergei telling him to run the bar by himself and walked away.

Confused, Sergei turned to Lena. "*Shcho? Ne rozumiyu.* (What? I don't understand?)"

Moments later, the head of the American Chamber of Commerce walked in with his wife. Spotting John sitting alone at a table, they walked over and sat down. "So, tell me John. How's everything going at The Kowboy Dance Hall and Saloon?"

"Don't ask me," John replied. "It's not my bar anymore. The Chechens have taken it over."

Up until that moment, the bar had been able to maintain the illusion that stories about Mafia involvement were only rumors, but now John was telling the head of the American Chamber of Commerce that the stories were true.

"Are you absolutely certain of what you're saying?" he asked. "Are you sure it was the Chechen Mafia?"

John confirmed that it was.

"Well, if the Chechens have indeed taken over, perhaps it would be wise to pack your bags and leave Kyiv as quickly as possible.

It must have sounded like good advice to John, because he left to do just that.

—

No sooner had John left when Valerie and Todd arrived. Seeing the head of the Chamber of Commerce they asked him if he had seen John. He looked visibly shaken and when he told them what John had told them they were horrified. In effect, John had just telegraphed the news to the entire Western community.

Between them, Valerie and Todd had sunk over sixty grand into The Kowboy and this kind of publicity would definitely put the future of the bar in question and their investments at risk.

Valerie and Todd immediately walked over to Sergei and asked him what had happened. Sure enough, John had handed over the keys to him and left the saloon.

—

Moments later, Rhett arrived. When he saw Todd and Valerie talking to Sergei, he walked over and asked, "Where's John?"

Valerie looked at him. "Wait a minute. Just go over there and sit down. We'll get right back to you."

He had heard that phrase much too much lately. Nevertheless, he was just as curious as anybody. So, he sat down and waited.

Twenty minutes later, he was still waiting.

Eventually, Rhett got up from the barstool and went to see what was taking Valerie and Todd so long. Lena informed him they had already left. To Rhett, for too long everyone in this deal had acted as if they were what Ukrainians termed as *Poop Zemlie* — roughly translated, "the center of the universe," literally translated, "the belly button of the earth." He was sick and tired of dealing with all the egos.

As he walked out he was cursing every American he could think of who had been involved with The Kowboy Dance Hall & Saloon.

—

Later that evening, Rhett returned to The Kowboy and found a radically different bar. The place was almost empty, John was conspicuously absent, and a blues band had replaced Toby and the Kowboy Bar Band. Nevertheless, Tatiana was still sitting behind the cash register. He ordered a drink.

Spotting Andrei standing in a corner, Rhett walked over and joined him. "Have you seen John tonight?"

"I believe John has left to go back to America."

Clearly stunned, Rhett stared at him. "Gone to America? What do you mean he has left to go back to America?"

"He was here earlier, but he left. The last I saw of him, he was walking out with a bottle of champagne in one hand and some Ukrainian girl under his arm."

"But he doesn't speak Ukrainian."

Andrei smiled. "He had an interpreter under the other arm."

Rhett smiled as he tried to picture the situation. "I bet that made an interesting trio. And Toby?"

"He is gone too. He left alone. I think he ran out of women."

"What do you mean?"

Andrei was laughing. "If a smart man sleeps around, he never sleeps with women who work together."

"Great!" Rhett muttered to himself. "Just great!"

—

Rhett sat alone in his apartment, a half-empty bottle of vodka by his side, when the phone rang. He picked it up.

There was a moment of silence . . . then he heard Dave's voice. "Rhett . . . Rhett!" His voice sounded panicked.

"Yeah, Dave. So tell me, what in the hell is going on?"

"Sergei has taken over the bar. There's going to be a fucking war!"

"What?" He figured it was just Dave shooting his mouth off again. "What do you mean there's going to be a war?"

Dave sounded hysterical. "I can't stop it! It's out of my hands now! I've already talked with John. He and Toby are supposed to be on their way to the airport. Sergei was going to take them hostages. Lena and her husband are leaving the country for Poland. I don't want them caught in the middle of this! Whatever you do, don't go down to the bar. They're going to be taking hostages! You need to get out of Ukraine as soon as you can!"

"Hold on, Dave. I can't just up and leave. Settle down for a minute and just tell me what's going on."

"Sergei took the bar away from John. The head of the Chamber of Commerce and his wife were there when it happened. He told them that the Chechen Mafia had just taken over. That's when he had told John to get out of the country. Todd and Valerie were there right after it happened."

"Well, I heard that they were gone, but I would like to know how come John didn't call me if everything was so goddamned serious?"

Dave didn't answer the question.

"Wait, wait — hold on a minute. I was in the bar when Todd and Valerie were there and they just left without telling me anything. Do you mean to tell me they just left me without telling me any of this?"

"I don't know about that, but I've already called them and warned them, too."

"What assholes!" Rhett was furious. "And what do you mean, John told the head of the Chamber of Commerce the Chechen Mafia was taking over? Sergei has nothing to do with the Chechens. Doesn't John even know who is who?"

"Listen to me, don't go down to the office either. They know where it is and they might come for you there."

"Listen, you dickhead! I have a lot of things in that office. I can't just leave everything there."

"If you go down there, I can't be responsible for what happens."

"Dave, I'm not going to just sit here in my apartment and hide. I need to go down to the office and see what's happening."

"Okay, but if you go outside, don't wear your cowboy hat. Don't wear anything that can link you with The Kowboy. Everybody knows who you are. I'm telling you, there's going to be a war!"

"Are you sure about that?"

"Sergei wanted the bar! Now he can have it! I don't want it! All they'll do is run it in the ground. Then he'll see I was right. Everyone will see I was right. Let him have it!"

"Dave, all I've ever heard out of Sergei is that he just wanted the bar to run like a normal business. He told that to John and Casey in front of me. Hell, Todd was even there."

"That's not according to what John told me. He said Sergei came and took the keys away from him."

"Bullshit! John gave him the keys. John's been part of your problem. He doesn't understand the language and he never knew what was going on. All I've seen him do for the past week is buy beer from the kiosks. The last thing I heard from one of the interpreters is they saw him leaving with a bottle of champagne under one arm and a young girl under the other."

"I don't want to talk about John right now. You just do whatever it is that you think you need to do. I'm just telling you to watch your ass."

"Okay. But I've been here for over three years and I've managed to hang onto it so far. Besides, they would be stupid to do anything to me. Too many people know me."

"I've got to go now. Just watch yourself. Bye." With that, Dave hung up. Rhett just sat there, trying to take it all in. "Fuck me!"

Dave had gone absolutely nuts and Rhett had figure out what he was going to do next. He picked up the bottle and poured another drink.

A t that moment Rhett was exactly as Salom described him, *Odeenokie Volk* — The Lone Wolf.

XII

Adios Ukraïna

The following morning, Rhett was still sitting in the chair. Two empty bottles lay on the table next to him.

Big Bad John and Toby the Texas Troubadour had packed their bags, skipped town and flown to America. Crazy Dave Seigal was raving like a lunatic in California leaving Rhett on his own without so much as an Adios Kiss My Ass!

The issue facing him was whether or not to wear anything that would link him to the Kowboy Dance Hall & Saloon. The question was, would he be a man or a mouse.

Rhett thought for a moment then muttered to himself, "Dave's nuts!" He put on his cowboy hat and left the apartment.

He took the same route he always did, keeping his eyes open and trying not to be paranoid. Nevertheless, everybody looked suspicious, but then again, this was Eastern Europe.

When he arrived at Republikanskie Metro Station, he tried to be aware of anything unusual. But again, this was Kyiv. Everything was unusual.

Nothing out of the ordinary happened.as he walked the two blocks to the office. When he arrived, he looked around and quickly unlocked the door.

The first thing he noticed were the pages of faxes on the floor. Rhett ripped them from the fax machine and started to read them.

The faxes were from Dave's government contractors. They contained requests for invitations for three treasury officials scheduled to arrive in Kyiv the following week. Lena usually handled these details, but there was no way of knowing whether she and her husband had fled to Poland or not. Rhett only knew what Dave had told him.

He called Lena's apartment. There was no answer. He placed a call to Dave back in the States and got a recorded message.

"Dave, I'm at the office. So far, everything appears to be normal. I haven't been taken hostage yet and you've received a butt-load of faxes from your government clients. Call me back."

Rhett then placed a call to Valerie. "Val, did Dave call you?"

"Yeah, he called me last night babbling like a maniac." She sounded completely put out by Dave's antics. "He was telling me about plans to assassinate Sergei. He said he had been talking it over with Salom. He even told me it was scheduled to happen by a certain date. I recorded it all on my answering service."

"Have you talked to John?

"Yeah. He and Toby both flew the coup."

"So tell me, Val, how come when everything was coming down at the bar, you and Todd left me there without telling me what was happening?"

Valerie didn't have much better of an answer than Dave. "Todd and I didn't think there was any danger and if there was, we figured you could take care of yourself.

"Thanks, a whole hell of a lot, Val." Valerie seemed not to notice the irritated tone in Rhett's voice.

"Do you have keys to the office?" She asked.

"I'm already here."

"Will you wait there for us? Todd and I want to come by and have a look at all of Dave's papers."

"I'm not going anywhere."

Just then, Igor stuck his head through the door. "Is anything happening yet?"

"Nope, just sitting here holding on to my dick waiting to be taken hostage."

—

A few moments later, Sergei's accountant arrived. It was evident by his face that he was clearly nervous. He knew something was wrong, but he didn't know what it was.

He was speaking in Ukrainian, but he was talking so fast, that Rhett turned to Igor and asked him to translate what he was saying.

Kolya apologized. "*Vybachte* (Sorry)."

Rhett wanted information and didn't have time for small talk. "So, tell me. What's the situation between Sergei and Dave?"

"They are partners," he replied in English.

"Did Sergei take over the bar from John?"

"No, all Sergei want was that the bar be run like a business. There were no books. John was buying everything with cash. If the tax people came for an inspection, we would be in a lot of trouble. That all. Sergei tried to tell John, then John gave him the keys. Why John and Toby leave?"

"Igor, tell him Dave called and told everybody there was going to be a war, that we were all going to be taken hostage by Sergei."

The accountant looked stunned.

"I'm just curious." Rhett continued. "Who is Sergei? Is he involved with the Mafia? Personally, I don't care. I just want to get to the bottom of all of this."

Rhett was being honest with him, hoping he would be honest in return.

The accountant acted surprised by the question. "Sergei's a businessman."

"That's what I thought."

"Sure, Sergei know people from the Mafia. That's normal here. He might do them favors from time to time, but he is simply a businessman."

For the most part, Rhett believed him.

They were still talking when Sergei stuck his head through the door. He also looked concerned and wanted to know what was happening as much as anybody. As he walked in, Rhett held out his hands together and laughed. "Are you here to take me hostage?"

"Shto?" (What?)

Rhett asked Igor to repeat the question in Ukrainian.

"What are you talking about?" He seemed shocked that Rhett would even consider asking him such a question.

Once again, Dave was exaggerating, making more out of everything than was necessary. It seemed that ever since he had gone "cold turkey" his ranting and ravings had gotten worse, Rhett just hoped that those tirades didn't wind up getting someone hurt.

"Igor, tell Sergei that Dave called me last night and said he had taken over the bar and that Sergei was planning on taking us all hostages." Rhett held out his hands out again.

Sergei slapped his forehead. *"Blyad!"*

Rhett knew what that word meant and it wasn't good. Rhett leaned back in his chair. "I didn't think so."

Sergei picked up the phone and dialed Dave's number in California. He also got the recording. He kept repeating over and over "Dave, *eta* Sergei . . . Dave . . . Dave . . . *Eta* Sergei . . . Dave!"

But Dave wasn't there.

Sergei was in a state of panic. He should have been. Dave had already told Rhett over the phone that "Sergei is a dead man." Valerie had also told him about Dave's plans for Sergei and Rhett knew that Dave wanted him out of the bar. Still, Rhett said nothing about it to Sergei. He figured it would only make things worse than they already were.

"Where's John?" Sergei asked.

"On his way back to America."

Sergei to his accountant and whispered something then he left.

Rhett knew in Dave's state of mind if talked to Salom, he could start his "war" in Kyiv from the comfort of his California home.

Rhett and Igor were still talking with the accountant when Dave's driver Boris walked in. He appeared uncomfortable around the accountant and asked to talk in private. Rhett and Igor followed him down the hall to a vacant office.

"I drive John to the airport. He act very afraid and look all around."

"Yes, I know he's gone. And Toby too?"

"Yes, Toby."

"Do you know where Lena is? Has she gone to Poland?"

"No, I don't think so. Not yet. She and her husband stay with her mother, but I think they leave soon. This is very bad thing, what Dave has done."

"I know. What do you plan to do now? Has Dave paid you?"

"Yes, he pay me, but only for last month. I no want work for Dave unless he pay me first. Then I work. I no trust him anymore."

"*YA rozumiyu* (I understand)."

"You know, last time he no pay me, my wife not eat for two days."

"I heard. Igor told me. I'm sorry."

"I want you know, I have no problem with you. But I sorry, I cannot be your driver unless Dave pay me."

"I understand. What are you doing now?"

346

"I work like taxi driver, but I no like. It not steady work. I need to work. I have chance for other job, but I no like it. It is bad work, very dangerous."

"Working for Dave can be dangerous too."

Boris smiled. "I know."

Rhett couldn't blame him. With Dave, late pay or no pay had become the norm.

Dave had finally overextended himself, traveling back and forth and throwing his money around like he was some wealthy big shot. By now, it was obvious to a lot of people he was anything but.

"Listen Boris, I don't know when Dave can pay. He has left no money with me. He has not paid me either. If I had any money, I would pay you."

I know you honest man. I trust you."

"*Spasybi* (Thanks)."

"I sorry. I have to go now. But if you need driver, call me. I be glad to help."

"Just take care of yourself, Boris."

"Don't worry, I be OK. But you . . . you be careful."

"I'll be all right." Rhett smiled. "Remember, I'm a cowboy." But Boris wasn't smiling when he shook Rhett's hand and left.

It was beginning to dawn on Rhett just how Dave had been handling his business. Everything he paid for, he paid for in cash. He had been collecting payments for the rental properties in hard currency.

Every time Dave departed for America, he always seemed to be carrying money in the lining of his luggage. Apparently, he had been smuggling the cash back into America for a while. Once he arrived in the U.S., he wouldn't declare it at customs. That way, Dave could avoid paying taxes, not only in Ukraine, but the U.S. as well.

And when he couldn't get cash, he had the rent on the other properties paid by wire transfer to some offshore bank account elsewhere. Consequently, nobody ever really knew how much money Dave actually made. Everyone was kept in the dark except for Lena. She was the only one who would have any idea, but Rhett doubted seriously if she knew everything. It was simply the way Dave did business . . . fast and loose.

Unfortunately, with the free spending he had become so famous for, he eventually lost control of his finances — and it had finally come back to haunt him.

When Rhett and Igor went back to the office, the accountant was gone. Then the phone rang. It was Dave.

"What's going on? I just got your message,"

"Well, Sergei was just by here and he didn't take me hostage. But he's clearly freaked out about everything."

"He should be. He messed with the wrong people. He's started a 'war' and there's going to be a bloodbath. He's a dead man. He just doesn't know it yet. Once Salom finds out about this, he's finished. I can't help him. Let him have the bar." Dave repeated his earlier statement. "He'll only run it into the ground. Then everybody will see I was right."

It was so typical of Dave to disavow everything. He had been the only one talking about "wars" or people getting killed and it was beginning to look like he just might just get his wish.

"Okay, okay. Let's quit talking about 'wars' and saying people are dead men, Dave. I have a lot of faxes here from government contractors. Has Lena really left for Poland?"

"Yes, I told her that her life was in danger and to get herself and her family to Poland and not to come back until I tell her it's safe."

There was no doubt about it to Rhett. Dave had absolutely gone around the bend.

"Okay, fine. Next question. What do you want to do about all these faxes?" Rhett read them to him one by one. "Do you want me and Igor to handle them? If you do, you have to give me some instructions. I don't know anything about this side of your business, but I think if you tell me where to find everything, I can handle things from here."

Dave gave Rhett instructions on what to find in the computer, the telephone numbers of his American contractors in Kyiv and told him to handle it.

"All right, Dave, I'll handle this for you. But if I get you through all of this, you are going to owe me big-time."

"Thanks, Rhett, I really appreciate it. I won't forget this."

"Don't! Now, next —" but Dave had already hung up.

Rhett realized that most people would he was insane and in ordinary circumstances, they would be right, but ever since he had arrived in Ukraine, nothing had been ordinary. The truth of the matter was, at this point Rhett didn't have much of a choice. He had too much on the line and there was nothing left for him back in Oklahoma.

Besides, he still had an office with a computer, printer and a fax machine. From there, he could continue pursuing other projects and stay in communication with the outside world. In any event, if he tried working out of his apartment, he would surely go stir crazy. Plus, Dave had promised to pay for his apartment and an airplane ticket back to the States. The only way Rhett was going to get that was to try to help the son of a bitch out of the hole that he had dug for himself. In other words, he didn't have much of a choice.

As Rhett started going through the stacks of papers, he realized that everything connected to the bar was a mess. Nothing he came across even remotely resembled anything that made sense. It wasn't representative of the way Davd handled his business affairs. He could see how Dave had gotten himself in such a pickle. Nothing was in its place, because nothing had a place. Everything was a mess. It was as chaotic as what had been happening at the bar.

Suddenly, Valerie, Todd and Sergei came bursting into the office. Valerie pushed Rhet aside and started rifling through Dave's papers.

Todd was going through Dave's computer file where he found a blank loan agreement that Dave used to get more money for the bar. It was impossible to tell how many shares Dave had been selling in the bar or who else might have a claim of part ownership.

They were frantically rifling through everything like a pack of junkyard dogs.

Rhett saw no reason to stop them and put his boots up on the desk. "Y'all be my guest and good luck." He was simply content to sit back and watch. After all, they were investors and considering how much money they had given Dave, he couldn't help thinking that they should have been concerned much earlier.

As for Sergei, he was back on the phone calling Dave again. He was beginning to sound like an old Cheech and Chong routine. "Dave . . . Dave!" But Dave's not there.

After getting anything they thought might be important, including some offshore account numbers, they left carrying a stack of papers.

As they walked out the door, Rhett cautioned them. "You know, if Dave does come back and finds all of those papers missing, he's not going to be happy."

Valerie turned. "We're not worried about Dave at this particular moment."

"Nevertheless," Rhett replied, "I suggest that if either of you talk to Dave, it might be better if you don't tell him that you've raided his office. In his current state of mind, there's no telling what he would do. It's just a suggestion Val . . . just a suggestion."

———

Later that afternoon, Rhett returned to The Kowboy and ran into one of the U.S. Government Treasury advisors that Dave was servicing through his government contracts. As they passed each other on the stairs he seemed surprised. "Well, Rhett, I see you're still here and all right."

"Yep! As you can plainly see, I'm alive and well."

"Tell me, is there any truth to the story that the Chechen Mafia had John and Toby lined up against the wall with machine guns pointed at their backs?"

"What? Oh, that's a rich." Rhett laughed. In fact, that's the best story I've heard all day."

XIII

The Lone Realtor

With the speed of light, the stories were suddenly all over Kyiv.

Evey week an article addressing the Mafia rumors would appear in some publication. It seemed that every English-speaking publication wanted to know what the real story was concerning the dust up that happened behind the scenes at the now infamous Kowboy Dance Hall & Saloon.

Rhett was deluged with questions about whether or not the Mafia was in control of The Kowboy. He was even getting calls at his apartment. The press knew they were on to something and every day it became harder and harder to deny the rumors, primarily because they weren't rumors at all.

One morning, he picked up the phone, only to wince when he heard the voice of a reporter from the Eastern Economist wanting to know if the rumors about the Chechen Mafia taking over were true.

"Let me say this, I don't deny there's a lot happening, but this story is far from finished." Rhett answered. "If you will just bear with me, I guarantee you there will be a story that's worth printing. Right now, it's too early to say anything yet, but believe me, I think things are going to get a lot better. You have to trust me on this."

For the most part, Rhett combined a little truth combined with wishful thinking while avoiding any questions concerning the Mafia. Sometimes people bought it, other times not so much, because there had been too many rumors and incidents to ignore. To make matters worse, John and Toby's rapid departure from Kyiv had only added fuel to the fire.

Later in the day, Rhett received a call from another reporter with the Economic Review. She had gone to The Kowboy over the weekend and was told that it was now a Ukrainian bar and Dave wouldn't be coming back. Rhett assured her that he had been talking to Dave on a daily basis, that he would be returning to Kyiv in a couple of weeks and that he was aware there were a few problems.

"A few problems my ass!" Rhett slammed the receiver down. It was getting to the point that he grimaced every time the phone rang, because there was most likely a journalist on the other end.

If Rhett had thought the bullets were coming fast a few weeks earlier, it was nothing in comparison to what was happening now. As a result, he decided it was about time to put out a press release of his own. The way he figured it, he might as well get in on the fun. As soon as it was written, he faxed it to every publication in Kyiv

CNN

THE COWBOY NEWS NETWORK

PRESS RELEASE

For Immediate Release

Dateline: Kyiv

It has been reported that "Dangerous" Dave Seigal will be returning to Kyiv in the near future. He wants to dispel those ugly rumors surrounding the now infamous Kowboy Dance Hall and Saloon. He also was quoted as saying, "I want to help out my friends, who are taking bets at 50 to 1 odds concerning my hiatus from the bar. Everyone wants to know whether or not I am ever coming back. Therefore, I plan on returning in order to help them make a few bucks."

Eternally the Dark Horse, Mr. Seigal cited the even odds that were being placed on his ever opening a Kowvboyskie Bar in Kyiv in the first place. However, he did point out, in fact, it did open. But nobody said anything about it staying open.

His beleaguered and badly battered public relations advisor, Rhett Avery (sometimes referred to as Duck Holiday, and who was arguably the first cowboy in Kyiv) was overheard saying, "In terms of public relation's nightmares, the Tylenol poisonings were child's play compared to this!"

When asked if bets were now being taken on Mr. Seigal's chances for survival upon his return, Avery declined comment. He simply quoted Yogi Bera's legendary remark, "It ain't over 'til it's over."

—

In the meantime, it appeared that Dave was beginning to come to his senses. He was starting to think about his cushy real estate business and all those lucrative government contracts he was about to lose. It was obvious; Dave's ass was in the soup. Nevertheless, when it came to money, he wasn't about to let all those sweet business deals go that easily. In the meantime, the U.S. Treasury Department had gotten wind of the rumors and were beginning to ask questions too.

—

It wasn't long before Rhett with his faithful Ukrainian companion Igor were handling Dave's business more efficiently than he ever had. As a result, since Rhett was handling everything for him in Kyiv, Dave figured he could play the part of the righteously indignant businessman, wronged by all of those ugly, unfounded rumors. Dave fired back with a fax of his own stating he had "everything under control."

Rhett was amazed at how the U.S. Government had no problems doing business with companies that had only a Post Office box as an address. In the meantime, everyone was faxing everyone, trying to save their own asses. The only problem, as far as Rhett was concerned, while everyone was playing SOA over their fax machines back in the States, he was holding on to his very real flesh and blood one in Kyiv.

Nevertheless, as far as Rhett saw it, he was now in the real-estate business.

—

"Rhett?" It was Dave calling from the States.

"So, tell me what's going on now."

"I've just been talking with John."

"Really? I guess he made it back home all right then."

"Yeah. He's all right, but he's royally pissed about what came down in Kyiv."

"Can't say that I blame him."

"He told me he's already hired some mercenaries."

"Mercenaries — did you say mercenaries?"

"He said that he's chartered a private jet."

"What for?"

"They're going to fly under Soviet radar over Siberia and into Kyiv, hunt down Salom and assassinate him."

"What!" Rhett cracked up. "Has he been watching "Firefox" or something? Does he know how far Kyiv is from Siberia? Does he even know Salom's address? And I'm sure the customs officials at the airport might be a little a little suspicious when a bunch of mercenaries arrive carrying automatic weapons through the metal detectors." Rhett was beginning to wonder if John had returned to California as deluded as Dave.

As soon as Rhett hung up the phone, the landlord walked into the office and pulled up a chair. He could see Rudy had something on his mind.

"Hello Rudy, what's up?"

"Tell me, Rhett, is it true what I have been hearing about Dave and the bar?"

Rhett took a deep breath and braced himself. "Well, exactly what did you hear?"

"I heard that Dave has taken the Chechen Mafia as partners. Is he crazy? Does he know that the Chechens never take on partners? Did he borrow money from them?"

"Well, I don't really know for sure Rudy. Dave doesn't say too much about his financial dealings."

"Let me tell you this." Rudy leaned closer to him. "If you borrow a dollar from a Chechen, the meter is running and by the end of the day, you'll owe him a thousand dollars. That's the way they do business. Do you understand what I'm telling you?"

Rudy went on for the next half-hour telling Rhett of the dangers of being involved with the Chechen Mafia. Rhett completely agreed with him, just like he had agreed with Volodomir and the former KGB director. He sat silently cursing Dave as Rudy went on and on.

"Do you know what they say about the Chechens?" Rudy lifted up his little finger. "If you just nick them here, they will chop your whole arm off." He made a gesture of an ax chopping off his arm. "You tell that to Dave!"

"I agree with you 100%, Rudy. But it's hard to tell a whore she's in the wrong business when her pockets are full of money. Maybe you should talk to Dave when he gets back. Maybe he'll listen to you. I've tried to tell him, but he doesn't seem to listen to me."

Rudy got up and started out the door, talking all the way. "You're goddamned right I'm going to tell him! I'm going to California in a few weeks and you're damned right I'll call him!"

"Thanks a lot, I would appreciate it. Come back any time. Always a pleasure Rudy . . . always a pleasure."

Rudy looked back and nodded before slamming the door behind him.

—

Over the following days, government faxes kept coming concerning advisors who were being sent to Kyiv. One in particular Rhett remembered from a memorandum from the Treasury Department. With all that was happening, Rhett assumed that he was probably being sent to find out just what the hell was going on with Dave Seigal and his Kowboy bar.

Rhett was reading the fax when he looked up and saw Oleg, the Ukrainian who had floated a loan to Dave a few months earlier, standing in front of him.

"Where's Dave?" He asked.

As it turned out, Oleg had been talking to a friend of his in America, who had told him there was an article in *Newsweek* about a bar called The

Kowboy Dance Hall & Saloon. It mentioned that Dave was the American owner and that he was having problems with the Mafia.

Rhett closed his eyes and whispered, "It just can't get better than this,"

"What?"

"Never mind."

Rhett told Oleg that he would be talking to Dave and would find out for sure whether it was true or not.

They shook hands and as Oleg walked out of the office, Rhett couldn't help but think that Oleg was in a surprisingly good mood, for a man who had loaned Dave twenty grand.

At that point, Rhett figured he had heard enough for one day. He left the office and headed for The Kowboy Dance Hall & Saloon. He needed a drink.

XIV

Odessa, America

As soon as Rhett walked into the bar, he noticed that most of the Marlboro ashtrays were gone and the Camel ashtrays were in their place. He picked one up and hurled it to the floor, shattering it into a thousand pieces. "Goddamnit!"

It got everyone's attention.

He saw one of Salom's security men jumped up and quickly moving toward him. The two men confronted one another, standing face to face when a young woman stepped between them.

She motioned for the security man to sit down. "I am the manager. Can I help you?"

"Do you know who I am?"

"I recognize you from the painting." She pointed to The Kowboys in Kyiv painting on the wall.

"Do you know why I did this?"

"No, sir, I do not understand."

Rhett explained the problems surrounding the sponsors and the legacy of Dave's little wars.

"I am very sorry. No one told me. I will straighten out the problem."

Suddenly, Rhett felt like a jerk. She was new and had no idea about anything that had been happening at the bar. He turned and walked out the door.

———

Then it all hit the fan at once. Within a week's time, it seemed as if every publication was running something about The Kowboy, the Mafia, Dave Seigal, or Toby and John's unexpected departure.

It started with a left jab coming from, all places, the American Chamber of Commerce newsletter:

Happy Trails? Not quite. Rhett Avery says rumors of Mafia wars at the Kowboy Bar in the Passazh are untrue. Yes, singer Toby Smith and manager John Hamilton have left says Rhett, the ad and PR director. Yes, owner Dave Seigal has taken a sabbatical. However, rumors of machine guns and a hostile takeover are unfounded. The Ukrainian and American investors are now trying to put a management team together and get things back on track.

Then came the right cross from the *Eastern Economist*.

COWBOY BAR AMERICAN FOUNDERS GO HOME

KYIV — Two of the three Americans who recently established The Kowboy, a western-style saloon in the Passazh off Khreshchatyk, have a least temporarily returned to the US. Principle Dave Seigal left day-to-day operations in the hands of his Ukrainian business partner, and a 19-year old Ukrainian cowboy impersonator. The third American, Rhett Avery, a former Peace Corps volunteer, can still be seen in the bar in his signature black leather coat and cowboy hat. He said, that Seigal, who had no previous managerial experience, was experiencing operational difficulties and had decided to spend the summer in his native California. He departed just after the Chicago Tribune profiled his saloon keeping in the Wild East.

Yes, Toby had returned to Texas, but within a week, he was on the phone desperately trying to get back to Kyiv. He had finally seen for himself what everybody had been telling him for weeks. Back home he was a nobody and there wasn't much demand for some nineteen-year-old kid who had been playing country music in some unknown bar in Kyiv.

He was calling Andrei, Todd, Valerie anybody who would give him another chance to come back and play at The Kowboy Dance Hall & Saloon. However, no one wasn about to pay Toby's asking price to come back and Dave, for damn sure, couldn't care less if he ever saw him again.

Then Rhett got another call from Dave. He was furious. It seems that Toby had been shooting his mouth off, talking to the newspapers back in his home town of Odessa, Texas. As it turned out, he was giving them quite an earful too.

Of course, according to Dave, Toby was a "dead man." Dave was going to have Salom kill him, just like he was going to have Salom kill anyone and everyone who happened to piss him off. Dave faxed a copy of the article to Rhett.

Sure enough, there he was, leaning back with his guitar, sporting a brand-new cowboy hat and wearing a shit-eating grin. Toby the troubadour, Kyiv's Country music star prominently displayed on the front page of the *Odessa American*. And he wasn't being modest about it either.

MUSICIAN TWO-STEPS THROUGH UKRAINE

Odessan returns home after teaching Ukrainians about the Cowboy way

By Deanna Barrymore, Odessa American

Toby Smith knows when to hold 'em, and when to duck out when the game's gone bad.

The 19-year-old Odessa guitar picker who introduced such country and western tunes as "Friends in Low Places" in Ukraine's first cowboy bar is back in the States after a brush with some unsavory characters.

When he was ordered "not to leave" Kyiv by the Russian and Chechnyan underworld last week in lieu of a debt owed by his American promoter, Smith thought it was best to pack his bags.

But when he tried to slip out of town, Smith was followed to the airport by a gang of suits slinging cellular phones and wearing menacing looks.

"It was kind of a ransom deal," said Smith, wearing a "Fear Not" T-shirt. There was a genuine concern in the situation."

But for Smith, who managed to return in one piece, the showdown ain't over.

For the man who helped open The Cowboy Bar in February is picking up his chips and heading back next month to join his fans.

"There's a huge market for American music and nobody there to fill it, except for me," said the musician. "I am the market, and I've got it cornered."

Smith's story began as a boy with a love of Russia. "I've always wanted to go to Russia, always, always, always," he said.

In November, Smith was in Levelland College studying country music as South Plains Junior College when he noticed an Internet job posting tacked to a teacher's door.

Could an American cowboy come and teach some classical Kyiv musicians country music?

"I'm your man." Smith replied and got the job.

So began Smith's 7-month lesson in cultural exchange. Armed with a black Stetson, a Washburn guitar and a suitcase full of CD's, he offered his band "some Texas guidance" - in George Strait, Garth brooks and his all-time favorite, Bob Wills.

Smith, who played classical piano twelve years and sang at Permian High School, was surprised at Ukrainian talent - one musician learned to sing in a drawl, another played the best lead guitar he'd ever heard. He was even more amazed at the Ukrainian response to country music.

"I will never forget their reaction, they just went nuts," he said of his first audience. "They were jumpin' up and down and yellin' I almost wanted to stop the song and say, 'We just don't act that way during country music.'"

People tried to steal the Stetson off his head.

But it was while playing at The Cowboy Bar, decorated frontier fashion, that things got a little rough. On its first night, one man was stabbed and hit over the head with a bottle and five men beaten in a brawl.

Smith said The Cowboy's promoter, a California real-estate developer, needed a "roof"- a local investor who greased the wheels for business.

Enter the rough guys.

And since two roofs are better than one, make room for the Chechnyan connection. "So, when the Chechnyans came in, it started a little turf war." Smith said.

Only the promoter didn't pay his bills, Smith said, to him or the thugs. Smith's phone was cut off. His band wasn't paid.

The mechanical bucking bull ordered from Dallas never arrived.

And each night, at least $1,000 was plucked from the tills by the hoodlums.

When Smith finally asked his promoter to furnish a phone so he could talk to his sick father, he was told that he could easily be replaced.

"You could put a howlin' dog up there and people wouldn't know the difference." the promoter told him, before leaving Kyiv, a mountain of debt and a few death threats behind.

But Smith's experience hasn't dampened his enthusiasm.

A devout Baptist, he's also a missionary for country music.

"Every day I say 'I'm not George Strait,' but every day, I just can't wait to get back."

Smith plans to return July 4 for a solo tour, without hoodlum interference and under one "roof" solid enough to support his band: "The KGB."

With the secret service greasing the wheels, Smith said, "we won't be having any problems."

All Rhett could say when he finished reading the article was, "Ouch!" And finally, with Dave's imminent arrival, the *Kyiv Post* chimed in with:

COWBOY BAR DISPELS RUMORS

Kyiv — Dave Seigal has returned to Kyiv to dispel the rumors surrounding the Kowboy Saloon on the Passazh, according to his public relations advisor Rhett Avery. A slew of rumors concerning the bar's finances and status have been circulating since Seigal and the bar's singer Toby Smith left town unexpectedly a few weeks ago.

The stage had been set for the return of "Crazy" Dave Seigal.

XV

No Such Thing as Bad Press

The phone rang. "Hey, I'm still alive!" David Seigal had returned.

"That's good to hear," Rhett answered. "I thought you were supposed to be here yesterday."

"Yeah, well, Salom picked me up at the airport. We went to his lawyer's dacha to have a barbecue and work out some details. Listen, I want you to meet me outside of the Kreschatik Metro at about one o'clock."

Before Rhett could answer, Dave hung up.

———

When Rhett exited the Metro station, he saw Dave standing there looking like a tourist in a Hawaiian shirt. Gone was the cowboy hat. As soon as he saw Rhett still dressed like a cowboy he started laughing.

"So, hey there cowboy! How's everything going?" Dave asked patting him on the back.

"Are you kidding?"

"Don't worry about it. I've got it all covered."

"So, what happened to the thousands of dollars that Salom's been siphoning off the bar?" Rhett asked.

"No problem, it's safe and being held for me. I talked to Salom and know where all the money is and how much. I can get to it whenever I need it."

As they walked down Kreshchatik Boulevard, Dave started filling Rhett in on his new plans.

"I've decided to make peace with Sergei. I was at the bar last night and of course, the business has dropped of drastically. Just like I predicted it would. There wasn't any country music to draw in the crowds. The food that Tatiana and her husband have been trying to serve at the restaurant is that simple Ukrainian garbage. Nobody wants it. Sergei tried to make things work too, but instead he's played into my hands."

It appeared to Rhett that Dave was under the impression that all he needed to do was to show up then everything would be normal again. As a result, he was ready to make his triumphant return to Kyiv and The Kowboy Dance Hall & Saloon.

However, Dave now needed Sergei. He needed him to show everyone that he was simply a misunderstood legitimate businessman — that he had no ties with the Mafia.

Nevertheless, Rhett was aware that Sergei didn't know anything about Dave's attempt to squeeze him out of the bar or even have him murdered. As far as Sergei knew, Dave had always been a loyal friend and business partner.

Still, Rhett knew that Dave would eventually have other plans for Sergei.

"So, what's the deal with John and those mercenaries?" Rhett laughed. "Ain't seen hide nor hair of 'em."

Dave became serious. "Watch what you say about John. I don't want any problems with him. I saw him in California. Right now, everything seems to be normal between him and me. So, I don't want anything else to happen to piss him off again."

"Well, that's not my problem. After he ran out without telling me what was coming down, I don't feel I owe him a damn thing."

"I'm telling you, be careful. He can be a dangerous character. He's already been tried for murder at least once; maybe even twice. I'm not really sure. I think he was also involved with the CIA in Vietnam. I'm telling you, you don't want to piss him off."

"That's interesting. John told me that he had never been to Vietnam."

"Well, he was. I'm not really sure what he was doing there, but he was with some covert group over in Cambodia or something. He told me, but I can't think of the name. All I know is, he was involved in some serious shit in Asia."

"You mean Air America?"

"Yeah, that was it."

Rhett changed the subject to address all the publicity surrounding the bar. "Well, even though there's been a lot of bad press lately, everything that has been printed was based on speculation and rumors, with the possible exception of John's boner. So, if you play your cards right, you just might rise from the ashes one more time."

Rhett then brought up the issue about the money for his rent and an airplane ticket back to the states.

Dave winced. "I'm sorry, I wish I could tell you something, but I can't just now. I didn't bring a lot of money with me. Let me see how things are at the bar and I'll get back with you on that. If worse comes to worse, maybe I can have my wife wire you the money."

"But what about all that money that you said Salom was holding for you?"

"It's kinda complicated." Dave squirmed like a child would when they made up an excuse.

"Well, you better figure out something, dammit!"

"Meet me tomorrow at the office. We'll iron out the details on the money and you can fill me in on what's happening with the real estate business. Right now, I gotta go and meet up with Salom and his lawyer." And with that, Rhett watched as Dave disappeared down Kreshchatik Boulevard.

———

The next morning when he met with the Cowboy Bar Band, Dave wanted to know where their loyalties lay. He knew Toby had been calling them and had Toby's *Odessa American* newspaper article prominently displayed on the desk in front of him.

"I want you to know that I'm back here to stay. I've got everything I own tied up in that club," he told them. "It's my life. So I need your decision now. Are you working for me or not?"

Since Dave owned half of their equipment, the band really didn't have much of a choice. They went with Dave.

As soon as they were out the door, Rhett brought Dave up to speed on what was happening with his realty business and the fact that a representative from the U.S. Treasury Department would be arriving in a few days to investigate the rumors about the Mafia.

Dave still considered himself a player and if push came to shove, he was ready to play it out with Treasury Department to the very end.

"Yeah, I already know he's be coming and as far as I'm concerned, if they want to cancel my contract, they're welcome to do it. I hold the leases to all their apartments and I'll simply tell them to move all their advisors out of my apartments. To my way of thinking, it's going be extremely difficult to explain to Washington why their advisors have been evicted from their residences in Kyiv."

When Sergei's bookkeeper came walking into the office, he informed him that Sergei had sent him to clear up some points about setting up the books. Dave told him to go and talk to Salom's bookkeeper. However, when the bookkeeper couldn't understand why he should be working with Salom's bookkeeper, it didn't take long before Dave reverted to his old ways.

He flew into a rage. "Goddamnit! You just tell Serge I'm in control. I've got everything tied up in that bar. It's my life and, by God, I know what I'm doing! If Sergei or anyone else doesn't like the deal, they'll wind up floating dead in the Dnieper!"

Dave had been back less than two days and already he was threatening to whack anybody and everybody who dare question his authority.

The bookkeeper explained that he was merely trying to get some information for Sergei. He quickly dropped the subject and left.

Then as Dave began looking through his papers, he turned to Rhett and started yelling. "Damnit! Where are all my records? I can't find anything! Has anybody been going through my files?"

Valerie had not heeded Rhett's advice to return Dave's papers to the office. "Have you talked to Valerie yet?"

"What do you mean?"

"I mean she's got some of your papers."

"What!? How could you let her?"

"Listen, Dave, you had gone around the bend. As a result, Val, Todd and Sergei came in trying to find out what was going on at the bar."

"They were with Sergei!?"

"Yeah. John and Toby had just left town. Nobody knew who was in control at the bar. What did you expect them to do?"

"That cunt! How dare she —"

"Okay, okay. Just settle down there." Rhett interrupted. "I want you to listen to me. I've heard you say that this bar is your life. Well, you're not the only one. There's a lot of people involved here. I know for a fact that Todd and Val have put over fifty-grand in that bar and remember, it was Sergei's place to begin with."

"I don't care! Why didn't you stop them? Whose side are you on?"

"Now, wait up just a damn minute! Seems like you got a mighty short memory. Maybe you forgot when everyone turned tail and ran, I was the only one who stayed and tried to hold things together. And believe me, it wasn't easy either."

This time, the intensity was rising in Rhett's voice. "I stepped in and kept Kyiv Realty operating. It was me who dispelled the rumors. Not Val, not Todd, and for damned sure, not that fucking Salom. Nobody else — *nobody!*"

Rhett looking at Dave squarely into the eyes, fists clenched at his sides.

"Don't you go questioning me about my loyalties. Besides, these people are supposed to be your partners. So, if you got a problem with Val, then you give her a call."

"Okay, okay. I didn't mean to suggest —"

"Then don't!"

"What do you need?" Dave's voice, for once, sounded apologetic. "You need some money? Because I didn't come back with a whole lot —"

"Just see what you can do about getting me an airplane ticket and make sure you pay Igor the twenty bucks a week you promised when you hired him. You can afford that, can't you? It's not that much and he's been a good employee, one of the few loyal sons-a-bitches you got around here. Promise me that."

"I will." Dave replied. "And Rhett, I want you to know I appreciate everything you did for me and I won't forget it either."

"Just try not to screw things up now that you're back."

Dave picked up the phone and called Boris to pick up the treasury representative at the airport. Boris agreed, but only after Dave agreed to pay him in advance.

He then turned to Rhett. "Listen up, Rhett, I want you to go with Boris and meet the Treasury rep. I'm going to be busy with Salom. You tell him that I'll catch up with him later.

———

As the Treasury rep exited customs he looked around for Dave, but the only person standing there to greet him was a stranger in a black cowboy hat.

"Hello, I'm Rhett. Unfortunately, Dave has been detained and I've been sent to take you to your hotel."

Boris took his bags and followed Rhett to the car parked just outside of Boryspol Airport terminal.

The drive to Kiev was more than a little awkward as Rhett was peppered with questions about Dave, the Mafia and the Kowboy. However, Rhett had heard them all so many times before, it was like same song, second verse. Nevertheless, he was relieved to get the rep checked into the hotel, at which point, he made a beeline for the bar.

He passed Salom and his men on the stairs as they were leaving. As for Dave, he found him behind the bar. "Listen, Dave, you'd better be prepared when you talk to that guy from Treasury. He's already asking questions about the bar and the Mafia."

Dave didn't appear worried and dismissed the warning. "Rhett, I already told you. I've got 'em by the balls. If push comes to shove, they can move their advisors out of my apartments. Don't worry, I'll straighten out everything. Trust me, I've got it all covered."

—

The next day, one of the reporters from the *Economic Review* tracked Dave down. He wanted to do an interview about The Kowboy and the rumors surrounding it.

When the subject of Toby Smith came up, Dave told him, "Toby was nothing more than a psycho. When I hired him. It was after he had been discharged from the Air Force during his flight training for mentally instability."

Once more, Dave's mouth would turn out to be his undoing. The following week, when the article appeared it was evident that the publication had called the states to verify Dave's accusations.

COWBOY BAR MANAGEMENT CLAIMS ALL IS WELL, BUT FORMER EMPLOYEE CITES MAFIA & DEATH THREATS.

Despite Dave Seigal's attempts to quell rumors about Mafia intrusion at the Kowboy bar on Kyiv's Passazh former employees maintain the rumors were largely true and that one employee's life was threatened.

Seigal returned on Saturday, June 15, to find his once successful bar empty due to rumors of a Mafia takeover.

"I can absolutely guarantee no move was made by the Mafia in regard to me or my business." Seigal said in an interview. "The Mafia problem in Ukraine has been blown completely out of proportion. I have been doing business in Ukraine for five years, and I have never paid protection money to anyone. I have a lot of connections in the Kyiv city government, and if anyone did come in here demanding money, I would be able to make a phone call to the authorities and get it stopped."

When asked how the rumors got started. Seigal responded that "I left my American manager, John Hamilton, in charge. John experienced some managerial problems, and my Ukrainian partner, Serhiy, jumped in to sort things out." (Although Seigal did not know Serhiy's last name when first asked, he later said it was Kornievskiy.)

Seigal said the management problems had to do with having "proper systems in place to deal with the success we were having."

But former bandleader, Toby Smith, reached in his hometown of Odessa, Texas by Economic review, said that Seigal left Ukraine at the end of May, having appointed Hamilton to manage the bar in his absence. "On the weekend of the Kyiv days," Smith said, *"we had $6,000 in beer sales alone. But the bookkeeper, Tatiana, handed over $3,000. She's a Mafia girl. John fired her, and then they re-hired her."*

Hamilton, now in southern California, confirmed Smith's version. On Kyiv Day, "Tatiana handed over $1,200, saying that Sundays are always slow. But I knew we had gone through 10 kegs of beer and we should have had at least $4,800. I fired her because she stole from the bar. They brought her back in the next day."

On Thursday, May 30, Hamilton and Smith were on the next flight home.

"We were going to leave on June 6," Smith said, "but that Wednesday the Mafia basically said 'Do this, this and this, and don't leave the country.' They threatened to kill one of my translators. So we changed our tickets and left the next morning.

When asked if his life was threatened, the translator, Kyiv native Andrei Kutlahmetov, said "yes."

On the day that Tatiana was fired, Kutlahmetov explained, "they tried to take over the bar. Before he left the bar, Tatiana's husband said to me, 'You have two choices: either leave the bar or we'll give you a lesson for the rest of your life.'"

(Neither Kutlahmetov, Smith nor Hamilton knew Tatiana's last name or her husband's first name.)

However, while Smith uses the word "Mafia" liberally in describing Seigal's business partners, Kutlahmetov is not so certain. When asked if they were Mafia, he responded. "No, I cannot say this. Probably they have Mafia connections. None of them carry a gun. For me they are just businessmen, and this was a misunderstanding between Dave, John and Serhiy."

Asked if he fears for his life, Kutlahmetov said, "I'm a big boy. I've been in to Kowboy bar since then. Look, if someone is really going to kill you, they don't tell you about it first."

None of which answers the question of why Seigal was out of town in the first place. On Thursday evening, May 23, an Economic Review employee was told by a doorman, "Dave Seigal is in America and he's never coming back to Ukraine."

Seigal's explanation? "I was out of the country for two weeks. I went to check on purchasing air conditioning, an electronic bull, and to set up for the new Mexican restaurant we're going to open."

Neither Smith nor Hamilton were certain why Seigal left the country originally, but they speculated that he was in the middle of a turf war between a Russian gang, led by Kornievskiy, and a Chechen gang, led by one "Salom."

"Dave has a habit of leaving when things get sticky." Smith said. "I'd been there since November, and there have been critical times when he just leaves."

"Dave brought in the wrong roof," Hamilton explained. "Everybody in that country has protection. It doesn't matter if it's a bar, restaurant or a T-shirt kiosk. Serhiy and Dave were partners from the beginning, but then Dave just crossed over to the wrong side. Serhiy owns [Carambol], which I understand is closed now, too. When Dave brought in the Chechen people to protect him, that

was a mistake. He should have stuck with the people who run things on the Passazh."

Hamilton also said that "they had threatened Dave's secretary Lena. He had to send her back to Poland. Dave doesn't know if he owns that bar, or if Serhiy or Salom owns it."

The problem, according to Hamilton, was that the bar was doing very well when run by Americans, but "Serhiy didn't want to pay us American salaries."

While Seigal said Hamilton is a "good guy," he said that as far as Smith is concerned, "The club opened on May 5, and on May 18 Toby came and said he wanted to leave on June 6. After I invested a lot of money in him, paying for five months of rehearsals."

Seigal also said that Smith was discharged from the military for mental instability. Hamilton, Smith and Smith's high school principal denied the allegation.

Smith, in fact, plans to be back in Kyiv playing with his band next week. Even Seigal admits that Smith has a lot of fans in Kyiv.

"I hope he knows what he's doing." Hamilton said.

As to Kowboy bar's future, business has picked up a little since Seigal's return. However, on Thursday, June 20, at a well-promoted party that Seigal had predicted would bring in 400 customers, only about 20 were present at 10:00 p.m.

Seigal is optimistic: "Toby left, but the band has decided to stay. I'm going to bring another cowboy singer in. I have already signed a lease for a new Kowboy bar to be built in Warsaw. We also hope to create production and a market for Kowboy bar accessories in Ukraine."

As soon as Dave read the article, he hit the roof. He was absolutely livid by the time Rhett walked into the The Kowboy Dance Hall ^ Saloon. "Son of a bitch! We got ambushed by the Indians at Intel news."

"What are you talking about." Rhett asked as Dave handed him the article. had yet to see the article.

All in all, the article was one big "he-said-they-said," but for the most part it exposed everything that Rhett had desperately been trying to cover up.

There was on line that surprised Rhett though and that was the one that said Tony was planning to return to Kiev in week to play with "his" band.

As he read the article, Rhett tried to listen to what Dave was raving about.

"They sent in this sweet little girl named Tess to take some pictures. Then they sent some other guy to sit at the bar and shoot the shit with the bartenders. Then ess came back about an hour later almost crying and said they set me up. She told me that they were going to do a story slamming me, Sergei, Salom, Lena, Tatiana and anyone else associated with the bar. That's exactly what they did!"

Speechless, Rhett looked up for a moment.

I guess they figured you had already left town so they left your name out of the article. Their inside source for everything was that little prick, Toby!" Dave's face was getting purple with rage. "I don't know why, but John had a lot to say too. He backed up every fucking thing that Toby said in his story!"

Dave's raised his hands as he looked upward. It was as if he was asking God for an answer. "I don't know why. I have never said anything against John and was even quoted in that goddamned article as saying he was a good guy."

Rhett had nothing to say. He just saw all his efforts go down the shitter. He simply sat and listened quietly to Dave.

"I need to call an attorney. We're going to — we're going to sue all those sons-a-bitches for slander. I guaran-god-damn-tee you Rhett, things are going to get pretty interesting around here!"

Dave's eyes were darting back and forth like a madman. He was literally spitting in rage as he tried to figure out what he was going to do next. Then he started talking to himself. "There no such thing as bad press. I'll tell you what I'm going to do. Yeah, that's exactly what I'm going to do. As a thank-you to that little shit Toby, I'm going to have Salom have his boys deliver him a one-way ticket."

Rhett could feel himself going numb.

"Fuck that *Economic Review*! I'll have Salom pay them a visit too. No, that won't be necessary. It only has a hundred subscribers anyway and you can't buy it anywhere . . . lucky for those pissants. But I'll tell you one thing, Rhett. I'm going to sue the pants of those cocksuckers. They'll rue the day they ever fucked with Dave-by-God-Seigal! They're going to pay, I tell you! They're all going to pay! Everybody's going to pay!"

But Rhett couldn't hear him. He couldn't hear anything. His eyes just glazed over as he stared off into nothingness.

XVI

The Kowboy Strikes Back

After Dave's meltdown, Rhett thought that it might be better not to bring up the issue of money for a few days. Instead, he and Igor kept the office running during the days since Dave was usually occupied with Salom and seldom came to the office.

Then, one afternoon, Rhett caught Dave at the bar with no Salom in sight. Since he appeared to be in a good mood, Rhett figured it was as good time as any to bring up the subject. "So how about my plane ticket?" He asked.

"Look, Rhett, I know I promised you, but I talked to Kathy and thanks to this insane phone bill and some medical bills from Kathy's little heart problem, I'm broke."

"Your wife's got a heart problem?"

"Didn't I tell you?"

"There's a lot you don't tell me Dave. Anyway, isn't the bar making money? I've been here and it's been packed almost every night."

"I know . . . I know, but all that money is going to pay bills in order to restock the bar."

"What about all those thousands you said that Salom is keeping for you?"

"It's a long story, but I can't get at it right now."

"Well then, what about your real estate business that Igor and I've been handling for you?"

"It's possible. If can rent a couple of my empty apartments this week, I might be able to get you some money. But I wouldn't bet your horse on it."

"Okay, then. What about your credit cards? You've been charging everybody else's trips. Use one of those." Rhett was trying to remain calm.

"Sorry, but my credit cards all maxed out. Kathy's having to borrow some money from her friends to get over here."

"Jeezus H. Christ! With all that's going down here, why are you thinking about bringing her over here for? Wouldn't she be safer back in the States?"

"I talked to Kath yesterday and she had already loaded the car with as many of our personal belongings as could fit, because our town is in the mountains and it is surrounded by wildfires. She told me they were evacuating all the people from the town."

"Christ Almighty! Isn't there someplace she can stay in the States until this is all over? What about John and Casey?"

Not a good idea after everything went down like it did.

"Great! Just great!" Rhett muttered under his breath.

"Look, when I last talked to her, it was right before she got on the plane."

Rhett simply glared back at Dave.

"Listen, Rhett. I've been talking things over with Salom. He assured me the plans for the other bars are 'all ahead full.' So, if you'll just bear with me this once, we'll be so knee-deep in money it will make up for what I'm not paying you. You've got to believe me. I really do have it all under control this time and I'm not going to screw it up.'"

"Then make sure you don't!" Rhett yelled. Then he turned and walked out of the bar.

—

That afternoon, Kathy arrived at Boryspol Airport, but Dave had completely forgotten and wasn't there to meet her. Instead of meeting his wife, Dave was off again with Salom. Eventually, she took a taxi into Kyiv and waited for him until he returned to the bar.

Confused and upset by the time that he showed up, Dave tried to convince her that it was merely an oversight. "I'm really sorry, honey. I was working on some important deals with Salom and it had merely slipped my mind."

"What do you mean it slipped your mind? You left me stranded forty kilometers outside of Kyiv."

"I know Honey, but everything's been so crazy."

She was on the verge of tears, yet she wanted to believe in him. "You know that I supported your decision to build the bar. And I have backed you on everything you have ever tried even when they didn't work out."

"Darlin', you know I couldn't do this without you."

"Well, I certainly hope so. I quit my job and traveled halfway around the world to be with you."

"I understand Babe, and you don't know how much I've missed you. I'm here all alone and every night I think about you. Please forgive me just this one time."

Eventually she forgave him, but she was beginning to have her doubts about her husband. Instead, she began to take out her frustrations out on everyone else. She didn't trust anyone. As far as Kathy was concerned, everyone was out to screw her husband out of everything he had worked so hard for. After all, he was the reincarnation of Peter the Great.

However, she had never seen the other Dave. The one who lived by night in the hotspots of Kyiv. The Dave who stayed out drinking all night, whoring with his buddies. Nobody was going to tell her, either.

—

One evening, as she sat in the apartment talking with Valerie, she began to soften. After all, Valerie was another woman and she need someone to talk to. If she had any doubts about Dave, she could confide her doubts to Valerie. She needed someone to tell her that Dave was a good man.

"Valerie, have you heard anything about Dave messing around while he's been in Kiev?"

It wasn't a question that Valerie necessarily wanted to hear, nor one she wanted to answer truthfully. She had a lot of money riding on The Kowboy. It already had enough problems. And she didn't want to add any more to the situation.

"Look, I merely know Dave from a professional standpoint," Valerie replied. "As far as I know, I've never seen Dave out with another woman or heard of him screwing around."

As vague as that answer was, it was enough for Kathy. She really didn't want to press any harder than that. She had heard what she wanted to hear.

—

A few days later, Lena returned from Poland. As soon as she called Dave. He told her to gather Sergei and quickly call a press conference to answer the accusations that had appeared in the *Economic Review*. His back up against the wall and Dave wanted to play the role of the outraged businessman one more time. It had worked for him in the past and he had every reason to believe that he could make it work for him again. Besides, he was news. Everyone wanted to know what was really going on at the Kowboy Dance Hall & Saloon. It afforded him a stage where he could rant and rave, act righteously indignant, and try to bluff his way out of the situation he had created for himself.

He even had a lawyer present to give the appearance that he was operating within the law. Only the *Kiev Post* showed up for the conference. The other publications were either too busy or had become bored with the whole soap opera that was enveloping the bar. One week later, Dave's final response was published.

THE KOWBOY STRIKES BACK

Owners of the Kyiv bar, the Kowboy, Dave Seigal and Sergei Komienko said that Thursday, June 27, they are filing a libel lawsuit against IntelNews in connection with an Economic Review article stating that Komienko has links to the Mafia.

"They have a history of doing dirty business here - there are many organizations, government organizations that will not speak to them because they misquote," said Seigal. "They've had scandals before in their newspaper because of their reporting, and I think it's time they stop."

Saying he built the bar as an example of successful investment in Ukraine, Seigal said he would "scream from the top of the roof that everything is OK."

"I have full authority and control of this bar, I have 100 percent control of management. I built it, and Sergei is my partner." said Seigal. He said that as an American he could survive bad press, but that Koimienko was deeply upset by the slander.

"Accusations that I am linked with the Mafia are completely unfounded," said Komienko. "These allegations are quite serious because they can lead to problems with government structures.

IntelNews ran an article in its June 24 Economic Review magazine reporting that while management claimed all was well, former employees of the Kowboy cited Mafia and death threats in connection with recent operations. Former bar manager John Hamilton was quoted as saying that a bar bookkeeper stole money and after firing her, she was rehired. Former bandleader Toby Smith confirmed the story, adding that his translator's life was threatened by the Mafia.

Economic Review publisher Christine Demkowych said Friday that IntelNews had not yet been contacted by Seigal and that it stood by the story. "The article was well-researched," Demkowych said.

However, on Monday, Seigal said he and Komienko met with lawyers and plan to bring the action against IntelNews within a week.

Seigal denied all allegations made in the article, saying, "all this reporting came from Toby Smith, a nineteen-year-old kid hired to teach Ukrainians how to play cowboy music. He had no knowledge of the financial aspects and he had no knowledge of what was going on in this bar. He worked 15 days and quit."

Seigal also said Smith later contacted Komienko and asked to be rehired. Smith reportedly asked for $4,000 monthly salary, four trips home a year and paid room and board - terms, which were refused. Seigal said he invested a lot of money in Smith, who claimed "he was the only reason people came to the Kowboy."

Admitting Smith was popular with the ex-pat crowd, Seigal nonetheless said he intended to get people back to the bar. He announced that as part of an upcoming American Independence Day celebration The Kowboy would kick off a weekend of live music, starting July 3rd with the Oregon band Dead Moon, followed by nights of live blues, rock-a-billy and a Sunday jazz fest.

It was interesting to note that the two newspapers differed on Sergei's last name. But then again, Dave never could seem to get anybody's name right.

——

The article, along with the concert, brought ex-pat community back and a few days later, the band Dead Moon played before a full house. Since Perekhid Media was sponsoring the show, they kept track of the receipts at the door. Tatiana and Salom stayed away and Dave took in the money at the bar. For all intents and purposes, it looked like Dave was fully in control and that the Mafia rumors had been blown out of proportion. The

385

weekend went off without a hitch and everyone thought that The Kowboy Dance Hall & Saloon was back in business.

After the concert, things began to pick up again. The bar was packed almost every night, although most of the traffic was there to see how Dave, who was now being referred to as "Al Capone," was faring.

—

After the concert, things began to pick up again. The bar was packed almost every night, although most of the traffic was there to see how Dave, who was now being referred to as "Al Capone," was faring.

Unfortunately for Dave, Salom quickly moved Elena back behind the cash register and she began doing the same thing to Dave that she had done to John. Even though Dave tried to fire her, Salom kept bringing her back and eventually, Dave, like John, realized he had no choice in the matter.

Left with no other alternative, Dave began to man the cash register himself, cramming as much money in a bag as he could every night. The bar now had two thieves.

Within a week, Dave had socked away close to seven grand. He kept it in a bag that he carried with him everywhere he went.

However, Salom wasn't too pleased. As far as he saw it, Dave was now stealing the money that he had been stealing from Dave and he wanted his money back! Although Dave didn't realize it, he was setting things in motion that were beyond anyone's control, with the possible exception of Salom.

—

A few days later, when Igor walked into the Kowboy, he found Rhett sitting at the bar.

"So how is our little Napoleon?" he asked.

"Who gives a shit?"

"Rhett, I'm sorry to bother you, but could you borrow me some money? I haven't had anything to eat today."

"What?" Rhett was shocked. "Hasn't Dave been paying you?"

"No, not yet."

"Haven't you asked him for your salary? How long has this been going on? Don't you see him at the office?"

"I haven't seen him very much. He hasn't been coming to the office much, but when he does, he's always with Salom."

"That son-of-a-bitch!" Rhett reached into his pocket and pulled out what money he had and gave Igor half.

"I'm sorry to have bothered you, Rhett."

"Fuck that! You haven't been paid and you're hungry. I promise you, I'll get your money for you. Now go get something to eat."

Igor left as Rhett ordered another drink and waited for Dave to arrive.

About an hour later, Dave walked into the Kowboy. He was with Lena and accompanied by Salom and his men . . . but this time Rhett didn't care. He immediately got up from the bar and walked straight toward Dave.

"You sorry sack of shit! Why haven't you been paying Igor as you promised?"

Dave was obviously taken aback and tried to maintain his composure in front of Salom. "I didn't have any extra cash."

"Bullshit! Rhett pointes to the bag on Dave's shoulder. "What are you carrying around in that satchel? You Cocksucker! While you and this asshole keep robbing each other blind, that kid has no money to buy food,

"Settle down. You're causing a scene in front of Salom."

"So what? You going to have me floating in the Dnieper by morning?"

"Just relax. I'll take care of him tomorrow."

"You're goddamned right you'll take care of him tomorrow, or I'm going to kick the shit out of you!"

Salom was watching intently as Dave continued trying to calm Rhett down. "Look, we really don't want to be doing this in front of Salom."

"Oh yeah . . . so what?" Rhett's temper and the vodka were outweighing his good sense. "Do I look like I give a rat's ass?"

"Although Salom couldn't understand what was being said, he understood the tone in Rhett's voice. *Staroshnya* (Be careful)."

Lena started to translate. "He said —"

"I know what he said!" Rhett then looked directly at Salom and sneered, "*Potsolooyu moyu zhoppu* (Kiss my ass)."

Rhett was furious as he turned around and returned to the bar.

While Dave was trying to assure Salom that everything was all right, Salom whispered something to one of his henchmen who nodded and left the bar.

———

It was after midnight when Rhett left the bar. Still angry,hHe was feeling no pain as he walked out of *The Passazh* and toward the Metro station.

As he walked through the glass doors, he noticed a group of young hooligans standing next to the entrance. Although they looked familiar, Rhett wasn't sure if he had seen them before.

Out of the corner of his eye, he saw them enter the Metro as he went through the turnstile. They followed as he rode the escalator down to the subway platform.

He slowly walked to the end of the platform pretending not to notice them. Nevertheless, they made him feel uneasy.

It seemed like an eternity as he waited for the train to pull in the station. He stepped back from the edge of the platform and could feel the wind in the tunnel pick up as the train approached.

The young men kept talking to each other, but every once in a while, Rhett would notice one of them looking in his direction.

Suddenly, the train came roaring into the station and screeched to a halt.

Rhett entered at one end of the car as the hooligans entered at the other. He looked straight ahead, pretending to be oblivious of their existence, but he continued to monitor their movements out of the corner of his eye.

The train roared into the next station. The doors opened as more passengers poured into the car. Rhett noticed that the young men were slowly moving closer to him. He continued to ignore them as the train picked up speed as it whisked through the darkened tunnel. A bead of sweat was beginning to trickle from under his hat and down the side of his face.

When the train stopped at the next station, Rhett quickly stepped out of the car. The group of young men quickly scrambled to get out of the door at the other end. As soon as they were on the platform, Rhett immediately stepped back in. Again, the group scrambled to get back inside before the doors closed. Then, before they could react, he stepped outside once again as the doors slammed shut behind him.

Rhett could see them looking at him from the widows. He simply smiled and tipped his hat as the train pulled out of the station.

He leaned against the cold granite wall and looked at the clock hanging above the tunnel's entrance. The time told him it was already too late to catch another train.

He rode the escalator up to the Metro's entrance, exiting on to *Universitat* Street into the cold darkness of Kyiv and began the long walk home.

VIA CON DIOS UKRAINE

"In every walk with nature, one receives far more than he seeks."   John Muir

I

A Walk in The Forest

The following morning as Rhett looked out the window of his apartment overlooking "The Avenue of Victory," he recalled the hooligans on the Metro and his late-night trek through the streets of Kyiv. Then he remembered telling Salom to kiss his ass.

As he started to get dressed to go to work, he began to have second thoughts. So, after considering the events of the night before, he thought it might be more prudent to take the day off."

—

What he didn't know was, early that morning, a man came to the office and told Lena he had been sent by Salom to take Dave to a meeting. Then as Lena got up to go with Dave, the man told her that her services wouldn't be necessary. Salom had already arranged for someone to handle the translations on this particular morning. For the first time since he had come to Kyiv, Lena would not be accompanying Dave as his trusted translator.

Dave didn't suspect anything. that there was anything unusual. He got up, grabbed the bag and left with the stranger. After all, he had already proven that the bar couldn't survive without him. Besides, Salom was his partner and he was in complete control of the situation. It would be the last time that Lena would see him.

One can only imagine what was going through Dave's mind as he got into the car and sped through the streets of Kyiv, then out of the city as it headed to a remote wooded area where a group of men were waiting.

Dave was in his own,

—

"What's going on? Where's Salom?" Dave asked. When one of the men tried to take the bag from him. he resisted. "What the hell are you doing?" The man slapped him and jerked the bag out of his hand.

"Do you know who I am?" Dave demanded. "Do you have any idea who you're fucking with? Do you know who my roof is?"

Nobody seemed concerned as the man counted the cash from Dave's satchel.

"Where is rest of the money?" The man asked in broken English.

"I don't know what you're talking about!" Dave was trying to act like he wasn't afraid, but the fear was beginning to show on his face as he began to tremble slightly.

Suddenly, he felt the wind being knocked out of him and he doubled over falling to the ground. There weren't many of them, but Dave was alone. As it turned out, he never was as tough as he had talked.

They said something to each other in Russian and began to laugh.

One grabbed him and jerked him up to his feet as another sucker-punched him. He collapsed again and lay on the ground doubled up in a feral position.

"Where's the money?"

Now, *they* were the ones who were making the demands.

"I don't have any money," Dave replied. Then one of them kicked him

"Who are your partners?" another asked.

"My partner is Sergei . . . Sergei!"

"Sergei who?" He slapped Dave across the face.

"Just a minute! Just a minute! Let me think." Dave never could get anyone's name right. He was frantic.

They slapped him again and again. His hands were above his head as he tried to protect himself from the blows.

"Uh, Sergei . . . Sergei. He owns the Carambol. Sergei . . . Komievsko . . . uh, Komiensko! No, no. It's Sergei Komievsko."

One of his captors said, in a flat, unemotional voice, "We want twenty thousand dollars, or we kill you and your family."

Even though he tried to hide it, he couldn't stop shaking. "I don't have twenty thousand dollars." He was petrified. It was beginning to show in his voice.

He was trying not to break down, but at this moment he was on the verge of tears.

"But you are famous owner of cowboy bar."

"I know, but I don't have that kind of money." Dave was pleading now.

"Then we have to kill you."

The man turned and went over to his car opening the trunk.

Dave didn't know what the man would pull out of the trunk or if they would put him in it. He'd seen this scenario a thousand times in movies. But now, this was happening in real life and it was happening to him. At that moment, small stream of piss started running down his leg.

The man pulled out a shovel and the laughing stopped. Dave thought the man was going to bash his head in and couldn't stop the shaking. It was beginning in his legs and starting to pulse throughout his entire body.

The man walked over to him and held out the shovel.

"What —? What do you want me to do?" He asked.

"Dig. Dig there." The man pointed to the ground in front Dave.

"What do you mean? I don't understand. Why?"

"Blyad!" The man pimp slapped him again. "You dig there. It is your — *kak skazat?*" he couldn't think of the word in English. He settled on "It is for you."

Then, at that moment, Dave understood. They were going to have him dig his own grave. The fear made him lose complete control over his bladder and he completely wet himself. The men looked on pointing to his soaked pant leg and began to laugh again.

"No, I can't. I mean, please. All right! What do you want?"

"We want twenty thousand dollars. You understand?"

"Da, I understand. What do you want me to do?"

"Give me telephone number of your partner," He snapped his fingers and held out his hand.

"Okay, but it's in my bag." Dave pointed to his bag and the man motioned for it to be brought to him.

Dave rifled through the bag and pulled out his little black desk planner. Frantically thumbing through the pages, he found Sergei's phone number. It was under "S" for Sergei.

He showed it to the man, who ripped it out of his hand and showed it to another, saying something in Russian.

The other man got into a car and drove off.

Dave just stood there. There wasn't anything he could do and he couldn't run. He was surrounded by a gang of hooligans and didn't even know where he was. Dave had sowed the wind and now it was time to reap the whirlwind . . . a time to atone for his actions.

After what seemed like an eternity, the car drove up to the clearing. The man who had gone to call Sergei got out and said something to the man in charge. He looked at Dave, then he walked over to him "No one answer. What you do now?"

Throwing the desk planner to the ground the man slapped Dave on the back of his head as one would to a child who had been caught in a bad act. He slapped him repeatedly before handing him the shovel again.

"Wair! Wait!" he was beyond desperation at this point. All he knew was how badly he wanted to get out of his predicament and save his sorry ass.

"I have another partner! He'll help me. I promise." Dave picked up the desk planner and showed him another number. "Here's his number. His name is Salom." Once again it was under "S." "Just call him, please! He'll help me I swear!"

The man looked at the phone number and said something else to the man who had just returned. They both turned and looked at Dave. The other man simply shrugged and got into the car again.

395

The gang worked Dave over on the rest of the morning and into the afternoon.

It was beginning to get dark by the time the other man returned. Dave was informed that Salom refused to talk to them.

Dave was now on his own. He was truly up shit creek — however, this time he had paddled most of the distance himself. He smelled of urine as he began to sob uncontrollably.

Suddenly, several Mercedes drove up. Dave looked up to see Salom and his men pouring out of their cars and attacking the men who had kidnapped him. Salom grabbed Dave and placed some keys in his hand and pointed to one of the cars. Although, Dave couldn't understand what he was saying, Salom was motioning for him to get into one of the Mercedes and drive away. Dave ran over to the car and jumped into it, but his hands were shaking so badly he had some trouble getting the keys into the ignition switch.

As he drove away, he looked in the back of his rear-view mirror and saw some men lying on the ground. He couldn't tell whose side they were on.

He only drove a short distance before he stopped. As afraid as he was at the moment, he was even more afraid of driving off and leaving Salom. He didn't dare drive away and leave him behind. Besides, Dave had no idea where he was.

His heart was pounding as he looked into the rear-view mirror to see if anyone was following him. He was terrified, yet relieved to be out of the hands of his captors. The inside of the car was beginning to reek of urine.

Suddenly, he saw a figure running toward the car. He couldn't tell who it was at first, but after a moment, he recognized it was Salom.

When Salom reached the car, he jumped in and signaled Dave to drive. They sped away, with Salom giving hand signals to direct him.

Salom smelled something, but he couldn't figure out where the smell was coming from. Not until he looked down and saw the yellow stains on Dave's pants.

Salom directed him into Kyiv and through the winding streets until they came to a building. He signaled for Dave to stop and to follow him inside.

As the two sat together, Dave pretended as if he understood what Salom was telling him. However, it was futile until an interpreter came to help them communicate. Nevertheless, it appeared to Dave that Salom had driven up out of nowhere and believed that Salom had risked his life to save him.

Although Dave was confused about the day's events, the was one thing he was sure of — finally he was scared. All the cockiness had been beaten out of him and the only thing he could think about was that he wanted to get out of Kyiv as fast as he could.

—

Kathy had been waiting at the apartment all day and had not heard a word from Dave. She was beginning to get worried. Her husband was missing and Salom was nowhere to be found.

She called Lena, but all that Lena could tell her was that Dave had left with someone to go meet Salom.

When she heard the phone ring and she quickly picked it up hoping it was Dave, but it was Valerie calling to ask her where Dave was. Kathy told her she didn't know, she hadn't heard from him and he had been missing all day.

Valerie could tell by the tone in her voice that something was wrong, but Val just figured it was simply Dave being Dave.

When the doorbell rang, Kathy told Valerie to hang on for a moment while she went to answer the door. It was Dave.

Kathy returned to the phone and told Valerie that she would call her back. She never did.

It was obvious that something was very wrong Standing in front of her was a man, badly bruised, dirty and reeking of urine. Dave wasn't so cocksure of himself anymore. He looked worried and scared.

The next morning, without a word to anybody — not even an *adios kiss my ass,* Dave was on an airplane bound for Amsterdam. He gave no thought to those he left behind in his wake. He just ran.

Gone was the man who had risen out of the ashes so many times in the past. Gone were the dreams that everyone had held for The Kowboy Dance Hall & Saloon. Kyiv had seen the last of "Crazy" Dave Seigal.

II

Via Con Dios Kyiv

The following afternoon when Rhett placed a call to the office there was no answer. Then he telephoned Igor who agreed to meet him in the center of the city. From there, they caught the Metro to *Republikanskie Stadium* and made their way to the office. It was the last place anyone had laid eyes on Dave.

When he unlocked the door, he was shocked to see that someone had cleaned out the office. Nothing was there. Except for the walls, it was empty.

Rhett stared for a moment in stunned silence. And then turned to Igor. "What the hell . . ."

He turned on his heel. Maybe Eudy would know what had happened.

When they arrived, a receptionist escorted them into Rudy's office. His security chief, Alexei, was standing next to him. He smiled at Rhett as he gave him a friendly greeting. It quickly became obvious that Rudy had no better idea about Dave's whereabouts than he did.

"That's what we're trying to find out." Rhett replied. "All I know is, the office is empty and it appears that Dave has vanished like a thief in the night.

Rudy whispered something to Alexei, who immediately placed a call on his cellular phone.

He turned back to Rhett. "You watch. You will see. It will not take my man long."

Within minutes, the security chief's pager went off. He pulled it from his belt and pushed a button and looked at the number that appeared on it. Then Alexei walked over to Rudy's desk, picked up the telephone, dialed, and handed the receiver to Rudy.

As soon as Rudy hung up he turned to Rhett. "So, it appears that Dave is in California."

"What? California?" Flabbergasted, Rhett looked at Igor who appeared as stunned as he was.

"I told you it would not take long. Does he really think he can cheat me by hiding in California? Ha! As far as Rudy was concerned, Dave could run, but he could not hide.

Rudy had made his point

———

As they left Rudy's office and walked back towards the Metro station, Rhett turned to Igor. "I am so terribly sorry. I really thought this was going work out for us and all I've done was to let you down."

"There is no reason to be sorry. You have not done anything."

"But, Dave. He never paid you."

"Do not worry about me. I will be okay. I started looking for work when I saw he could not pay you. I found a job two days ago."

"*Slova Bog* (Thank God) for that." Although it was a minor consolation, Rhett was relieved. "You know, Igor? Americans are a strange breed. They always hold themselves above everyone else, especially when they're out of their element. They think they have all the answers and go around preaching ethics as if America invented it. But the truth is, they're all too easily corrupted . . . just like anyone else."

"I know, I have seen it ever since the Americans came to my country. It appears to me there is not that much difference between Americans and Ukrainians."

Rhett shook his head. "I don't know what to say. Can you ever forgive me?

There is no need to forgive you for anything. I believe you are an honest man and have a good heart. Maybe you drink a little too much sometimes, but you have been my friend and I know you love my country almost as much as I do."

Rhett looked down at the pavement. He didn't want Igor to see the tears welling up in his eyes. "And you have become like a son to me."

"We have shared a great adventure together, but now it has come to an end. My job is waiting and I must go. *Slava Ukrayini* — Glory to Ukraine — my friend." Igor extended his hand.

As they shook hands, Rhett replied, "*Vse naykrashche miy drookh* (All the best, my friend)."

Then he watched Igor as disappeared in a crowd of people.

—

As soon as he got back to his apartment, Rhett picked up the phone and dialed Dave's number in California. "The number you dialed has been disconnected. Please check to see if . . ."

He hung up then dialed Valerie's number. "What are you doing here?" She seemed to be completely surprised to hear his voice.

"Have you talked to Dave? I tried to call him, but his number has been disconnected."

"Didn't anybody tell you?"

"Tell me what?"

"Well, it seems that Dave was taken to the forest outside of Kyiv and had the shit beaten out of him. He's gone back to California."

"Yeah, I was at Rudy's office this afternoon and he told me Dave was in California. Who told you that Dave was beaten?"

"Lena. She's been in contact with Kathy in California."

"Well, has anyone talked to Dave?" Rhett asked.

"No!" Her voice was angry. "But I talked to Kathy and she told me about what happened to Dave."

Rhett listened in astonishment as Valerie conveyed Kathy's account of what happened to Dave including Salom's daring rescue.

"That's a hell of a story, but have you talked to Dave?"

"No, according to Kathy, Dave's seriously ill and spending time in some clinic down in Mexico somewhere."

"Yeah, right!" Rhett scoffed. "He's either going through detox or he's down there whoring like he always did here. If you ask me, he's most likely hiding out because he's too humiliated to talk to anyone."

Dave might have gotten off lucky to get off with only a beating before scurrying off to California, but seeing how easily Rudy had located him, perhaps he wouldn't be so lucky after all.

Valerie continued. "As I was talking to Kathy, she told me that she and Dave had been discussing things over and they had come to the decision."

"Yeah, so what decision did they come to?"

"That Dave would probably not be returning to Kyiv."

"Yeah, no shit!"

Valerie then told Rhett about a conversation she had with Kathy when she was in Kyiv about how she was asked if Dave was sleeping with other women.

"And what did you tell her?"

"What do you think I told her? I sidestepped the issue as well as I could, but you know as well as I do. When Dave was in Kyiv, he was a free man. Nevertheless, I think she may have suspected enough to affect the outcome of 'their decision.'"

"Pullin' that ole' Tammy Wynette and standing by her man, is she? It was probably safer for her to have Dave closer to home in California where she could keep an eye on him."

Valerie's conversation was confirming what everybody was beginning to realize. Dave had skipped town.

"I've been talking with Lena." Valerie continued. "She was still hoping that she was going to hear from Dave until I told her that he had given instructions not to give his number to her. That was when she broke down in tears."

"Leaving her out in the cold like that? No money, no job, not even the courtesy of a phone call. That's pretty harsh even for Dave. So, where does that leave all the investors and the bar?"

Obviously, I'm out a lot of money, but Lucy's situation is even worse. She convinced her family to invest their life savings and they lost their home. Lucy's now living in a little one-room flat with her father on the outskirts of Kyiv. Other than Lucy, Todd and myself, I have no idea who else has invested in that bar.

"Do you know Oleg?"

"No, who's that?"

"He was some guy loaned Dave twenty grand for a percentage of The Kowboy. I was there when he gave Dave the money." The phone went silent. "Val, are you there?"

Rhett heard a voice on the other end quietly say, "Jesus!"

Rhett was thinking what the Mafia had done to Dave was nothing compared to what he had done to those who trusted him. In the short span of a few months, Dave Seigal had destroyed the lives of those close to him, as well as the image of the American Cowboy.

"Have you been to The Kowboy?" Rhett asked. "Do you know what's going on there?"

"I don't feel like going right now. Meet me there tomorrow night. I've got a lot more to tell you." Then Valerie hung up.

III

Y'all Come Back Saloon

The following night, it was raining when Rhett arrived at The Kowboy. As he descended the stairs, he glanced at Kyrill's painting. Somebody had put a cigarette out on his likeness.

As he walked through the swinging doors, he could see Salom's henchmen sitting at the bar. They turned and looked at him as if he were the last member of a lost command. A big heavyset one turned and looked at him for a minute. Then he got up and approached Rhett.

With the way things were going, Rhett wasn't sure what to expect until he extended his hand and smiled. *"Odeenokie Volk! Privyit, Gde Dave* (Hello, Where's Dave)?"

Rhett simply shrugged as he looked around. The place was like a ghost town. There were a few Ukrainians and even fewer Americans. The business that everyone dreamed about had simply vanished.

Tatiana steered clear of him. Walking past her, he threw some money on the counter and ordered a drink. She may have been a lot of things, but she wasn't dumb, and was fully aware that he didn't like her any more than she liked him.

Rhett turned to see a young man wearing a cowboy hat walking toward him.

Shaking Rhett's hand, he introduced himself with a smile. "My name's Caleb. How do you do. You must be one of the cowboys."

"How could you tell?"

"I recognized you from the painting that's hanging on the wall at the entrance."

"Well, I guess that was a dead giveaway . . . and who are you exactly?"

"Like I said, I'm Caleb. I'm the temporary replacement singer, until they bring a new one back from the States. I heard that the last singer left town in kind of a hurry."

"I suppose you could say that. So, who hired you?"

"I don't really know for sure, but I think it was one of Dave's partners. I never got the chance to meet Dave Anyway, somebody told me that they needed a singer. So, I thought I would come down and audition. Actually, I'm an accountant and work for a tax firm during the day."

"Well, don't quit your day job."

"Oh, you don't have to worry about that. I'm just doing this for fun."

"So, how's it been going so far?"

"Not too bad. It's kind of slow, but I've only been here for a couple of nights." Caleb leaned over and whispered, "There's a lot of Mafia activity going on here, you know."

"Now that you mention it, I think I've heard that somewhere."

"I used to be a gospel singer, so I've never really performed country music before. My brother's an evangelist."

"Funny you say that. Our last musician was a missionary of sorts too."

"So, what's the deal? I've heard a lot of stories going around. What really happened to Dave?"

"Nobody really knows for sure. That's what I'm trying to find out."

"Like I said, I've heard a lot of stories. But you know . . ."

"So, tell me Caleb. What are they paying you?"

"We really haven't settled that question yet, but if they don't pay me soon, I'm out of here."

"Wise decision."

"Well, I better be going now. Nice meeting you. Stick around for a set."

"Sure. See you later. Good luck."

Rhett turned to see Valerie walking toward him. She took one look at him in his cowboy hat and immediately broke out into laughter. "Once a cowboy, always a cowboy, right?"

"Yep, that's right, Val. Dave may have run like a rabbit, but I'm not about to. I'll be damned if I'm going to allow his screw-ups to change all that. Besides, I've been walking through Kyiv like this for a long time and I never had any problems until Dave and this goddamned bar. I guess that makes me the last living cowboy in Kiev."

"I suppose you are. So, what do you think of our little gospel singer?"

"He's not so bad, I guess."

Although Caleb was singing a country song, it sounded more akin to one of those Sunday-go-to-meetin' tent revivals.

"Well, he's no Toby Smith," Valerie added.

"Whatever you say. Jeezus Val! I don't know what you all thought was so great about Toby. It was the band and as far as I'm concerned, I'm glad that that little peckerwood is gone."

"I didn't think he was that bad. Besides, he was popular with the crowds. In fact, he called Todd the other night and asked him to send a thousand dollars so he could buy a plane ticket back to Kiev."

"Well, I hope you told him to have Toby go and take a flying fuck. He was paid to come to Kyiv and perform Two weeks after the bar opened, he decided to go home."

"Pretty much. I told Todd he could do what he wanted, but Toby screwed us almost as much as anyone. I told him if Toby wants to come back to Kiev so badly, let him spend some time flipping burgers to pay for his own ticket."

For once, Rhett thought Valerie made sense. "Anyway, I want to get rid of this guy as soon as possible and get somebody else in here with a little more twang in their voice."

"Yeah, good luck with that." Rhett scoffed. "So, do you have any idea what the hell is going on here?"

"Todd and I were scheduled to have a meeting this afternoon with Sergei and the Chechens, but neither of them showed."

"Then who's in control of the bar and why is that bitch Tatiana still here? She was the one who was stealing the money. John and I saw her."

"It's okay. She likes me now." Valerie replied. "She and her husband had me over and fixed me dinner last night. We sort of bonded. I'm her best friend now."

For the life of him, Rhett could not understand the logic behind that statement. If Valerie thought being her "best friend" made any difference, she was as deluded as Dave.

Moments later, Tatiana came over and whispered something into Valerie's ear. Then she got up and followed her to the Cantina. When she returned, she told him, "Tatiana told me business has been terrible and that they need help."

"Ya think, Val?"

"Anyway, Todd and I are trying to find buyers for the bar. We've been talking to some Westerners who might be interested. But of course, nobody is going to want the Chechen Mafia for partners. So, we need to convince Salom that he should sell his part outright and move on."

"Really, and how's that going?"

"The problem is that Salom said he invested fifty thousand dollars in the bar. But, no one knows for sure whether he really did invest that money or if he just made it up."

"Well, I can tell you that's bullshit." Rhett sneered. "I was there when Dave asked Salom to loan him twenty thousand and I know that Salom only gave him ten. I also remember Salom made him give him back that money a week later."

"Rhett, you know as well as anybody the way Dave handled his business. It was all in cash. He didn't really keep any books or records that we can check."

"Look Val, Salom's not the kind of guy to simply fork over fifty grand. He's too smart for that. On the contrary, Salom is the kind of person who would sit back and wait to plunder the bar's assets, which is exactly what he's doing."

Dave's American investors had no choice if they wanted to recoup their investment. There was no alternative. They had to find a buyer and pay Salom whatever he wanted. Maybe they would get their investment back. Maybe they wouldn't.

However, in all probability, their chances were slim at best.

Rhett thought Salom might have been the only one who had any brains to begin with. In principle, he had gotten what he wanted and now controlled a piece of prime real estate in the center of Kyiv and could exchange it any time he wanted to for a hefty sum without investing one kopek. All he had to do was to sit back and wait. If Valerie and Todd couldn't bring him some sucker, sooner or later, some chump would come his way.

It was becoming obvious to Rhett that Valerie didn't know what was going on, any more than anyone else.

"Well, I've got to go now. I'm having a meeting at my place on Sunday. We're all going to sit down and see what we can salvage out of Dave's businesses." Valerie got up from the table. "As an afterthought, she turned to Rhett. "If you want to come, you're welcome."

Rhett scowled. "Thanks a lot, Val. You're a real goddamn sweetheart."

Rhett eventually got tired of the employees coming up to him and asking when Dave would be coming back so they could get paid. Unfortunately, there was nothing he could tell them. It only made him feel more depressed. As a result, he didn't stay long.

On his way out, he waved goodbye to the gospel singer who returned the gesture with a nod of his head looking as if he were asking folks to come down to the stage for a "late night benediction at the Y'all Come Back Saloon.

IV

The Mavens of Misfortune

Rhett was running low on cash. As a result, he decided to go to the meeting at Valerie's apartment. Besides, no matter what Val or Todd thought, Dave had screwed him out of a lot of money too, and it was money he had been counting to pay rent and a plane ticket back to Oklahoma.

When he arrived, he found the Americans discussing how they were going to split up what remained of Dave's businesses. Like a flock of vultures, they were trying to salvage anything they could from the disasters Dave had left in his wake.

Although Rhett couldn't figure out why Mike had become a player in this scenario, it appeared that he was leading the discussion. "I've done a little investigating and I figure Dave has about twenty leases on apartments in the city. Of course, we'll have to fix a few up and pay some bills. However, if we can renegotiate the leases, I figure it could bring us about thirty grand a month."

Rhett sat quietly listening as Mike continued.

"I've already sent off a fax to the government contractors informing them that Dave has gone out of business and we're now in charge. The way I figure it, due to all the bad publicity surrounding Dave and his antics, they won't want to damage their reputation any more than has been done already."

"Well, Lena has talked to the woman who owns the apartment where Toby was staying." Valerie interjected. "Apparently, he trashed the place before he left and she's looking at a few thousand dollars in phone bills."

"This is true." Lena added, "She cannot get the phone turned back on until she pays the outstanding bill. She does not know what she will do. She cannot rent the apartment without a telephone."

Mike picked up on the woman's misfortune and saw an opportunity just waiting to be taken advantage of. "Maybe if we wait, she'll become desperate. Then when we've made enough money off the other places, we can renegotiate the lease for a lower price. The way I see it, she won't have much of a choice. So, what about Dave and John's apartments?"

"The women who own those apartments are very angry too." Lena answered. "They also have very high telephone bills. Plus, Dave never paid her for a couple of months and when Toby moved in with John, he made a lot of phone calls to America. In addition, they are complaining that there was some broken furniture and other damage."

Mike thought for a moment. "If we play our card right, we might just come out of this making a pretty penny. As I recall, those were really nice places. Lena, tell them that we will fix the damaged furniture and replace whatever was damaged. In exchange, try to get them to renegotiate their leases at a lower price too." One could almost see him licking his lips at another's misery.

"Speaking of John and Toby," Valerie interrupted, "I got a call from John last night and apparently, he wants to come back to Kyiv."

"Really? Is he coming with or without the mercenaries?" Rhett laughed.

Clearly confused, Valerie looked at him. "What are you talking about?"

"Never mind, you wouldn't believe me if I told you. It was something he told Dave about assassinating Salom. So, let me get this straight Val. You're saying not only does Toby want to come back, but after all that's happened John wants to come back too?"

"That's what he said. Evidently, Kyiv has gotten into his blood."

"You have got to be kidding. And Toby? What's his story?"

"According to John, Toby had become engaged to his sweetheart back in Texas and he asked her to return with him to Kyiv. However, after she read the story in the *Odessa American* about the Mafia, she told Toby that she decided it was safer to stay in Texas."

"Evidently she has more sense than Toby." Rhett laughed. "So, what was Toby's reaction?"

"He broke off the engagement, flew to California and moved in with John."

"What a guy." Rhett shook his head. "Even if he didn't get bounced out of flight school for being nuts, it's plain to see that he's not playing with a full deck."

Valerie continued, "For some reason, I think Toby has become a sort of surrogate son to John and they've been trying to devise a plan that will get them back to Kyiv."

"Okay you two, cut it out." Todd interrupted. "Let's get back to business. What are we going to do about The Kowboy?"

"Well, something's got to be done if we ever want to get our investments back." Valerie chimed in. "The American Embassy has put out the word and everyone in the foreign community has been warned to stay away. And after what happened to Dave, nobody in their right mind is going to take on the Mafia as partners."

"I've been talking to Salom," Todd interjected. "He wants to know how to contact Dave. He told me he found someone interested in buying The Kowboy and wants to give Dave his share of the money from the sale of the bar."

"Rhett scoffed at the idea. Yeah, right! Look, if you think Salom is going to pay Dave anything from selling this place, then it will be a true sign that economic reform had taken hold in Eastern Europe."

"Listen, Rhett, you weren't there," Todd interjected.

"Maybe not, but you guys are welcome to believe whatever you want," Rhett snapped back. "But I sure as hell ain't buying any of that crap."

"Oh, Rhett, why do you have to be so negative?" Valerie added.

Rhett couldn't believe what he was hearing and gave her an incredulous look. "Jeezus H. Christ! Get a reality check, Tinkerbelle! Have any of you thought that maybe Salom's daring rescue wasn't all it appeared to be . . . that maybe that whole thing had been staged? Think about it for a minute. Dave was in the middle of nowhere, for Chrissake. How did Salom know where to find him? Last time I checked, there aren't any addresses in the middle of the forest. So, ask yourselves what are Salom's real reasons for wanting to find Dave in California? Think about it. What if Salom told Dave some things that he doesn't want anyone to know about."

At that moment, Mike came forth with another revelation. "I've been doing some checking on Salom and it seems that he is not really the head of the Chechen Mafia after all. Apparently, Salom and his gang work for one of the eight Mafias that control Kyiv. He's actually an enforcer for a powerful government figure . . . someone called Lazarenko."

The mention of Lazarenko's name sent a palled chill through the room. Rhett didn't know exactly why, but he recognized the name from the conversation he had with John about his trip to Yalta.

"So, what's the deal with Sergei?" Rhett asked. "Has anybody talked to him? After all, he was Dave's original partner."

"I think Sergei's somewhere behind the scenes, trying to regain control of the place." Todd added, "He got caught in the middle when Dave brought Salom and his gang onto *The Passazh*."

"So where is he?" Rhett asked.

"I don't know for sure." Todd answered. "I haven't talked to him, but I think that the Mafia that controls *The Passazh* may have held him accountable for what's happened and they're punishing him by refusing to give him any backup to regain control of this place."

Rhett still wasn't satisfied. "Well, shouldn't someone be talking to him? After all, it was Sergei who originally owned that place"

"I think Sergei is irrelevant at this point. Look, Tatiana and I are on best terms. She trusts me and I think I can use that to help us deal with Salom, Then Todd and I can see what we can work out with him."

Rhett couldn't believe what he was hearing. Valerie and Todd were picking up where Dave had left off. They were going to dump Sergei, choosing to deal with Salom instead. In their own way, Valerie and Todd had been corrupted too.

V

Chaos on the Mean Streets

It was the middle of the night when the phone rang. A friend was calling from the States who wanted to know if Rhett knew a businessman from Oklahoma named Paul Tatum. It was reported he had just been assassinated in a Mafia-style killing outside of a Metro station in Moscow.

According to news reports, Tatum had been involved in a property dispute over the Radison Hotel with the Moscow city government. The deal had gone sour and he had been in a virtual state of siege somewhere in the center of Moscow. Nevertheless, with eleven bullets in his back, all that didn't seem to matter much anymore.

The unofficial word was that Tatum was pretty much of an asshole who had been playing all sides. The reports also said that the hotel had been a well-known hangout for the Mafia. And, like Dave, it was rumored that he had been involved with Chechens.

The unwritten code of never killing a Westerner had been broken and Tatum had become the first American to fall victim to the shady dealings that was beginning to typify doing business on the mean streets of former Soviet Union.

That very same day, news reports of an assassination attempt on Ukraine's Prime Minister Pavlo Lazarenko hit Kyiv. It made all the news wires and was broadcast all over the world.

According to reports, a bomb had been planted by the side of the road and had exploded only seconds after his car had driven by. There were minor injuries, but Lazarenko had escaped shaken but not stirred.

The only thing that seemed suspicious was the immediate denial of any involvement from the head of the regional administration of the Donetsk Oblast Valery Sherbanye.

The media had alluded to a bitter rivalry between the two men and after the bombing incident, Sherbanye refused to meet Lazarenko at the airport in Donetsk when Lazarenko's plane arrived. Nobody knew what it meant or why, but it foreshadowed what the future would bring for the relatively peaceful situation that had existed in Ukraine.

Although there was speculation that the Mafia had been involved, nobody really knew for sure. However, whatever it was, Rhett knew that it couldn't be good.

Things like that happened in Moscow but not Kiev. It meant the complexion of Ukraine was taking a turn for the worse. It was beginning to catch up with the mayhem that was occurring in its more violent neighbor to the north.

Part of the problem stemmed from the historical and cultural differences that had existed between the eastern and western regions of Ukraine for decades. The eastern regions Ukraine, which included the Donetsk Oblast, spoke Russian and had always felt closer to Russia. On the other, the Ukrainian language had similar characteristics to Polish having been part of Poland off and on over the centuries. As a result, western Ukraine wanted closer ties with the West.

As it turned out, Lazarenko owned part of an energy consortium, which controlled most of the energy industry in Ukraine and had approved a deal to purchase inexpensive coal from Poland, rather than the more expensive coal from Sherbanye's Donetsk region.

Once again, Rhett remembered Lazarenko's name and the chill that Valerie and Lena felt when his name was mentioned suddenly became all too clear.

—

A few days later, Rhett was summoned to Volodomir's office. After hearing the rumors Volodomir wanted to question him about what was happening at The Kowboy Dance Hall & Saloon.

"So, Rhett. We have been friends ever since you arrived in my country and I expect you to be to be honest with me. What happened to Dave Seigal and who is in charge of the bar?"

When Rhett told him, Volodomir was furious. "Do you know, who was responsible for Dave's attack?"

"Honestly, nobody really knows who beat the hell out of Dave and quite frankly, I don't think anybody seems to care. There were a lot of people who loaned him money in exchange for part ownerships in the bar. If any one of them came to the realization that Dave was screwing just about everyone, who could really blame them."

"What about his Ukrainian partner?" Volodomir replied. "What has happened to him?"

"If you are talking about Sergei, I haven't seen him around lately. Especially after Dave was talking about having his Chechen partner assassinate him."

"What? Are you serious?"

"I heard him. In fact, Dave always got a thrill whenever he talked about having someone killed or when he used the word Mafia. It seemed that it made him feel tough."

"And what did Dave's partner think about this?"

"As far as I know, Sergei never knew anything about it. However, if he had he ever found out about Dave's true intentions, he would have been more than justified to take him out to the woods, and Dave certainly would have had it coming."

"Tell me Rhett. Why did you not do something about this?"

"I tried Volodomir. I swear to you, I really tried. I told Dave about your offer to arrange for the *Militsia* as security for the bar, but he wouldn't listen."

"And what about John? Why did he not listen to my advice?"

"Because he believed whatever Dave would tell him. Believe me when I tell you, I kept telling everyone that working with the Mafia was a bad idea. Unfortunately, John wouldn't listen even when I told him that I had been picked up and questioned by the Ukrainian Security Service."

"I know. It was my hope that Mikhail could talk to you and you would pass on his warning about doing business with the Mafia."

Rhett was not surprised considering Volodomir's connections with the intelligence community.

"By the way, Mikhail said he liked you. He told me he thought you were an honest man."

"So, tell me Volodomir. Just how powerful are the Chechens in Kyiv?"

Volodomir snorted derisively. "Most were taken out to the forest by our Secret Service and executed years ago. Why do you ask?"

"Because I was at a meeting with the American investors a few nights ago and they were talking about trying to get back their investment by working with the Chechens instead of working with Dave's partner, Sergei."

""*Duraki!* (Fools)" Volodomir exclaimed. "And what did you tell them?"

"Basically, the same thing I have been telling everyone ever since I got involved with this nightmare. Unfortunately, I don't think that they were listening either. Look Volodomir, Americans have had this love affair with the Mafia long before the Godfather movies. They like the idea of breaking the rules and getting away with it. Unfortunately, what many don't realize is the Mafia is not exactly as they are portrayed and romanticized in the movies."

"Rhett, if I may. Let me explain something. When we were part of the Soviet Union the Black Market was controlled by our Committee for State Security, which the West knew as the KGB. It was the government's way of providing the people with Western goods without compromising Communist doctrine.

"However, when the Soviet Union collapsed the Black Market split into various factions. Still, some members our Security Service continue to maintain contacts within criminal organizations. Consequently, when Western businesses becomes involved with a Mafia the government is usually aware. And when Westerners lose their businesses what can they do? They certainly cannot complain to the authorities."

"I learned when I was London and met someone who did business in Eastern Europe. Before that, like most Americans, the only thing I knew about the Soviet Union was what I saw in James Bond movies. Still, I can see what you mean. What better way to weed out the likes of Dave Seigal?"

Volodomir smiled. "Over the years I have come across many fast-talking Westerners and what they don't seem to realize is, we have more than our share of fast-talkers too. In fact, they can talk just as fast as any foreigner, especially when they cannot understand our language. Many come to my country under the assumption that they can take all us "Russkies" for everything we have. Really, who do they think we are — chimpanzees?"

"Yeah, I knew a couple of them back in the States. They're called "Okies." Anyway, at a meeting the other night, Dave's American partners were saying that Salom works for someone named Lazarenko. I also heard that name from John. Do you know who he is?"

"I assume you are referring to Pavlo Lazarenko. He is the Prime Minister of Ukraine."

"Is he the same one who survived an assassination attempt?"

Volodomir's tone suddenly changed. "He is, and I am somewhat surprised you are aware of that."

"Well, it was on all the news wires and I also read something about him having a problem with someone named Valery Sherbanye from the Donetsk region."

Volodomir leaned over his desk and looked Rhett directly in the eyes. "Sherbanye is no longer a problem. This morning he was gunned down at the airport in Donetsk.

At that point, Volodomir stood up to shake Rhett's hand indicating the meeting had come to an end and that he did not want to pursue the matter any further.

"I am glad we had this chance to talk Rhett, because I will be travelling in Europe for several weeks. However, when I return, I'm sure we will have a chance to speak again."

"Hopefully I will know a little more by then." Rhett replied. "In fact, Dave's American investors told me they are supposed to meet with Salom and his Chechens tonight."

Rhett started to turn around, but Volodomir would not let go of his hand. "Listen to me carefully. You need to be careful my friend. I would not like anything to happen to you."

As he walked out of the Ministry building, a flood of thoughts came surging into Rhett's mind. He knew in all probability that no one would ever know who was responsible for what happened to Dave. Maybe it was the Mafia, maybe it was the government. The distinctions were becoming too shady and blurred to tell the difference anymore. The truth was, probably nobody except those who were directly involved would ever know.

As he made his way to The Kowboy, he kept thinking how Americans tended to forget the game being played when they're doing business in a foreign country. How when they're not playing on their turf more times than not, they're playing by somebody else's rules and they don't realize it.

—

When he arrived at The Kowboy, he saw Valerie, Todd and Mike sitting at a table in the corner talking to Lena.

"Kowvboi! Yak spravee (How're you doing)?*"* Rhett turned to see a young Ukrainian Marine from the American Embassy motioning him over.

"Nee pohano (Not bad).*"* He extended his hand. The young marine's grip was like a vice as Rhett gritted his teeth and attempted a smile.

"I no see you for long time. You own this place?" Rhett's hand was throbbing as he pulled it from the young marine's grip.

"Not quite. Excuse me, but I have to meet with some people over there. Let me buy you a beer and when I'm finished. Okay?"

"You have deal!" He slapped Rhett on the back.

—

The three Americans looked up as Rhett approached their table. "So, has anybody figured out what's going on with this silly saga yet?"

Valerie was the first to answer. "Dave called Lena last night. I think he's trying to make things right with her."

"Yes, he did." Lena said earnestly. "He told me if Salom wants to give him his share, he should give it to Todd. Then Todd can wire it to him in California."

Rhett's eyes rolled back. It was the first time that Dave had placed a call to Lena since he had deserted her. However, Rhett knew if there was the slimmest chance for Dave to make a buck while hiding out in California, he certainly wasn't about to miss out on claiming his share.

"So, what's happening with John and Toby's reunion tour back to Kyiv? Have you heard anything more from them?"

Valerie was already shaking her head. "It seems that Toby wouldn't do any work or look for a job, so John told me he kicked him out. Surrogate son or no surrogate son, Toby was getting too expensive for John to take him in to raise."

"Well, I suppose it's Via Con Dios Toby Smith then." Rhett laughed. "I guess he's been left to wander the wastelands of America with only the memories of his fleeting success in the former Soviet Union. All I can say is good riddance to bad rubbish."

"So, what are you planning to do now, Rhett?"

"At this point, I figure I'm pretty well screwed too. Besides, as far as I'm concerned, Oklahoma is like the gateway to purgatory and goin' back there is pretty much out of the picture. However, I did get a call from the states a couple of nights ago and there seems to be a lot of interest in Eastern European Mafia stories."

"Well, with the exception of Lena, I suppose you were around Dave more than anyone else. You've been like the fly on the wall while all this was happening." Valerie replied.

"You're right Val. I've seen things that no one else has. Look, for months you, Todd and just about any other Westerner involved in this mess have been saying that one day you're going to write the story of what happened at The Kowboy Dance Hall & Saloon. So, while everybody was talking about it, I've been writing about it, because I figured if I didn't, nobody else was going to."

"How much have you written?" Todd asked.

"So far? About a hundred pages or so. Every time something happened here, I would write something down."

Valerie laughed. "You may be the only one to make any money out of this mess."

Rhett shook his head as he replied. "I'm just sorry that Dave was only abducted and beaten before they rode his sorry ass out of town. It would have made a much better story if someone had shot the bastard."

Todd looked surprised. "Really? Where is it?"

"It's in Dave's computer. Problem is, I don't know where that computer is."

Lena spoke up. "I have it."

Rhett turned to Lena. "You have it?"

"Yes. I do."

"Well, I have been sort of keeping a chronology of all the events too."

"Really? What have you got Val?" Rhett asked.

"Actually, I only have a couple of pages. I kinda write mainstream of consciousness, you know. Then later, I organize everything as I write. Listen, Rhett," Valerie continued, "I know a journalist for the *Wall Street Journal*."

Rhett leaned toward. "Yeah?"

"Anyway, she's expressed an interest in writing down my — I mean *our* — story. You know, all of what's happened here and maybe turning it into a novel. I think you should talk to her and turn your material over for her to look at."

"Are you suggesting that I'm not up to the task Val?"

The question caught her off guard. "Uh — well, of course not. It's just that —"

"Yeah, yeah. I get it. Other than advertising copy, I'm not really a writer. Is that what you mean? Look, I don't pretend to be some novelist, but I do have a story to tell. Besides, I've put in a lot of work writing everything down and after what I've been through —"

"Of course you have." Valerie placed her hand reassuringly on Rhett's forearm, "But let's just think this thing through for a minute. Now, and this is only my opinion, don't you think this story would be better written by someone who has an objective viewpoint? Besides, there might be some legal ramifications if real names were used."

Todd had another idea. "You know what, Rhett? I've got a friend who lives in L.A. Maybe I can connect you with him. He writes comedy scripts for television."

"Hey, I'm open to any ideas," Rhett replied. "Like I said, I know I'm not a writer and I'm sure I'm going to some need help. So, I'm willing to talk to him. Why not?"

"If the story is on a computer disc, why don't you give it to me? Then I could e-mail it to him."

"Like I told you, it's on Dave's computer. If you want, we can go to Lena's apartment and you can make a copy of what I have."

It was becoming apparent to Rhett they weren't really interested in his story. They were only interested in whatever information was on the computer disc.

Suddenly, Rhett was aware that no one was talking and were fixated on something behind him. He turned around to see Salom, Tatiana at his side and a group of his gangsters standing behind him.

Tatiana glared at Rhett.

He glared back.

"Well, I guess that's it for our meeting, Rhett," Valerie blurted out. "We have to go and talk to Salom right now. Keep in touch. We'll talk again sometime."

Then the three quickly stood up and followed Salom into a back room, leaving Rhett alone at the table.

"Yeah? Well, fuck you too!" Rhett pulled a flask from the inside pocket of his duster and took a swig of *Samahon*.

—

Todd, Valerie and Mike were listening intently, trying to understand every word of what was being said. When it became too difficult, they relied on Lena to clarify the points.

"Have you found Dave yet?" Salom asked.

"Uh . . ." Todd didn't know what to say. He did know Dave's new phone number, but after what Rhett said, he was reticent to give Salom the information he wanted.

"We're still trying to locate him," Valerie answered.

"Well then, what about my fifty thousand dollars?"

Salom looked in Mike's direction. "And who is this?"

"Excuse me," Todd answered, "this is my friend Mike. He is helping us straighten out some of Dave's business problems."

"Ocheen Priyatna (Very pleased). *"* Salom nodded in Mike's direction.

"Ocheen Priyatna, " Mike answered.

"Where is 'Lone Wolf'?" Salom asked.

"Who?" Valerie didn't understand.

"I saw him out there. Why isn't he with you?"

"Oh, you mean Rhett. He's not really with us. We were just talking to him. He worked for Dave, not us. We're not associated with him. He has nothing to do with our business."

Salom smiled. It was evident that these Americans had loyalty to no one. They were as weak as Dave.

"Well, I need to know where Dave is if I am to give him his share of the money."

"Oh, we can handle that," Todd answered. "If you give us the money, we will make sure that it gets to Dave."

"But how? I thought you just said that you do not know where he is."

"Well, uh — I'm sure that he will contact us eventually," Valerie answered.

"Then, when he does you will let me know?"

"Absolutely . . . of course we will. As soon as we know, we'll tell you." Valerie continued

"So, tell me Salom, who are these people you say want to buy the bar?"

"They are some foreigners I know."

"And how much do you think they will pay?"

"I believe they are willing to pay at least two hundred thousand dollars."

"That's great . . . in fact, that's really excellent! We have also been trying to find buyers, but there is one problem."

"What is that?"

"People are very nervous about doing business with the Mafia."

"What Mafia?" Salom was beginning to enjoy toying with these Americans.

"Well, Dave told us certain things about your business dealings and . . ."

Salom's smile quickly disappeared. "Forget what Dave told you! He told many people many things. It was not good for business. Look out there. There are no Americans, no foreigners. Business has been very bad."

Valerie thought she could get him to see things from her point of view. "All I'm saying is that if you let us take over The Kowboy, everything will look better and we can have a better chance to sell it. Then we will all get our money back."

"This is true." Todd agreed.

"Absolutely!" Mike added.

Valerie thought she had another card up her sleeve and decided to play it. "Listen, Salom. The Kowboy has had a lot of bad publicity and it was Rhett — I mean *Odinokie Volk,* he was the one who was responsible for our public relations. Unfortunately, he just told me that he was writing a story about The Kowboy. In fact, he has been going around Kyiv talking to people and asking many questions and I'm sure that we cannot afford another story like the one in the *Eastern Economist.*"

"Then you should talk to him." Salom suggested.

"We tried, but remember he worked for Dave. He will not listen to us."

"Do not worry about him." Salom replied.

"I just wanted to be honest with you, Salom. All we want is to sell this place and get our money back. I simply think that Todd and I have a better chance to do it."

"I will consider this matter." Salom replied.

"Okay." Valerie was obviously trying to gain Salom's trust. "I just want you to know that we are on your side and we just want for everyone to get along and work together."

"I understand."

Considering everything settled, Valerie stood up. "Well, if that is all, then we must go. We have other business to take care of."

The others stood up too and they all made for the door. "We'll be in touch," Todd added.

"Da, kaneshnya (Yes, of course)*,"* Salom answered.

———

Rhett was talking to the Ukrainian Marine when the Americans left the bar. He didn't notice as they walked out the door, nor did he notice the five young men passing them on their way out.

"Val," Todd asked, "do think that was a good idea, to tell Salom that Rhett was writing a story about The Kowboy?"

"Don't worry about it. It's no big deal. I figured if Salom thought there might be more bad publicity about him and his involvement with this place, then perhaps he'd be more cooperative, that's all."

"But what about Rhett?"

"Do you really care about him?"

Todd thought for a moment. "Not really."

"Then why are we even having this conversation? Besides, Rhett's a big boy. He can take care of himself."

———

The young men walked directly over to Salom who pointed to Rhett and said something. Then he and his bodyguards walked out of the saloon.

Rhett had been talking to the young Ukrainian Marine and was unaware that he was the only American left in the place.

"You want a *peevo* — a beer?" Rhett asked.

"Sure, *kowvboy. Chomu Bini* (Why not)?"

"Just a minute, I'll be right back." Rhett walked over to the bar and was waiting to be served when the five young men walked up behind him. As he turned around, Rhett found himself surrounded. He instantly recognized them as the same ones he eluded from the night they followed him on the Metro.

One of snatched Rhett's cowboy hat and placed it on his head, smiling as if he had just won a trophy. Rhett's natural instincts took over as he grabbed it back. The smile left as the young hooligan shoved Rhett backwards. Rhett shoved back.

The young tough took a swing as Rhett ducked, but before he could respond with his own punch, Rhett suddenly found himself in the middle of a melee. All five jumped him, kicking and beating Rhett as he tried to fend off their assault. He felt the full force of a kick as it hit him in the ribs. It was all he could do to bob and weave. It was one lone cowboy against five. Time after time he was pummeled with fists and kicks. He tried his best to defend himself, but could feel his knees start to buckle.

It seemed like an eternity before he caught something out of the corner of his eye. It was the young marine stepping in, pulling the hooligans off Rhett. His powerful fist caught one square in the face, sending him reeling backwards. The others dispersed, quickly running up the stairs and out of the bar. When it was all over, Rhett was still on his feet, a little worse for wear, However, he still had his hat and gained a certain degree of respect.

"Molodetz kowvboy!" The young marine congratulated him with a thumbs-up. "You still standing."

Rhett noticed Tatiana standing behind the bar. She had witnessed the entire incident and was smiling. *"Dai mene vodka!"* he demanded, holding up two fingers.

She poured the drinks as Rhett slammed the money down on the bar. He spit out a small stream of blood. It splattered on the bar and onto Tatiana.

"Boodmo!" he exclaimed as he toasted the young marine who had come to his rescue.

Although he was trying to keep a game face, the beating had taken more out of Rhett than he let on. Shortly thereafter, he excused himself and limped to the Metro to catch the subway home.

When he arrived at his apartment, he pulled out the bottle of *Samahon* and poured himself a stiff drink. It burned as it passed over his bloodied lip,

He turned on the television and sat down. The only light in the room was coming from the TV screen, giving everything an eerie glow. Rhett found himself watching a crime show. It was much more graphic than anything he had remembered in the States. He sat watching the mayhem screen. It was an infant with half its head blown away; its lifeless little body lay in a bloodied crib. A grandmother lay dead a few feet away, an ice pick protruding from her chest. It had been a Mafia hit, but Rhett had no way of knowing the child was Sergei's or that the old woman had been his mother. It was a sign of the mayhem and violence that would come to define the mean streets of the former Soviet Union.

VI

Where the Hell is Oklahoma?

Rhett awoke with a start as the empty bottle rolled off the table and crashed onto the floor. He was still sitting in the chair as the first rays of the morning sunlight began to creep into the apartment. The television was still on, but there was nothing on the screen, nothing but the white snow.

He winced with pain and grabbed his ribs. His head felt like someone had taken a mallet to it. Then he remembered the beating he had been dealt at the hands of the five young hooligans.

Slowly he got out of the chair and made his way to the bathroom. Turning on the light, he looked in the mirror and saw a bruised face staring back at him.

He let out a chuckle. "Well, as cowboy movies go, I guess it could have been worse. They could've had a rope."

Rhett pulled up his shirt to examine the damage. His chest and abdomen were covered in hues of purple and blue from the bruising kicks he had suffered in the fight.

He pulled a bottle of Soviet painkillers off the shelf and limped into the kitchen to make some coffee. He poured a cup and downed a half-dozen pills, washing them down with the coffee. Then he walked back to the living room, pulled a bottle of cognac from the cabinet and liberally laced his coffee.

Rhett waited until mid-morning, when he picked up the phone and dialed Valerie's number.

"*Slooxhayoo* (I'm listening.)," Valerie's voice answered in Russian.

"Val."

"Look, I can't talk right now. I'm busy. I'm in the middle of my Russian lesson."

"But —"

"Sorry, gotta go now. I'll call you later." She hung up, leaving Rhett listening to a monotonous dial tone.

"Yeah, thanks a lot ... bitch!" Rhett muttered as he put the receiver down and took another drink of his coffee and cognac.

Two hours later, she hadn't called back. Rhett called again. When he got no answer, he called Todd and got a recording. He left a message, but Todd never returned his call.

—

Although, the idea of returning to Oklahoma seemed distasteful, it appeared he had little choice.

Changing his clothes Rhett traveled by Metro to the offices of Air Ukraine to book a flight out of Kyiv. He had reached the end of his rope.

When he arrived, the agent asked for his passport and visa. She took one look at it, shook her head and handed it back.

"Sho (What)*?"* He asked.

She pointed to the date. His visa had expired a week earlier. In all of the pandemonium, Rhett had forgotten to renew it.

"Horasho, Ya panemeiyoo. Odnaka, pazhalzda dai menee pokupiti moi billet? (Fine, I understand. However, please let me buy my ticket)."

Rhett slid his last remaining credit card under the window, smiled and placed his hands together as if he were praying.

The agent looked at him, smiled back and shrugged. *"Horasho."*

She took the card and ran it through the computer as Rhett nervously looked around.

A look came over her face — it wasn't a look that Rhett particularly wanted to see.

She handed the card back saying, *"Eesvaneeti, eto nee rabotayet* (Sorry, it doesn't work). *"*

"It can't be. Surely there has to be some kind of mistake."

Rhett asked her to try again. *"Pozhaluysta, dayte mne posledniy shans* (Please, give me one last chance). *"*

Rhett must have looked like a sad case, because the woman seemed to take pity on the lonesome cowboy. She ran the card through one more time.

The result was the same. She pointed to the screen as she moved it around for Rhett to see, and there it was on her computer — *Credit Denied!*

"Izvinite, ya nichego ne mogu sdelat," she said. (Sorry, I can do nothing). *"*

"Ya paneemaiyou, spaceeba bolshoi (I understand, thank you very much) *"*

Rhett took back his card and walked away as the agent watched the cowboy disappear out the door.

———

Left with no alternative and little choice, Rhett figured it was time to pack his bags and call his sister. Although they had never been close, but he was hoping that perhaps he could rely on her to come up with enough money to make it back to Oklahoma.

As soon as he returned to his apartment Rhett picked up the receiver and placed a call to the States. It seemed like an eternity, as he heard the telephone ringing over and over again. Finally, the ringing stopped, but before he could say anything, he realized he was talking to a recording.

When the message stopped, he waited for the beep. "Hello, Melanie. It's Rhett. I went to buy a plane ticket, but my credit card's been denied. Anyway, I'm in serious trouble if I can't get a ticket out of here. So, please. When you hear this, call me back as soon as possible."

He opened another bottle of vodka and waited. He waited all afternoon and into the night. He was still waiting four bottles and two days later. Nobody called back.

What Rhett hadn't realized was how life in America had changed. The idea of e-mail, the Internet, and how people lived their lives on the computer were alien to him. He didn't know that America had changed its way of communicating with one another or that his sister was busy "surfing the net," talking on chat rooms and looking for another husband. Consequently, she didn't check for messages on her answering machine anymore. He had no concept that America had entered the information age and like the Tower of Babel, America was busy building its Information Super Highway.

Like many a cowboy before him, Rhett had simply fallen out of step with the times. He was like a rider of the pony express in the age of technology. he had been left him behind.

He was on his own, waiting for the call that would never come, stuck in Ukraine, no money, no visa, no plane ticket and no way out.

—

That evening as Rhett sat in his apartment, alone in the dark with a bottle of brandy and a pack of cigarettes with cockroaches as his only companions. They freely ran across the walls and over the tables. It was as if it were more their home than his — perhaps it was. At least they had been born here. Whoever said, "When nothing is left, there will be the rats and cockroaches" must have been thinking about a place like this. Rhett felt like he was living in a "roach motel." He had checked into Ukraine, but he couldn't check out.

One crawled over his leg, as if he were a piece of furniture. He took his finger and flipped it sending it disappearing into the darkness. Rhett heard it hit the wall then listened as it scurried away as if it were only a minor inconvenience.

Every time he heard footsteps in the corridor, he wondered if someone might be coming for him. He didn't know if Salom knew where he lived. Would he be paid a visit like the one Dave had been paid in the end?

He really didn't give a shit about anything anymore. Besides, if Salom and his henchmen didn't get him, the drinking would. He too had become polluted, sick of all the greed and tired of watching everyone screwing everybody out of everything.

—

The power had been shut off again in his region of Kyiv. Ukraine was deeply in debt. Part of the problem was the mass corruption that had become so pervasive in the government. It was cold and raining and they owed millions to Russia for energy they couldn't afford.

Although Chernobyl had been scheduled for another shutdown according to an agreement between the government and the European Union, it all came down to money and Rhett knew that Chernobyl would be operating again, supplying Kyiv with much of its power.

For the life of him, Rhett could never figure out who was greedier, the people that ran this country or the Westerners who had been sent to help them. Soviet Totalitarianism had given way to the corporate feudalism of the multinational corporations.

He lit a cigarette, took another drink, got up, walked to the window and looked out over the darkened boulevard. *"Prospect Pobedy* . . . Avenue of Victory. What a fucking joke!"

Like everyone else, Dave had left him in quite a fix.

It was getting late. Rhett didn't really know why, but he put on the now infamous cowboy hat and duster and left the apartment. Once more, he headed to The Kowboy Dance Hall & Saloon.

He took the Metro to the center of Kyiv. The people on the subway were all staring blankly off into nothingness. They either looked like zombies or were drunk to the point of passing out. Rhett was a little drunk himself.

It had begun to rain again as he exited the Metro at *Maiydan Nezolezhnosti* and walked the short distance to The Kowboy.

He passed an old woman sitting on the street. Her arms were outstretched, begging for a few *kopeks*. He dropped a few coins in her hand as she crossed herself and said, *"Dai Bog* (Go with God). *"* Rhett saw a tear running down the side of her haggard and wrinkled face. As he stood there looking at her, he couldn't help but think, while the members of Parliament, the Mafia and Westerners lived like royalty, the people of Ukraine suffered.

And at that moment, he knew why it was called the almighty dollar. He had seen the face of God and knew exactly what he looked like. He looked just like Benjamin Franklin.

———

Rhett turned and walked toward The Kowboy. Descending the stairs, he could hear some mournful Ukrainian singing the blues. A doorman was taking money for the cover charge. He looked at the painting, then at Rhett and said nothing as he walked past him and down into the darkened bar.

About a dozen of Salom's Chechens were sitting in various places, firmly entrenched and in complete control.

It was obvious to Rhett that Sergei had little or no power here. Perhaps Sergei was thinking that if he could only sit and wait on the sidelines foolishly hoping for Dave to return — to make everything right, but Rhett knew there would be no Dave.

A few of the Chechens turned in Rhett's direction, looking startled, looking as if they had seen a ghost. "Behold the pale rider . . ."

Rhett walked past them and smiled. They smiled back. He shook hands with a few of them as they asked where Dave was.

"Ya ne znayou. Tse ne moiya problyema (I don't know. It's not my problem), *"* he answered.

"Where's Dave? Dave's not here." Once again, there was that old Cheech and Chong joke.

Not far from the stage, Rhett spotted Andrew, the male model. He looked up with glazed eyes. He was drunk. "OH! Rhett. It good to see you. When Dave come back?"

"Dave's never coming back."

"This place is bad now. Mafia here. Everything spoiled. I no like it. Dave not come back?"

"Never . . . *Neekole,*" Rhett repeated. "Dave's gone."

"Oh, look! My friend bring me back this cowvboy hat from America and this shirt and this . . . this . . ."

"It's called a bolo."

Andrew took his hat off and showed Rhett the name printed on the inside. "It from Shepler's. You know this place?"

"Yeah, I know it. It's the biggest cowboy shop in America."

"This from Dallas, Texas. See?" He pointed to the label again.

"Yeah, I know jt. There's one in Oklahoma too."

"But shirt not Wrangler. I want Wrangler." He then put his finger up to his lips. "Shhh. Let's not talk here. You come with me. Okay?"

They walked back up into the entryway of the bar. Rhett pointed to the cigarette burn on his face in the painting. "Who?'

"I don't know. All bad here. We talk Ukrainian . . . American. You and me. Okay?"

"Okay." Rhett answered. Then began the strange dialogue in half Ukrainian/Russian, half American/English.

Andrew was determined to know more about Dave. "Where Dave?" he asked again. "He no come back? Only Mafia here. It no cowvboy bar now."

"Dave went back to America. He's in California and he's not coming back. The Mafia were his partners. You understand? Dave did this."

"But it is very, very bad."

Rhett looked at him. "Well, Andrew, it looks like I'm the last cowboy in Kyiv."

"I know you are real cowvboy. I remember, you first cowvboy in Kyiv."

Rhett needed another drink. "Let's go back in the bar, Andrew. Okay?'

As they descended the stairs and back into the bar, Rhett could hear the musician still playing the blues and singing in Ukrainian. In a way, it reminded him of little ditty Dave used to sing . . . "The Ukrainian Bar Blues."

Rhett walked over to one of Salom's men. "This is Salom's place now, isn't it?"

"Da."

"Where's Salom?"

"He not here tonight. He be back on Monday. You want talk to him?"

"*Mozhet Beet* (Maybe)." Rhett replied.

"Nyet problema."

"Rhett shook his hand, patted him on the arm and smiled. Then he turned back toward Andrew standing a few feet away at the bar.

"Rhett," Andrew asked. "You buy me drink, okay?"

"Sure, why not?" Rhett laid money on the counter.

Another Ukrainian came up to the bar and ordered a bottle of cognac.

Andrew turned to Rhett. "It is his birthday. We drink to his birthday, okay?"

Andrew asked for two glasses and the man poured two shots of cognac.

He then introduced Rhett. "This is my friend. He is real cowvboy."

Rhett lifted glass and asked in Russian, "I wish you happiness, health and luck."

He nodded back and answered in English. "Thank you."

Then he took his bottle and walked away.

Truth be told, Rhett barely noticed the man who had been talking to Salom's lieutenant. He was busy talking to Andrew as the man walked out of the bar.

"Rhett, you know? My friends now call me cowvboy, Cowvboy of Kyiv. "But I want real cowvboy hat like yours. This not real. And I want these, these — how you call it?" Andrew motioned as if something was wrapped around his legs.

"Chaps?"

"Yes . . . yes, I want chaps like you have. My friends, they say to me, 'Andrew, you cowvboy of Kyiv.' I know you cowvboy. I want to buy hat like yours. How much cost?"

Rhett gave him a wry smile. "So, they call you cowboy, do they?"

"Yes, I am Cowboy of Kyiv."

"Well, I suppose somebody's got to do it."

"What?"

"Nothing, it's not important."

Rhett then took his Resistol off and placed it on Andrew's head.

"How much?"

Rhett simply shook Andrew's hand and answered back in Ukrainian. "My friend, I wish you luck. Goodbye."

And with that, Rhett turned and walked out of The Kowboy Dance Hall & Saloon for the last time. The dream was finished. He was finally leaving Dave, his Chechens, Kyiv and everything else behind."

—

Rhett walked out into the rain. It had cleansed the night air and it felt good.

He began walking down *The Passazh* and past the alley where Salom had been stabbed the night of the hell or high water party. He saw someone standing in the shadows, but didn't really care who it was or why he was there. He just walked past him and down the rain soaked street.

Suddenly, Rhett thought he heard an explosion, followed by a sudden flash. Then he felt a pain in the back his head and felt himself floating downward.

When he opened his eyes, he was lying on the street, his face looking up into a black sky. All he felt was confusion. "I can't be that drunk. I hadn't had that much to drink. Shit! Where's my cowboy hat?"

He felt something warm on the back of his neck, wet and flowing out onto the street and was aware that someone was going through his pockets. Taking everything — his passport, his identification, what money he had left.

Everything.

Rhett tried to move his arms, to pick himself back up, but for some reason they didn't respond. He couldn't seem to move.

The pain came back. It was excruciating, but only for a moment. Then all of a sudden it went away and he felt himself floating again as he let out a sigh.

Rhett lay on his back, blinking and looking upward into the rain . . . into the blackness of the night.

For a moment, he thought he was saying something, but he couldn't hear his voice. What he was trying to say was, "Where the hell is Oklahoma?"

Epilogue
NOTES FROM KYIV
Monday, October 06, 2003

One sign of change is the infamous Cowboy Bar is no more. It has been closed. A "Temporary Closed" sign is now on its door, but there is nothing as permanent in Kyiv as a temporary closed sign. The location of the gunslingers of Kyiv painting featuring Rhett Avery is unknown.

The Men That Don't Fit In
Robert Service

There's a race of men that don't fit in,
  a race that can't stay still;
So they break the hearts of kith and kin,
  And they roam the world at will.
They range the field and they rove the flood,
  And they climb the mountain's crest;
Theirs is the curse of the gypsy blood,
  And they don't know how to rest.
If they just went straight, they might go far;
  They are strong and brave and true;
But they're always tired of the things that are,
  And they want the strange and new.
They say: "Could I find my proper groove,
  What a deep mark I would make!"
So they chop and change, and each fresh move
  Is only a fresh mistake.
And each forgets, as he strips and runs
  With a brilliant, fitful pace,
It's the steady, quiet, plodding ones
  Who win in the lifelong race.
And each forgets that his youth has fled,
  Forgets that his prime is past,
Till he stands one day, with a hope that's dead,
  In the glare of the truth at last.
He has failed, he has failed; he has missed his chance;
  He has just done things by half.
Life's been a jolly good joke on him,
  And now is the time to laugh.
Ha, ha! He is one of the Legion Lost;
  He was never meant to win;
He's a rolling stone, and it's bred in the bone;
  He's a man who won't fit in.